Praise for Patricia Davids and her novels

"The little bit of mystery thrown in is a welcome
addition to this tale of Englisch and Amish coming
together in times of tragedy."
—*RT Book Reviews* on *Amish Redemption*

"Davids' deep understanding of Amish culture
is evident in the compassionate characters and
beautiful descriptions."
—*RT Book Reviews* on *A Home for Hannah*

"[A] lovely romance between two strong-willed,
intelligent people."
—*RT Book Reviews* on *The Doctor's Blessing*

Praise for Emma Miller and her novels

"The pace is just right in this enjoyable tale."
—*RT Book Reviews* on *A Husband For Mari*

"There is warmth to the characters that will leave
readers looking forward to seeing more."
—*RT Book Reviews* on *A Match for Addy*

"[A] heart-warming romance."
—*RT Book Reviews* on *Courting Ruth*

After thirty-five years as a nurse, **Patricia Davids** hung up her stethoscope to become a full-time writer. She enjoys spending her free time visiting her grandchildren, doing some long-overdue yard work and traveling to research her story locations. She resides in Wichita, Kansas. Pat always enjoys hearing from her readers. You can visit her online at patriciadavids.com.

Emma Miller lives quietly in her old farmhouse in rural Delaware. Fortunate enough to be born into a family of strong faith, she grew up on a dairy farm surrounded by loving parents, siblings, grandparents, aunts, uncles and cousins. Emma was educated in local schools and once taught in an Amish schoolhouse. When she's not caring for her large family, reading and writing are her favorite pastimes.

USA TODAY Bestselling Author

PATRICIA DAVIDS

Amish Redemption

&

EMMA MILLER

A Husband for Mari

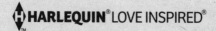

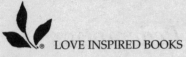

LOVE INSPIRED BOOKS

PLEASE RECYCLE
THIS PRODUCT IS RECYCLABLE

Recycling programs
for this product may
not exist in your area.

ISBN-13: 978-1-335-14500-0

Amish Redemption and A Husband for Mari

Copyright © 2017 by Harlequin Books S.A.

The publisher acknowledges the copyright holders
of the individual works as follows:

Amish Redemption
Copyright © 2015 by Patricia MacDonald

A Husband for Mari
Copyright © 2016 by Emma Miller

CONTENTS

AMISH REDEMPTION   7
Patricia Davids

A HUSBAND FOR MARI   227
Emma Miller

AMISH REDEMPTION

Patricia Davids

The book is lovingly dedicated
to all my readers. Thanks for
making my writing dreams come true.

Attend unto my cry; for I am brought very low: deliver me from my persecutors; for they are stronger than I. Bring my soul out of prison, that I may praise thy name: the righteous shall compass me about; for thou shalt deal bountifully with me.
—*Psalms* 142:6–7

Chapter One

Joshua Bowman's parole officer turned the squad car off the highway and onto the dirt lane. He stopped and looked over his shoulder. "You want me to drive to the house or do you want to walk from here?"

The immaculate farmstead with the two-story white house, white rail fences and big red barn at the end of the lane had never looked so beautiful. It was like many Amish farms that dotted the countryside around Berlin, Ohio, but this one was special. It was home.

Joshua cleared his throat. "I'd rather walk."

It was kind of Officer Oliver Merlin to allow Joshua's family reunion to take place in private. It was about the only kindness he had received from the *Englisch* justice system. He struggled to put that bitterness behind him. It was time for a new start.

Officer Merlin leveled a hard look at him. "You understand how this works. I'll be back to meet with you in two weeks."

"I'll be here."

"After that, we'll meet once a month until the end of your sentence, but I can drop in anytime. Deliberately miss a meeting with me and you'll find yourself back in prison. I don't take kindly to making long trips for nothing." The man's stern tone left no doubt that he meant what he said.

"I'm never going back there. Never." Joshua voiced the conviction in his heart as he met the officer's gaze without flinching.

"Obey the law and you won't." Getting out of the car, Officer Merlin came around to Joshua's door. There were no handles on the inside. Even though he was on his way home, he was still a prisoner. The moment the door opened, he drew his first free breath in six months.

Freedom beckoned, but he hesitated. What kind of welcome would he find in his father's house?

Officer Merlin's face softened. "I know this is hard, but you can do it, kid."

At twenty-one, Joshua was not a kid, but he appreciated the man's sympathy. He stepped out clutching a brown paper bag that contained his few personal possessions. A soft breeze caressed his cheeks, carrying with it the smells of spring, of the warming earth and fresh green grass. He closed his eyes, raised his face to the morning sun and thanked God for his deliverance.

"See you in two weeks." Officer Merlin closed the door behind Joshua, walked around the vehicle, got in and drove away.

Joshua immediately sat down in the grass at the edge of the road and pulled off his boots and socks. Rising, he wiggled his toes, letting his bare feet relish the cool softness beneath him. Every summer of his life, he had worked and played barefoot along this lane and through these fields. Somehow, it felt right to come home this way. Picking up his bag and carrying his boots in his other hand, he started toward the house.

Set a little way back from the highway stood his father's woodworking shop and the small store where his mother sold homemade candy, jams, jellies, the occasional quilt and the furniture his father and brothers made. The closed sign still hung in the window. His mother would be down to open it as soon as her chores were done.

Joshua had painted the blue-and-white sign on the side of the building when he was fifteen: Bowmans Crossing Amish-Made Gifts and Furniture. At the time, his father thought it was too fancy, but Joshua's mother liked it. The bishop of their congregation hadn't objected, so it stayed. The blue paint was fading. He would find time to touch it up soon. Right now, he had to face his family.

Joshua was a dozen yards from the house when he saw his brothers come out of the barn. Timothy led a pair of draft horses harnessed and ready for working the fields. Noah, the youngest brother, walked beside Timothy. Both big gray horses raised their heads and perked up their ears at the sight of Joshua. One whinnied. His brothers looked to see what had caught their attention.

Joshua stopped. In his heart, he believed he would be welcomed, but his time among the *Englisch* had taught him not to trust in the goodness of others.

Timothy gave a whoop of joy. He looped the reins over the nearby fence and began running toward Joshua with Noah close on his heels. Their shouts brought their oldest brother, Samuel, and their father to the barn door. Samuel broke into a run, too. Before he knew it,

Joshua was caught up in bear hugs by first one brother and then the others. Relief made him giddy with happiness, and he laughed out loud.

The commotion brought their mother out of the house to see what was going on. She shrieked with joy and ran down the steps with her white apron clutched in her hands and the ribbons of her Amish prayer *kapp* streaming behind her. She reached her husband's side and grasped his arm. Together they waited.

Joshua fended off his brothers and they fell silent as he walked toward his parents. He stopped a few feet in front of them and braced himself. "I know that I have brought shame and heartache to you both. I humbly ask your forgiveness. May I come home?"

He watched his father's face as he struggled with some great emotion. Tall and sparse with a flowing gray beard, Isaac Bowman was a man of few words. His straw hat, identical to the ones his sons wore, shaded his eyes, but Joshua caught the glint of moisture in them before his father wiped it away. Tears in his father's eyes were something Joshua had never seen before. His mother began weeping openly.

"Willkomme home, *mein sohn."*

Joshua's knees almost buckled, but he managed to stay upright and clasp his father's offered hand. "*Danki*, Father. I will never shame you again."

"There is no shame in what you did. You tried to help your brother. Many of our ancestors suffered unjust imprisonments as you did. It was God's will." He pulled Joshua forward and kissed him on both cheeks.

When he stepped back, Joshua's mother threw her arms around him. He breathed in the scent of pine cleaner and lemon. Not a day went by that she wasn't scrubbing some surface of her home in an effort to make it clean and welcoming. She had no idea how good she smelled.

Leaning back, she smiled at him. "Come inside. There's cinnamon cake and a fresh pot of *kaffi* on the stove."

"We'll be in in a minute, Mother," Isaac said.

She glanced from her husband to her sons and nodded. "It's so *goot* to have you back."

When she returned to the house, his father began walking toward the barn. Joshua and his three brothers followed him. "Do you bring us news of your brother Luke?"

"He is doing as well as can be expected. I pray that they parole him early, too." It was Luke's second arrest on drug charges, and the judge had given him a longer sentence.

Samuel laid a hand on Joshua's shoulder. "We never believed what they said about you."

"I was in the wrong place at the wrong time. My mistake was thinking that the *Englisch* police would believe me. I thought justice was on the side of the innocent. It's not."

"Do you regret going to Cincinnati to find Luke?" Noah asked.

"*Nee*, I had to try and convince him to come back. I know you said it was his decision, Father, but I thought I could persuade him to give up that wretched life and return with me. We were close once."

In the city, Joshua had discovered his brother had moved from using drugs to making and selling them. Joshua stayed for two days and tried to reason with him, but his pleas had fallen on deaf ears. He'd been ready to accept defeat and return home when the drug raid went down. In a very short time, Joshua found himself in prison alongside his brother. His sentence for a first offense was harsh because his brother had been living near a school.

His father regarded him with sad eyes. "The justice we seek is not of this world, *sohn*. God knows an innocent heart. It is His judgment we must fear."

"Do you think this time in prison will change Luke?" Timothy asked softly.

Prison changed any man who entered those walls, but not always for the better. Joshua shrugged.

His father hooked his thumbs through his suspenders. "You are home now, and for that we must all give thanks. Timothy, Noah, Samuel, the ground will not prepare itself for planting."

Joshua smiled. That was *Daed*—give thanks that his son was home for five minutes and then make everyone get to work.

Joshua's brothers slapped him on the back and started toward the waiting team. Timothy looked over his shoulder. "I want to hear all about the gangsters in the big house tonight."

"I didn't meet any," Joshua called after him, wondering where his brother had picked up such terms.

"Not even one?" Noah's mouth fell open in disbelief.

"Nope." Joshua grinned at his little brother's crestfallen expression. Joshua had no intention of sharing the sights he'd seen in that inhuman world.

"Come. Your mother is anxious to spoil you. She deserves her happiness today."

Joshua followed his father inside. Nothing had changed in the months Joshua had been away. The kitchen was spotless and smelled of cinnamon, fresh-baked bread and stout coffee. Standing with his eyes closed, he let the smells of home wash away the lingering scent of his prison cell. He was truly home at last.

"Sit," his mother insisted.

He opened his eyes and smiled at her. She wasn't happy unless she was feeding someone. She bustled about the kitchen getting cups and plates and dishing up thick slices of coffee cake. He took a seat at the table, but his father remained by the desk in the corner. He picked up a long white envelope. Turning to Joshua, he said, "Mother's *onkel* Marvin passed away a few months ago."

Joshua frowned. "I don't remember him."

His mother set a plate on the table. "You never met him. He left the Amish as a young man and never spoke to my family again."

"It seems Mother has inherited his property over by Hope Springs." His father tapped the letter against his palm.

"I didn't even know where he lived. His lawyer said he was fond of me because I was such a happy child. Strange, don't you think? Would you like *kaffi* or milk?" she asked with a beaming smile on her face.

"Coffee. What kind of property did he leave you?"

"Forty acres with a house and barn," his father replied. "But the lawyer says the property is in poor repair. I was going to go to Hope Springs the day after tomorrow to look it over, but you know how I hate long buggy trips. Besides, I need to get the ground worked so we can plant. Joshua, why don't you go instead? It would take a load off me, and it would give

you a little time to enjoy yourself before getting behind a planter again."

Hope Springs was a day's buggy ride from the farm.
The idea of traveling wasn't as appealing as it had once
been, but doing something for his father was. "I'd be
glad to go for you."

His mother's smile faded. "But Joshua has only just
gotten home, Isaac."

Joshua rose to his feet and planted a kiss on her
cheek. "You have two whole days to spoil me with your
wunderbar cooking before then. I'll check out your
property, and then I'll be home for good."

"Do you promise?" she asked softly.

He cupped her face in his palms. "I promise."

"Mary, I have just the *mann* for you."

Resisting the urge to bang her head on the cupboard
door in front of her, Mary Kaufman continued mixing the lemon cake batter in the bowl she held. "I don't
want a man, Ada."

*Don't want one. Don't need one. How many ways
can I say it before you believe me?*

Except for her adopted father, Nick Bradley, most of
the men in Mary's life had brought her pain and grief.
However, the prospect of finding her a husband was
her adopted grandmother's favorite subject. As much
as Mary loved Ada, this got old.

"Balderdish! Every Amish woman needs a *goot*
Amish husband." Ada opened the oven door.

"The word is *balderdash*."

Ada pulled a cake out using the folded corner of
her black apron and dropped it on the stove top with
a clatter. "*Mein Englisch* is *goot*. Do not change the

subject. You will be nineteen in a few weeks. Do you want people to·call you an *alt maedel*?"

"I'll be twenty, and I don't care if people call me an old maid or not."

Ada frowned at her. *"Zvansich?"*

"Ja. Hannah just turned four. That means I'll be twenty." Mary smiled at her daughter playing with an empty bowl and wooden spoon on the floor. She was showing her dog, Bella, how to make a cake. The yellow Lab lay watching intently, her big head resting on her paws. Mary could almost believe the dog was memorizing the instructions.

Ada turned to the child. "Hannah, how old are you?"

Grinning at her great-grandmother, Hannah held up four fingers. "This many."

Patting her chest rapidly, Ada faced Mary. *"Ach!* Then there is no time to lose. Delbert Miller is coming the day after tomorrow to fix the chicken *haus*. You must be nice to him."

Mary slapped one hand to her cheek. "You're right. There's no time to lose. I'll marry him straightaway. If he doesn't fall through that rickety roof and squish all our chickens."

She shook her head and began stirring again. "Go out with Delbert Miller? Not in a hundred years."

"I know he is *en adlichah grohsah mann*, but you should not hold that against him."

Mary rolled her eyes. "A *fairly* big man? *Nee*, he is a *very* big man."

"And are you such a prize that you can judge him harshly?"

Mary stopped stirring and stared at the cuffs of her long sleeves. No matter how hot it got in the summer, she never rolled them up. They covered the scars on her wrists. The jagged white lines in her flesh were indisputable evidence that she had attempted suicide, the ultimate sin. Shame washed over her. "*Nee*, I'm not a prize."

A second later, she was smothered in a hug that threatened to coat her in batter. "Forgive me, child. That is not what I meant. You know that. You are the light in this old woman's heart and your dear *dochder* is the sun and the stars."

Mary closed her eyes and took a deep breath.

God spared my life. He has forgiven my sins. I am loved and treasured by the new family He gave me. Bad things happened years ago, but those things gave me my beautiful child. She is happy here, as I dreamed she would be. I will not dwell in that dark place again. We are safe and that evil man is locked away. He can never find us here.

Hannah came to join the group, tugging on Mary's skirt and lifting her arms for a hug, too. Mary set her bowl on the counter and picked up her daughter. "You are the sun and the stars, aren't you?"

"*Ja*, I am." Hannah gave a big nod.

"You are indeed." Ada kissed Hannah's cheek and Mary's cheek in turn. "You had better hurry or you will be late for the quilting bee. I'll finish that batter. Are you taking Hannah?"

"I am. She enjoys playing with Katie Sutter's little ones." Mary glanced at the clock in the corner. It was nearly four. The quilting bee was being held at Katie's home. They were finishing a quilt as a wedding gift for Katie's friend Sally Yoder. Sally planned to wed in the fall.

"Who else is coming?"

"Rebecca Troyer, Faith Lapp, Joann Weaver and Sarah Beachy. Betsy Barkman will be there, of course, and I think all her sisters will be, too."

Betsy Barkman was Mary's dearest friend. They were both still single and neither of them was in a hurry to marry—something few people in their Amish community of Hope Springs understood. Especially Betsy's sisters. Lizzie, Clara and Greta had all found husbands. They were impatiently waiting for their youngest sister to do the same. Betsy had been going out with Alvin Stutzman for over a year, but she wasn't ready to be tied down.

"Sounds like you'll have a wonderful time. Make sure you bring me all the latest gossip."

"We don't gossip." Mary winked at her grandmother.

"*Ja*, and a rooster doesn't crow."

Shifting her daughter to her hip, Mary crossed the room and gathered their traveling bonnets from beside the door. She stood Hannah on a chair to tie the large black hat over her daughter's silky blond crown of braids. As she did, she heard the distant rumble of thunder.

Ada leaned toward the kitchen window to peer out. "There's a storm brewing, from the looks of those clouds. The paper said we should expect strong storms today. You'd better hurry. If it's bad, stay with the Sutters until it passes."

"I will."

"And you will be nice to Delbert when he visits."

"I'll be nice to him. Unless he squashes any of our chickens," Mary said with a cheeky grin.

"Bothersome child. Get before I take a switch to your backside." Ada shook the spoon at Mary. Speckles of batter went everywhere much to Bella's delight. The dog quickly licked the floor clean and sat with her hopeful gaze fixed on Ada.

Laughing, Mary scooped up her daughter and headed out the door. Bella tried to follow, but Mary shook her head. "You stay with *Mammi*. We'll be back soon."

Bella gave her a reproachful look, but turned around and headed to her favorite spot beside the stove.

Mary soon had her good-natured mare harnessed and climbed in the buggy with Hannah. She glanced at the rapidly approaching storm clouds. They did look threatening. The sky held an odd greenish cast that usually meant hail. Should she go, or should she stay home? She hated to miss an afternoon of fun with her friends.

She decided to go. She would be traveling ahead of it on her way to the Sutter farm and Tilly was a fast trotter.

Mary wasted no time getting the mare up to speed once they reached the highway at the end of her grandmother's lane. She glanced back several times in the small rearview mirror on the side of her buggy. The clouds had become an ominous dark shroud, turning the May afternoon sky into twilight. Streaks of lightning were followed by growing rumbles of thunder.

Hannah edged closer to her. "I don't like storms."

She slipped an arm around her daughter. "Don't worry. We'll be at Katie's house before the rain catches us."

It turned out she was wrong. Big raindrops began

hitting her windshield a few minutes later. A strong gust of wind shook the buggy and blew dust across the road. The sky grew darker by the minute. Mary urged Tilly to a faster pace. She should have stayed home.

A red car flew past her with the driver laying on the horn. Tilly shied and nearly dragged the buggy into the fence along the side of the road. Mary managed to right her. "Foolish *Englischers*. Have they no sense? We are over as far as we can get."

The rumble of thunder became a steady roar behind them. Tilly broke into a run. Startled, Mary tried to pull her back but the mare struggled against the bit.

"Tilly, what's wrong with you?" She sawed on the reins, trying to slow the animal.

Hannah began screaming. Mary glanced back and her heart stopped. A tornado had dropped from the clouds and was bearing down on them, chewing up everything in its path. Dust and debris flew out from the wide base as the roar grew louder. Mary loosened the reins and gave Tilly her head, but she knew even the former racehorse wouldn't be able to outrun it. They had to find cover.

The lessons she learned at school came tumbling back into her mind: *get underground in a cellar or lie flat in a ditch.*

There weren't any houses nearby. She scanned the fences lining each side of the road. The ditches were shallow to nonexistent. The roar grew louder. Hannah kept screaming.

Dear God, help me save my baby. What do I do?

She saw an intersection up ahead.

Travel away from a tornado at a right angle. Don't try to outrun it.

Bracing her legs against the dash, she pulled back on the lines, trying to slow Tilly enough to make the corner without overturning. The mare seemed to sense the plan. She slowed and made the turn with the buggy tilting on two wheels. Mary grabbed Hannah and held on to her. Swerving wildly behind the horse, the buggy finally came back onto all four wheels. Before the mare could gather speed again, a man jumped into the road, waving his arms. He grabbed Tilly's bridle as she plunged past and pulled her to a stop.

Shouting, he pointed toward an abandoned farmhouse that Mary hadn't seen back in the trees. "There's a cellar on the south side."

Mary jumped out of the buggy and pulled Hannah into her arms. The man was already unhitching Tilly, so Mary ran toward the ramshackle structure with boarded-over windows and overgrown trees hugging the walls. The wind threatened to pull her off her feet. The trees and even the grass were straining toward the approaching tornado. Dirt and leaves pelted her face, but fear for Hannah pushed her forward. She reached the old cellar door, but couldn't lift it against the force of the wind. She was about to lie on the ground on top of Hannah when the man appeared at her side. Together, they were able to lift the door.

Mary glanced back and saw her buggy flying up into the air in slow motion. The sight was so mesmerizing that she froze.

A second later, she was pushed down the steps into darkness.

Chapter Two

Pummeled by debris in the wind, Joshua hustled the woman and her child down the old stone steps in the hope of finding safety below. He had discovered the cellar that afternoon while investigating the derelict property for his father. He hadn't explored the basement because the crumbling house with its sagging roof and tilted walls didn't look safe. He couldn't believe anyone had lived in it until a few months ago. Now its shelter was their only hope.

The wind tore at his clothes and tried to suck him backward. His hat flew off and out of the steep stairwell to disappear in the roiling darkness overhead. The roar of the funnel was deafening. The cellar door banged shut, narrowly missing his head and then flew open again. A sheet of newspaper settled on the step in front of him and opened gently as if waiting to be read. A second later, the cellar door dropped closed with a heavy thud, plunging him into total darkness.

He stumbled slightly when his feet hit the floor instead of another step. The little girl kept screaming but he barely heard her over the howling storm. It sounded

as if he were lying under a train. A loud crash overhead followed by choking dust raining down on them
changed the girl's screaming into a coughing fit. Joshua
knew the house had taken a direct hit. It could cave in
on them and become their tomb instead of their haven.

He pressed the woman and her child against the
rough stone wall and forced them to crouch near the
floor as he huddled over the pair, offering what protection he could with his body. It wouldn't be much if the
floors above them gave way. He heard the woman praying, and he joined in asking for God's protection and
mercy. Another crash overhead sent more dust down
on them. Choked by the dirt, he couldn't see, but he felt
her hand on his face and realized she was offering the
edge of her apron for him to cover his nose and mouth.
He clutched it gratefully, amazed that she could think
of his comfort when they were all in peril. She wasn't
screaming or crying as many women would. She was
bravely facing the worst and praying.

He kept one arm around her and the child. They both
trembled with fear. His actions had helped them escape
the funnel itself, but the danger was far from over. She
had no idea how perilous their cover was, but he did.

He'd put his horse and buggy in the barn after he
arrived late yesterday evening. One look at the ramshackle house made him decide to sleep in the backseat of his buggy while his horse, Oscar, occupied a
nearby stall. The barn, although old and dirty, was still
sound with a good roof and plenty of hay in the loft.
His great-uncle had taken better care of his animals
than he had of himself.

Joshua hoped Oscar was okay, but he had no way
of knowing if the barn had been spared. Right now, he

was more worried that the old house over their heads wouldn't be. Had he brought this woman and her child into a death trap?

Terrified, Mary held Hannah close and prayed. She couldn't get the sight of her buggy being lifted into the sky out of her mind. What if they had still been inside? What if her rescuer hadn't appeared when he did? Was today the day she was to meet God face-to-face? Was she ready?

Please, Father, I beg You to spare us. If this is my time to come home to You, I pray You spare my baby's life. But if You must take Hannah, take me, too, for I couldn't bear to be parted from her again.

The roar was so loud and the pressure so intense that Mary wanted to cover her aching ears, but she couldn't let go of Hannah or the apron she was using to cover their faces. The horrible howling went on and on.

Make it stop, God! Please, make it stop.

In spite of having her face buried in the cloth, thick dust got in her eyes and her nose with every breath. Hannah's small body trembled against her. Her screams had turned to whimpers as her arms tightened around Mary's neck. The roar grew so loud that Mary thought she couldn't take it another moment. Her body shook with the need to run, to escape, to get away.

As soon as the thought formed, the sound lessened and quickly moved on. Was it over? Were they safe?

Thanks be to God.

Mary tried to stand, but the man held her down. "Not yet."

She could hear the wind shrieking and lashing the trees outside, but the horrible pressure in her ears was gone and the roar was fading. In its place, groaning, cracking and thumps reverberated overhead. A thunderous crash shook the ceiling over them and the old timbers moaned. Hannah clutched Mary's neck again. Mary glanced up fearfully. She couldn't see anything for the darkness and the man leaning over her.

He said, "Stay close to the wall. It's the safest place."

She knew what he meant. It was the safest place if the floor above them came down. She huddled against the cold stones, pressing herself and Hannah into as small a space as possible, and waited, praying for herself, her child and the stranger trying to protect them. After several long minutes, she knew God had heard her prayers. The old boards above them stayed intact.

"Is the bad thing gone, *Mamm*?" Hannah loosened her stranglehold on Mary's neck. Her small voice shook with fear.

Mary stroked her hair and kissed her cheek to soothe her. Somewhere in their mad dash, Hannah had lost her bonnet and her braids hung loose. "*Ja*, the bad storm is gone, but keep your face covered. The dust is very thick."

Hannah was only quiet for a moment. "Can we go outside? I don't like it in here."

Mary didn't like it, either. "In a minute, my heart. Now hush."

"We must let the storm pass first," the man said. His voice was deep and soothing. Who was he? In her brief glimpse of him, she had noticed his Amish dress and little else beyond the fact that he was a young man without a beard. That meant he was single, but she didn't recognize him from the area. He was a stranger to her. A Good Samaritan sent by God to aid her in her moment of need. She wished she could see his face.

"Is Tilly okay, *Mamm*?"

"I don't know, dear. I hope so." Mary hadn't spared a thought for her poor horse.

"Who is Tilly?" he asked.

"Our horse," Hannah replied without hesitation, surprising Mary.

Hannah rarely spoke to someone she didn't know. The current situation seemed to have erased her daughter's fear of strange men, or at least this man. It was an anxiety Mary knew she compounded with her own distrust of strangers. She tried to accept people at face value, as good, the way her faith required her to do, but her dealings with men in the past had left scars on her ability to trust as well as on her wrists. Not everyone who gave aid did so without an ulterior motive.

"I think your horse is safe. I saw her running away across the field. Without the buggy to pull, she may have gotten out of the way." There was less tension in his voice. Mary began to relax. The worst was over and they were still alive.

"But Tilly will be lost if she runs off." Hannah's voice quivered.

"*Nee*, a *goot* horse will go home to its own barn," he assured her. "Is she a *goot* horse?"

Mary felt Hannah nod vigorously, although she doubted the stranger could see. "She's a *wunderbar* horse," Hannah declared.

"Then she'll likely be home before you."

Hannah tipped her head to peer at the man. "Did your horse run off, too?"

"Oscar is in the barn. He should be okay in there."

Mary heard the worry underneath his words. In a storm like this, nowhere aboveground was safe.

Hannah rested her head on Mary's shoulder. "Are *Mammi* Ada and Bella okay?"

"They are in God's hands, Hannah. He will protect them." The twister had come up behind them. Mary had no idea if it had touched down before or after it passed over the farm. She prayed for her dear grandmother.

"I want to go home. I want to see *Mammi* Ada and Bella."

"Is Bella your sister?" the man asked.

"She's my *wunderbar* dog."

He chuckled. It was a warm, friendly sound. "Have you a *wunderbar* cat, as well?"

"I don't. Bella doesn't like cats. She's going to be worried about me. We should go home now, *Mamm*." Mary hoped they had a house waiting for them.

"We'll get you home as soon as the storm has moved on," the young man said as he stepped back.

Mary's eyes were adjusting to the gloom. She could see he was of medium height with dark hair, but little else. She knew that without his help things could have been much worse. He could have taken shelter without risking his life to help them. She had his bravery and quick action to thank for getting them out of her buggy before it'd become airborne. Just thinking about what that ride would have been like caused a shiver to rattle her teeth.

He gave her an awkward pat on her shoulder. "I think the worst is over."

She tried not to flinch from his touch. Her common sense said he wasn't a threat, but trusting didn't come easily to her. "We are grateful for your assistance. God was merciful to send you when He did."

He gave a dry bark of laughter. "This time I was in the right place at the right time."

What could he find funny in this horrible situation?

Joshua was amazed at how God had placed him exactly where he needed to be today to save this woman and child, and yet six months ago the Lord had put him in a position that sent him to prison for no good reason. Who could fathom the ways of God? Not he.

"I am Mary Kaufman and this is my daughter, Hannah."

He heard the hesitation in her words and wondered at it. "I'm Joshua Bowman."

"Thank you again, Joshua. Do you think it is safe to venture out?"

A loud clap of thunder rattled the structure over them. "I think we should wait awhile longer."

The thunder was followed by the steady ping of hail against some metal object outside and the drone of hard rain. The tornado had passed but the thunderstorm had plenty of steam left.

"I reckon you're right." Abruptly, she moved away from him.

"I'm sorry. I didn't mean to be overly familiar." Close contact between unmarried members of the opposite sex wasn't permitted in Amish society. Circumstances had forced him to cross that boundary, but it couldn't continue.

"You were protecting us." She moved a few more steps away.

She was uncomfortable being alone with him. He

couldn't blame her. She had no idea who he was. How could he put her at ease? Maybe by not hovering over her. He sat down with his back against the old stone wall, refusing to think about the creepy-crawly occupants who were surely in here with them.

She relaxed slightly. "Do you live here?"

"I don't, but my great-uncle did until he died a few months ago."

"I'm sorry for your loss."

"*Danki*, but I never knew him. He was *Englisch*. He left the family years ago and never contacted them again. Everyone was surprised to learn he had willed the property to my mother. She is only one of his many nieces."

"He must have cherished a fondness for her."

"So it would seem. My father sent me to check out the place, as the letter from the attorney said it was in rough shape. *Daed* wants to find out what will be needed to get it ready to farm, rent out or sell. Unfortunately, it's in much worse condition than we expected."

That was an understatement. His father would have to invest heavily in this farm to get it in working order, and the family didn't have that kind of money. They would need to sell it.

"From the sounds of things, it will need even more repair after the storm passes."

He chuckled at her wry tone. "*Ja*. I think the good Lord may have done us a favor by tearing down the old house. I just wish He had waited until we were out of the way."

His eyes had grown accustomed to the gloom. He could make out Mary's white apron and the pale oval of her face framed by her black traveling bonnet. She sat down, too, pulling her child into her lap. Together, they waited side by side in the darkness. At least she seemed less afraid of him now.

The thunder continued to rumble, punctuating the sound of the wind and the steady rain. They sat in tense silence. Even the child was quiet. After a while, the thunder grew less violent but the rain continued. Was it going to storm all night? If so, he might as well find out what was left of the property and see if he could get this young mother and daughter home.

He rose to his feet. "Stay here until I'm sure it's safe to go out."

She stood, too, holding her little girl in her arms. "Be careful."

He made his way to the cellar door and pushed up on it. It wouldn't budge.

He pushed harder. It still didn't move. Something heavy was blocking it. He worked to control the panic rising in his chest. He couldn't be trapped. Not in such a small place. It was like being in prison all over again. His palms grew damp and his heart began to pound.

"What's wrong?" Mary asked.

The last thing he wanted was to scare her again, but she would soon find out what was going on. He worked to keep his tone calm. There was no point in frightening her more than she already was. "Something is blocking the door. I can't move it. Can you give me a hand?"

He sounded almost normal and was pleased with himself. If she knew differently, she didn't let on. Having someone else to worry about was helping to keep his panic under control.

"Hannah, stay right here," Mary said, then made her

way up the steps until she was beside him. She braced her arms against the overhead door. "On three."

She counted off and they both pushed. Nothing. It could have been nailed shut for all their efforts accomplished. He moved a step higher and braced his back against the old boards. He pushed with all his might, straining to move whatever held it. Mary pushed, too, but still the door refused to budge.

This can't be happening.

"Help! Help, we're down here," she yelled, and beat on the door with her fists. He wanted to do the same.

Don't think of yourself. Think of her. Think of her child. They need you to be calm.

He drew a steadying breath. "There isn't anyone around to hear you. This farm has been deserted for months."

"There must be another way out."

He heard the rising panic in her voice. He forced himself to relax and speak casually. "There should be a staircase to the inside of the house. Hopefully, it isn't blocked."

"Of course. Let's find it. I don't want to stay down here any longer than I must. All this dust isn't good for Hannah."

She started to move past him, but he caught her arm. "You could get hurt stumbling around in the dark. Stay here with your daughter. I'll go look. I've got a lighter, but I'm not sure how much fuel is left in it. Shout if you hear anything outside. No one will be looking for me, but your family will be looking for you, right?"

"They will, but not soon."

That wasn't what he wanted to hear. "Maybe someone will see your buggy out there and come to investigate."

"My buggy isn't out there. Didn't you see it get sucked up and carried away?"

"I didn't. I had my eyes fixed on you."

"No one is going to know where to look for us, are they?" Her voice trembled.

"It won't matter once I find a way out. I'll be back as quick as I can." It was an assurance he didn't really feel.

He tried to remember the layout of the building he had surveyed for his father. Although he had looked in through the windows that hadn't been boarded over, he hadn't ventured inside to explore thoroughly since his father was more interested in the land and its potential. Joshua didn't remember seeing a door that might be an inside entrance to the cellar. Some older houses only had outside entrances. The most logical place for the stairs would be near the kitchen at the other end of the house.

As it continued to rain, water began pouring through cracks in the floorboards overhead. That wasn't good. It meant a part of the house had been torn open, allowing the rain to come in. How sound was what remained? The steady rumble of thunder promised more rain. Would the saturated wood give way and finish what the tornado had started? He looked over his shoulder. "Mary, stay near the wall or in the stairwell, okay?"

"I will."

Joshua surveyed what he could in the darkness. The cellar itself wasn't empty. The only clear place seemed to be where they were standing. The cavernous space was piled high with odds and ends of lumber, boxes, old tires and discarded household items. His great-uncle, it seemed, had been a hoarder as well as a recluse.

Joshua had put a lighter in his pocket before leaving the farm in case he ended up camping out. It had come in handy last night and now he pulled it out, clicked it on and held it over his head. Gray cobwebs waved from every surface in the flickering light that did little to pierce the gloom. He couldn't keep the lighter on for long before he burned his fingers, so he quickly identified a path and let the light go out.

Stepping around a pair of broken chairs, he pushed aside wooden boxes of unknown items. When his shin hit something, he flicked on the lighter again. A set of box springs blocked his way. Most of the cloth covering had rotted away. Mice had made off with more. Skirting it as best he could without stepping on the springs, he continued along the cellar wall. A set of shelves on the far side was lined with dust-covered cans, jars and crocks, but he saw no stairs. He finished the circuit and moved back toward where Mary was standing. He flicked on his light.

"Have you discovered a way out?" Her voice shook only slightly, but he saw the worry in her eyes.

They weren't going anywhere until someone found them. He had no idea how long that might take. They could be down here for hours, days even. The thought was chilling. He stopped a few feet away from her and let the light go out. How did he tell a frightened woman she was trapped in a cellar with a man who'd spent the past six months in prison?

When Joshua didn't answer her question, Mary's heart sank. She knew he hadn't found an exit. She bit her thumbnail as she considered their predicament. Her friends would be concerned when she didn't arrive at the quilting bee, but they might assume she had stayed home to wait out the storm. When she didn't return home this evening, Ada would become concerned, but she might think Mary had decided to spend the night at the Sutter farm. Ada might not even know about the tornado if it had formed this side of the farm.

Mary hoped that was the case. Ada had a bad heart and didn't need such worry. It could be morning before she became concerned about them and perhaps as late as noon before she realized they were missing.

Mary's adoptive parents, Nick and Miriam Bradley would begin looking for them as soon as their absence was noted. Miriam stopped at the farm every morning and Nick dropped by every evening on his way home from work without fail. He would know about the tornado. He would stop by the farm this evening to make sure she and Hannah were safe. Would he go to the Sutter farm to check on them when he found they weren't home? She had no way of knowing, but she prayed that he would.

It might take a while, but Nick would find them. Mary had no doubt of that. But would he find them before dark? Or was she going to have to spend the night with this stranger?

Chapter Three

Mary shivered as she looked around the old cellar. If she had to spend the night in here, she wouldn't like it, but she could do it. She would depend on God for His protection and comfort. In the meantime, she had to be brave for her child and make the best of a bad situation for Joshua's sake, too. He was trying to hide his fear, but she saw it in his eyes.

"I noticed an old lantern hanging from a nail by the cellar steps. We should check and see if it has any kerosene in it." She spoke calmly, surprised to find her voice sounded matter of fact.

"Good idea. I'll see if I can find an ax or something useful to chop open or pry up the door." Joshua flicked his lighter on. He located the lantern, took it down from the nail and shook it. A faint sloshing sound gave Mary hope.

Hannah tugged on her skirt. "I'm hungry. Can we go home now?"

Joshua leaned toward her. "You mean you want to go home before our adventure has ended?"

Hannah gave him a perplexed look. "What adventure?"

"Why, our treasure hunt." He raised the glass chimney of the lantern and held his lighter to the wick. It flickered feebly for a second and then caught. He lowered the glass, wiped it free of dust with his sleeve and turned up the wick. The lamp cast a golden glow over their surroundings. It was amazing how much better Mary felt now that she could see.

"What kind of treasure hunt?" Hannah sounded intrigued by the idea.

"We're all going to hunt for some useful things," Mary said.

Joshua nodded. "That's right. Let's pretend that we are going to make this cellar into a home. What do we need first?"

"Chairs and a table," Hannah said.

"Then help me look for some on our pretend shopping trip." He glanced at Mary. She nodded and he held out his hand to Hannah. "I think I saw some chairs over this way. Don't you like to go shopping? I do. This storekeeper needs to sweep out his store, though. This place is as dirty as a rainbow."

Hannah scowled at him. "Rainbows aren't dirty. They're pretty and clean."

He held his lantern higher. "Are they? Well, this place isn't. It's as dirty as a star."

"Stars aren't dirty, Joshua. They twinkle."

"Then you tell me what is dirty."

"A pigpen."

"Yup, that is dirty, all right, but this place is worse than a pigpen. What else is dirty?"

"Your face."

Mary choked on her laugh. Hannah was right. His face was covered in dirt. There were cobwebs on his clothes and bits of leaves and grass in his dark brown hair. It was then she realized how short his hair was. It wasn't the style worn by Amish men. Joshua must still be in his *rumspringa*.

Mary had left her running-around years behind a few short weeks after Hannah was born. She had been baptized into the Amish faith at the age of sixteen, the time when most Amish teens were just beginning to test the waters of the English world.

Joshua seemed to notice she was staring at him. He rubbed a hand over his head in a self-conscious gesture and shook free some of the clinging grime.

Mary looked away. She wiped down her sleeves and brushed off her bonnet, knowing she couldn't look much better. Oddly, she wished she had a mirror to make sure her face was clean. It wasn't like her to be concerned with her looks, but she did wonder what Joshua thought of her.

That was silly. He would think she was a married woman with a child, and that was a good thing. She glanced at him again.

He wiped his face with both hands but it didn't do much good. He spoke to Hannah. "This isn't dirt. It's flour. I was going to bake a cake."

Hannah giggled at his silliness. "It is not flour."

"Okay, but this is a table and we need one." He held his find aloft. The ancient rocker was missing a few spindles in the back, but the seat was intact.

Hannah planted her hands on her hips. "That's a chair."

"It's a good thing I have you to help me shop. I'd

never find the right stuff on my own. Let's go look for a donkey."

Hannah giggled again. "Joshua, we don't need a donkey in our house."

"We don't? I'm so glad. I don't know where it would sleep tonight."

His foolishness made Mary smile. He was distracting and entertaining Hannah. For that, she was grateful. Mary turned her attention to finding something to collect the rainwater. She had no idea how long they might be down here, but Hannah was sure to be thirsty soon.

She found a metal tub hanging from a post near the center of the room. It had probably been a washtub at one time. Using her apron, she wiped it out and positioned it under the worst of the dripping. Next, she found an empty glass canning jar and rinsed it out the same way. She put it in the center of the tub. Once the jar was full, the overflow would accumulate in the tub and leave her something to wash with later.

The plink, plink, plink of the water hitting the bottom of the jar was annoying, but they would be grateful for the bounty before morning. She refused to think they might be down here more than one night.

Taking off her bonnet, she laid it aside. Then she held the cleanest corner of her apron under a neighboring drip until it was wet and unobtrusively used it to scrub her face.

At the end of their shopping trip, Joshua and Hannah came back with two barely usable chairs, a small wooden crate for a third seat and another washtub with a hole in the side for a table, but no ax or tools. Joshua set the furniture up in their corner, allowing Hannah to arrange and rearrange them to her satisfaction in her imaginary house.

While her daughter was busy, Mary spoke quietly to Joshua. "I will be fine until we are rescued, but Hannah will be hungry soon. Do you have anything to eat?"

"Nothing. I'm sorry. Everything I have is out in my buggy in the barn. There are some cans and jars on the shelf back there. Want me to take a look?"

"*Nee*, you're doing a wonderful job keeping Hannah occupied. I'll go look." Normally leery of strangers, Mary didn't feel her usual disquiet with Joshua. She assumed their current circumstances made him seem like less of a stranger and more like a friend in need.

He pulled a candle stub from his pocket. "I found this along with a couple of others in a pan. It was the best one." He lit it, dripped a small amount of wax on the overturned washtub and stuck the butt in it to hold the candle upright. Then he handed Mary the lantern.

"Someone was probably saving them to melt down to reuse." She didn't have a mold to form a new candle, but she could make one by dipping a wick in the melted wax. A strip of cotton cloth from her apron or from her *kapp* ribbon would make an adequate wick. She would work on that before the lantern ran out of fuel. Sitting in the dark was the last thing she wanted to do.

Hannah began jumping up and down. "I hear a siren. Do you hear it? It's Papa Nick!"

Mary's spirits rose until the welcome sound faded away. Nick wasn't coming for them. He had no idea where she was. It might not even have been him. How much damage had been done by the tornado? Were others in need of rescue?

A few moments later, she heard the sound of another

siren on the highway. Were they ambulances rushing to help people injured by the twister? She had been praying so hard for herself and for Hannah that she had forgotten about others in the area. This part of the county was dotted with English and Amish farms and businesses. How many had been destroyed? How many people had lost their lives? She prayed now for all the people she knew beyond the stone walls keeping her prisoner. It was the only thing she could do to help.

Lifting the lantern, she moved across the crowded room to the shelves Joshua had indicated and searched through the contents. She glanced back to see him placing the tub as Hannah instructed in her imaginary house. The lantern flickered and Mary turned up the wick. She hated being trapped, but at least she didn't have to face the situation alone.

A dozen times in the next half hour the eerie wailing of sirens rose and fell as they passed by on the highway a quarter of a mile away from the house. Each time, Mary's hopes sprang to life and then ebbed away with the sound. She met Joshua's eyes. They both knew it was a bad sign.

Joshua noticed the growing look of concern on Mary's face. It didn't surprise him. He was concerned, too. He had no idea when rescue would come. Would anyone think to search an old house that had been abandoned for months? Why would they? He racked his brain for a way to signal that they were here, but came up empty. Someone would have to come close enough to hear them shouting.

Hannah came to stand in front of him with her hands

on her hips. "Joshua, we need a stove and a bed now. Take me shopping again."

She looked and sounded like a miniature version of her mother. He had to smile. "You are a bossy woman. Does your mother boss your *daed* that way?"

Hannah shook her head. "He died a long time ago. I don't remember him. But I have Papa Nick."

At first, Joshua had assumed Papa Nick was *Englisch* because Hannah connected him to the siren she heard. However, the siren could have belonged to one of the many Amish volunteer fire department crews that dotted the area. Was Papa Nick her new father, perhaps? He glanced to where Mary was searching the shelves and asked quietly, "Who is Nick?"

"He's my papa Nick," the child said, as if that explained everything.

"Is he your mother's husband?"

"Nee." She laughed at the idea.

He glanced at Mary with a new spark of interest. She wasn't married, as he had assumed. It was surprising. Why would the men in this community overlook such a prize? Perhaps she was still mourning her husband. Joshua rubbed his chin. He noticed a bit of cobweb dangling from his fingers and shook it off. He needed to concentrate on getting out of this cellar, not on his interest in Hannah's mother.

He patted Hannah's head. "We will go shopping as soon as your *mamm* returns. Let's wait and see if she brings us any treasures."

"Okay." Hannah sat on her makeshift chair, put her elbows on her knees and propped her chin in her hands. "I wish Bella was here."

Joshua sat gingerly in the chair with a broken arm.

He sighed with relief when it held his weight. Remembering the black-and-white mutt that had been his inseparable companion when he was only a little bit older than Hannah, he asked, "What kind of dog is she?"

"She's a yellow dog."

Joshua smothered a grin and managed to say, "They're the best kind."

"Yup. She was *Mammi* Miriam's dog, but when I was born, Bella wanted to belong to me."

Mary returned with several jars in her hand. "These pears are still sealed and the rings were taken off so they aren't rusty. If worst comes to worst, we can try them, but they are nearly three years old from what I can read of the labels."

He grimaced. "Three-year-old pears don't sound appetizing."

"I wasn't suggesting they were, but I've known people to eat home-canned food that was older than this."

"Really? How can you tell if it's bad?"

"If the seal is intact, if the food looks good and smells okay, it should be okay…" Her voice trailed off.

He folded his arms over his chest. "You go first."

She rolled her eyes and he smiled. He could have been trapped with a much less enjoyable companion. "Come on, Hannah. We're going shopping for a bed. I think I saw one earlier that might go with our decor."

"What's decor?" Hannah asked, jumping off her chair.

He gestured toward his clothing. "It means style."

"What is your style?" Mary asked with a gleam of amusement in her eyes.

"Cobwebs and dust. What's yours?" He leaned toward her. "How did you get your face clean?"

She blushed and looked down. "There is plenty of water dripping in on the other side. You could wash up if you'd like."

"Good idea. Come on, Hannah. Let's get some of this decor off of us."

"*Ja*, it's yucky."

Mary stopped Hannah. She lifted the girl's apron off over her head, tore it in two and handed him the pieces. "Use this to wash and dry with. It's the cleanest thing you'll find down here."

"*Danki.*" As he took it from her, his fingers brushed against hers, sending a tiny thrill across his skin. She immediately thrust her hands in the pockets of her dress and her blush deepened.

She was a pretty woman. He liked the way wisps of her blond hair had come loose from beneath her *kapp* and curled around her face. He liked her smile, too. Would he have noticed her if they hadn't been forced together? In truth, he wouldn't have looked twice if he saw her with a child. He realized he was staring and turned away. The last thing he wanted was for her to feel uncomfortable.

After washing Hannah's face and his own, Joshua returned to find Mary had put the candle stubs he'd seen in a small jar. She was melting them over the flame of the candle on the tub. Hannah had found a worn-out broom with a broken handle. She began using it to sweep the floor of her house. "We didn't find a stove, *Mamm*."

Joshua gestured toward Mary's jar. "Are you going to make me eat wax for supper because I don't want your ancient pears?"

Using a piece of broken glass, she cut the ribbons off her *kapp*. "*Nee*, I'm making more candles."

"Smart thinking." The lantern had been flickering. It would go out soon and he hadn't found more kerosene.

She flashed him a shy smile before looking down. "I have my moments."

He noticed she had opened one of the jars of fruit. "Did you eat some of that?"

She nodded. "If I don't get sick, it should be fine for the two of you."

"I'm not sure that was smart thinking. Were they good?"

"As sweet as the day they were canned, but kind of mushy. Would you like some?"

"I'll pass. I might have to take care of you if you get sick. Besides, I'm not hungry."

She glanced up. "I feel fine. Did you find a bed for Hannah?"

He sat down in the chair. "Just some rusty box springs and a pile of burlap sacks. I'll bring them over later. It's not much, but it will have to do. I'm sorry I couldn't find anything for you."

"The rocker will suit me fine." She dipped her ribbon in the melted wax and pulled it out. Letting it harden, she waited a little while and then dipped it again. Each time she pulled it out, the candle grew fatter. Hannah came over and Mary allowed her to start her own candle.

It was pleasant watching them work by lantern light. Mary was patient with her daughter, teaching her by showing her what to do and praising her when she did well. Outside, the sound of rain faded away. The storm was over. Would someone find them soon?

"You mentioned you were here inspecting the property. Where is home?"

He gingerly settled back in his chair. "My family has a farm and a small business near a place called Bowmans Crossing. It's north and west of Berlin."

"Do you have a big family?" Hannah asked.

"Four brothers, so not very big."

Hannah gave a weary sigh. "I want a brother *and* a sister, but *Mamm* says no."

Joshua chuckled.

Mary refused to look at him. "You have Bella. That's enough."

He couldn't resist teasing her. "Your *mamm* needs a husband first, Hannah."

Hannah's eyes widened and she held up a hand. "That's what *Mammi* Ada says. She says *Mamm* will turn into an old *maedel* if we don't find her a husband soon."

Joshua tipped his head to the side as he regarded Mary's crimson cheeks. "I think she has a few years yet. Tell your grandmother not to worry."

"I wish you two would stop talking about me as if I weren't here. Your candle is thick enough, Hannah. I think Joshua should make up a bed for you."

Hannah looked at her in shock. "You mean we have to sleep here?"

Mary cupped her daughter's cheek. "I'm afraid so."

"I sure wish this adventure was over. Can I have supper now?"

Mary glanced at Joshua. He shrugged. "If you feel okay, I don't see why not."

Hannah enjoyed eating sticky pear halves with her fingers while Joshua fixed a makeshift bed for her. It wasn't much, but it would keep her off the cold damp floor. She made a face as she crawled onto the burlap bags. Mary checked the edge of her apron and found it was dry now. She pulled it off and used it to cover Hannah. It wasn't long before the child was asleep. The lamp died a few minutes later.

Joshua lit the candle that Mary had made and stuck it to the middle of the tub. It would burn out long before the night was over. Mary settled in the rocker, but he knew she didn't sleep any better than he did. The long night crawled past. He had no way to tell time. He simply had to endure the darkness, as he had done in prison.

The distant rumble of thunder woke him some time later. He lifted his head and winced at the pain in his neck. Opening his eyes, he realized he was still in the cellar. It was dark, but he could make out Mary's form in the other chair.

She sat forward and bent her neck slowly from side to side. "Is it morning?"

"I think so."

"It's raining again."

"Ja."

"I was dreaming about bacon and eggs."

His stomach rumbled. "I was dreaming about three-year-old pears."

"Really?"

"Nee, I wasn't dreaming at all. If I was, I'd wake up and find I was at home in my own bed."

"Wouldn't that be nice?"

They both stood and stretched. She looked at him. "What's the plan for today?"

He rubbed his bristly cheeks with both hands. "I thought you had a plan."

"I'm sure it's your turn to come up with something. I thought of making the candles."

He nudged the broken rocker with his boot. "Which was good, but I thought of finding furniture for our snug little home. It's your turn to be brilliant."

"I've never felt less brilliant in my life. What would you like for breakfast? I believe we have more three-year-old pears or some four-year-old peaches."

"Peaches," Hannah said, sitting up on her make-shift mattress.

"Peaches," he agreed. "Provided they look safe."

After their meal, they spent more time exploring for a way out without success. By noon, the rain had moved on and a few narrow beams of sunlight streamed through cracks in the floorboards overhead, allowing them to see their dismal surroundings a little better.

Joshua studied the cracks for a while. "I think I might be able to knock some of the floor planks loose if I can find something sturdy to reach them."

"I knew you would have a plan." Mary began to search through the piles of junk and he joined her.

The best thing he could come up with was a post about five feet long and two inches thick. He chose a spot overhead, wrapped some cloth around one end of the wood to prevent slivers and began thrusting it upward. Mary and Hannah stood nearby watching him. After half an hour, his arms were aching, the end of the post was beginning to splinter and the floorboard above him had only been displaced by an inch. It was something, but it wasn't enough.

Mary reached for his battering ram. "Let me work on it for a while. Do you think we'd do better to try and knock a hole in the cellar door?"

He handed her the wooden post. "It's reinforced with metal straps and I didn't see any light shining in through it. There's no telling what's on top of it. I know it's open above me here."

They took turns working for several hours and had the ends of two planks above them loose when Mary suddenly grabbed his arm. "Wait. Stop. I hear a dog."

The barking grew louder.

Hannah got up off the floor and began jumping. "I hear Bella."

Joshua gave a mighty heave and the floorboard broke, leaving a narrow space open. They looked at each other. "Neither of us can fit through that," he said, his excitement ebbing away.

"Hannah might be able to."

The sunlight dimmed and Joshua looked up. The head of a large yellow dog was visible above him. The dog barked excitedly. Hannah rushed to Joshua's side. "I knew I heard Bella."

"I hear voices, too." Mary began shouting. A few moments later, the dog was pushed aside.

An English woman with brown hair knelt down to look in. "Mary, is that you? Is Hannah with you?"

Tears of joy streamed down Mary's face. "We're okay, Miriam, but we can't get the cellar door open."

"Thank God you are safe. We'll get you out. Don't worry. Nick, I found them!" She disappeared from view. The dog came back to the opening. She lay down and woofed softly.

Mary threw her arms around Joshua in an impulsive hug. "I knew they would find us. I just knew it."

Bella barked again. As if Mary realized what she was doing, she suddenly stepped away from Joshua and crossed her arms. "It's Miriam and Nick, my adoptive parents. Nick will get us out of here."

Joshua heard activity at the door and the sounds of something heavy being dragged aside. "Looks like our prayers have been answered."

Mary picked up Hannah. Joshua followed them as they hurried to the stairwell.

From the other side, a man said, "Everyone stand clear."

"We are, Nick." Mary replied. The sound of an ax striking the portal was followed by splintering wood. A hole appeared in the top of the door and grew rapidly. Through it, Joshua could see the leaves and limbs of a large tree that must have been holding the door shut. Mary's father was swinging the ax like a madman. Joshua ached to help, but he could only stand by and wait.

Finally, the top section of the door broke free and a man's hands reached in. "Give me Hannah."

Mary handed the child over and then waited until the opening was enlarged. Joshua boosted her up and then climbed out on his own. The sunshine and the fresh air was a blessed relief from their dark, dank room. He blinked in the brightness and focused on Hannah in the arms of a woman in her early thirties. Mary was in the embrace of a man in a brown uniform. It wasn't until he released her that Joshua realized he was an *Englisch* lawman.

Mary turned to him with a bright smile, but he

couldn't smile back. "Joshua, this is my adopted father, Sheriff Nick Bradley."

A knot formed in the pit of Joshua's stomach as dread crawled up his spine.

Chapter Four

Mary's father was the *Englisch* sheriff!

It was all Joshua could do to stand still. He hadn't done anything wrong, but that hadn't made any difference the last time he'd had a run-in with the law. Cold sweat began trickling down his back.

"The storm came up so suddenly. I didn't know what to do when I saw the funnel cloud. Then Joshua stopped Tilly and pulled us into the cellar. God put him there to rescue us." Mary was talking a mile a minute until she turned to look at the house. Her eyes widened.

Joshua turned, too. Only part of one wall had been left standing. The rest was a pile of jagged, splinted wood, broken tree limbs, scattered clothing and old appliances. A small round table sat in one corner of what must have been a bedroom. There was a book and a kerosene lamp still sitting on it. The remainder of the room had been obliterated.

Hannah reached for Nick. He took the child from Miriam, who promptly drew Mary into her embrace.

"We're so thankful you're safe. God bless you, Joshua." Miriam smiled her thanks at him.

Hannah threw her arms around Nick's neck. "I'm so happy to see you, Papa Nick."

"I'm happy to see you, too, Hannah Banana," he said, patting her back, his voice thick with emotion.

She drew back to frown at him. "I'm not a banana."

He smiled and tweaked her nose. "You're not? Are you sure?"

She giggled. "I'm a girl."

"Oh, that's right."

It was apparently a running gag between the two, because they were both grinning. The sheriff put Hannah down and held out his hand to Joshua. "Pleased to meet you. My heartfelt thanks for keeping my girls safe."

Joshua reluctantly shook the man's hand and hoped the sheriff didn't notice how sweaty his palms were. "No thanks are necessary."

Nick's eyes narrowed slightly. "You aren't from around here, are you? I didn't catch your last name."

Here it comes. Joshua braced himself. "Bowman. My family is from over by Berlin."

"The name rings a bell. Who is your father?" Nick tilted his head slightly as he stared at Joshua intently.

"Isaac Bowman." Joshua held his breath as he waited to be denounced as a criminal. What would Mary think of her rescuer then? He wasn't sure why it mattered, but it did.

Miriam lifted Hannah into her arms. "Stop with the interrogation, Nicolas. Let's get these children someplace safe. We still have a lot of work to do."

"Is Ada okay?" Mary asked, looking to Miriam.

Nodding, Miriam said, "She's fine except for being

worried about you and Hannah. The house was only slightly damaged, but her corncribs were destroyed."

"Oh, no. Who else was affected? We heard the sirens last evening."

Miriam and Nick exchanged speaking glances. Nick said, "A lot of people. The Sutters' house was damaged. Elam has minor injuries. Katie, the kids and the women who were gathered for the quilting bee are all okay. I'm sorry to tell you that Bishop Zook was seriously injured. They took him to the hospital last night and into surgery this morning. We're still waiting for word about him. He lost his barn and his house was heavily damaged, but his wife is okay."

"Oh, dear." Mary's eyes filled with tears. Miriam hugged her.

Nick cleared his throat. "The tornado went straight through the south end of Hope Springs. Ten blocks of the town were leveled. We're only beginning to assess the full extent of the damage in the daylight. I need to get back there. We've still got a search-and-rescue effort underway. As of noon, we had seven people unaccounted for, but that goes down to five now that we've found you and Hannah."

Mary took Hannah from Miriam. "How did you find us? We were supposed to be at the Sutter place."

Nick said, "When Ada saw your mare come home without you, she got really worried. She walked to a neighbor's house to use their phone to call me last night. We checked with Katie and learned you never arrived. Your buggy was found in Elam Sutter's field at first light this morning. When we saw you weren't in it, we picked up Bella in the hopes that she could locate you and tried to retrace your path. She led us here."

"She must have heard us pounding. She couldn't have followed our scent after all that rain," Mary said.

"I don't know how she knew, but she did." Miriam patted the dog and then began walking toward the road, where a white SUV sat parked at the intersection with its red lights flashing. The sheriff followed her.

Grateful that he hadn't been outed, Joshua caught Mary's arm, silently asking her to remain a moment. She did. Their brief time together was over and he needed to get going. "I'm glad things turned out okay for you and Hannah."

"Only by God's grace and because you were here."

"You were very brave, Mary. I want you to know how much I admire that. You're a fine mother and a good example for your daughter. I'm pleased to have met you, even under these circumstances."

She blushed and looked down. "I have been blessed to meet you, too, and I shall always count you among my friends."

"I need to get going. My folks are expecting me home in a day or two. When they hear about this storm they'll worry." He took a step back.

Mary's eyes grew round as she looked past him. "Oh, no."

"What?" He turned and saw the barn hadn't been spared. Half of it was missing and the rest was leaning precariously in hay-covered tatters. He'd been so shaken to see the sheriff that he had forgotten about his horse. He started toward what was left of the building at a run.

Mary was tempted to follow Joshua, but she knew he might need more help than she could provide. Instead, she ran after Nick. She caught up with him and quickly explained the situation.

Nick said, "I'll help him. Let Miriam drive you and Hannah home and then she can come back for me."

"Absolutely not," Miriam said before Mary could answer. "I'm not leaving until you and that young man are both safe."

He kissed her cheek. "That's why I love you. You never do what I tell you. Call headquarters and let them know what's going on. I don't want them to think I've gone on vacation."

"I will. Be careful."

As Nick jogged toward the barn, Mary said, "I'm going to see what I can do."

"No, the men can manage."

"More hands will lighten the load." Mary raced after Nick. When she reached the teetering edge of the barn, she hesitated. She couldn't see what was holding it up as she slowly made her way inside the tangled beams and splintered wood. Everything was covered with hay that had spilled down from the loft. It could be hiding any number of hazards.

Once she reached the interior, she no longer had to scramble over broken wood, so the going was easier. She saw the flattened remains of Joshua's buggy beneath a large beam. Ominous creaking came from overhead. Joshua and Nick were pulling debris away from one of the nearby stalls. A section of the hayloft had collapsed like a trapdoor, blocking their way. She reached Joshua's side and joined him as he pulled at a stubbornly lodged board.

He stopped what he was doing and scowled at her. "Get out of here right now."

"You don't get to tell me what to do." She yanked on the board and it came free. She tossed it behind her.

Joshua turned to Nick. "Tell her it isn't safe."

"It isn't safe, Mary," Nick said.

"It is safe enough for you two to be in here." She lifted another piece of wood and threw it aside.

"See what I have to put up with, Joshua? None of the women in my family listen to me."

Mary heard a soft whinny from inside the stall. "Your horse is still alive, Joshua."

He said, "We're coming, Oscar. Be calm, big fella."

They all renewed their efforts and soon had a small opening cleared. The gap was only wide enough for Mary to slip through. Joshua's horse limped toward her. He had a large cut across his rump and down his hip.

"Oh, you poor thing." Mary stroked his face. He nuzzled her gently.

"How is he?" Joshua asked.

"He has a bad gash on his left hip, but the bleeding has stopped. How are we going to get him out of here?"

Nick said, "Even if we free him from the stall, he can't climb over the debris to get out the way we came in."

"Can you cut through the outside wall?" To her, it looked like the fastest way out.

"The silo came down on that side and left a few tons of bricks in the way."

Looking around from inside the stall, Mary saw only one other likely path. "If you can get into the next stalls and pull down the walls between them and this one, we could lead him through to the outside door at the far end of the building."

"It's worth a look," Nick said.

He and Joshua headed in that direction. She heard Joshua call to her. "Mary, if the upper level starts shifting, I want you to leave the horse and get out as fast as you can."

"I will," she called back. She patted Oscar's dusty brown neck and said softly, "Don't worry. We'll get out of this together."

The sound of her father's ax smashing into wood told her they were starting. She looked up, ready to scurry through the gap if she had to.

She hadn't been waiting long when the chopping stopped. She heard voices but couldn't make out what they were saying. Oscar whinnied. From outside, more horses answered. The sound of a chain saw sent her spirits soaring. Someone had joined Nick and Joshua.

It took less than five minutes before she saw her new rescuer cutting through the adjoining stall. It was Ethan Gingerich, a local Amish logger. Oscar began shifting uneasily. She realized he was frightened by the sound and smell of the chain saw. He tried to rear in the small space with her. She barely had room to avoid his hooves.

"Ethan, wait! He's too fearful."

Ethan killed the saw's engine. Oscar quieted, but he was still trembling. Mary patted his neck to reassure him and spoke soothingly.

"Use this to cover his eyes." Ethan, a bear of a man, unbuttoned the dark vest he wore over his blue shirt, slipped it off and handed it to Joshua. Joshua climbed over the half wall with ease and quickly tucked the vest into Oscar's halter, making sure the horse couldn't see any light. Although the horse continued to tremble, he didn't move. Without the roar of the saw, Mary could hear creaking and groaning from the remains of the hayloft.

Joshua kept his hold on Oscar and gave Mary a tired smile. "I've got him now. Thanks for your help. You would be doing me a great favor if you went outside."

His shirt was soaked with sweat and covered with sawdust and bits of straw. He'd been working to the point of exhaustion to get to her, not just to his horse. She nodded and watched relief fill his eyes. "I reckon I can do that."

He moved closer to the half wall and bent his knee. She stepped up and swung her leg over the wide boards. Nick caught her around the waist and lifted her down. She brushed off her skirt, straightened her *kapp* and went down the length of the barn through the openings they had cut. Behind her, she heard the chain saw roar to life again. She was tempted to stop and make sure all the men got out safely, but she knew they didn't need her.

Outside, she saw Miriam standing a few yards away beside the team of huge draft horses that belonged to Ethan. She had Hannah by the hand. When Hannah saw her, she dropped Miriam's hand and raced forward. "*Mamm*, Bella chased a rabbit into the field and she won't come back. I called her and called her."

"That naughty dog." She swung Hannah up into her arms.

Miriam crossed her arms and glared at Mary. "Bella is not the only naughty member of this family. Go wait for us in the car, Hannah."

Mary put her daughter down and watched her run to the vehicle. Hannah loved to ride in Papa Nick's SUV. He often let her play with the siren. Smiling, Mary turned back to Miriam, but her adoptive mother's face was set in stern lines. Mary sought to defend herself. "I had to help. You would have done the same."

"No, I wouldn't have. They could have managed without you. You have a kind but impulsive nature, Mary. It's better to think things through than to rush into something only to find bigger trouble. You should know that better than anyone. Nick wouldn't have come out of there without you no matter how dangerous it became. He would have left the horse if he had to."

Miriam almost never scolded her, and she never brought up Mary's past. Chastised, Mary stared at the ground and whispered, "I'm sorry."

She felt Miriam's hand on her shoulder. "I know you are. I just want you to think with your head and not let your emotions rule you. Just be more cautious."

Mary heard trepidation in Miriam's voice. She was more upset than Mary's action warranted. "I'm sorry I frightened you. You must have been worried sick all night long."

Miriam pulled her close. "I was. Promise me you'll be more careful."

"I promise."

When Miriam held her tighter and didn't release her, Mary knew something else was troubling her mother. "What's wrong?"

Miriam sighed. "I didn't want to tell you this now after all you've been through, but there is something you need to know."

"What?"

"Kevin Dunbar is coming up for parole."

Mary's gaze shot to lock with Miriam's as dread seeped into her heart. "What does that mean?"

"If he is granted parole, it means he will be released from prison."

"But they sentenced him to ten years. It's only been four."

"I know, and Nick and I will speak at the hearing and object to his early release, but it may not be enough."

Mary crossed her arms tightly. "Will he come here?"

"He doesn't know where you live. He doesn't know your new name. He doesn't know that I adopted you or that I married Nick. I don't see how he could find you and Hannah."

"He said he would make me pay for speaking against him in court." She bit her lower lip, but it didn't stop the taste of fear that rose in her mouth.

Miriam laid both hands on Mary's shoulders. "He won't find you. Nick and I will see to that. We wanted you to know so it wouldn't come as a shock if he does get an early release, but we don't want you to worry. Here come the men. Why don't you join Hannah in the car?"

"I want to speak to Joshua first. His buggy was crushed and his horse is injured. He has no way to get home. I'm sure Ada won't mind if he comes home with us."

"I'm sure she won't, but it wouldn't be proper for you to offer him a place to stay. You are a single woman. I'm married. I can suggest he stay with my mother."

"But—"

"No buts, Mary. Don't argue about this. An Amish woman is not outspoken. She is modest and humble. You need to cultivate those virtues or you will be perceived as prideful. Don't forget, your actions reflect on Ada, too. Nick spoils you. He's a good man, but he doesn't understand Amish ways."

Mary sighed deeply. Miriam had been raised Amish and knew what was expected of each member. While Miriam had chosen to live English, Mary had freely chosen the Amish way of life. It wasn't an easy path, but she felt called to follow it. The freedoms she enjoyed by having English parents shouldn't cause her to lose sight of what it meant to live a Plain life. She had placed her life totally in God's hands. She would remain His humble and obedient servant.

Ethan approached them with his chain saw balanced on his shoulder. Miriam said, "Thank you for your assistance, Ethan. Is your family safe?"

"Glad I could help. The storm wasn't bad at our place. I heard about the twister when Clara came home last night from the quilting bee. I went out this morning to see if anyone needed me, or my team. I've cut through a lot of trees blocking lanes and roadways and hauled them aside. I was on my way home when I saw the sheriff's SUV and thought I'd see what he was up to out here."

"I'm glad you did," Nick said as he and Joshua came up beside them.

Mary pinned her gaze to the ground. Joshua must think she was a frightfully forward woman after the way she had acted. "Have you heard if Betsy is safe?" she asked, knowing her friend, whose oldest sister was Ethan's wife, had been headed to the same quilting bee at Katie Sutter's home.

"*Ja,* she is fine. I took Clara and the *kinder* to Wooly Joe's first thing this morning. All the girls were at their grandfather's place. You've never heard such squawking as those sisters do when they have something exciting to talk about. They were getting ready to take food and supplies into Hope Springs."

Mary smiled at him. "I'm glad they're okay. God is *goot*."

"Indeed He is. I need to get my team home. They've had a tough day." Ethan bade everyone farewell and left.

Mary began walking toward Nick's vehicle. She tried not to look back to see if Joshua was watching, but she couldn't help herself. He was.

Joshua watched Mary walk away and a strange sense of loss filled him. This was probably the last time he would see her. He was shocked to realize just how much he wanted to see her again. Under normal circumstances.

Nick laid a hand on Joshua's shoulder. "You must be exhausted."

He tried not to flinch from the man's touch, but it brought back the way the police and the prison guards had grabbed him in the past. "A little," he admitted. His strength was draining away now that the crisis was over.

Miriam glanced toward the car and then turned to him. "Unless you have other plans, why don't you come back to my mother's home with us? You can clean up and have a hot meal, spend the night and then decide what to do in the morning."

As much as he wanted to accept, he didn't want to spend any more time in the sheriff's company. "*Danki*, but I don't think so."

"Suit yourself," Nick said.

Miriam laid a hand on Joshua's arm. "You need a place to stay until you can sort things out and get home. My mother will welcome you. She is Amish, so I know you'll be comfortable there. Not another word—you're coming with us."

She walked away to join Mary and Hannah. Joshua stood rooted to the spot. He hadn't expected this kindness from outsiders. He swallowed hard and hitched a thumb over his shoulder toward the barn. "I have some clothes and a few things in what's left of my buggy that I need. Let me get those and see to my horse."

Nick said, "Leave him tied up here, and I'll have someone bring a trailer and take him to our vet."

"I would appreciate that, if it's not too much trouble." Joshua wasn't sure he had the money to pay for a vet, but his father would send more to cover the bill. Isaac Bowman never skimped on taking care of his animals. It was a lesson he had drilled into his sons.

"No trouble," Nick said. "I've had reports from all over about loose and injured livestock. I have nearly a dozen volunteers with stock trailers helping wherever they are needed and taking all sorts of animals to our vet's clinic. Doc Rodgers has already asked for help from other veterinarians in the state. He'll have someone to look after your horse."

After agreeing to the arrangement, Joshua tethered Oscar where he could reach green grass and water and covered him with a blanket to keep the flies out of the gash. Then he extracted his duffel bag and his few belongings from his crushed buggy and joined Mary's family in the SUV. Hannah greeted him with a big smile. "Bella came back."

Joshua glanced over his shoulder. The Lab mix was

in the back of the vehicle panting heavily. "It looks like she had a good run."

"She was chasing a rabbit. She's not supposed to do that," Hannah told him in a low voice.

"Did she catch him?" Joshua asked in a whisper. He shared a smile with Mary, but she quickly looked away.

Hannah shook her head. "She never catches them. She's not very fast. What about your horse?"

"Nick said he'll have someone take him to the vet clinic."

Mary continued to avoid looking at him. He fell silent and remained that way. The sudden change in their circumstances left him feeling tongue-tied and awkward. Or maybe it was because her father kept glancing at him in the rearview mirror. Perhaps going to Mary's home wasn't a good idea.

He hadn't been able to think of a reason to refuse under the sheriff's steely gaze earlier. He didn't want to raise the man's suspicions.

Joshua's parole agreement said he couldn't leave the area without notifying his parole officer. Was he in violation of that even if he was still in the same county? He should have checked before he left home.

The radio crackled and came to life with a woman's voice. "Sheriff, do you read me?"

Nick picked up the mic. "I read you, dispatch."

"We found the missing Keim children. The boys are fine."

Nick grinned at Miriam. "That's great news. Where were they?"

"At their aunt's house. They had gone fishing. They ran to take cover there when the storm cut them off from home. It took her family a while to dig out afterward and gather their scattered horses and cattle before they brought the kids home."

"That only leaves the McIntyre family unaccounted for."

"Nope, they weren't home. They were out camping in the woods. They came back to town about an hour ago. That's everyone who was unaccounted for, and FEMA is now on scene."

"Good. Let Deputy Medford know. Lance is in charge until I return."

"He already knows, sir."

"Have you had any word on Bishop Zook?"

"He's out of surgery and is expected to make a full recovery."

"The blessings just keep coming. Thanks. I'll be at Ada's house in a few minutes. You can get me on my cell if I don't answer the radio."

"Roger that." The radio went dead.

Joshua glanced at Mary. With her eyes downcast and her hands clasped, she was a lovely sight. Even with the smudges of dirt on her face. Was there anyone special in her life?

He caught sight of Nick watching him in the mirror and looked away, but like a magnetic needle that was always drawn to the north, Joshua's gaze moved back to Mary's face.

He might be attracted to her, but he only had one option where the sheriff's daughter was concerned: go home and forget all about her.

Chapter Five

"Do I have dirt on my face?" Mary didn't look up. She could feel Joshua's gaze on her and wondered what he was thinking. Since entering the car he had been so serious, so worried.

"You do, but I was staring at the destruction out there." He gestured toward the view beyond with his chin.

She looked out the window beside her and gasped. They were driving parallel to the tornado's track. The land bore an enormous scar of destruction. Everywhere the twister had encountered trees, only denuded trunks with stripped and snapped limbs remained. Where the trees had been toppled whole, huge mats of roots stuck in the air. As the storm had passed through wheat fields, it was if an insane harvester had mowed down random sections. Even the grass had been torn out of the pastures, leaving a path of churned dirt in the funnel's wake.

"That's the Keim farm," she said as they rolled past the once neatly tended Amish home. The entire front of the building and the roof was missing. It resembled a dollhouse more than a home. She could see into the rooms of the upper stories, where beds sat covered in bright quilts and clothes still hung on pegs. Below, the stove was all that was left in the remains of the kitchen. Some two dozen Amish men and women were working to clear the rubble. It was one advantage of large Amish families—when someone was in need, there were lots of aunts, uncles and cousins to come help.

Mary pressed her hand to her mouth. "This is so terrible."

Nick said, "It's pretty much the same all the way into Hope Springs. The tornado stayed on the ground for five miles. At times, it was half a mile wide. I've never seen anything like it."

He slowed the SUV and turned in to Ada's lane. The tornado had missed the house by a quarter of a mile. Most of the wind damage was confined to the fields and the crops that had been planted by the young farmer who rented Ada's land. There were shingles missing from the roof of the house and many of Ada's flowers had been blown down.

Nick stopped the vehicle by the front porch, where Ada stood waiting for them. The worry on her face transformed into a bright smile when Mary opened the door and let Hannah out. The child raced up the steps straight into Ada's embrace. Mary followed her.

"I thank *Gott* you are both safe," Ada said as she hugged Mary. "You hadn't been gone more than twenty minutes when the storm hit. When I came outside and saw the twister had gone the same direction you were heading, I dropped to my knees and prayed for you."

"God heard you. He sent Joshua Bowman to help us. You must thank him, as well," Mary replied, turning to introduce her grandmother to him as he got out of her father's vehicle.

Miriam said, "Joshua's buggy was destroyed and his horse was injured. He's a long way from home. I'm hoping you can look after him until he has a chance to sort out what to do next."

Ada raised a hand and beckoned. "Of course. Everyone, please come inside. I've been keeping supper warm in the oven. I must hear what happened to you."

"I can't stay," Nick said. "I have to get back to the command post we have set up in Hope Springs."

"I can't stay, either," Miriam added. "The Red Cross needs volunteers. As a nurse, I know they'll have use for me. I don't know when I'll be back, *Mamm*."

Ada nodded. "I understand."

After another round of hugs from Nick and Miriam, Mary waved goodbye from the porch steps and then led the way into the house. The kitchen smelled of fried chicken and fresh bread. Hannah proceeded to tell her great-grandmother all about their adventure. Ada was shocked and amazed at their narrow escape. Finally, Hannah said, "And then Bella found us. I'm really hungry. Can we eat now?"

Mary laid a hand on her daughter's shoulder. "We should get cleaned up before we sit at the table. Come on. Let's find some decor-free clothes for you." She glanced at Joshua and saw him smile. Pleased by it, she led Hannah away to clean up and change.

When she returned, Joshua was coming in through the front door. He had washed up and changed, as well. His face was clean shaven and his hair was still damp. The house had only one bathroom, so she knew he must have washed at the pump outside. He had a blue plastic basin in one hand.

Joshua offered the basin to Ada. "Thanks for the hot water. It made shaving a whole lot easier."

"*Goot.* You are welcome to stay with us for as long as you like. I have a spare bed and you won't be any trouble. Now, sit and let me get some food on the table. Mary, slice some bread and fetch a jar of pears from the pantry."

"No pears," Mary and Joshua said together. They shared an embarrassed glance.

Looking confused, Ada said, "I have some peaches if you would rather."

Mary tried not to laugh. "Don't we have some plums?"

"*Ja*, we do."

Mary kissed her grandmother's wrinkled cheek. "Plums will be fine. It's so good to be home."

While Mary and Hannah were busy getting the table set, Ada began pulling pans from the oven. "Joshua, where is your family from?"

"A place called Bowmans Crossing. It's north and west of Berlin. About a day's buggy ride from here."

"I don't know it, but then I've only been in Hope Springs a few years. I moved here from Millersburg. Do you have someone special waiting back home?"

"Not yet."

"So you haven't met the right girl, is that it?"

Mary sent her grandmother a sour glance, but Ada ignored her. Joshua grinned at Hannah. "I've met her, but she's not quite old enough to marry. I'm going to have to wait a few years."

"He means me, *Mammi*." Hannah put the last plate on the table. "I'm not going to be an old maid."

"At least one of my girls has some sense. What does your family do, Joshua?"

"They farm and run a small business."

"And how did you end up here?"

"He came to look over some property for his father. I think he has answered enough questions for one day." Mary took her place at the table.

"I'm just making conversation and trying to put the poor boy at ease." Ada carried her pan to the table and dished out the creamy potatoes.

When Ada was finished, she took her place at the table and everyone bowed their heads in silent prayer. Because Joshua was the only man at the table, the women waited until he signaled the prayer was finished. Mary hadn't realized how hungry she was until she dug into her grandmother's mouthwatering, crispy fried chicken. It was one of the best meals Mary had ever eaten.

When Joshua was finished, he leaned back in his chair and patted his stomach. "That was mighty *goot*, *danki*."

Ada smiled at him. "It does my heart good to see a man enjoy my cooking. Mary is a fine cook, too."

"I can help clean up," he offered.

Mary and Ada exchanged amused glances. Very few men offered to help with kitchen chores. "I can manage," Ada said. "It would please me if you would read from the Good Book for us when I'm done here."

"It would be my pleasure. Hannah, do you have a Bible story that you like?"

"Noah. I like the story about Noah and all the animals."

Ada smiled. "Very appropriate. As Noah and his family were delivered from a great storm, so were you and your mother. *Gott* is merciful."

Their evenings were often spent with Mary reading passages while Ada caught up with her needlework. It was a pleasant change to have someone else reading to her. Mary listened to the sound of Joshua's voice and realized once again how soothing it was. He had a strong, firm voice. He read with ease and with understanding, pausing occasionally to ask Hannah about something that he had read. She listened intently, seated on the floor in front of him with Bella at her side. He seemed to be a man devoted to his faith, but Mary knew not everyone was what they seemed to be.

When it was time for bed, Ada showed Joshua to the spare room while Mary took Hannah up to her room. She knelt beside Hannah as the child recited her bedtime prayers. Overwhelmed with gratitude for their deliverance, Mary gazed at her child and gave silent thanks. She would never again take moments like this for granted.

Hannah got into bed and pulled the sheet to her chin. "I like this bed much better. It smells *wunderbar.*"

Mary tucked her in. "I agree."

"Will Joshua be here in the morning when I wake up?"

"*Ja*, he will be here."

"I'm glad. I like him. Don't you?"

Mary smiled at her daughter and planted a kiss on her forehead. "I like him, too." Maybe more than she should.

"How old will I have to be before I can marry him?"

Mary bit her lower lip to keep from laughing. "Very old, I'm afraid."

"As old as you?"

Mary chuckled. "At least as old as me."

"Okay. *Guten nacht, Mamm.*"

"Good night and sweet dreams, *liebschen.*" Mary stepped away. Bella took her usual spot on the blue rag rug beside the bed. Mary patted the dog's head. "And sweet dreams for you, too, Bella. You are a very *goot hund.*"

The following morning, Mary was up bright and early. By the time Ada came out of her room, Mary already had breakfast underway. Although she would have denied it if anyone asked, she wanted to impress Joshua with her cooking skills. Just a little. She pulled a pan of cinnamon rolls from the oven and set it to cool on the counter.

It wasn't long before he came in. "Something smells delicious. I hope it tastes as good as it smells."

"It will. How do you like your eggs?"

"Less than three years old." He tried to pinch off a piece of cinnamon roll, but she batted his hand away.

"Sit down and behave yourself or all you'll get is eggshells."

"Is there coffee?" He glanced hopefully at her.

"In the pot."

He helped himself to a cup and sat at the table. She could feel him watching her. It should have made her nervous, but it didn't. Somehow, it felt comfortable having him in the same room. It shouldn't, but it did, and she wondered why.

What was it about him that made him different from other men? She studied him covertly as she tried to put her finger on it.

His face wasn't particularly handsome, but he had a strong jaw and a square chin that made him look dependable. She finally decided his eyes were what made him so interesting. They were a soft, expressive brown. They crinkled at the corners when he smiled. She liked that. It proved he smiled often. And he didn't mind being quiet.

Ada and Hannah came in a few minutes later and Mary regretted the loss of her time alone with Joshua.

Did he feel the same? Or was he anxious to leave and get home? Of course he was. Why would he want to spend more time with her?

Ada poured some coffee and leaned her hip against the counter. "We will take food and supplies into Hope Springs when our chores are done. Our neighbors are in need. *Englisch* and Amish alike. We must do what we can."

Mary nodded, ashamed to admit she had forgotten for a little while the tragedy that had struck her community.

They had barely finished breakfast when Bella barked and trotted to the door, wagging her tail. Mary heard the sound of a buggy pulling up outside. Ada rose and went to the window. A bright smile transformed her face as she turned to Mary. "With all that has happened, I clean forgot Delbert Miller was coming by today. I must go out and make him welcome. Mary, you should come, too." Ada hurried out the front door.

Mary dried her hands slowly on a kitchen towel. "As if I had any choice in the matter."

* * *

After the women went out the door, Joshua leaned toward Hannah. "Who is Delbert Miller?"

"*Mammi* says he is the perfect *mann* for *Mamm*. He's going to fix the chicken house roof, but *Mamm* is afraid he'll fall through and squish our chickens."

The perfect man? Joshua rose to his feet and sauntered toward the door to get a look at the paragon.

The buggy in front of the gate was tipped heavily to one side. When the driver got out, Joshua understood the reason. Delbert Miller was a man of considerable size, with a jovial smile and a booming voice to match.

"Good morning, Ada. Good morning, Mary. I see the storm caught you, too."

"Not as bad as some, I hear. What about your place?" Ada asked.

"Not even a branch knocked down."

"You were blessed," Mary said quietly.

"Indeed, I am." Delbert gave Mary a bright smile. His gaze lingered on her face.

Joshua studied Mary closely, looking for her reaction. To his eyes, she didn't look happy to see the perfect man, and that pleased him.

A team of horses pulling a wagon came up the lane, driven by two young Amish men. The wagon was loaded with lumber.

"Have you brought help?" Ada asked.

Delbert gestured in their direction. "I met Atlee and Moses Beachy on the road. They were on their way home from the Weavers' sawmill with lumber for the town. They insisted on following me in case you needed some repairs."

"That was mighty kind of them, but all I need is a few shingles on the porch roof."

"We have some with us," one of the twins said.

Hannah came outside, but the child stood behind her mother, peeking around the edge of her skirt.

The two young brothers, identical twins, got down from the wagon. "Has anyone seen Hannah Banana?" asked the one who had been driving.

"Could be she got blown away in the big wind," the other one said as they looked around pretending to seek her.

Hannah stepped out from behind Mary. "I almost got blown away. Did you see the tornado? It smashed Joshua's house, and we got stuck in the old cellar. *Mamm* and me and Joshua had to stay there all night. It was full of cobwebs and yucky."

"You don't say?" Delbert looked to Mary for more of an explanation.

Mary, her cheeks glowing pink, gave an abbreviated account to their visitors and introduced Joshua to the men. She sent Hannah back into the house before the little girl could repeat more of the story.

Ada spoke to the twins. "You can get out on the porch roof from the upstairs window. I'll show you. Delbert, I have some cinnamon *kaffi* cake I baked yesterday. Come up to the house when you're finished and have some."

"I'd love to, but it will have to wait. There's a lot of people in need today and the twins and I should get going when we are finished here."

"I understand. Mary will show you what we need done to the chicken *haus*."

Joshua caught Mary's slight hesitation before she nodded. "Come this way."

"Why don't I give you a hand," Joshua offered. He was rewarded with a grateful look from Mary. It appeared that she didn't want to be alone with Delbert.

"I don't reckon I'll need any help." Delbert frowned at Joshua.

"Many hands make quick work," Mary said brightly. She led the way to the henhouse beside the barn.

The structure had seen better days. There was a hole in the roof where some of the shingles had rotted away. The red paint was faded and peeling from the walls. Joshua suspected a number of boards would need to be replaced. Mary pointed out where the chicken wire around the fenced enclosure was loose and sagging. She opened a gate to the enclosure and stepped back. The black-and-brown hens scurried past her and spread out across the barnyard in search of insects. A large rooster crowed his displeasure, but when all the hens were gone, he followed them and took up a post on the corral fence, where he crowed repeatedly until one of the twins shooed him away.

Delbert turned to Mary. "I'll need a ladder to get up on the roof. Do you have one I can use?"

She pointed toward the barn. "Of course. It's right inside the main door."

Delbert looked disappointed that she didn't offer to show him in person, but he went to fetch it alone.

"I think Hannah might be right," Joshua said, trying to hide a smile.

Mary frowned at him. "About what?"

"She said Delbert was the perfect man for you."

Her eyes narrowed in displeasure. "There's no such thing as a perfect man. Only God is perfect."

"True enough, but I think you were right about the rest."

"I have no idea what you're talking about."

"If he gets up on the roof of that chicken house, he's going to go right through it."

A reluctant smile tugged at the corner of her pretty mouth. "Why do you think I let all the hens out?"

Delbert returned, carrying the ladder under his arm. He propped it against the building, but before he could climb up, Joshua caught him by the arm. "Why don't you let me go? You and Mary can hand me the supplies I'll need once I am up there."

Delbert looked ready to argue, but thought better of it. "I reckon it would be better for a skinny little fellow like you to test those old boards."

Joshua slapped him on the back. "Exactly what I was thinking. Would you mind if I borrow some of your tools?"

Once he was on the roof of the henhouse, Joshua pried loose the rotted shingles with Delbert's hammer. A section of the plywood roof had to be replaced, but the underlying rafters were sound. Mary handed the new shingles to Delbert, who stood on the ladder and handed them over to Joshua. When Joshua came down, Mary excused herself and went up to the house, leaving the two men alone.

"I can give you a hand restretching the wire fencing," Joshua offered.

"Sure."

Joshua set to work pulling the old staples that held

the wire onto the wooden fence posts. "Have you known Mary long?"

"Since she first came here. Four years now, I guess it is."

"Did you know her husband?"

"*Nee*, I'm not sure she was married. If that's the case, I don't hold it against her. We all make mistakes. She's a fine woman, and her little girl is as sweet as they come."

Joshua mulled over that startling bit of information. Did it change the way he felt about her? He wasn't sure, and that shamed him. "Hannah said her father has gone to heaven."

"That is what Mary told Bishop Zook when she joined our congregation. He was an *Englisch* fellow, and that's all I know about him."

Joshua stared at the house. "Does she mourn him still?"

"That I cannot tell you, but she doesn't go to the singings and she has turned down a lot of fellows who have tried to ask her out. Some people say she's too particular. I think she'll come around when the right fellow shows an interest."

Joshua glanced at his companion. "It could be the right fellow doesn't live around here."

Delbert stared at Joshua for a long moment, then he burst out laughing and slapped Joshua on the back hard enough to make him wince. "Only God knows the right one for each of us. If He has someone in mind for her, then that's the one she'll wed, and it won't matter where he's from. We should finish this pen right quick. Others need my help today."

The man had a big heart to match his big frame. "Delbert, I need to find a way to get to Bowmans Crossing as soon as possible."

"Why can't you get home the same way you got here?"

"My buggy was wrecked in the storm and my horse was injured."

"Sorry to hear that. I know a fellow in Hope Springs that drives Amish folks. I'll take you by his house. If he can't take you, well, you're handy with a hammer. You'll be most welcome to join the rest of us in the cleanup."

Joshua was ready to get home. He would miss his growing friendship with Mary, but it was better to leave before the attachment deepened. He had no illusions about his chances with her and the less he had to do with her father, the better. She wasn't the one for him. Joshua didn't believe Delbert was the man for her, either, but he wished the big fellow well in his pursuit of her.

Delbert looked around and lowered his voice. "I should warn you about the Beachy twins."

Joshua looked toward the porch roof, where the two young men were finishing the last of the repairs. "What about them?"

"They have a knack for playing pranks on folks. Harmless pranks for the most part, but beware. You might sit down on a chair and get up to find a red bull's-eye painted on the seat of your pants. It happened to me and I never did figure out how they did it."

Joshua laughed outright at Delbert's pained expression. "I'll beware of them. *Danki*."

* * *

"What can be so funny?" Mary stood at the window watching Delbert and Joshua out by the henhouse.

"What's that, child?" Ada asked. She was at the kitchen table wrapping sandwiches and packing them into boxes.

"Joshua and Delbert are out there slapping each other on the back and laughing like a pair of fools." It was an exaggeration on her part, but she had a sneaking suspicion that they were laughing at her expense.

"The Lord has blessed Delbert with a *wunderbar* sense of humor. The man likes to make other people smile. There's nothing wrong in that. Would you pack the plates for me? I expect there will be a lot of hungry people working in Hope Springs today. We'll need to fill some jugs with water, too."

Mary turned away from the window. If the town had seen the same kind of destruction she had witnessed, it would be bad. She was foolish and vain to be worrying about what Joshua Bowman thought of her. She put him out of her mind and began helping Ada prepare lunches.

A few minutes later, Joshua walked in the door. "I wanted to thank you for your hospitality. I'm going to ride into Hope Springs with Delbert and check on my horse, then I'm going to try and find a ride home."

The twins came down the stairs. Atlee patted Hannah on the head. "That should keep the rain from coming in, Hannah Banana. Take care." They doffed their hats and went out.

Joshua went to collect his gear. When he returned, Ada handed him a large box. "Take this with you and tell Delbert to leave it at the Wadler Inn in Hope

Springs. The twins said it is still standing. We don't have room for everything in our little cart and our pony Fred can't pull a bigger wagon."

Joshua nodded. "I'll be happy to do that for you. Anything else?"

"*Nee*. Bless you for all your help and for taking care of Mary and Hannah."

"It was my pleasure."

Mary didn't want to say goodbye to him. Not yet. Berlin wasn't that far away. He could find an excuse to return if he wanted to. Did he want to?

"Will we see you again?" she asked quickly, and then looked at her feet. That was too bold of her.

"I would like that," he said quietly.

Her cheeks grew warm. She knew she was blushing. Then she realized he didn't know anything about her. Not really. When he learned her history, he'd run the other way, and that was fine. She didn't need a fellow to like her. Only—wouldn't it be nice if he did?

Hannah ran and bounced to a stop in front of him. "Goodbye, Joshua. When will I see you again?"

"That's hard to say. I live a long way from here."

"But you could come for a visit. He's welcome to visit, isn't he, *Mamm*?"

"Of course he is," Ada said when Mary remained silent.

"*Danki*, Ada. Goodbye, Hannah. Goodbye, Mary."

"Goodbye." Clenching her fingers together until they ached kept Mary from saying anything else. She was a terrible judge of men. The ones she'd thought cared for her had hurt her unbearably. It was better to keep the memory of Joshua's kindness rather than count on him and have him fail her.

When she found the courage to look up, he was already out the door. Her spirits plummeted. Would she ever see him again?

"He was a nice young fellow," Ada said from behind her.

Mary crossed the room to look out the window. "*Ja*, he was."

"I'm gonna miss him," Hannah said and left the room with Bella on her heels.

Mary watched Joshua climb into the buggy with Delbert. The vehicle still tipped heavily to one side. She smiled at the thought of Joshua hanging on to the edge of the seat to keep from sliding into Delbert's lap all the way into Hope Springs. He would make Hannah laugh when he told her the story.

Only he wouldn't be back to share it with her.

And it was better that way. Wasn't it? She didn't want her daughter growing to depend on someone who would let her down.

That was true, but protecting Hannah from disappointment wasn't the whole reason Mary didn't date. The sobering fact was that she didn't want to like someone and then find out he wasn't what he seemed. She was terrified of making another mistake. It was better to depend on God and her family. It was enough. Although she was lonely sometimes.

Mary watched until the buggy was out of sight. She wasn't missing Joshua already, was she? That was ridiculous. They'd known each other for less than two days. A few extraordinary hours. It was foolish to think he'd return to see her and more foolish to wish he would. He surely had a girl waiting back home. He hadn't mentioned one, but it was the Amish way to keep such things private.

He'd been kind to her and to Hannah. It was silly to read anything else into that kindness.

"The Lord provides," Ada said.

Mary shot her grandmother a quick look. "The Lord provides what?"

"All that we need." Ada wore a self-satisfied smile. Humming, she returned to the table to finish packing supplies for their trip into town.

"You're right. He does." Mary joined her grandmother at the table. The Lord had supplied a kind man to come to her rescue in the storm and that was all there was to it. She was grateful, but she wouldn't expect anything more.

Chapter Six

As Joshua rode into town with Delbert, the extent of the destruction became increasingly evident. Where the tornado had reached the town, it had obliterated everything in its path. Houses had been leveled. Mangled cars had been rolled into buildings and trees lay everywhere. Pink insulation and articles of clothing fluttered from the remaining branches of denuded trees that were still upright. It was almost impossible to take in the scope of the damage.

A National Guard soldier had them state their business, and then allowed them to go on after warning them that the town would be closed at 6:00 p.m. and everyone would have to leave unless they were a resident with a habitable house.

A few blocks later, Delbert stopped his horse in front of a building that was little more than a pile of pale bricks. A single wall with an arched window remained standing. The grassy area around the building was covered with brightly colored books.

Delbert whistled through his teeth. "I heard it was bad, but I didn't know it was this bad."

"Was this the library?" Joshua had come to value books in his time behind bars. They'd become a solace during the long days and longer nights in his small cell.

Delbert nodded. "Across the street is the *Englisch* grade school."

That building was in the same condition as the library. A group of women and children were picking up books and papers off the ground and placing them in large blue plastic bins. Up ahead, Ethan Gingerich had his team of draft horses hitched to a fallen tree that had obscured most of a house. At a word from him, the horses leaned into their collars and pulled the massive trunk into the street. A battered white van emerged from the foliage. It had been crushed against the home. An elderly man moved to look it over.

Delbert sighed. "I reckon Samson Carter can't take you to Bowmans Crossing today."

"Why not?"

"Because that is Samson and that is his van. We can ask him if he knows anyone else who can give you a lift if you want?" Delbert waited for Joshua to make a decision.

An elderly woman joined Samson and the two of them stood with their arms around each other surveying the damage to the house and vehicle. She was crying. Everywhere Joshua looked, he saw people picking through the debris of what had once been a town but now resembled an enormous trash heap. Looking down, he noticed an open book on the sidewalk beside the buggy. Its pages fluttered in the breeze. He got out and picked it up. It was a second-grade reader that belonged to a girl named Ann. His mother's name was Anna.

He turned to Delbert. "I reckon I wasn't meant to go home today."

"I thought you had to get back?"

"I have to be home by next Thursday for certain, but my family will understand that I'm needed here until then. I'll write and let them know."

"I'll keep an ear out for anyone going that way."

"I'd appreciate it." Holding the book in his hand, Joshua crossed the street and joined the volunteers at the school.

Mary's eyes brimmed with unshed tears as she made her way past ruined fields and damaged farms to the outskirts of Hope Springs. Ada clutched Hannah close to her side and kept patting the child's back to comfort her. Mary knew her grandmother needed comforting as much as Hannah did. Ada loved the community that had welcomed her wholeheartedly when she first arrived.

Ada had once belonged to a strict, ultraconservative Old Order Amish congregation that didn't allow their young people a choice—they were expected to join the Amish faith. Because their daughter chose to live English, Ada and her husband were forced to shun Miriam. The split was painful for everyone. After Ada's husband died, she knew the only way she could have contact with Miriam was to leave the community she had lived in for sixty years. Hope Springs became a place of healing for both Ada and Miriam, and ultimately for Mary, too.

She loved the community for the same reason— unconditional acceptance from the gentle people who lived devout plain lives amid the rolling farmland and tree-studded hills. Now the village they both loved had been all but destroyed.

The closer they got to town, the more damage they saw. Broken tree limbs and whole uprooted trees blocked the streets and lanes. At the edge of town, houses and businesses were simply gone. Only rubble remained. They heard the sound of chain saws long before they saw the men working to clear debris. Several large vans with brightly painted letters on their sides were lined up along the road. A group of people stood beside them. Long black cables snaked around them and satellite dishes adorned the tops of the vehicles.

Two young men in military uniforms motioned for Mary to stop at the edge of town. Bella lay on the floorboards of the cart with her head on her paws, but she sat up when they stopped.

One soldier approached the cart. "I'm sorry, ladies. We've just been told not to allow anyone down this road. There's a gas leak. Until the utility company can get in to shut it down, it's too dangerous. You'll have to go around."

"We have food for the volunteers. Sheriff Bradley is expecting us," Mary said.

A helicopter buzzed low overhead. Hannah looked up. "What are they doing?"

"They're from one of the television stations. They're taking video of the storm damage."

Hannah gave him a puzzled look. "What's a video?"

He smiled. "Pictures for television."

"Why?"

"Because this is news." He pointed toward a side street. "The command post has been set up at the Wadler Inn. If you go two blocks west, you might be able to go north from there. There are still a lot of downed trees and power lines, but I think you can get your buggy through. The power is off to the whole town, so don't worry about touching the lines. Just be careful."

"We will. *Danki*." Mary started to turn Fred and head the way the young soldier had indicated. The group from the news van approached. One of them carried a large camera on his shoulder aimed in their direction. They were blocking Mary's way. A woman in a bright red dress came to the side of the cart and held a microphone toward Mary. "Vanetta Jones of WWYT News. Can you tell us how the Amish community is reacting to this disaster?"

The pony, frightened by the commotion, shied away. Mary had trouble controlling him. "We're here to help our neighbors however we can."

Ada turned her face away from the camera and held up her hand. "Please, no pictures." Mary struggled to control the pony, who was threatening to bolt. "Please, let us pass."

The cameraman and reporter stepped aside. Mary urged her pony forward, happy to leave the intrusive people behind her.

"I can't believe this is the same town," Ada said quietly. "I don't recognize it. I'm not sure which street we're on."

Mary wasn't, either. Nothing identifiable remained among the piles of debris. A sea of broken tree limbs blocked her way. Crushed cars were scattered helter-skelter among roofless and wrecked homes with large red *X*s painted on them. Halfway down the second block, an English family sat huddled together on concrete steps. A mother and father with three children, one a baby in the mother's arms. The baby was crying. The whole family wore dazed expressions. Their clothes were dirty, and only two of them had shoes on. A damaged van sat nearby. The house the steps once led up to was completely gone. Only the bare floors remained. All the nearby homes were in a similar state.

Mary stopped the buggy, handed the reins to Ada and got out. Although she was leery of strangers, she couldn't pass by these people in need. She pulled a box from the stack behind her seat and carried it to the young couple.

"We have some food and some water for you."

The man took the box. "Thank you. I don't know you, do I?"

"We've never met. Do you have somewhere to go?"

"We slept in our van last night but it doesn't run. We can't leave."

Mary's heart ached for them. "We're on our way to the inn. If they have room, I'll send word."

"We don't have the money to stay there. I don't know where my wallet is." He looked around as if expecting to see it on the ground.

"You won't need money," Ada said quickly. "God commands us to care for one another. There won't be any charge."

Bella hopped out of the cart and trotted up to the young boy and girl seated beside the man. Hannah followed her. The big dog sat and offered her paw to shake. The boy tentatively reached for her foot and shook it. He was rewarded with a quick lick on the cheek.

Hannah said, "This is my dog, Bella. She's sorry

your house got blowed away." All the children began to pet her. Their faces slowly lost their hollow expressions.

Mary spoke to the young mother. "What do you need for the baby?"

She glanced around. "Everything. Diapers, formula, a crib."

"All right. We'll be back later. For now, I have some dry blankets and some kitchen towels you can use as cloth diapers until we return." Mary got the supplies from the back of the cart and gave them to her.

"Bless you." The young mother started crying and her husband pulled her close.

"Hannah, come on." Mary held out her hand.

"Can we help them look for their cat, *Mamm*? It ran away in the storm."

"We'll worry about Socks later," the father said to his children.

"There is an animal collection station being set up at the vet clinic north of town. Your cat may be there. If it is, someone will look after it until you claim it," Mary said.

The father gave her a tired smile. "Thanks. That's one less worry."

Mary returned to the cart and lifted Hannah onto the seat. Bella jumped in and lay down on the floorboards again. Ada kept the reins and clicked her tongue to get Fred moving.

They made their way toward the Wadler Inn, leaving the street in a few locations and traveling over people's lawns to get past downed trees. When they arrived at their destination, they witnessed a beehive of activity. Buggies and carts were lined up along the street next to pickups and cars. Amish and English worked side by side carrying in supplies and donations. A large Red Cross tent was being set up down the street at the town's small park. From here, it was easy to see most of the town remained intact, but the tornado had cut a path through the southwest end with merciless ferocity.

An Amish boy about ten years old ran up to the cart. "I'll take care of your pony if you're staying a spell." He pointed toward the outskirts of town. "We're putting them in Daniel Hershberger's corral."

"*Danki*. How did your family fare?"

"We didn't have much damage. Just a few trees down, nothing like here. God was good to us."

"Something good will come from all of this, too," Ada said, stepping down and handing him the reins. "Troubles are God's way of getting our attention. They remind us that this world is not our eternal home and our time here is not our eternal life. Tie the pony to the hitching rail, but leave him harnessed to our cart for now. We'll need him to bring another family here."

"Okay." The boy did as she instructed, then crossed the street to where another Amish buggy had pulled up in front of the hardware store.

Inside the lobby of the inn, Mary and Ada found Emma Yoder and her mother, Naomi Shetler, directing the placement of supplies and sending tired first responders and volunteers up to the guest rooms for a few hours of rest. Both women looked exhausted. Emma owned and operated the inn with her husband, Adam. Naomi had worked at the inn for years until her marriage to Wooly Joe Shetler, a reclusive sheep farmer and Betsy Barkman's grandfather.

Ada greeted each of them and said, "What can we

do to help? We've brought water, sandwiches, cakes and extra bedding. Who needs to be fed?"

Emma swept a few stray hairs back from her forehead. "Bless you. Take the food around to the café entrance. Betsy and Lizzie are preparing lunches there. Give the bedding to Katie and Nettie. They're upstairs. We had forty souls sleeping on the floor in here last night. There won't be that many tonight. A lot of folks have relatives who are taking them in, but we will still have some with nowhere to go."

"Have you room for a family of five?" Mary asked. "We passed them on our way here."

Emma gave her a tired smile. "We'll make room."

"They have a newborn baby."

"I'll have Adam bring our son's cradle down from the attic. Where is that man?" She turned and went in search of him.

Mary caught sight of Betsy coming in from the café. When Betsy saw her, she raced across the room and threw her arms around Mary. "I'm so glad you're okay. You can't know how worried I was when I heard your empty buggy had been found. I didn't know you were safe until late last night when Ethan brought us word."

"It was quite an adventure. I'll have to tell you about it when we have the time."

Betsy nodded. "That may be a while."

She turned toward Naomi behind the front desk. "I've got six dozen cookies and sandwiches made along with three gallons of tea and lemonade. Shall I take it to the Red Cross tent or will we be serving people here?"

"Go check with the Red Cross and see what they want us to do. We'll be happy to serve people here if they need us to. Hannah, I know you'd like to see your friends. The Sutter *kinder* are upstairs with their mother helping fold linens and sorting donations. Would you like to join them?"

Hannah looked to Mary. "May I?"

"*Ja*, but I don't want you going outside. There is too much going on and too many things you could get hurt on."

"Okay." She darted up the stairs as fast as she could.

Ada and Mary went outside and brought in their contributions. After giving them to Naomi, Mary turned to Ada. "I'm going to go back and pick up that family."

Ada nodded. "*Goot.* I will see what I can do here."

Mary returned to the cart and retraced her way to the family without a home. They were still sitting on the steps, but the baby wasn't crying. She stopped the pony on their lawn. "There is room for you at the inn. I can take you there now."

The husband shook his head. "We can't take your charity. We will manage."

"How?" his wife asked.

He scowled at her. "I can take care of this family."

"Please," Mary said. "We have a place for you to stay, but we are in need of many hands to help. It will not be charity. We will put you to work."

"This is very kind of you," the young mother said as she got up from the stoop. She handed the baby to Mary, got in and took the baby back. The father sighed and followed. He loaded the two older children in the rear of the cart and climbed up beside his wife.

When they arrived back at the inn, Mary turned the young family over to Emma's capable hands and went to the kitchen. Betsy was back from the Red Cross tent.

She was packing sandwiches into a large box. "We are going to take half of these to the other end of the park and set up there. I'll take this basket. You grab a box and come with me. I can't wait another minute to hear about your adventure."

The two women walked side by side down the street and across the park. Mary gave Betsy a carefully edited version of her time with Joshua. Although she thought she had done a good job of downplaying the incident, Betsy wasn't satisfied.

"Tell me more about this young man. Wasn't it scary to be alone with a stranger?"

"I wasn't alone. I had Hannah with me. I was thinking about her, and about how to make things less frightening for her. He was, too. I wasn't thinking about myself."

Betsy peeked at Mary through lowered lashes. "Was he nice-looking?"

"I suppose he was. He was kind. That matters more than looks." He had been kind. And funny. And good with Hannah. All the things she dreamed a man should be. He had appeared in time to save them and now he was gone. She'd likely never see him again. She knew it was probably for the best, but it didn't feel that way.

"It's too bad that he left before I had the chance to thank him for taking care of my very best friend and her daughter."

Just then, Mary caught sight of Nick and Miriam. They were speaking to the woman in the red dress who had tried to interview her. Betsy said, "I heard that we made the national news."

"What a sad way for our town to become famous.

They tried to interview Ada and me on our way into town."

"Did they? We'll have to find somewhere to watch the news. Maybe you'll be on it."

"We can't watch TV even if we wanted to."

"No one from the church will object if we happened to see it at an *Englisch* friend's home. Who has a television? The hardware store has one they keep on in the back."

"No one in town has electricity, Betsy. The power is out."

Betsey giggled. "That's right. I forgot. We're just used to being without it, so I didn't notice. I'm sure they'll have generators running soon. The *Englisch* can't do much without electricity."

Mary saw several members from her church setting up benches and tables. "I think that's where we're supposed to be."

She put her box on the nearest table. Betsy opened her basket and began setting out plates and a platter of cookies. Mary began unpacking the sandwiches and piling them on a plastic tray.

"I didn't think we would meet again so soon."

Mary looked up in astonishment. Joshua stood in front of her with a plate in his hand. "Joshua! What are you still doing here? I thought you were going home?" Her heart began fluttering like a wild bird in her chest.

"Delbert took me to Samson Carter's place, but his van is out of commission. It had a rather large tree on top of it. When I saw how much work needed to be done here, I thought I might as well stay for a few days longer. I dropped a note to my family in the mail so they won't worry about me. Happily, the post office is in one piece."

Flushing with pleasure at seeing him again, Mary continued setting out the sandwiches. "That's very kind of you to stay."

"Are you Mary's mystery man?" Betsy regarded him across the table.

"I'm not much of a mystery." He reached for a sandwich and a couple of cookies.

"Betsy, this is Joshua Bowman. Joshua, this is my friend Betsy Barkman." It was silly, but it felt odd introducing him to her friend as if he were an old acquaintance. They barely knew each other.

"I'm grateful you were able to rescue Mary and Hannah. I'm so glad I have a chance to tell you that. Oh, I see Alvin over there. I need to find out how his mother is doing. She was knocked down when a tree branch slid off the roof of a house and hit her this morning."

Betsy hurried away, but looked back with a wink for Mary before catching up with Alvin. The two of them had been dating for several years, although Betsy said she wasn't sure he was the one.

"This must be hard for you," Joshua said.

Mary ducked her head. How could he possibly know how confused and excited she felt when he was near? "Why would seeing you again be hard for me?"

"I meant it must be hard for you to see your community in ruins."

She felt like a fool. "It is sad, but look how everyone is working together. Friends are helping friends. Strangers are helping strangers. It will take a lot of work, but we'll get through this."

"I was wondering if your grandmother's offer of a place to stay was still open? If not, I'm sure I can find another family to put me up."

"Ada and Hannah will be happy to have you stay."

"And you, Mary? Will you be happy if I do?" His voice was low enough that only she could hear him.

She quickly looked down. She was excited at the prospect, but it also gave her pause. She already liked him too much. Her track record with liking and trusting the wrong men made her leery of repeating those mistakes. She chanced a glance in his direction. He was watching her with a small grin on his face that set butterflies loose in her midsection. She was trying to think how she should answer him when a group of volunteers arrived and began helping themselves to the food. Joshua moved aside. Maybe she should pretend she hadn't heard his question.

Someone called his name. Mary saw Ethan Gingerich gesturing to him from the back of a wagon. Joshua waved to acknowledge him.

Looking at Mary, he tipped his head toward Ethan. "I need to get back to work."

"But you haven't finished your lunch."

"I'll take it with me."

She tried for an offhand tone to make it seem as if she didn't care where he stayed. "Our cart is at the Wadler Inn. You can find us there when you're ready to call it a day. Unless you find someplace else you'd rather stay."

Joshua tempered his disappointment. He could hardly expect Mary to be overjoyed about spending more time with him. He was little more than a stranger, but at least she hadn't rescinded the invitation. That was something.

He wasn't sure what it was about Mary, but he was drawn to her in a way he had never been drawn to another woman. Maybe it was the circumstances of their first meeting. Maybe when their lives weren't hanging in the balance and the world wasn't smashed beyond recognition he would be able to see her in an ordinary light and this strange attraction would fade.

Or maybe she would always be special in his eyes.

For now, he was happy he hadn't been able to return home today. Seeing her again made the whole day brighter.

He glanced toward the command tent and found Sheriff Bradley watching him. A chill settled between Joshua's shoulder blades. If her father learned of his record, Joshua could kiss his chances of spending time with Mary goodbye. And maybe even his freedom.

Was he being a fool to risk it?

Chapter Seven

Joshua caught sight of Mary several times during the day while he avoided being anyplace near where the sheriff happened to be working. Like many of the women, Mary manned the food stations and helped wherever she was needed. More than once, he saw her loading smashed lumber, chunks of insulation and broken Sheetrock into the waiting trucks lined up along Main Street. Late in the afternoon, he saw her with her arms full of dirty toys as she carried them toward the lost-and-found area. She worked tirelessly, as did most of the residents and volunteers who had flooded in to help the devastated town.

After a long, hard day of sorting books, cutting up trees and clearing the streets of debris so that vehicles could get through, Joshua was bone tired when he arrived at the inn for a ride to Mary's house. He found her sorting through papers and photographs that had been brought in by the volunteers. She looked up and caught sight of him. A smile brightened her face before it quickly became blank. She looked down and resumed her work.

Every time he thought she was glad to see him, she retreated just as quickly.

He crossed the lobby, stepping around people rolled up in blankets and sleeping bags. He spied Ada sitting in a large wing-back chair by the fireplace. She was asleep. Bella lay quietly beside her. He didn't see Hannah. When he reached Mary, he spoke quietly so as not to disturb the people trying to rest. "They told us to go home. The National Guard is locking down the town for the night soon. No one's going to be allowed in after curfew. They are asking only residents to stay."

"All right." Mary brushed the back of her hand across her forehead. "The rest of this can wait. I'm sure there will be more by morning. A woman from New Philadelphia brought in a photo album and a checkbook. She said she found them in her rosebushes. That's thirty miles from here. The checkbook belongs to Bishop Zook, but no one here knows who the photograph album belongs to."

"There are so many people trying to protect what is left of their homes that they haven't had time to search for missing items. We must have covered fifteen damaged houses with tarps this afternoon alone. Have you heard any more about your bishop's condition?"

"He's in intensive care, but he's improving. One of his ribs punctured his spleen."

"I'm sorry. Let us hope God speeds his healing. If you want to keep working, I'll find a place to wait until the Guard makes us leave."

She shook her head. "Let me tell Emma and Miriam that we're going."

He looked around. "Where is Hannah?"

"She is out back with Katie and her little ones. I'll go get her and then wake Ada."

"Does she know I'm coming home with you?"

"I told her you might. I wish we could let her nap a little while longer. I'm afraid she did too much today."

"Maybe you can convince her to stay home with Hannah tomorrow."

"I'll try. Sometimes convincing Ada to do something that's for her own good can require delicate maneuvering."

He chuckled. "It must run in the family."

She rolled her eyes. "If you want to be helpful, go outside and find the boy who stabled our pony."

"Consider it done."

Joshua found a pair of boys sitting on the curb. One of them knew which pony belonged to Ada. He left at a run and returned a few minutes later with Fred. Joshua had the pony harnessed to the cart by the time Mary came out. He helped Ada up onto the seat. She was almost too tired to make it.

"*Danki*, Joshua. These old bones don't work as well as they used to. I'm glad you chose to stay with us."

He helped Mary up next, lifted Hannah up to her and then climbed in himself. Bella wanted on the floorboard but he made her get in back. It was a tight squeeze with all of them on the bench seat, but he didn't mind being pressed close to Mary. There was something comforting about her presence.

As he drove out of town, he was forced to stop as a police officer directed some heavy equipment across the road. A news van sat beside them on the shoulder of the road. The reporter, a man with gray hair, was speaking to the camera. "As you can see behind me,

Amish families like this one have poured in to help this community in horse-drawn wagons, buggies and carts. Although very few Amish live in this town of two thousand people, it hasn't made any difference to them. Helping their neighbor goes far beyond the confines of religion and town limits."

Joshua ignored the camera that swung to include them. Mary and Ada turned their faces away. Hannah looked around him and waved. A woman behind the cameraman waved back. When the heavy equipment was safely over the road, they were allowed to go.

Something the reporter said stuck in Joshua's mind as he urged Fred into a trot down the highway. Joshua glanced at Mary and Hannah sitting beside him. The man had thought they looked like a family.

It was growing dark by the time they finally reached home. Hannah had fallen asleep in Mary's arms several miles back. Now her arm was numb from holding her daughter. Ada got down and headed for the house with lagging steps. Bella hopped out and loped toward the barn. Joshua noticed that Mary was having trouble.

"Here, let me take her." He lifted Hannah off her lap.

Mary rubbed some feeling back into her arm. "She's getting heavy. I don't know how she has grown up so quickly."

"My mother used to threaten to tie a brick on top of my hat so I wouldn't grow so fast." Joshua settled Hannah over his shoulder and extended a hand to help Mary down from the cart.

"Did it work? Maybe I'll try it."

"It didn't work for any of her sons."

Mary hesitated to take his hand, but her common

sense won out. He was just being kind. She had to keep reminding herself of that. She allowed him to help her down and then quickly stepped away from him, still rubbing her tingling arm. She reached for Hannah, but Joshua shook his head.

"I'll take her to bed if you'll show me the way."

"All right." She walked up to the house and held the door for him.

Ada was unpacking the baskets they had taken into town. Mary said, "Leave them, Ada. I'll take care of them as soon as I get Hannah into bed."

"*Danki*, child. I don't know why I'm so tired."

"It was an emotionally difficult day," Joshua said.

"It was. *Guten nacht*, all." Ada walked down the hall to her bedroom at the rear of the house.

Mary led Joshua up the narrow staircase to the second floor. She opened the door to Hannah's room and turned on the battery-operated lamp she kept on Hannah's bedside table. Joshua laid Hannah gently on her bed and stepped back.

He treated her daughter with such tenderness. If nothing else about him appealed to her that would. The trouble was *everything* about him pleased her.

Mary removed Hannah's prayer *kapp* and shoes and quickly changed her into her nightgown without waking her. Joshua crossed to the window and opened it to let in the cool night air as Mary tucked the sheets around Hannah and kissed her forehead.

"She's a sweet child," he said softly.

"She is the sun and the stars."

They left the room together. Mary closed the door quietly. Then it was just the two of them in the dark hall. His nearness sent a tingle of awareness across her skin like a soft evening breeze. He smelled of wood shavings and his own unique scent that she remembered from their time together in the cellar. She stepped back and crossed her arms. "I hope you are comfortable in the spare room."

"Compared to the backseat of my buggy and the chairs we tried to sleep in night before last, the spare bed felt *wunderbar*."

"Was it only two days ago? It seems like ages." She began walking down the stairs.

"A lot has happened since then. I got to meet Delbert."

Mary tried to smother her smile but it broke free, anyway. "Was the ride with him comfortable?"

"I wouldn't say it was comfortable. My arm was mighty tired of hanging on to the edge of the seat by the time we reached town."

"Delbert is a good man. I shouldn't make fun of him."

"He's a hard worker. Not fast, but he gets the job done."

Crossing to the stove, she stoked the coals and placed a kettle over the back burner when the embers flared to life. Although the *Ordnung* of their church allowed propane stoves, Ada refused to get rid of her wood-burning one.

"Would you like some tea?" Mary wanted to prolong their time together. She shouldn't. She should go to bed and forget he was even in the house.

Like that's going to happen.

"I would love some tea. *Danki*." He took a seat at the table.

Suddenly nervous, Mary finished unpacking the

baskets, making a mental list of the things she would need to take with her in the morning. After putting out a pair of white mugs, she placed a tea bag in each one. She could feel Joshua's gaze on her as she moved around the kitchen. He didn't speak. Thankfully, the kettle began to whistle. She took it from the stove and filled the waiting mugs.

She carried them to the table and handed him one. "I would've thought you could have found a ride to Berlin with some of the *Englisch* volunteers."

"I did think of that, but by then I had seen the extent of the destruction and I wanted to help. I can stay a few days. The vet told me Oscar won't be fit to travel for at least a week unless I have him trailered home. You wouldn't believe the number of injured horses and cattle that have been brought in. To say nothing of the dogs and cats."

"So you're staying for a week?" A flicker of excitement shimmered through her.

"Oh, I don't have to stay here for that long. I can find somewhere else."

Don't make it seem important.

"I reckon the chair in your great-uncle's basement is still available."

Joshua chuckled. "As a last resort, I'll keep that in mind."

Mary took a sip of her tea. "You can stay with us. Ada won't mind and Hannah will love having you. I can ask Nick to have Oscar brought here. We can look after him for you. We have room in the barn. It's the least we can do."

"That would be great. I'll pay you for his keep."

"There are plenty of chores you can do. The corn-cribs are going to have to be rebuilt before fall."

"I'll see what I can do after I get back from Hope Springs tomorrow."

Mary sighed deeply. "This is not what I imagined I'd be doing a week ago."

"What do you mean?"

"Sorting through the wreckage of people's homes and lives, looking for something to salvage for them."

"It's not something anyone imagined. It's just what needs to be done."

"You sound very practical."

"Do I? My family often accuses me of being the dreamer. The fellow who always thinks he can make things better, help people change."

"Do I detect a hint of bitterness?"

He dunked his tea bag up and down without looking at her. "Sometimes people don't want to change."

"Sometimes they don't know how," she said gently.

"He knows how. He just won't."

"Someone in your family?"

Joshua shook his head. "I don't want to bore you with our problems."

"You saved my life. Feel free to bore me. Sometimes talking helps."

He hesitated, then said, "I have a brother who left."

"Left the Amish?"

Joshua hunched over his cup, staring at it intently. "*Ja.* Luke got in with bad company. He got into drugs."

"It happens." She rubbed the scar on her wrist. Her past was checkered with bad company and all the trouble it had brought her. Hannah was the only good thing to come out of that horrible time.

Joshua sat back. "*Nee*, Mary, it doesn't just happen. My brother made a choice. He hurt a lot of people."

"Including you?"

"Including me and everyone in our family."

"I'm sure he regrets that."

Joshua sneered. "Not that I can see."

"Where is he now?"

"Far away."

He looked so sad. She wanted to reach out and comfort him, but she held back. "I'm sorry."

"*Danki*, but it doesn't matter. He is my brother and I love him, but he is lost to us."

"Perhaps not. With God, all things are possible. I'll pray for him."

"You are a good woman, Mary."

The look he gave her warmed her all the way through. She basked in the glow of his compliment. When had she started needing someone's praise?

When he started giving it. When he called her brave outside the cellar.

Had it only been yesterday morning? It seemed as if she had known him for years.

He took a sip of tea. "Tell me how you ended up being adopted by two *Englisch* people? That's got to be unusual for an Amish girl."

She came back to reality with a thud. When he learned about her past, he would know she wasn't good and she wasn't brave. She took one last sip of her tea and carried the mug to the sink. "It's a long story. I think I will save it for some evening when I'm not so tired."

"Sure. I understand."

She left him sitting at the table and went to her room, but it was a long time before she fell asleep.

* * *

Someone was patting his face. Joshua cracked one eyelid. Hannah was bending close.

"Are you awake?" she whispered.

"Maybe." He glanced toward the bedroom windows. Only a faint pink color stained the eastern horizon.

"*Mamm* said I wasn't to bother you until you were awake."

He sat up stiffly and rubbed his face with both hands. "Okay. I'm awake. What do you need?"

"The wagon has a broken wheel."

Did they have a wagon as well as a cart? He didn't remember seeing one. How did a wheel get broken at this hour? "Do you mean the cart has a broken wheel?"

"*Nee*, my wagon does." She shoved a wooden toy in front of his face.

He took it from her and held it out where he could focus on it. The rear axle was broken and the right rear wheel was split in half. "This looks bad."

She held her hands wide. "I know. I can't take my chickens to market without it."

He heard the faint clatter of pans in the kitchen downstairs. Was Mary up already? He sighed heavily. He'd gotten out of the habit of rising early when he was in prison. There was no point. He stared at the broken toy. "How did this happen?"

Hannah spun to glare at Bella, sitting quietly behind her. "She got in it and she was too big."

The Lab perked up and wagged her tail happily.

The image of the eighty-pound dog trying to fit in a toy wagon that was only ten inches wide made Joshua look closely at Hannah. Something wasn't right. "Are you sure that's how this happened?"

Hannah stared at her bare feet. "I wanted her to get in, but she wouldn't. So I showed her how to jump in and the wheel broke."

"You jumped in the wagon?"

"Only because Bella wouldn't do it."

"I think the results would have been the same either way, but it's not right to blame Bella for something you did."

"I know. But can you fix it? *Mamm* says she can't."

He could if he was home and in his father's workshop. He didn't have the tools he would need to fashion the parts here. He hated to admit he couldn't help so he tried a different approach. "I'm afraid we'll have to take it to a wheelwright. Is there a buggy maker in these parts?"

"Levi Beachy makes buggies in Hope Springs."

"If his business hasn't blown away, I'll take your wagon in and see what he can do. It needs a new axle as well as a wheel. But Hannah, a lot of folks need their wagons and buggies repaired, too. Ones that aren't toys. It might take a while for it to get fixed."

"Okay. I guess I'll take my chickens to market next week."

"I'm sorry I couldn't be more help."

She picked up a cardboard box with paper cutouts of chickens in it and headed to the kitchen. "That's okay. *Mamm*, Joshua is awake!"

Mary peeked around the door frame. He managed a little wave. She gave her daughter the same look Hannah had turned on Bella. "Did you wake him up?"

"Bella did."

He couldn't let that slide. "Hannah, what did I tell you?"

Her little shoulders slumped. "That it's not right to blame Bella for things I do."

Mary frowned. "So you did wake him."

"Only because Bella wouldn't do it. Do I have to go to the corner in the kitchen now?"

"*Ja,* right this minute." Mary pointed toward the stairs. Bella followed Hannah with her head down and her tail between her legs.

Mary dried her hands on her apron. "I'm sorry, Joshua. You can go back to sleep for a while. She won't bother you again."

"I'm awake. I might as well see what can be salvaged of your corncribs after I take care of the horses."

"All right. Would you feed the chickens and the cow, too, while you are out there?"

"Sure. Do you want me to milk the cow?"

"Ada will milk her. They get along. She likes to kick everyone else."

"Ada does?"

Mary giggled. He adored the sound. "*Nee,* Rosie the cow does."

"Then I'll leave milking Rosie to Ada."

Mary turned around and left. Scratching his head and yawning, he headed for the bathroom. If he kept moving, he'd wake up. Every muscle in his body ached. It had been months since he'd done as much physical labor as he'd done yesterday, and it showed.

Twenty minutes later, he was wide-awake and pitching hay from the open door of the barn loft down to the horse, the pony and a doe-eyed brown-and-white Guernsey cow. His stiff muscles were loosening up and the fog had lifted from his brain. A decent night's sleep could do wonders for a man. As could walking outside without seeing high barbed-wire fences and guard towers.

He had stayed up late last night writing a letter to his parents. He wanted to share his thoughts, and he knew it would ease his mother's mind to hear more from him. It had been hard to describe the damage he saw and how the lives of people had been altered in Hope Springs, but it had been easy to write about Mary, Ada and Hannah. He might have written too much about Mary, but everything seemed to revolve around her.

He drew a deep breath as he leaned on his pitchfork and watched dawn break over the land. The springtime air was fresh and crisp. Thick dew covered the grass and sparkled where the sunlight touched it. If he faced south from the hayloft door, he could see fields of young corn just a few inches tall. By late summer, it would be higher than a man's head and by winter it would be stacked in rows of shocks waiting to feed the cattle. It was good land. A man could make a fine living for his family farming it. At the moment, it was green and brimming with the promise of new life.

"Joshua, breakfast is ready," Mary called from the front porch.

"Coming." He tossed one more forkful of hay to the animals and went down the hayloft ladder. When he came out of the barn, he saw the sheriff's white SUV coming up the lane.

Joshua's joy in the morning vanished as dread seeped in to replace it. The one thing he hadn't included in his letter was Mary's relationship to an Englisch lawman.

The vehicle rolled to a stop in front of the house. The passenger-side door opened and Miriam stepped out with a friendly smile on her face. "Good morning, Joshua. I thought you would have been well on your way home by now."

Nick got out, too. His smile wasn't near as friendly. Joshua fixed his gaze on the ground. "I thought I would stay for a few days and help with the cleanup."

"All help is appreciated," Nick said. He and Miriam both looked weary.

She sighed deeply. "Yes, it is, and sorely needed. I don't know how the town will ever recover from this."

Joshua couldn't think of anything to say. Fortunately, Hannah came flying out of the house just then. "Papa Nick, can you fix my wagon?"

He scooped her up in his arms. "What happened to your wagon?"

"Bella—" Hannah glanced at Joshua and lowered her face. "I mean—I jumped in it and it broke. Bella didn't do it."

"You are just in time to eat," Ada said from the doorway. "Come in."

"I was hoping you'd ask." Nick set Hannah on the ground and they all went toward the house.

Joshua followed slowly.

Breakfast was a feast. Mary had prepared bacon and scrambled eggs. There were fresh hot biscuits with butter and honey and oatmeal with brown sugar and cinnamon. He picked at his food. It was hard to have an appetite when he was seated beside the sheriff. Every bruise, every humiliation Joshua had suffered during his arrest and time in prison came back to choke him. He rubbed his wrists at the memory of handcuffs chafing his flesh. Bile rose in his throat.

Ada poured coffee into the cup in front of him,

bringing him back to the present. A rich, enticing aroma rose from the steaming liquid. He grasped the cup and raised it to his lips. It was hot, but the slightly bitter brew settled the nausea in his stomach. He looked up to thank her and noticed that she still had dark circles under her eyes.

Nick seemed to have noticed, as well. "Miriam and I'll head into town after we're done with breakfast. Ada, you and Mary don't need to come in today. There will be plenty of volunteers to help."

"I think I will remain here. I've gotten behind on my own work." Ada sat down at the table.

Hannah popped up. "Can I go to town with you, Papa Nick?"

"Nee." Mary shook her head. "Papa Nick has too much to do to look after you in all that chaos. Besides, I need you to stay home and help *Mammi.*"

"But how will I get my wagon fixed?"

"I'll see to it," Joshua assured her. She seemed content with that.

Miriam laid a hand on Mary's sleeve. "Are you going back today?"

"I am. Betsy and I have signed up for shifts at the food station."

"You can ride with us," Nick offered.

"That's all right. I know you need to get going, and I'm not ready. Joshua and I will take the cart."

Nick sent Joshua a sharp glance. "As long as you are both careful. The place is a zoo."

"We will be," Mary assured him. Joshua kept his gaze on his half-eaten eggs.

"May I have another biscuit? How long are you staying, Joshua?" Nick asked.

"I have to be home by Thursday so I need to leave by Wednesday."

Mary passed the plate of biscuits to Nick. "Can you have Joshua's horse brought here? We can look after him, and that will free up space at the vet clinic."

"Sure. I'll see to it. Will you be staying here, Joshua?"

He couldn't tell from Nick's tone what he thought about the idea. He glanced at Mary to gauge her reaction. She kept her eyes downcast. Joshua cleared his throat. "Yes, if it's not too much trouble for Ada and Mary."

"It's no trouble," Ada declared. "I'll put you to work. I need wood cut for the stove. I need my corncribs fixed. I have plenty to keep you busy."

Nick nodded slowly, but didn't say anything. Joshua had the impression he wasn't pleased, but there was little he could do about it.

Joshua shifted uneasily in his chair and took another sip of coffee. Had the sheriff noticed his nervous attitude? Hopefully he hadn't, but something in the man's intense gaze made Joshua doubt he missed much.

The sheriff and Miriam left shortly after that, much to Joshua's relief. Later, as he waited beside the cart for Mary to join him, his spirits rose with a growing sense of anticipation. The ride would only take thirty minutes or so, but it would give him thirty minutes alone with Mary, and he liked that idea.

That became the pattern for the next several days. Joshua took care of the animals in the mornings, then headed to breakfast, where Nick and Miriam joined them at Ada's insistence. She wanted to be kept apprised of the progress and needs in the community and she said no one was better informed than Nick. Miriam was able to pass along updates on Bishop Zook and the other injured people. Joshua strongly suspected part of Ada's plan was to insure her daughter was getting enough food and rest and not working herself into the ground.

After breakfast, Joshua would drive Mary into Hope Springs. They would go their separate ways in town, but they often found each other for a quiet lunch in the park. The work was exhausting and sad, but nearly everyone worked to keep each other's spirits up. One afternoon, an impromptu singing took place when five teenage Amish girls began a hymn in the park. They were soon joined by a group of young men, and for thirty minutes the cares of the volunteers and townspeople were lifted away by the sweet voices of the a cappella group.

In the evenings, Joshua rebuilt Ada's corncribs and read from the Bible after supper. Once Ada went to bed, he and Mary talked about their day over a mug of tea at the kitchen table. When he was alone in his room, he wrote to his family each night. He found himself writing more about Mary and Hannah than about the storm damage and recovery.

As he sealed the envelope of his current letter, he stared at it and wondered what his family would make of Mary if they met. Would they like her as much as he did? Would they approve of her adoptive parents?

He sighed as he realized he could easily go home now. There were plenty of helpers in Hope Springs, but he didn't want to leave.

Not just yet.

Chapter Eight

$\mathcal{M}$ary sat down on the cart seat beside Joshua on Saturday morning and worked hard to control her nervousness. It was another simple wagon ride into town just as they had done all week. It wasn't like riding with a young man in his courting buggy. They were on their way to help people affected by a disaster. They were not on a date. Yet a happy sense of anticipation gripped her.

Joshua had chosen to harness Tilly that morning. The mare stepped along brightly in the ground-eating trot that Standardbreds were famous for. Traffic along the rural highway was heavy for a Saturday morning. It seemed that people from all over were converging on the town in cars, pickups and wagons. Mary saw several license plates from neighboring states.

A large flatbed truck with a bulldozer on the bed followed them at a crawl for a half mile before it could pass on the hilly road. Joshua pulled over to give the traffic more room as it flowed by them. The large white van that passed them last was from Pennsylvania. It was loaded with young Amish men and women.

"It hasn't taken long for the word to get out among

the Amish." He guided Tilly back to the center of their lane when the way was clear.

"The town will be grateful for the extra help. I heard yesterday that the Mennonite disaster relief people were on their way."

"They always find a way to help. I'm sure more Amish will be coming, too. The recovery will take months."

"So many groups rushing to help. It restores my faith in people."

He cast a sidelong glance her way. "Do you doubt there are good people?"

"Sometimes. I know it's wrong, but it's hard to accept people at face value."

"Our faith teaches us otherwise, but I know what you mean. It's hard for me, too."

"You are thinking about your brother and the people he became involved with."

"In part, but I was thinking about something else."

She waited for him to elaborate. He didn't. "Something that happened to you?"

He shook his head. "It's not important."

"Now you have made me doubly curious."

He glanced at her and smiled. "I see where Hannah gets it."

"Which is a polite way of telling me to mind my own business. Very well. Tell me about Bowmans Crossing. What's it like?"

"It's nowhere near as big as Hope Springs. It's more a collection of farms and small Amish-run businesses than a true town. When my family first settled in the area, they built a house by the river and ran a ferry crossing for their neighbors. That's how the place got its name. There is a bridge over the river now, but folks still call it Bowmans Crossing."

"You said your parents farm there."

"*Ja.* My *daed* was the youngest son, so he inherited the home farm. Two of his brothers own a buggy-making business. Another sells harnesses."

"Do they live nearby?"

"All within a mile. You can't throw a rock in any direction without hitting one of my cousins."

"It must be nice to have a big family."

"I guess it is. I've never known anything else."

"What will your father do with the land your mother inherited?"

"I'm not sure. My youngest brother will inherit the home place, so maybe one of us will take over my great-uncle's property here."

Would Joshua be sent to farm it? The idea that he might settle in the area brought on mixed emotions—happiness that he might remain close by, worry about what that would mean if her attraction to him grew unchecked.

"Delbert mentioned that you moved to Hope Springs a few years ago. Where was home before that?"

"I grew up near New Philadelphia." The edge of Hope Springs came into view and she quickly changed the subject. "I hope the television cameras are gone."

"I only see one."

A gray-haired man in the uniform of a county deputy stopped them. He held a large clipboard. "Are you residents?"

"We are volunteers," Joshua said.

"Names?"

He wrote down their information and then pulled

two yellow bracelets from a box. He handed them to Joshua. "I know the Amish don't wear jewelry of any kind. You don't have to have this on, but you need to have it somewhere on your person so you can prove you are here legitimately. The numbers match your name, so be sure and check out with a sentry when you leave town. Please accept my gratitude for coming to help. I went to school here, way back when. It breaks my heart to see so much of the town in ruin."

"The town will recover." Mary tried to comfort him with her words.

"I know it will. There are some mighty fine, mighty strong people here. If we didn't know that before, we sure know it now." He waved them through.

She looked at Joshua. "I'm to meet Betsy and some of the other women at the Red Cross tent in the park. You can drop me at the inn. What will you be doing?"

"The volunteers were asked to meet in the park, too. Most of the streets have been cleared and all of the damaged roofs have been covered, so I think we're starting a house-by-house cleanup of debris."

"When our shift is over, Betsy and I will lend a hand."

He glanced at her feet. "Did you wear sturdy boots? You'll need gloves, too."

"I'm wearing Ada's work boots and two pairs of socks so I won't get blisters. I have gloves in my pockets. I'll be fine."

"Where is the buggy maker's shop? I promised Hannah I would see about getting her wagon fixed and she reminded me this morning that I hadn't done it."

"Follow the street that runs behind the Wadler Inn

to the west side of town. You can't miss Levi Beachy's place. I should warn you about the twins."

Joshua laughed. "I've already been warned about Atlee and Moses. I'll try not to fall prey to one of their pranks. The way folks talk, you would think the tornado was their doing." He pulled Tilly to a stop in front of the inn.

Mary got down before he could help her. "It wouldn't surprise me if they had something to do with it. Can you deliver these supplies to the Red Cross tent, too?"

"I sure can. See you later." He slapped the reins on Tilly's rump and drove away.

Betsy came out of the inn with a huge load of towels in her arms. "The two of you looked quite cozy riding together."

Mary knew she was being teased. "It's not a very big cart. I would look cozy if I'd only had a broom with me."

"Not that cozy. Is he still staying with you and your grandmother? What does she think about him? He's single, after all."

"Ada has her eye on Delbert Miller for me."

Betsy's eyebrows shot up. "You can't be serious."

"She's getting desperate. I'll be twenty next Sunday, so the pressure is on."

"I know that feeling." Betsy adjusted the load in her arms.

"How is Alvin's mother?" Mary took half the towels from Betsy and they began walking toward the park. The persistent sounds of chain saws had been replaced by the rumble of heavy machinery and countless hammers boarding up windows and repairing roofs. The smell of diesel exhaust hung heavy in the air.

"She's getting as antsy as Ada. Lots of talk about the grandbabies everyone else is having while she may be in the grave before she has any. She told Alvin the tree branch that slid off the roof and hit her was God's way of telling him to speed things up."

"And is he?"

Betsy paused and looked around to make sure they couldn't be overheard. "He proposed last night."

Mary's mouth fell open. "He did? What did you say?"

"I told him I'd rather that he ask me because he loves me and not because his mother got hit by a tree limb. It wasn't that big a branch."

"You said no?"

"Not exactly."

"You said yes? You were going to stay single until you were twenty-five. I've heard you say that a dozen times."

"I know what I said. I told him maybe. It would be nice to have a home of my own. When I see my sisters Clara and Lizzie with their babies, I think it would be nice to have a baby, too."

"Take my advice. Don't make the same mistake I did. Have a husband first. It makes life a lot less complicated."

"Don't tell me you see Hannah as a mistake, because I won't believe you. No one could love their little girl more than you do."

"I never think of her as anything but the most precious gift God could give me. I made my share of mistakes, but she is my redemption. How did Alvin take your answer?"

Betsy sighed heavily and shook her head, making the ribbons of her *kapp* dance. "Not well. He has stopped speaking to me."

"He'll get over it. He's head over heels for you."

"I thought he was, but now, I'm not so sure."

They reached the tent. It was busy as volunteers manned stations of water, ice and food. The hum of a generator could be heard outside. Orange electric cords stretched across the floor, held down with strips of duct tape. A small television at a desk in the back flashed with images of the destruction taken by helicopters and reporters on the ground.

There was little time to talk as Betsy and Mary passed out food, water and hot beverages to a steady stream of volunteers. A few were merely sightseers, not interested in working. They had come to gawk. The rest, young Amish people from neighboring communities, college students and off-duty first responders from as far away as Kansas, were all there to give freely of their time simply because they wanted to help someone in need.

Moving tons of rubble was backbreaking work, as Mary learned after her four-hour shift at the tent ended. She was loading bricks from a collapsed chimney into a wheelbarrow when she saw Joshua approaching. She straightened and brushed her gloves together. "Did you get something to eat? They still have sandwiches at the food tent."

"I finished my break a few minutes ago. I'm on my way back to work, but I've been sent on a mission to find you."

"Me? What for?"

"I met a local fellow named Alvin. When he learned

I was staying at your place, he enlisted my help to gather some information about a friend of yours."

"Betsy."

"*Ja.* He seems like a nice fellow, so I thought I would help him out." Joshua began picking up bricks with her.

"Oh, dear. What exactly does he want to know?"

"Is she seeing someone else?"

Mary threw a brick in the wheelbarrow and glared at Joshua. "Of course she isn't. She's been seeing Alvin for ages."

Straightening with a brick in each hand, Joshua tipped his head to the side. "Then I am a little confused. I thought he wanted to go out with her."

"He wants to marry her."

"Then he should ask her."

"He did."

"Now I'm even more confused. Did she give him an answer?"

"She said maybe."

"Now I get it." He tossed his bricks on top of hers. "He's wondering if she is waiting for someone else to ask the same question. Otherwise, she would've said yes or no."

The wheelbarrow was full, so Mary grabbed the handles. "She said maybe because she isn't ready to marry. She wants her freedom for a while longer."

"Can I tell him that?"

"Since he hasn't figured that out for himself, you can. And he should inform his mother." She began walking toward the street.

Joshua followed her with an armload of bricks. "I think I'll draw the line at telling him what he should say to his mother. I don't mind helping a fellow find out if a girl is interested, but this relationship sounds more complicated than I am equipped to handle."

She grinned at him. "It's a wise man who knows when he is in over his head."

Joshua stopped in his tracks. She had such a pretty smile. It made her eyes sparkle, and his heart stumbled over itself when she aimed it at him. He knew for a fact that he was getting in over his head because he sure wanted to see her smiling a lot more. At him.

He hurried to catch up with her. "What are we doing with these bricks?"

"We're stacking them on a pallet in the driveway. They'll be taken to be cleaned and reused to repair Mrs. Davis's chimney by a local bricklayer who has volunteered his services."

"Nice guy." Joshua began stacking the bricks tightly together.

"I think so, too. Mrs. Davis doesn't have family to help her. She is watching us from the window, by the way. I have heard she's afraid to leave her home and hasn't been out since the storm."

"It had to be frightening to see this destruction up close and then have the place overrun with strangers."

Joshua glanced toward the house. The curtain at the window fell back into place. A second later, it parted again as a yellow cat settled itself on the window ledge to watch them. Joshua casually bent to tie his boot-laces and glanced covertly toward the window. A small white-haired woman holding a gray cat in her arms pulled the curtain aside again.

A tall *Englisch* man came striding down the street toward them. "Let me give you a hand with those."

Mary straightened, put her hands on her hips and stretched backward. "This is the last of the unbroken ones. Joshua, this is Pete Metcalf. He's the bricklayer I was telling you about."

"Good to meet you." Pete held out his hand. Joshua shook it.

Mary pulled off her gloves. "How are your wife and family getting along?"

"It's still crowded at the inn, but we're really grateful that we have a place to stay. Thank you for insisting we go there. The baby is doing great. She is the center of attention when she's awake. It's like having two dozen babysitters. The only problem is that we can't find our cat. The kids have been all over town and they are brokenhearted. We even took your suggestion and checked at the veterinary clinic, but she wasn't there."

"You should have the children check with Mrs. Davis. She is a cat lover. I think she has taken in some strays. I noticed some open cans of cat food on her steps."

Pete hiked a thumb toward the house. "Mrs. Gina Davis, the lady whose chimney I'm fixing?"

"*Ja.*"

"I'll go ask her now."

"*Nee*," Mary said quickly, stopping him. "Send the children."

"Why the kids?"

"They are less frightening than a strange man would be. When people are scared and anxious, small children can help them overcome that fear."

He shrugged. "Okay, I'll have them come over."

When he left, Joshua moved a step closer to Mary. "Why didn't you ask her if she had their cat?"

"I don't need a place to stay or someone to care for me or about me. Mrs. Davis and Pete's family both need those things. Maybe a cat can bring them together."

He tipped his head slightly and regarded her with a bemused expression. "You know she has their cat, don't you?"

"The children came by the Red Cross tent earlier. They were showing people a drawing of a gray cat with three white feet. The little boy drew it since they didn't have any photographs. They were hoping someone had seen her."

"And we just saw Mrs. Davis holding a cat like that."

Mary grinned. "It might not be the same cat. Then again, it might be. Or it might be another cat that needs children to love."

"And my family thinks I'm the optimistic dreamer. They should meet you. They would adore you."

Mary blushed a rosy red.

The moment the words were out of his mouth, Joshua regretted them. What was he doing? He wouldn't be in town for more than a few more days. He had no business implying he wanted her to meet his family. That wasn't going to happen. He was on parole. Her father was an *Englisch* lawman. His family wouldn't be comfortable with that.

The last thing he needed was to fall for this woman with a sweet daughter and an even sweeter smile. It couldn't work between them. As much as he liked her, he wasn't able to trust her father.

Maybe when his sentence was up. Maybe when he wasn't afraid of being sent back to prison. Maybe. All his life he'd been taught to avoid the *Englisch* and shun their worldly ways except when he had to do business with them. His time in prison had taught him to fear them. Mary's father was polite and it was clear he loved Mary and Hannah, but Joshua couldn't bring himself to trust the man. He avoided Nick when he could and stayed silent when he couldn't.

Stepping away from Mary, Joshua said, "I should get back to Alvin. I'm sure he's on pins and needles waiting to hear what I learned."

"Tell him Betsy needs time to think over his offer. I'm sure she loves him, but I think she's afraid to admit that. She isn't ready to settle down now, but she will be one day."

"I'll tell him that. *Danki.* How will I find you when I'm done for the day?"

"I'll be in the Red Cross tent with Miriam or Nick."

Joshua nodded. Hopefully, her father would be out working elsewhere.

Just then, Pete returned with his son and daughter. He waited at the foot of the steps while they went up to the door and knocked. When the door opened a crack, the little boy held up a piece of paper. "This is our cat, Socks, and she's missing. Have you seen her? We miss her an awful lot."

The door opened a little wider. Joshua strained to hear the woman's reply. "I have seen a cat like that, but she's not so fat."

The boy turned his picture around to stare at it. "I'm not a very good artist. Where did you see her?"

"Wait here." Mrs. Davis closed the door. When she opened it again, she held the gray cat in her arms.

The little girl began jumping and shouting, "That's Socks. Socks, we found you." She held up her arms.

Mrs. Davis came out on to the porch and sat on a

green painted bench. "She's been very scared. You have to be quiet so that you don't frighten her even more."

The little girl cupped the cat's face between her hands and rubbed their noses together. "I missed you so much."

The little boy stroked the cat who was purring loudly. "Thank you for taking care of her."

The little girl gathered the cat in her arms. "I'm going to take you home now."

"Except we don't have a home," her brother reminded her gently.

From the bottom of the steps, Pete spoke. "We appreciate you taking care of Socks. Our house was destroyed and we are staying at the inn. Could you continue to look after her until we find someplace more settled? We can pay you to board her, although it will be a few days before I have the money from our insurance settlement."

"But, Daddy, Socks wants to stay with me." His daughter looked ready to cry.

"I know, honey, but we don't have a safe place to keep her. A lot of people are coming and going at the inn. She could get out and get lost again. You don't want that."

"No."

Mrs. Davis rose to her feet. "She can stay here. Why don't you children come inside and visit with Socks for a while? I have other cats. Would you like to meet them? If that's okay with your father," she added quickly.

"That would be great. Thank you. I'll get this mess in your yard cleaned up as soon as possible. Do you have other damage?"

"My attic window is broken."

"There's a fellow with glass and cutting tools over by the school. I'll let him know you need some work done."

Mrs. Davis opened the door and followed the children inside. Joshua gave Mary a wry smile. "You were right. Children can help."

"The way having Hannah with us helped you when we were in the cellar."

That surprised him. Had Mary noticed how fearful he'd been that day? "It did help. I hate small places, but knowing Hannah and you needed me to remain calm gave me a way to control my fear."

Mary fisted her hands on her hips. "I reckon I'll help Pete clean this yard so the children can play out here without getting hurt."

"I'm on my way to the Hope Springs Fellowship Church."

She smiled at him. "We'll meet up again later."

Joshua thought a lot about Mary as he walked toward the church. She had a knack for understanding people who were afraid. She saw ways to help them. His admiration for her grew. When he reached his destination, he saw a dozen men working on the roof of the white clapboard church that had sustained serious damage. The young pastor was the only *Englisch* fellow among the Amish men with their shirtsleeves rolled up. Joshua stepped into line and carried a bundle of shingles up a ladder to where Alvin was hammering them into place. He stopped working when he saw Joshua.

"Well? Is she seeing someone else? Did you find out anything?"

"Mary was very helpful. Betsy is not seeing anyone other than you. She isn't in a hurry to marry, and pressing her probably isn't the right thing to do." Joshua laid the bundle of shingles where others could reach them.

"I don't understand why she won't marry me. Her

sisters are all married. That can't be the reason. Even her grandfather recently married, so it's not because she has to take care of him. I don't get it."

"Mary says to give her time." Joshua pulled his hammer from the tool belt Alvin had loaned him and began setting the shingles in place. The two young men, both the same age, were quickly becoming friends after meeting that morning at the command center, where they'd been assigned to the same tasks for the day. The rat-a-tat-tat of hammers filled the air around Joshua as he and the other men made short work of the project.

Alvin drove the next nail in with unnecessary force. "I'm tired of waiting. There are a lot of young women who would be pleased to go out with me."

"And yet none of them are Betsy."

Alvin put his hammer down. "That's the truth. I like you, Joshua Bowman. You've got a good head on your shoulders."

"There are others who don't think so."

"How long are you staying?" Alvin positioned the next shingle.

"I need to be back in Bowmans Crossing before Thursday. I'll have to hire a driver or take the bus if one goes that way."

"With all the people that have showed up to help, I'm sure someone from your neck of the woods is here. There's a message board at the inn. You can put a note there asking for a ride."

"Good idea. *Danki*."

"Don't mention it. It's the least I can do after sending you to question Mary. I appreciate it. I could've asked one of my friends or cousins, but I thought since you knew Mary so well she might tell you something she wouldn't tell them."

"I don't know her that well. We only met the day of the tornado."

"Is that so? But you're staying with her and her family."

Joshua related the story of their night in the cellar while they worked.

Alvin slipped the last shingle in place. "She's a nice girl. She befriended Betsy when she and her sisters moved here. Have you got a girl back home?"

"I don't. You're blessed to have found the right one."

Alvin shook his head. "Only if she'll marry me."

"Don't give up. Looks like we are done here. What do we do now?"

"Go back to the command center and see what else they need us to do."

Would Mary be there by now? Joshua discovered he was eager to find out. It was sad—no matter how hard he worked at convincing himself he should stay away, he was ready to jump at the chance to see her again.

He followed the group of men back to the center of town to find where to go for their next project. He spied Mary standing by Miriam and Nick at the back of the Red Cross tent. Both women wore shocked expressions. Nick's angry scowl made Joshua hesitate, but Mary's distress pulled him to her side. "What is it? What's wrong?"

She looked at him with tear-filled eyes. "I was on the news. My face was on television and so was Hannah's."

Chapter Nine

Mary noticed Joshua's perplexed expression. He didn't understand how serious this was. How could he? She hadn't told him anything about her former life. She was starting to like him too much. She didn't want him to know what a foolish girl she'd been.

What if Kevin Dunbar had seen her picture? Numbing fear made her heart pound. If he had, then he knew where she lived. Where Hannah lived.

"I'm going to have them stop airing it." Nick pulled his cell phone from his pocket and stormed out of the tent. As upset as she was, Mary couldn't help noticing Joshua's relief at Nick's departure. Did he dislike her father? Was it because he was the English law? Many Amish distrusted Nick in the beginning, but they soon came to see he was honest and sensitive to their ways even when those ways conflicted with the law he was sworn to uphold.

Miriam's phone went off. She read the text and shoved the phone in her pocket. She gripped Mary's hand. "I'm needed at the medical tent. I'll be back as soon as I can."

After Miriam left, Joshua took a step closer. His eyes were filled with compassion. "Your church members will understand that you weren't seeking notoriety. The news cameras must have captured many Amish people." He pointed to the television. "Look, there's Delbert helping clean out someone's house."

The camera was panning a particularly hard-hit area of homes. It wasn't a close-up of Delbert, but his size made him recognizable. There were several Amish men and women in the scene. Joshua believed she was upset because the Amish shunned being photographed. She wanted to explain but she couldn't. Miriam and Nick had decided years ago to keep her past and her old identity a secret. The fewer people who knew, the safer she and Hannah would be.

Besides, Mary didn't want to involve Joshua. This was her father's business. She needed to let him handle it.

"It isn't just you, Mary. I see the girls from the singing, too. Their faces are recognizable. You are worried for nothing."

She drew a deep breath. "You're right. It's foolish to be upset."

After all, what were the chances that Kevin had been watching? He was still in prison.

A few moments later, Miriam came back. "Nick said he has taken care of it. The clip won't run again. Joshua, would you take Mary home? I'm sure that Hannah is missing her, and I'd like someone to check on Ada. I have to stay. I'm the only nurse on duty right now."

"I don't mind at all," he said quickly. He seemed relieved to have something to do. "I'll go get the cart and meet you out front in a few minutes."

Mary clutched Miriam's arm when Joshua was out of sight. "Do you think Kevin might have seen this? Would he have television in his cell?"

"Not in his cell, but there is a common room where the men can watch programing the warden deems suitable. This news channel is probably one of those. Even if he saw this, he's still behind bars. He can't hurt you."

"I'm afraid and I shouldn't be. My life is in God's hands. It has always been. I know that. He is my protection. He is Hannah's protection."

Miriam pulled Mary close for a quick hug. "I believe that, too, but I can't help worrying about you. Kevin may have friends on the outside. There is a multitude of strangers here. I think it would be best if you didn't come back to help."

Mary pulled away, shamed by her doubts. "These are our friends, Miriam. I can't hide when I see how much still needs to be done for our community. To remain at home would be cowardly."

"My Amish upbringing tells me you are right, but I've been married to a cop for too long. I know that evil exists."

"But it is not stronger than our faith."

"You are so brave."

Mary smiled at her adoptive mother. "I've had good examples to follow."

Miriam's phone went off again. She quickly scanned the text. "I have to go. More people have been hurt by nails and saws, falls and falling limbs in the last two days than were injured by the tornado itself. Let Ada know that Nick and I won't be by tonight or tomorrow morning. Nick is worn to the bone. He needs what little rest he can get. He's been going nonstop since this whole thing happened. If I can steal an extra half hour of sleep for him, I'm going to do it. He gets cranky when he's sleep deprived."

"I'll tell her."

"*Danki.* Give Hannah our love."

"I will." Miriam left and Mary went outside to wait for Joshua.

Betsy stood by a card table handing out donated gloves. She was pointedly ignoring Alvin standing nearby. Mary walked over to her and whispered an old Amish proverb. "Keep your words soft and sweet in case you have to eat them."

Shooting Alvin a sharp look, Betsy turned to Mary. "That's why I'm not talking to him. At all. Where are you going?"

"Home. Miriam thinks Ada needs a break from watching Hannah, but I'll be back Monday morning. What about you?"

"I'll be here. My sister Lizzie has decided the family needs something fun to do after all this work. She proposed we have a picnic by the lake next Saturday. I'd love it if you would join us."

"That's very kind. I know Ada is always happy to visit with your grandmother."

"*Goot.* I'll see you tomorrow at the prayer meeting. It's at Adrian Lapp's place. At least they didn't have any storm damage."

"Am I invited to the picnic?" Alvin asked. He had moved closer while they were talking.

"I reckon," Betsy replied without enthusiasm.

He stuck out his chin. "If I'm not busy, I might come."

"Don't fret about it. If you can't make it, you won't

be missed." Betsy threw down the pair of gloves she held and marched away.

Joshua pulled up with the cart. Mary gave Alvin a sympathetic look. "Don't worry, Alvin. She'll come around."

He glared at Betsy's retreating back. "The question is will I be around to see it." He walked away in the opposite direction.

Mary climbed in beside Joshua and he set Tilly in motion. "Things are still not going well for them?"

"*Nee*, and I'm afraid Betsy is just digging in her heels now."

"That's a pity. Are you okay?"

She knew he was referring to the newscast. "I am. It's not likely that there will be trouble because of it. It was just a shock. I had already been scolded for being too forward and then to see my face plastered on the television screen was upsetting." It was true, but it wasn't the whole truth.

"I don't find you forward. Who scolded you?"

Mary folded her hands in her lap and kept her eyes down. "Miriam. She is right—sometimes I am too bold in my speech. She thinks that Nick is a bad influence on me, but he isn't."

"I don't find you bold at all. I find you refreshing."

She didn't know what to say to that. She noticed a cardboard carton beneath his feet and decided to change the subject. "What's in the box?"

"Hannah's wagon."

"I'm surprised that Levi Beachy had time to fix it."

"He didn't, but he let me use his tools."

"Did you?" How kind was that? In the midst of all

this destruction, he'd made time to repair her daughter's toy. He was a good, kind man.

"It didn't take long. I had such a big breakfast that I didn't need a lunch break."

"I remember you just picking at your breakfast this morning. I thought maybe you didn't like my cooking."

That was the wrong thing to say. Now he would think she was fishing for compliments.

"Your cooking is good, but it's not like my *Mamm's*."

That put her firmly in her place. "I'll try to do better."

He grinned. "You don't have far to go."

Okay, that was nice. "Thanks again for fixing Hannah's wagon. She loves pulling that thing around."

"I noticed she had some paper chickens she wanted to take to market. Does she have other animals?"

"She used to have a cow, but its head was accidently removed by Bella."

He laughed. "Better a paper cow than the real one."

Mary smiled at him, her fright forgotten for a moment as she relaxed in his company. "You haven't tried to milk Rosie. You might change your opinion about that."

He laughed again and her spirits rose. Joshua Bowman was good company inside and outside of a cellar.

Seeing the worry fall away from Mary's face made Joshua happy. He still didn't understand why she had been so upset about appearing on the news. There had to be more to it than what she was sharing with him. He'd seen the flash of fear in Nick's eyes, too, before anger replaced it.

Joshua was curious, but it wasn't any of his business, so he kept quiet.

A car honked behind them. Joshua urged Tilly to a speedier pace. The road was still filled with traffic and many drivers grew impatient when they had to creep along behind an Amish wagon or buggy. He didn't want to cause a wreck. Unfortunately, it meant they arrived at Ada's farm that much quicker and his time alone with Mary was cut short.

And soon the rest of his time with her would be cut short, too. He would have to head home by Wednesday at the very latest. It wouldn't do to miss his first meeting with his parole officer, even for another day in Mary's company.

When they reached the farm, he stopped the cart by the front gate and got out. He held out his hand to help her down. Her fingers closed over his with trusting firmness. Hannah darted out of the house, letting the screen door slam behind her. Tilly flinched at the sound, jerking the cart. Mary lost her balance. She would have fallen if he hadn't caught her by the waist and pulled her against him. She clutched his shoulders to steady herself.

He gazed into her wide eyes as he slowly lowered her to the ground, reluctant to let her go. His hands spanned her tiny waist with ease. Color bloomed in her cheeks. An overpowering urge to kiss her hit him. What would she do if he tried?

Hannah shot down the porch steps. "Joshua, you're back. Did Levi get my wagon fixed?"

Joshua slowly released Mary. Her hands slid down his arms in a soft caress before she stepped away. He drew an unsteady breath and turned his attention to

Hannah. Ada was at the screen door watching them with a knowing little smile on her face.

Feeling foolish, he gave Hannah his full attention and dropped to one knee to address her. "I went to the buggy shop, but as I suspected, Levi was too busy to work on your wagon."

Her hopeful expression fell and her lower lip slipped out in a pout. "Oh. Well, that's okay. Lots of people need their real buggies fixed. I can pretend my shoe box is my wagon for a little while longer."

"I'm glad to hear you say that, Hannah. It means you believe in putting the needs of others before yourself."

She tipped her head slightly. "It does?"

"It does. Thinking of others has its own rewards." He rose to his feet and withdrew the box from beneath the seat. Setting it on the ground in front of her, he waited for her to open it. Mary looked on with a pleased expression.

Hannah glanced up at him. "What's this?"

"A reward for putting others first."

She opened the flaps of the cardboard box. "My wagon! It did get fixed."

She pulled it out and then stared in the box with a puzzled frown. "Someone left their toys in here."

He grinned. "They are your toys. I made them for you."

"You did?" She reached in and came out with a handful of wooden animals.

"Look, *Mamm*, Joshua made me a cow and two horses and three pigs, and here is Bella!"

The toys were little more than crude wooden cutouts, but he'd had a chance to sand them smooth. They were recognizable animals even if they weren't detailed. "Do you like them?"

"They are *wunderbar*! Did you make some chickens?"

"I didn't because you already had some." And because they might have taken more skill than he could muster with Levis' jigsaw.

She loaded the animals in her wagon and ran toward Ada. "*Mammi*, look what Joshua made for me."

"They are very nice. Did you thank him?"

"*Danki*, Joshua."

"You're welcome."

Ada held open the screen door so Hannah could come inside. "Joshua is making both my girls smile today."

Feeling pleased with himself, he propped his arms on the gate. "Ada, you are the only Kaufman woman I want smiling at me."

"You are a flirt." She rolled her eyes and blushed before she disappeared into the house.

"Only because you tempted me with your fried chicken," he called after her.

He turned to put the horse away and found Mary watching him with her arms crossed and a tiny smile curving her lips. "How do you do that?"

"How do I do what?" He strolled back to stand in front of her with his thumbs hooked under his suspenders.

"How do you make us all like you so easily?"

Joshua leaned closer to gaze into her sky-blue eyes. He saw the chasm opening under his feet, but he was powerless to keep from falling in. Why did the first woman to turn him inside out have to be a sheriff's daughter? "Do you like me?"

"I can't decide."

"Guess that means I'll have to try harder." He leaned closer still, but instead of trying for the kiss he wanted, he slipped past her, grasped Tilly's bridle and led the mare to the barn. He knew Mary was watching.

Inside the barn, he found Oscar waiting for him in the first box stall. The big brown horse whinnied a greeting. He limped forward and Joshua saw the large dressing covering his hip. "Looks like the vet took care of you."

He led Tilly into an adjacent stall, unharnessed her and began to rub her down.

The barn door opened and Ada came in with a basket full of bandages and ointments. "Before you flustered me, I was going to tell you that your horse arrived."

"I'm sorry I teased you, but your fried chicken is the best. I mean that. Better than my mother's, and that takes some doing."

"Stop with the flattery."

"If I must."

"The vet sent instructions on how to take care of your horse's injury and some supplies. I'll leave them here." She put them on a workbench beside the barn door.

"Danki."

Her face grew serious as she walked toward him. "I know it is not our way to interfere in the lives of our young people, but I'm an old woman with a bad heart, so I hope you will forgive me."

"For what?"

"Are you a free young man?"

He stopped brushing the mare and stared at Ada. His stomach flip-flopped. Had she found out about his prison record? "What do you mean?"

"Don't flirt with Mary unless you are prepared for her to take you seriously."

Laying his currycomb aside, he came to the stall gate and leaned on it with his arms crossed. "I would never knowingly hurt Mary."

"I'm sure that's true, but she has endured many heartaches. I don't want to see her suffer another if I can help it. Do you know what I mean?"

"I like Mary. I think we can be good friends."

"But not more than friends?"

"I have to return home. It may be a long time before I can come back."

She sighed deeply. "I'm glad you are honest about it. You are a likable young fellow, but don't encourage her if you don't mean it with all your heart. I have never seen her smile at anyone the way she smiles at you. I don't want to see her get her heart broken. Supper will be ready soon."

"Can I ask you something, Ada?"

"Ja."

"Is Mary still mourning Hannah's father?"

"She does not mourn him. He did not treat her well, but through him, God gave her Hannah, and for that gift we are all grateful."

"Why hasn't she gone out with some of the local fellows?"

"Because a man must win Mary's trust before he can win her heart, and she does not trust easily."

Ada left the barn and he mulled over her words as

he finished taking care of Tilly. Was he being unfair to Mary? He liked her. He wanted to spend more time with her. If she felt the same, what harm was there in their friendship?

He wasn't prepared to admit his feelings were stronger.

He left the stall and picked up the supplies for Oscar. He briefly read through the vet's instructions. It was simple enough. He entered Oscar's stall with the intention of changing the dressing as per the vet's instructions. He noticed the grain in the horse's feed bucket hadn't been touched, but his nose was wet from getting a drink.

"What you doing?"

Joshua looked over Oscar's back to see Hannah had climbed to the top of the stall gate and was watching him. "I'm checking to make sure Oscar is comfortable. He's in a strange new place and he's had a lot of scary things happen to him."

"He looks okay to me."

"Looks can sometimes be deceiving. He hasn't eaten anything, but he has been drinking water, so that's good. I think he'll be okay in a day or two."

"*Mammi* says you are going to be leaving soon."

"That's right. I have to go home."

"You are coming back, aren't you?"

"I hope I can. Will you look after Oscar for me until he can come home?"

"I think *Mamm* should do that. He's pretty big."

"What is it that you think I should do?" Mary asked as she leaned on the gate beside her daughter. Joshua's heart jumped up a notch, as it always did when he caught sight of her. He was kidding himself. What he felt was much more than friendship.

"Joshua wants you to look after Oscar until he comes back because he's going to be leaving soon."

Mary met his gaze. "I reckon I can do that, if he will show me what needs to be done."

"I was about to change the dressing, if you want to watch. The vet left me detailed instructions."

She opened the gate and slipped into the stall, making Hannah giggle as she swung it wide and then closed it. Hannah grinned at her. "That's fun. Can we do it again?"

"After Joshua shows me what needs to be done." Mary moved to stand near him. She kept her arms folded tightly across her middle. He tried to keep Ada's warning at the forefront of his mind. He didn't want to hurt Mary. He would be more circumspect in his dealings with her.

"First thing is to remove the old bandage."

She stepped up beside Joshua to read the paper he held. Her nearness caused him to lose his train of thought. "Then what?" she asked.

He forced his attention back to the horse. "The vet stitched the wound, so you want to check and make sure none of the stitches look infected." He pulled the dressing off and revealed a swath of shaved skin with a neat set of sutures down the center. The cut itself was about eight inches long.

"It looks good to me."

"Me, too." He softly pressed along the wound. "You want to check for hot spots or lumps that would indicate an infection is forming deep in the tissue." Yellowish fluid oozed from the lowest stitch when he pressed beside it.

Mary placed her hand next to his and followed with an examination of her own. "I don't feel anything unusual. What about this drainage?"

"The vet says we need to wash it down with cool water and he suggests putting some petroleum jelly on the skin below where it is seeping. He sent along some ointment to put on the dressing to keep the edges of the wound moist. Mostly, I'm worried about Oscar rubbing it against the boards when it starts itching."

Mary rubbed her left wrist. "I remember how much they itched before the doctor took them out."

"You've had stitches? I never have. What happened?"

She looked away and tugged her cuff lower. "I got cut with a piece of glass."

"On your wrist? That could've been serious."

"I was fortunate." She folded her arms again and wouldn't make eye contact.

Something told him there was more to the story, but he didn't press her. "Other than a dressing change every other day, he shouldn't need anything special. The vet doesn't want him out where he can run, but I hate to see him confined to a stall."

"I can walk him."

"That would be great." He applied the ointment and a clean dressing, and then patted Oscar's shoulder.

"Do you know when you'll be leaving?" Mary followed him out of the stall.

He swung the gate wide several times, making Hannah laugh as she held on. He plucked her off and set her on the floor. "I must be home by Thursday. I'll stay as long as I can."

Hannah skipped out of the barn ahead of them. Mary walked slowly. "When do you think you'll be back?"

He had to be honest. He stopped walking and she paused beside him. "I'm not sure when I'll be back, or if I'll be back."

"I see." Some of the light in her eyes died.

"A lot depends on the man I'm meeting on Thursday. If I can't return, my father will send one of my brothers to collect Oscar."

"I hope you come back." She bit her lower lip and looked down, as if she were afraid she had said too much.

He lifted her chin with his fingers until she was looking at him. "I hope I can, too. But I can't make you any promises."

She laid her hand against his cheek. "I'm not asking for a promise."

The longing in her eyes was too much for him to resist. He leaned forward and gently kissed her.

Chapter Ten

Mary knew she should turn aside, but she didn't. Joshua gave her a chance to do just that. He hesitated, only a breath away from her. She didn't move. She wanted to know what his mouth would feel like pressed against hers. She closed her eyes.

His lips were firm but gentle as he brushed the corner of her mouth. She tipped her head slightly and he took advantage of her willingness. His kiss deepened and it was more wonderful than she had imagined, than anything she remembered. Her heart raced. She gripped his shoulders to steady herself and kissed him back.

A few seconds later, he pulled away. She opened her eyes to stare up at him. His face mirrored her wonderment. She didn't know how to react or what to say.

Regret filled his dark eyes. "I'm sorry, Mary. I shouldn't have done that."

She pressed her hand to her lips. They still tingled from his touch. "Don't be sorry."

She turned and raced out of the barn, determined to regain her self-control. Something she couldn't do when he was near.

After all this time. After all the heartaches she had endured, the Lord had finally sent someone to make her believe in love again.

Only she knew it couldn't be love she felt. It had to be infatuation. She barely knew Joshua and he barely knew her, but for the first time in years, she believed it was possible to care about a man and have him care about her in return. A man who was kind and generous. Someone who could make her heart flutter with just a look.

When she reached the house, she paused and looked back. He was standing in the barn door watching her. He didn't look happy. Her common sense returned, pulling her silly girlish fantasy out of the clouds.

He was sorry he had kissed her. He was leaving. By his own admission, he might not come back. She was a fool to let her feelings get so far out of hand. Miriam had warned her to think with her head and not to let her emotions rule her. She hadn't listened.

It wouldn't happen again.

It couldn't happen again.

If Joshua had known how much a simple kiss would change his relationship with Mary, he would never have given in to the impulse.

Supper was strained. Mary wouldn't look at him. She barely spoke. She barely touched her food. Even Hannah seemed to notice that something was wrong. She kept glancing from her mother to him with a questioning look in her eyes, but she didn't say anything.

Ada kept up her usual running chatter. Had Mary told her what he'd done? He didn't think so. If Ada thought he was trifling with Mary, he was pretty sure that she would sic Bella on him. He half believed that he deserved it. After professing that he would never hurt Mary, he'd gone right ahead and made a very stupid move.

The thing was, he didn't regret that kiss at all.

Mary's smile was sweet, but the taste of her lips was even sweeter. They were soft and delicate, like the petals of a rose.

And he had to stop thinking about it right this second. It couldn't happen again.

When he went into the living room to read the Bible after supper, Mary excused herself, claiming a headache, and went to bed early.

Hannah played quietly with her wagon and wooden animals for an hour, and then Ada took her up to bed. Joshua was left alone with his thoughts. They weren't happy ones. His impulsive gesture might have cost him a friendship he valued deeply. Was there a way to make it up to her? Would apologizing again help? Or only make things worse? He was afraid to find out.

He wandered into the kitchen. He missed having tea with Mary. He missed the quiet, intimate moments they shared across the red-and-white-checkered tablecloth. Leaving the kitchen, he climbed the stairs. He glanced at Mary's closed door, then kept walking until he reached his room. He didn't write home. Instead, he lay down on the bed and folded his arms behind his head as he tried to figure out his next move. The full moon rose and cast a bright rectangle of light through the window. He watched the moonbeams' slow crawl across the floor for hours and still didn't have an answer.

Sunday morning dawned bright and clear and Mary was thankful she could finally get out of bed. Attempting to sleep had been a futile exercise until the wee hours.

She saw Joshua's door was open when she stepped out into the hallway. His bed was neatly made and empty. He was already up, too. She paused at the top of the stairs. What would she say to him? What would he say to her?

Could they pretend the kiss had never happened and go back to being friends?

She was willing to try.

She had breakfast well underway by the time he came in from taking care of the animals. She smiled cheerfully. "Good morning. How is Oscar?"

A bemused expression flashed across his face before he turned to hang his hat on a peg by the door. "His hip is draining more. I changed the dressing again."

"Do you think we should have the vet out to look at him?"

Joshua washed up at the sink. "I don't think it's that bad. If it's not better by Monday, then maybe we should."

After drying his hands on a towel, he folded it neatly on the counter. "Is your headache better?"

"All gone."

"Mary, about yesterday. I'd like to explain."

Pasting a false smile on her face, she said, "It was just a kiss, Joshua. It wasn't my first one. In case you haven't noticed, I have a daughter."

"I just want you to know that I didn't mean to offend you. I value your friendship. I hope I haven't lost that."

"You haven't lost a thing. I'm still your friend." She turned away. It was too hard to keep up the pretense while he was watching.

"I'm thankful for that. It won't happen again."

Oh, but she wished it would. "Go ahead and pour your own coffee. I'm going to get Hannah and Ada up. We'll have to hurry if we don't want to be late for church." There was plenty of time, but she left the room, anyway.

Since they hadn't yet been able to purchase a new buggy, they journeyed in the cart to the home of Adrian and Faith Lapp about three miles away. The main doors of the red barn had been opened wide. Men were unloading backless wooden benches from a boxlike gray wagon the congregation used to transport them from home to home on the day of the services. A number of men recognized Joshua and called out a greeting. Atlee and Moses Beachy had been put in charge of the horses. They came up to the cart as Joshua helped Mary down.

Ada gave the young men a stern look. "No tricks from you boys today."

Atlee and Moses smiled at each other. Atlee said, "Everybody has been telling us that. A good joke is only funny when you least expect it. We couldn't get away with anything today. Everyone is watching."

Ada poked her finger toward them. "I'm keeping my eye on you just the same. Any funny business and you'll have to answer to me."

Mary tried to hide her smile, but she caught Joshua's eye and saw he was struggling to keep a straight face, too. A giggle escaped her. Ada could no more keep up with those two boys than she could fly, but that didn't stop her from giving them what for.

Joshua managed to cover his chuckle with a cough. He handed Mary the baskets of food from the back of the cart. "Find me when you're ready to leave. It doesn't matter to me how long we stay."

The service would last for at least three hours. Afterward, a light noon meal would be served. Afternoons were usually spent visiting with friends and neighbors while the children played hide-and-seek and the teenagers got up a game of volleyball. Families didn't normally leave until late afternoon. If the hosting family was having a singing that night, many of the young set would remain until dark.

Ethan Gingerich came up to Joshua. "How is your horse faring?"

"The wound is still draining more than I would like. Have you any suggestions?"

The two men walked away discussing equine medicine. Mary sighed deeply. Joshua seemed right at home among them. It was a pity he was leaving. She would miss him dreadfully.

Ada grasped Mary's arm to steady herself as they walked across the uneven ground. "What's the matter, child?"

"I just realized that Joshua is going to find out today that I've never been married."

"Why do you say that?"

"Because I will be sitting in my usual place with the unmarried women. He'll know I wasn't married to Hannah's father."

"And how will he know the women around you are single? He doesn't know them."

"He knows Betsy. We always sit together."

"Well, isn't it better that he finds out sooner rather than later?"

"I know, but I don't want him to think badly of me."

"Our mistakes cannot be undone, child. We face them, we admit them and then we strive to do better. The sins of your past were all forgiven when you were baptized. If Joshua thinks less of you, then he is not a man to worry over, he's a man to be forgotten. There are plenty of Amish men in this community who would prize you as a wife."

"I'm not sure that's true, but you are kind to say so. Only I don't fancy any of them."

Ada turned to face her. "And do you fancy Joshua Bowman?"

"I'm not sure, but I think I do."

Mary thought Ada would begin shouting for joy. She was always pressing Mary to find a man. To her surprise, Ada ignored her comment and said, "Let's take this food into the house and enjoy praising our Lord on this beautiful day. We have much to be thankful for. I wonder who will preach the service since Bishop Zook is still in the hospital?"

After delivering the food to the kitchen and chatting briefly with the women gathered there, Mary, Hannah and Ada went out to the barn and took their places on the benches provided.

The sun shone brightly beyond the barn doors. They had been propped open to catch the warm rays on the cool spring morning. Rows of wooden benches in the large hayloft were filled with worshipers, men on one side, women on the other, all waiting for the church service to begin. Large tarps had been hung from the rafters to cover the hay bales stacked along the sides. The floor had been swept clean of every stray piece of straw.

Mary sat quietly among her friends with Hannah beside her. Glancing across the aisle to where the men sat, she caught Joshua's eye. He was near the back among the single men. He smiled at her and she smiled back shyly. If he realized the significance of where she was sitting, it didn't appear to bother him. Had she been worried about nothing? When would she learn to leave her fears in God's hands?

As everyone waited for the *Volsinger* to begin leading the first hymn, Mary closed her eyes. She heard the quiet rustle of fabric on wooden benches, the songs of the birds in the trees outside and the occasional sounds of the cattle and horses in their stalls below. The familiar scent of alfalfa hay mingled with the smells of the animals and barn dust as a gentle breeze swirled around her. She opened her eyes and saw a piercing blue sky above the green fields outside. It was good to worship the Lord this close to His creations.

The song leader started the first hymn with a deep clear voice. No musical instruments were allowed by their Amish faith. Such things were seen as worldly. More than fifty voices took up the solemn, slow-paced cadence. The ministers, the deacon and the visiting bishop were in the farmhouse across the way, agreeing on the order of the service and the preaching that would be done.

Outsiders found it strange that Amish ministers and bishops received no formal training. Instead, they were chosen by lot, accepting that God wanted them to lead the people according to His wishes. They all preached from the heart, without a written sermon. They depended on the Lord to inspire them. Some were good preachers, some more ordinary and some, like Bishop

Zook, were truly gifted at bringing God's word alive on Sunday morning.

The first song came to an end. The congregation sat in deep silence. The Lord's Day was a joyful but serious day. Everyone understood this. Many in the community had suffered, but God had spared many more. All of them were here to give thanks.

After a few minutes of silence, the *Volsinger* began the second song. When it ended, the ministers and the visiting bishop entered the barn. As they made their way to the minister's bench, they shook hands with the men they passed.

For the next several hours Mary listen to the sermons delivered first by each of the ministers and then by the bishop. They spoke of sharing the burdens that had been placed on the community. She tried to absorb the meaning of their words. There had been many times when she felt burdened by the vows she had taken, but today wasn't one of them. She belonged to a special, caring people.

She closed her eyes and breathed deeply. This day she felt the warmth of God's presence. She gave thanks for the goodness He had bestowed upon her and her family and begged His forgiveness for all her doubts and faults.

Facing the congregation, the bishop said, "Galatians, chapter six, verses nine and ten. 'And let us not be weary in well doing: for in due season we shall reap, if we faint not. As we have therefore opportunity, let us do good unto all men, especially unto them who are of the household of faith.'

"The Lord has made it clear that it is the duty of everyone present to aid our members in need. As you know, Bishop Zook was injured in the storm. He remains in the hospital, but by God's grace he will soon be released. We will be taking up a collection for the medical bills he can't meet. His barn was also destroyed in the same storm. I have met with other area bishops and we are planning a barn raising for him a week from Monday. Everyone is invited to help to the extent that they are able." He gave a final blessing and the service was over.

The scrabble of the young boys in the back to get out as quickly as possible made a few of the elders scowl in their direction, including Ada. Mary grinned. She remembered how hard it was to sit still at that age. It was harder still because the young people knew they would be spending the rest of the day visiting with their friends and playing games. Although the young girls left with more decorum, they were every bit as anxious to be out taking advantage of the beautiful spring day. She let Hannah follow them.

Mary happened to glance in Joshua's direction and caught him staring at her. All the other men were gone.

Betsy elbowed her in the side. "Will you stop looking at that man like you are a starving mouse and he is a piece of cheese?"

Mary rose to her feet. "I'm not a starving mouse."

"You could've fooled me." The two of them went out together and soon joined the rest of the women who were setting up the food. The elders were served first. The younger members had to wait their turn. When Joshua came inside to eat, Alvin was with him. Betsy saw him, muttered an excuse and quickly left the room.

Alvin put his plate down. "I reckon I've lost my appetite."

He left and Joshua looked at Mary. "Is there anything you can think of that would aid his cause? He's miserable. He's been talking about her nonstop for the last half hour."

"Betsy is miserable, too. I don't know how to help."

"I might have an idea. It's my turn to have a plan, right?"

She smiled. "I think it's my turn, but you go ahead."

"Is Betsy the jealous type?"

"I wouldn't know. Alvin has been stuck to her side ever since they met. She's never had to worry about him straying."

"Let's see how she reacts if he shows an interest in someone else."

Mary bit her lower lip. "I don't know. That doesn't seem right."

"If this blows up in our faces, it's your turn for a plan."

"Oh, make it worse and then hand it to me. *Danki.* What girl will go along with this? Don't look at me."

"Just make sure Betsy is where she can see the barn door on the south side in half an hour. Can I borrow your traveling bonnet?"

"What for?"

He gave her a big grin. "Because my helpers didn't bring theirs."

"I have no idea what you are talking about, but I left mine on the seat of the cart."

"Okay. Thirty minutes."

"South barn door."

"Right." He winked and went out.

Betsy returned shortly. When it was their turn to eat, they carried their plates outside and joined Betsy's sisters on several quilts spread in the shade of an apple tree. The alpacas that Adrian and Faith raised were lined up at the fence watching the activity. Mary found them adorable, especially the babies. The adults, with their freshly shorn bodies and fluffy heads, were comical. The south barn door was in easy view from where she was sitting.

"Betsy, where is Alvin?" her sister Lizzie asked.

"I don't know, and I don't care," Betsy declared.

Her three sisters shared shocked looks. Clara, the oldest, gaped at Betsy. "Since when?"

"Since ages ago. I don't have to share everything with you just because you're my sisters."

Greta touched Mary's arm. "Did you know about this?"

"I know she's been miserable since he stopped talking to her."

"I have not. And he didn't stop talking to me. I stopped talking to him."

Mary saw Joshua and Alvin standing just inside the barn door. The bottom half of the split door was closed, but the top was open. A tall woman in a black bonnet was standing with them. She was turned so Mary couldn't see her face. She appeared to be in an animated conversation with Alvin.

Lizzie noticed at the same time. "He's not having any trouble talking to that woman. Who is that?"

Betsy swung her head around to look. "I don't know."

Alvin laughed at something the woman whispered in his ear. Her bonnet dipped and her shoulders jiggled as if she were giggling. Clara said, "She's very tall. I don't know who it could be."

Joshua stepped out of the barn and came toward them. Alvin slipped his arm around the woman's shoulder and they disappeared from view inside the barn.

Betsy shot to her feet. "Who was that with Alvin?"

Joshua shrugged. "I didn't catch the name, but they seem to know each other well."

He sat down beside Mary. "Are you about ready to go?"

She tried to keep a straight face. "Not yet."

Betsy fisted her hands on her hips. "Is it one of those Pennsylvania Amish girls that came to help in town? She should stay in her own state."

Joshua shook his head. "That's unkind, Betsy. Alvin was just being nice."

"I saw how nice he was being. I'm going to give him a piece of my mind."

"But you aren't speaking to him," Mary reminded her.

"You're right. I'm not." Betsy sat down, but she couldn't keep her eyes off the barn. Alvin and his friend never reappeared.

Later, when they were getting ready to leave, Joshua was helping Ada into the cart when Atlee and Moses brought Tilly to them and hitched her up. Ada scooted to the far edge of the seat. "You boys were good today. I'm glad to see you've grown out of your need to play pranks."

Moses grinned at her. "I wouldn't say we've outgrown it."

Atlee handed Mary a bundle of cloth. "Thanks for the use of your bonnet. Alvin found it very becoming on my brother."

The boys punched each other in the shoulder and

walked off laughing. Ada shook her head. "I'm glad they aren't mine."

Mary smoothed out her bonnet and took Hannah as Joshua handed her up. "Really? Moses, Alvin and my bonnet? That was your plan?"

He climbed in and took the reins. "I think it worked. Betsy was stunned. At least Alvin knows she isn't indifferent."

"You got her attention, I'll give you that."

"Now all Alvin has to do is keep it." He slapped the reins against Tilly's rump and the mare took off.

Relieved that his relationship with Mary seemed to be on the mend, Joshua was eager to return to work in Hope Springs. On Monday, he and Mary made the trip again. There were fewer volunteers in town. The initial storm and media coverage had brought in hundreds of people wanting to help. Now that the nitty-gritty of rebuilding was getting underway, there was less need for general cleanup and more need for skilled carpenters. The Amish and Mennonite workers remained as the backbone of the recovery effort.

After leaving Mary at the Wadler Inn, Joshua crossed the now barren blocks toward the church. He and several others would be rebuilding the portico that morning. As he passed by Gina Davis's home, he saw she was out pruning her rosebushes. Pete's children were playing in the yard. The front door of the house opened and a woman with a baby in her arms called for the others to come in. He saw Pete on the roof setting the last of the chimney bricks into place. Pete saw him and waved. "How's it going?"

Joshua stopped and tipped back his hat. "Not bad. And you?"

"I'm done here. I'll start at the school tomorrow. I've been hired by the school district to repair the building. It was an offer I couldn't refuse."

"The laborer is worthy of his hire. Are you still staying at the inn?"

Pete gathered his tools and came down the ladder. "Actually, we're staying with Mrs. Davis until we can get a new house built. It's working out for both of us."

Exactly as Mary had hoped it would. Joshua touched the brim of his hat. "Have a *goot* day."

He started to walk away, but Pete stopped him. "You might want to keep an eye out for anything odd. They told us in the town meeting this morning that some of the stores have been looted. The police have set up a tip line folks can call if they see something. Just when it seems the goodness of mankind toward one another is overwhelming, a few have to prove there are still miserable people out there."

Shaking his head in disbelief, Joshua walked on. Instead of following the winding street, he took a short-cut through a wooded area that surrounded the rocky outcropping behind the church. A small stream cut through the woods. It led to the bubbling spring that had given the town its name. There was a small bridge over the brook behind the church, but he had no trouble jumping across using a couple of convenient stones. He was about a block from the church when he saw two men slipping through the trees ahead of him. Something in their stealthy demeanor caught his attention. He watched as they entered the back door of a vacant house with faded paint and boarded-over windows that had fallen into disrepair years before the tornado arrived. He was tempted to walk on, but his curiosity drew him to follow them.

He approached the house and had his hand on the back doorknob when he heard voices coming from a broken basement window off to the side below him. "I stashed the weed here. Nobody's gonna check an old wreck like this place. How much do you want?"

"How much do you have?"

"Enough. If you want stronger drugs, I can get that too. I borrowed some from the pharmacy last night. The place was easy pickings. Their security system didn't even have power."

Joshua's skin crawled when he realized what was going on. He took a step back and his heel crunched a piece of broken glass.

"What was that? Check it out." The voice became a harsh whisper.

Joshua walked away quickly and hurried out to the street. At the corner, he saw Nick in his patrol car. Joshua hesitated. Should he tell Nick what was going on? Would Nick assume he was involved?

It would be better to say nothing. It wasn't Amish business. It had nothing to do with him. He hurried on toward the church. A few minutes later, he heard the sound of a siren behind him, but he didn't look back. He kept his head down and walked faster. He only slowed when Nick shot past him without stopping. Joshua blew out a long breath and waited for his racing heart to return to a normal pace.

It took him and his coworkers three hours to finish the new entryway for the church. Pastor Finzer came out of the rectory to view the finished project. There were tears in his eyes.

"Gentlemen, I can't thank you enough for your work here. It's wonderful to see the house of the Lord ready to welcome worshipers again. A little paint and elbow grease by yours truly and I don't think people will know the difference between the old and the new parts of the structure. It's beautiful."

He shook everyone's hand. "Please let me buy you lunch at the Shoofly Pie Café. It's the best Amish cooking for miles around."

Knowing that Mary was working at the inn that day, Joshua agreed and walked along with a group as they headed that way. Passing the section of woods where he had seen the men, Joshua slowed to see if Nick had gone that way. There was no sign of him.

The pastor noticed Joshua's interest. "That place belonged to the family that founded this town. It's a shame it was allowed to fall into ruin."

"I saw two men go in there earlier."

"Teenagers, perhaps. They've been known to hold parties there. I'll check it out."

The thought of the gangly young pastor stumbling into a dangerous situation forced Joshua to reconsider keeping silent. He stopped walking. "They weren't teenagers. I got the impression they didn't want to be seen."

Pastor Finzer stopped, too. Concern creased his brow. "Are you sure?"

"I heard there has been some looting around town."

"Sadly, that's true. Perhaps I should mention this to the authorities."

"You must do what you think is best. The fellow

staying with Gina Davis said there is a tip line folks can call."

"That's right. I almost forgot. Go on to the café. I'll catch up with you." The minister walked rapidly back toward the church and Joshua breathed a sigh of relief.

At the inn, he checked at the front desk and learned Mary was running an errand. She wasn't expected back for half an hour. He found a seat at the café counter, ordered lunch and waited for Pastor Finzer to join him.

A hand clamped down on his shoulder. "Step outside right now," Nick growled.

Chapter Eleven

Joshua wanted to knock Nick's arm aside, but resisting would gain him nothing. He should have told Mary about his record when he had the chance. It would've been better coming from him than from her father. Now it was too late.

"I said, come outside."

Joshua turned on the bar stool. "Say what you need to say here. I am not ashamed."

"Outside!" Nick walked out of the building. Joshua followed slowly. He didn't have a choice. At least he wasn't being hauled away in handcuffs.

The sheriff didn't stop walking until he was half a block up the street. Then he turned on Joshua. "I knew there was something about you the minute I laid eyes on you. If I hadn't been so busy with this mess, I would have run a background check on you sooner. Not many Amish men turn up in my database. Imagine my surprise when Joshua Bowman was at the top of the list when I checked this morning."

Joshua pressed his lips shut. Nick didn't want to hear anything he had to say.

Nick glared, but drew a deep breath. "Have you told her?"

"I thought I would leave that to you."

"Don't get smart with me. Have you told Mary that you're a convict?"

"That I was wrongly imprisoned? *Nee.*"

"I didn't think so."

"I was going to tell her. Not that I expect you to believe me."

"You were picked up for dealing drugs. What do you know about a burglary last night at the pharmacy?"

Joshua folded his arms and glared. "If I know something, I must be involved. If I'm involved, that means I violated my parole, and I'm on my way back to prison, which is exactly what you want, isn't it?"

"Where did you get that chip on your shoulder?"

"Your justice system gave it to me."

Nick reined in his temper with visible difficulty. "I skimmed through your case file."

"Then you know everything. I won't waste my breath explaining."

Folding his arms over his chest, Nick relaxed slightly. "It left me with some unanswered questions. I would've handled the investigation differently."

"My story would've been the same no matter who asked. I didn't do the things they accused me of doing."

"Just like that, I'm supposed to believe you? You had a dozen chances to tell me you are out on parole. Why didn't you?"

"Because I knew exactly how you would react. Like this. Besides, I didn't see what difference it made. I came to look over some property for my father. I didn't choose to be trapped with Mary, but I started liking her. And this community. After I saw the extent of the damage here, I wanted to help these people rebuild."

"I think you're done helping. Hope Springs can get along fine without you."

"Don't you mean Mary will get along fine without me?"

"You're a smart fellow. That's exactly what I mean. Mary has had enough trouble in her life. She doesn't need to get involved with you."

"I happen to care for Mary a lot. If she were your *Englisch* daughter, I would say that you are right. But Mary is Amish. She knows that forgiveness comes first. She knows a thing that is forgiven must also be forgotten."

"You don't know anything about Mary."

Joshua reined in his own rising temper. "I know her better than you think. I also know you want to protect her."

"That's right. That's why you are leaving. I have a car waiting that will take you to Ada's place so you can pick up your stuff, and then my deputy will take you home. I'm also going to let your parole officer know that you were here without his knowledge. He's not going to like that, and he's going to keep a closer eye on you from now on."

Joshua strove to put his bitterness aside. He didn't want this animosity between himself and Mary's father. Not if there might be a future with her. He hung his head, trying to be humbled before God and this man. "When my sentence is finished, may I come back?"

"I'd rather you didn't."

Joshua looked up. "Because you don't want the criminal element in your town? Or because you don't want Mary seeing some guy you don't like? It's her choice. The Amish understand that. They don't interfere in the courtship of their children."

"Someday when you have a daughter, remember this conversation." He pointed up the block where an unmarked white car was waiting. "There's your ride. Get going."

Mary learned that Joshua had been looking for her when she returned from her errand. She checked in the café, but he wasn't there. She combed the area she thought he might be working in several times without seeing him. When she spotted Delbert cutting lumber at the back of the grocery store across the street, she approached him and waited until he finished the cut and the saw fell silent. "Delbert, have you seen Joshua? He was looking for me a while ago and now I can't find him."

"I saw him talking to the sheriff. They went that way." He pointed up the block.

"Danki."

She walked in that direction and saw Nick at the drugstore on the next corner. He was standing with his deputy, who was busy writing a report. The store owner was gesturing wildly. There was no sign of Joshua. She walked up to Nick. "I'm sorry to bother you, but have you seen Joshua?"

"He's gone home," Nick said without looking at her.

"Back to the farm?"

"Back to Bowmans Crossing."

"I thought he wasn't leaving until Wednesday."

"Something came up and he caught an early lift."

"What came up?" She tried to wrap her mind around the fact that he was gone.

Nick looked at her then. "You knew he was going to leave sooner or later."

Sooner or later, yes, but not without saying good-bye. Mary turned away to hide her distress. What a foolish woman she was to think she meant something special to him. "You're right. I knew he was leaving. I just didn't want him to go."

Tears stung her eyes as she walked away from Nick. When she turned the corner and there was no one to see, she broke down and sobbed.

Joshua received a heartfelt hug from his mother when he arrived home. No one had expected him until Thursday. His father and brothers were all out working in the fields. He looked forward to doing the same. To getting back to a simple life with plenty of hard work and little time to mourn the loss of Mary's company.

His mother gestured toward the table. "Sit down. I've just made some brownies. We have been reading about the damage at Hope Springs in the newspapers. It must be terrible."

"It is. The community is making progress, but a third of the homes were destroyed. Electricity has been restored to many of the English businesses and homes that are left, but some of them are still living Amish."

That made her chuckle. "It's good to have you home. Will the town recover?"

"The people are determined. There's still a lot of cleanup that needs to be done. Mary thinks it will take years for the place to look normal again. I think she's right."

"Mary is the woman you wrote about? The one you were trapped in the cellar with?"

"She's the one." He tried to remember exactly what he'd said about her. Probably too much. She occupied a central place in his mind.

His mother got down a plate and began cutting her brownies. "Is she pretty, this girl you couldn't leave behind?"

"Not as pretty as you, and I did leave her behind." He bitterly regretted that he hadn't been allowed to tell Mary goodbye. Would she think he didn't care enough to find her, or would Nick tell her the truth? Was she grieving or was she relieved to have Joshua Bowman out of her house and her life? Would he ever know?

His mother put a plate in front of him. "What will you do now?"

"I want to go back to Hope Springs. There is still so much work that needs doing." And Mary was there. Mary and Hannah, the two people who had come to mean the world to him.

His mother took a seat across from him. "Your father and I have been talking about that."

"You have?"

"Our bishop made a plea for supplies and money to aid the Amish folks there. You know they will share the financial burdens among themselves, but the expenses will be high and some families will suffer because of it. We must help if we can. Your brothers have agreed. I wish I could go along, but your father and your brothers could not do without me. I would like to meet your Mary."

"She's not my Mary and there is something I haven't told you about her."

"So serious. What is it?"

"She is adopted. Her parents are *Englisch*."

"That is not a terrible thing, although it is unusual."

"The woman that adopted her is married to Sheriff Nick Bradley."

Sitting back, his mother stared at him with wide eyes. "Perhaps we should not mention this to your father just yet."

"As much as I want to go back, it isn't up to me. I'll need to convince Officer Merlin it isn't a risk to let me go there. I don't think he'll agree. Nick Bradley doesn't want me seeing Mary."

"Is she a good Amish woman?"

"She reminds me a lot of you."

"I could be a better Christian."

"Mary isn't perfect, but she has an Amish heart. She is a good mother. She cares for her elderly grandmother with tenderness. She is sometimes outspoken, but she repents when she steps over the line. She would do anything for her friends and neighbors in need. *Ja*, she is a good Amish woman."

Better than he deserved. Maybe he shouldn't go back. Maybe this was God's way of telling him that she was better off without him.

"Let us pray about this and wait to see what the Lord wills. Your father can be a very convincing man. I should know. He convinced me to marry him when I had three other perfectly good offers."

Joshua laughed. "*Mamm*, were you a wild girl with a string of fellows?"

"I was. Until I wed. Eat your brownie and don't fret. God has a plan for us all. We must have faith in that."

* * *

"Why wasn't I informed that you were away from home?"

Officer Oliver Merlin sat at the kitchen table in the Bowman home on Thursday morning as promised. He finished the last bite of a cinnamon roll and licked his lips. Joshua's father and mother sat with him. Joshua was too nervous to sit in one place. He leaned against the spotless kitchen cabinets. He knew his brothers would be hovering nearby outside.

"My son was only doing what dozens of other young Amish people were doing. He was helping those in need. It was God's will that he was in Hope Springs when this disaster struck. He was not involved in any crime."

Officer Merlin dabbed his face with a napkin, then folded his hands together and leaned on his forearms. "I am not your son's enemy, Mr. Bowman. Nor am I your enemy. I am required to keep detailed records of my parolees' activities. My job is to see that Joshua can become a functioning member of society and stay out of trouble."

"Would you like another cinnamon roll, Oliver?" Joshua's mother pushed the plate in his direction.

"Don't mind if I do. These are just about the best I've ever had."

"*Danki.* You are too kind."

Isaac frowned at his wife before he leaned forward, too. "You can put my son back in prison with a word."

"My opinion can sway the court for him or against him, that's true, but it's his behavior that forms my opinion and that is what a judge will evaluate."

"My son is already a good member of our Amish

community. He adheres to our ways. He needs no judge but God."

"I appreciate your religious convictions. I admire the Amish. I don't want to be intrusive, but I don't have the all-seeing eye of God. I need to observe Joshua at home as well as at work. I may show up at any time. I can even visit his friends to make sure they aren't involved in criminal activities. Joshua is motivated to do well, but he has a chip on his shoulder where law enforcement is concerned."

"Can you blame me?"

Joshua moved to brace his arms on the edge of the table and glare at his parole officer. "I didn't do anything wrong. I was there to convince my brother to come home. The police who arrested me wouldn't listen. No one believed me. The prosecutor made it sound as if I had been making drugs for months. The woman who said I did this, under oath, did it to get her own sentence reduced. People acted like we were freaks. I saw the papers—Amish Brothers Arrested for Cooking Meth by School. Buggies Used to Smuggle Drugs to Rural Teenagers. I wasn't with my brother until two days before I was arrested. Do I have a distrust of English law enforcement? *Ja*, I do."

It wasn't until his father laid a hand on his shoulder that Joshua realized he was shaking with anger. His father spoke quietly in Pennsylvania Dutch. "We forgive them. We forgive them all as our Lord forgave those who persecuted Him unto death."

Joshua nodded, shamed by his outburst. "Forgive me."

"I'm not here to retry your case, Joshua. Do innocent men go to jail? Yes, they do. Do guilty men go free? All the time. I'm here because I don't want you to go back to prison. I want your family and your friends to understand that. They may think they are protecting you by clamming up when I ask questions, but they aren't. If we can't be honest and forthcoming with each other, this may not work. I don't want that. I like it when my people stay out of trouble."

Joshua's mother placed her folded hands on the table. "What about Luke? Can he come home soon?"

"I can't make that determination. I can report that he has a stable home environment waiting and his family will be supportive if I'm called on to testify."

Joshua walked to the window. He stared outside without seeing his father's farm. It was Mary's face he envisioned. "Will I be allowed to return to Hope Springs and continue with the recovery efforts?"

"Do you have an address where you will be staying?"

"I'm not sure. There's a place called the Wadler Inn. They are giving rooms to workers. I'm sure you can find their telephone number. They will know how to reach me if I find lodging elsewhere."

"I'd like a little more concrete information."

Joshua turned away from the window. "The town was nearly leveled. Some people still don't have electricity. They don't have water. Many don't even have a roof over their heads. I'm sure I'll be staying with an Amish family, but the Amish don't have telephones. The phone number for the inn is the best I can do. If you say I can't go, then that is that. But know there are people in desperate need there."

He wouldn't be able to stay with Ada and Mary. He was sure Nick wouldn't allow it. Joshua turned back to the window. How could he miss them all so deeply after only a few days? He missed Hannah's energy and Ada's cooking and teasing. He missed everything about Mary, but mostly he missed her smile.

Officer Merlin folded his black notebook and zipped it closed. "All right. You can return to Hope Springs. Check in with Sheriff Bradley when you get there. If I decide to drop in and see how you're doing, I'll expect the people at the inn to tell me where you're staying."

"Sheriff Bradley doesn't want me in his town. I was… I was seeing his daughter."

Oliver rose to his feet. "I noticed he was quite sharp on the phone."

"He can be more so in person."

"It's a free country. You have limits because of your parole status, but Sheriff Bradley can't stop you from returning to Hope Springs if I give my approval. However, I would suggest you give serious thought to avoiding his daughter. I'll be at the inn in Hope Springs on Saturday evening. You will be there."

"I will." Joshua hoped his face didn't reveal his relief. He would see Mary again. He would explain everything and pray that she understood and forgave him. He would find out if the Lord had a plan for the two of them. He prayed it was true. All he wanted was to see her again.

When Officer Merlin drove away, Isaac sighed heavily. "I wished only the best for my children. How have I failed them?"

Joshua came and laid a hand on his father's shoulder. "You did not fail us. We have failed you."

"Life is long. I pray I will see all my sons around this table again one day." He rose to his feet. "I made arrangements with the *Englisch* horse hauler to get your animal brought home, but he can't pick him up until Saturday. Would you write to Ada Kaufman and tell her that?"

"I will." Could he explain what happened in a letter to Mary? No, it was better to see her face-to-face.

After his parents went into the living room, Joshua stayed in the kitchen. Samuel came in carrying the mail. "Was the *Englischer* satisfied with your behavior?"

"Well enough, I reckon. He'll be here again in two weeks and he will check on me in Hope Springs."

"*Daed* and I have loaded a wagon with furniture and lumber for you to take with you. It's not a lot, but we have some to spare for those less fortunate." His voice trailed away as he stared at the envelope in his hand.

"What is it?" Joshua asked.

"It's a letter from Luke. He's never written before."

"That will please Mother."

Samuel held it out. "It's not addressed to Mother. It's addressed to you."

"To me? Why would he write to me and not to *Mamm* or *Daed*?"

"You'll have to open it and see." Samuel laid the letter on the counter. "I've got a rocking chair to finish and a harness to repair. I could use your help."

"I'll be out in a minute." Joshua picked up the letter and tore it open. It was short and to the point—Luke needed to see him. There was no other explanation. Something was wrong.

"You'll get over him. Men can't be trusted. Women are better off without them."

"You don't mean that, Betsy." Mary looked up from

the supplies she was restocking in the Red Cross center and glanced around. The temporary tent had been taken down and the relief center now occupied the basement of the town hall. A new truckload of donations had arrived that morning. The first boxes contained much-needed necessities like soap, toothpaste and shampoo. Some of the men, including Alvin, were setting up tables and folding chairs in the room down the hall that would serve as a place of relaxation and a meeting room when needed.

"Maybe I do mean it. Just a little. Some men can't be trusted. And those are the ones we are better off without."

Mary didn't feel better off without Joshua and she didn't want to talk about it. The ache was too new, too raw. She prayed that he would write and tell her why he left without a word. There had to be an explanation. "Does that mean you haven't made up with Alvin?"

Betsy glanced down the hall. It was empty. "He was flirting with another woman. You saw it."

"Betsy, you turned him away. He has been faithful to you for two years and you turned him away because you are afraid to commit to marriage. You tell him to go away, and when he does, that makes you angry? Do you know how ridiculous you sound?"

Betsy snapped the lid closed on a cooler filled with water bottles. "Okay. I didn't like seeing Alvin interested in someone else, but I don't know what I want. Do you?"

Oh, yes, she did. Mary wanted to see Joshua again. She wanted to know that the friendship and affection she thought they shared wasn't one-sided. She wanted to believe she could have a chance at a normal life and not have to live out her days alone. Joshua had opened her eyes to that possibility, but now he was gone.

"We aren't talking about me, Betsy. It doesn't make any difference what I want. Alvin is still here. You are the one who has a choice."

"But what if it's the wrong choice? How can I tell that I'll like him in ten years, let alone still love him in fifty years?"

"Ada says marriages are made in heaven, but husbands and wives are responsible for the upkeep."

"It's a wise Amish proverb, but what does it really mean?"

"It means you won't love him in fifty years if you aren't determined to love him every day from now until then. Answer me this. Can you see your life without him in it?"

"I don't know. I just don't know."

Alvin came around the corner with a set of folding chairs in his hands. He dropped them on the floor with a clatter. "I know what I want, Betsy Barkman. I want to have children with you and grow old with you and lie down in the earth beside you when my time comes. That's what I want. That won't change in ten years and it won't change in fifty years. Maybe you can see a life without me, but I can't see one without you. I love you, and I don't care who knows it!" He turned to look at the room but it was empty.

Mary hid a smile and picked up the supplies. "I'm going to take these to the closet."

Betsy snatched the box from her hands. "I'll take them. Alvin, would you give me a hand?"

His face turned beet-red and he rushed around the end of the counter to take the box from her. Together, they vanished into the supply room that was so full of donations there was barely enough room for one person, let alone two.

When they came out ten minutes later, Betsy's lips were puffy from being kissed and her cheeks were bright red. Alvin wore a look of bemused satisfaction. He picked up the chairs and hurried down the hall with them.

"Well?" Mary knew the answer. Betsy's eyes sparkled like stars in the night sky.

"A fall wedding. He loves me." She whirled around once and hugged Mary.

As happy as she was for her friend, Mary couldn't help the stab of jealousy that struck her. Would she ever find that kind of love?

Nick walked in through the front door, pulled off his sunglasses and came over to the two women. "How's it going?"

Betsy composed herself and gestured to the counter. "Two boxes of much-needed things like soap, and one box of shoes that contained two pairs of red high heels and six pairs of flip-flops. Not the best footwear for working in a disaster zone. What are people thinking?"

He chuckled. "We'll never know. Mary, I thought I would see if you'd like to join me for lunch. We haven't had a chance to spend much time together lately. I'm sure Miriam can join us."

Shaking her head, Mary said, "I'm not really hungry. You go on."

"Mary, you have to eat. He isn't worth getting this upset over."

She knew he meant Joshua. She looked down. "I'd rather not talk about it."

"He wasn't who you thought he was," Nick muttered.

She looked up quickly. "What do you mean by that? What aren't you telling me?"

Chapter Twelve

The following afternoon, Joshua once again faced the gray walls and high wire fences of Beaumont Correctional Facility. The driver his father had hired for the day agreed to be back to pick Joshua up in an hour. Although Joshua dreaded walking in the doors, it was considerably better to come as a visitor than it was to be a prisoner. He was searched and led into a small waiting room. A second door opened and Luke came in. His brother was all smiles, but Joshua knew something was up.

"It's good to see you, little brother. Mother's home cooking agrees with you."

"You're looking thin." Joshua sat down at the table.

"The food here stinks. You haven't forgotten that so quickly." Luke paced the room.

"What's up, Luke? Why am I here?"

"Maybe I wanted to apologize for getting you in trouble in the first place."

"I appreciate that. You know you have been forgiven. The family will welcome you—surely you know that."

Smirking, Luke said, "I know the Amish forgive sinners. I've heard it all my life."

"It's not something we say. It's something we do." Something Joshua was learning to do.

Luke looked at him sharply. "You're really beginning to sound like our old man."

"I pray that is true. Our father is devout and wise."

"Mom wrote that you've been working in Hope Springs."

"I've been helping with the tornado cleanup. There's still a lot to be done."

Luke brightened. "Are you going back?"

Joshua nodded. "Our family is donating some lumber and furniture and *Mamm* is sending canned goods. I'm headed back tomorrow with the wagon."

He hoped that Mary would forgive him for his sudden departure when he explained why he'd left without saying goodbye. She had the right to be upset that he hadn't told her about his prison time, but he believed she would understand. He was anxious to see her again. He dreamed of her at night and thought about her every hour of the day.

Luke sat down at the table. "That's just great. I was wondering if you met a woman there named Mary Shetler."

"*Nee*, the name isn't familiar."

Luke's left leg tapped up and down. There was a hollow look in his eyes. Joshua scowled at him. If he didn't know better, he would suspect Luke was using drugs again, but how could he get them in here?

Luke frowned and bit thumbnail. "That's too bad. I need you to do me a favor when you go back. I need you to find her."

"Why?"

"I've got a friend in here. His name is Kevin Dunbar. Joshua, he saved my life. There was a fight in the yard and I would have been stabbed if Kevin hadn't knocked the knife out of the guy's hand. I owe him. You understand that, don't you?"

"If he saved you, he was an instrument of God's mercy. I'm grateful for his intervention, but what does this have to do with finding someone in Hope Springs?"

"Kevin had a girlfriend, an ex-Amish girl. She was pregnant with his baby when he was locked up. She hasn't contacted him. His letters have all been returned unopened. He thinks she returned to the Amish. Her name is Shetler, Mary Shetler. He wasn't sure where she went. He had some friends looking for her in her hometown, but they never found her. He about gave up hope until he saw her on the news about Hope Springs."

"If she didn't answer his letters, maybe she doesn't want to see him."

"He still loves her. He respects her decision. He doesn't hold it against her. He just wants to know that they are both okay. Joshua, the man doesn't know if he has a son or a daughter. He's made mistakes, but he deserves to know his child is okay."

"She might not be living in Hope Springs. Many Amish came from other places to help. I don't know, Luke. The fellow is *Englisch*. His business is none of ours."

"You know it's important in here to have someone who can watch your back. This isn't Bowmans Crossing. Things can get ugly in here. This guy is my friend. He's helping me out."

"How?"

"He's taking care of me. Making sure I'm okay."

"Is he getting you drugs?"

"That's not a very Amish thing to say. He's going to get me a job with a couple of his old pals in Cleveland when I get out of here."

"Making meth again?"

"You are the suspicious one now. They run a salvage yard. I want to help a friend just the way you want to help the people in Hope Springs. Some of them are *Englisch*, too, aren't they? This is no different. All you have to do is ask around quietly and see if you can locate her. You don't even have to speak to her. He just wants to know that she's okay."

Joshua thought of Mary. He longed to know how she was. He hungered for any word of her. He could understand a man wanting to know his child and the woman he loved were safe and happy. "Okay, I'll ask around."

"Great. That's all you have to do. You are doing me a big favor. I owe you for this, little brother. When I get out of here, we are going to have some good times together, you and I."

"Does this mean you'll come home?" Joshua asked, fearing he already knew the answer.

Luke rubbed his face with his hands, shot to his feet and began pacing again. "You know the Amish life isn't for me. I don't want to be stuck in the Dark Ages. I want to be surrounded by life and fun."

"We Amish have life and fun all around us, Luke. We aren't stuck in the Dark Ages. We work hard and live a simple life so that we may be close to God and to each other."

"Like I said, you sound like *Daed*. So tell me about

this girl you're seeing in Hope Springs. What's she like?"

"How do you know about her?"

"*Mamm* forwarded all of your letters. You know how she loves to keep circle letters going in her family. You sound quite taken with Mary Kaufman and her daughter, Hannah. Is Mary pretty?"

"She's very pretty and very sweet." His heart ached to see her again.

"And Amish. *Mamm* must be over the moon about it."

Joshua sobered. "Not as much as you might think."

"Why not?"

"It's complicated."

"What's complicated about love? It's spring. It's in the air, unless you're locked in this place."

"In my case, a lot. Mary is Amish, but she was adopted by an *Englisch* couple when she was a teenager."

"So?"

"Her father is the sheriff."

Luke burst out laughing and slapped the tabletop. "My ex-convict brother is dating the daughter of a sheriff. That has to be the funniest thing I've ever heard. What does her *daed* think about you?"

"Nick Bradley doesn't care for me."

"I can imagine. Are you going to call him Papa Nick after you marry his little girl, or will it always have to be Officer Nick? You might have been better off taking a ride in the tornado."

"I'm glad it's a joke to you. For me, it's serious."

"I'm sorry. I don't mean to tease you. All you have to do is ask around for Mary Shetler when you get back to Hope Springs and let me know as soon as you hear anything. Kevin is going to be paroled soon. You don't even have to come see me. Just call. Do this favor for me and I'll come home when I get out. I promise. What do you say?"

It was late in the afternoon by the time Nick turned into Ada's lane. Mary sat beside him quietly. Their relationship had become strained over the past few days and Joshua was the reason. Nick knew something about Joshua's sudden departure, but he wouldn't talk about it. Mary never doubted how much Nick loved her and Hannah, but somehow, his feelings about Joshua were driving a wedge between them. She hated it, but she didn't know what to do about it.

In the yard, she saw a wagon piled high with lumber. Two gray draft horses stood with their heads down at the corral fence. They looked as weary as she felt.

Nick stopped the car. "Looks like more Amish contributions are on their way to Hope Springs. It must be someone who knows Ada."

They opened the car doors and got out. Hannah came flying down the steps and threw herself into her mother's arms. "*Mamm*, guess what? Joshua is here. He came back."

Mary's heart stopped for an instant and then raced ahead as joy welled up inside her. He was back. He had come back.

It was hard to breathe.

She looked toward the porch and saw him standing with Ada. Mary choked back a sob. She was so happy she was ready to cry.

Joshua came down the steps with his hat in his hand.

It was then she noticed that he didn't look happy to see her. He looked worried. Her joy ebbed away.

Nick moved to stand beside her and crossed his arms as he glared at Joshua. "I'm surprised to see you here."

"I just stopped to rest the horses and to let Ada know a horse hauler will be here Saturday to pick up Oscar. I'll be heading into town after I speak to Mary. If that's okay?"

The men were staring daggers at each other. Mary's confusion grew. "Of course you can speak to me, Joshua. What's going on?"

His expression grew puzzled. "I wasn't sure you would want to see me after the things Nick told you about me."

"Things? What things? Nick, what's he talking about?" Something was going on, and she had no clue what it was. She didn't like the feeling. She put Hannah down. "Run inside and tell Ada to put on some tea, will you, dear?"

"Sure." Hannah dashed away.

Mary glanced at Joshua and saw confusion in his eyes. He was staring at Nick. "You didn't tell her."

"I thought I would leave that up to you if you had the courage to come back."

Mary fisted her hands on her hips. "Someone had better tell me what's going on?"

Nick looked down at the ground. "Don't make me regret this, Joshua. She is a pearl beyond price and more dear to me than my life. I don't know what I would do if anyone hurt her." He kissed Mary's cheek and walked to his vehicle.

He opened the door, but paused and looked back at Joshua. "I arrested a couple of guys on suspicion of burglary yesterday. We got a tip from Pastor Finzer about where they were staying. He said you had seen something suspicious. I appreciate it when citizens look out for each other. It makes my job easier." He got in and drove away.

Joshua looked ready to fall down. Mary rushed to his side. "Are you okay?"

"I believe I would like that tea now. I have a few things to tell you, Mary, and Ada should hear them too."

"Finally. Come inside." She took his arm and led him toward the house.

When they were settled in the kitchen, Mary sent Hannah to play in the other room. Ada glanced back and forth between Mary and Joshua without comment.

He drew a deep breath. "The reason I had to get home was so that I could meet with my parole officer."

Mary sucked in a sharp breath. Of all the things she expected him to say, this wasn't among them. Ada frowned. "What is a parole officer?"

Joshua gave her a lopsided smile. "He watches over people who have been released from prison early to make sure they are walking the straight and narrow."

Ada's mouth fell open. "You were in prison?"

Mary was equally stunned. "Why?"

"Do you remember me telling you about my brother? The one who left the Amish."

Mary nodded. "His name is Luke."

"Luke had been in and out of trouble for a while. His first arrest for drugs nearly broke my mother's heart. He went to jail and we thought when he got out that he would come home. But he didn't. My parents believed that he was lost to us. I couldn't accept that."

"Of course not. You love him," Mary said softly.

"I went to see him. I went to try and convince him to come home. He had gone from using drugs to making and selling them. I couldn't make him see how much he was hurting everyone. I couldn't get through to him. After two days, I gave up. Before I could leave, there was a drug raid. Luke had sold meth to an undercover cop. I was there when it happened. I wasn't making drugs. I wasn't using drugs. I wasn't selling drugs, but that didn't matter to the men who arrested us. The house was across the street from a school. I don't know how my brother could have been so stupid."

"Why would being near a school make a difference?" Ada asked.

"The penalty for endangering children is much higher."

Kevin had always made sure he stayed far away from them when he was selling drugs. Mary looked at Joshua. "Didn't your brother tell them you were innocent?"

"He did but no one believed him. No one believed me. The district attorney was eager to get a double conviction. One of the women Luke supplied was arrested on another charge. In exchange for a lower sentence, she testified that I had been helping Luke for months." He took a sip of his tea.

"She lied?" Ada stared at him in disbelief.

He set down his mug. "Drugs are a powerful and evil master."

Mary leaned toward him. "Why didn't you tell me this to begin with?"

"If you remember, you were trapped in a cellar with a total stranger and you were scared to death."

"And later? When we got out of the cellar?"

He stared into his tea as if it contained some important information. Suddenly, she knew the answer to her own question. "Nick."

Joshua nodded. "It seemed the wisest course was to keep silent. I wasn't sure if I had violated my parole by coming here. I *was* sure Nick wouldn't like the idea of a convict staying with you."

"He found out and that's why you left early."

"It was Nick's…suggestion."

Ada sighed and gave him a bright smile. "Well, you are back now and things are as they should be. I'll get fresh sheets for your bed."

Joshua shook his head. "There's no need. I won't be staying here. I'll come by to visit often, but I'm going to stay in town."

Mary reached across the table and laid a hand on his arm. "You can stay with us. I can handle Nick."

Joshua could barely believe the blessings the Lord had bestowed on him. Nick had not turned Mary against him. Joshua was guilty of misjudging the man. Mary and Ada accepted his explanation and were still willing to open their home to him. It was more than he had dared hope for. Until now, he'd cared for Mary and valued her friendship, but seeing the determination in her blue eyes sent a rush of deeper emotion through his chest. He was in love with her. It didn't matter that he hadn't known her long. He wanted to spend a lifetime getting to know her, earning her trust, providing for her and caring for her for the rest of his days.

That was his goal, but he knew he had to start with small steps. She liked him, but Ada had warned him that Mary grew to trust people slowly. "I'm sure you can handle Nick, but I don't want to cause friction between you. I would love to stay, but it's best if I go on into town. Besides, my parole officer will be checking in with me at the Wadler Inn."

He loved that she looked disappointed. "Okay, but you are staying for supper tonight."

"I can't, but I will be back tomorrow morning to do the chores and to finish fixing your corncribs, Ada. After that, I'll be working in town. But first, I have to deliver this lumber to your bishop's home before dark."

Mary pulled her hand away. "Your family's contribution is most generous."

He wanted to be alone with her. To show her how much he had missed her. He rose to his feet. "I should go check on my team. How is Oscar getting along?"

Mary shot to her feet with her hands clenched in her apron. "I was just going to change his dressing."

Ada smiled. "I thought you did that this morning?"

Mary blushed. "Did I? That's right, and I felt the drainage was worse, so I was going to check it again. Joshua, why don't you take a look and tell me what you think. It's your decision if we need to call the vet."

"Sure. I'll take a look at him." He followed Mary to the door.

Ada chuckled. "That's going to be the most pampered horse that has ever lived in my barn."

Joshua made a pretense of checking over his team before he entered the barn. As soon as Mary came in behind him, he held out his hands. "I missed you so much."

She took his hands and squeezed them. "I missed you, too. I was so afraid I would never see you again."

He drew her into his embrace. She rested her cheek against his chest. For a long time, they simply held each other. He had never known such happiness. Unfortunately, he couldn't hold her forever. He lifted her chin and brushed a kiss lightly across her lips. "As much as I want to stay, I had better get on the road. I don't want to be driving my big wagon after dark."

"Promise me you won't vanish again without telling me where you're going."

"That's an easy promise to make."

"Thank you for your honesty in the house. I should be honest with you in return. There are things about me that you need to hear."

"They won't change how I feel about you."

"You won't know that until I'm finished."

Hannah came through the barn door. He and Mary quickly stepped apart. "*Mammi* wants to know how Oscar is."

He shared a knowing smile with Mary. "*Mammi* wants to make sure we are behaving ourselves." He tweaked Hannah's nose. "Oscar is fine. You have been taking good care of him. I missed you."

"I missed you, too. *Mammi* says we're going to have a picnic at the lake tomorrow for *Mamm's* birthday." She hopped up and down with excitement.

"That sounds *wunderbar*. I'm sure you'll have a good time."

"You can come with us." Hannah clapped her hands.

"Happy birthday, Mary. That's awful nice of you to invite me, Hannah, but I think the picnic is just for your family."

"Nonsense," Ada said as she came into the barn. "I expect you to join us. We aren't leaving without you.

Not after all the work you have done in this community. There will be several families there, not just ours."

"Please say you'll come," Hannah begged.

"I don't see how I can refuse such a kind invitation." He caught Mary's eye. Maybe he could find some time alone with her.

She looked away first. "You don't have to come if you would rather do something else."

"I can't think of anything I'd rather do than go on a picnic with you. I'd love to take a long stroll around the lake."

Ada laughed. Mary didn't smile.

When Ada and Hannah left the barn, Joshua took Mary's hand again. "I'm listening now. What did you want to tell me?"

She stepped away from him. "It can wait until tomorrow. You should leave before it gets too late."

"I'm not in a hurry, Mary."

"Tomorrow. We'll talk tomorrow." She hurried out of the barn, leaving him puzzled.

Was she that worried about what she had to tell him? What could be so bad?

Chapter Thirteen

On Saturday morning, Joshua picked up Mary, Hannah, Ada and Bella for the short wagon ride to the Shetler farm. Mary sat quietly beside him. He'd spent the night wondering what she needed to tell him, determined to convince her it didn't matter. He hoped he wouldn't have to wait long to get her alone.

At the Shetler farm, they joined Joe and Naomi Shetler, along with all the Barkman sisters and their husbands and children on the shore of a small lake in Joe's pasture. The green hillsides around the lake were dotted with white sheep and playful lambs. After helping Mary and Ada out of their buggy, Joshua joined the men standing in the shade of a tall oak tree. Hannah and several of the children ran to the water's edge and threw a stick for Bella. The Lab raced in, splashing the children urging her on. When she came out, she put the stick down and shook from head to tail. While she was busy, a large black-and-white sheepdog darted in and stole the stick and the chase was on.

Mary produced a bottle of soap and some wands and the children were soon blowing bubbles. The dogs gave up chasing each other and launched themselves at the orbs floating in the air. The other women, chatting and bustling about, were busy setting out the quilts and chairs and arranging the food on the tailgate of Joe's wagon.

Joe stroked his gray beard. "I've learned it's best to stay out of their way until they tell us it's ready."

Joshua surveyed the lake. "Is the fishing any good here?"

Nodding, Joe gestured toward the north end. "There's some mighty good fishing all along this side. Would you like a pole? I have several extras."

"I might take you up on that later." Joshua was watching Mary laughing with the children. It was good to see her so carefree.

"After you've had time to walk out with Mary, you mean." Joe chuckled.

Joshua gave him a wry smile. "Am I that obvious?"

"You forget that I've had a houseful of granddaughters all finding mates in the last two years. I know the look of a man who is smitten. Alvin and Betsy are slipping away now. You should take Mary in the other direction."

"I will. Speaking of granddaughters, I've been meaning to ask if you're related to a girl named Mary Shetler?"

"I've no relative named Mary. Why do you ask?"

"My brother knows an *Englisch* fellow who is looking for a girl by that name. Apparently, she was an old girlfriend. He thought he saw her on the television here in Hope Springs helping after the tornado."

"I'm the only Shetler in this community, but there are plenty of them over by New Philadelphia, although they are only distantly related to me. Maybe she's from one of those families. Mary is a common name. I don't know how to help you find her."

"New Philadelphia. I'll let my brother know."

"If she is Amish and left this *Englisch* fellow, it may be best that he not find her."

"I've thought of that, but they had a child together that he never met. A man should know his child."

"Perhaps this woman had a good reason for leaving him."

"Perhaps. *Danki*, Joe." Joshua saw Clara had taken over supervising the children. Mary was strolling toward the water's edge. He left Joe chuckling behind him and went to join her.

She smiled shyly when he stopped beside her. He gazed out over the lake. Fleecy white clouds in the blue sky floated above their flawless reflections in the water, as if the beauty was too great for the heavens to hold. "This is a pretty place, don't you think?"

"*Ja*, it's peaceful here." She began walking and he fell into step beside her. He could tell she was nervous.

They strolled for a while until a bend in the shoreline took them out of view of the others.

He found a fallen log beside a blooming dogwood tree and sat down. Mary joined him.

He glanced at her sitting beside him. He wanted to kiss her more than he wanted anything else in his life. He wanted the right to hold her in his arms. In the depths of his heart, he believed she was the woman God had fashioned for him alone. It didn't matter that he wasn't her first love. It only mattered that she loved him now. He took her hand. It was small and soft and it fit his perfectly. "Mary, I have come to care deeply for you. I need to know that you feel the same."

She pulled her hand away and stood. "There are things I need to tell you before you say more. You aren't going to like hearing them."

He tried to take her hand again, but she pushed away. "Please, don't touch me. If you do, I may falter."

"I'm sorry. Mary, I don't know why you are afraid of me. I would never hurt you. Nothing you can say will change my feelings for you."

Mary wanted so much to confide in him, but she was scared. Scared it would matter. "I'm not afraid of you, Joshua. I'm afraid of the way I feel when I'm with you."

He took her hand and squeezed gently. "And how is that?"

"I feel like there might be a chance for me. A chance at happiness."

"That's how you make me feel. Why does that scare you? You deserve happiness."

"I'm afraid I'll reach for it and it will burst like one of Hannah's soap bubbles on the grass."

"There's more to it, isn't there? Is it me? Do you think I won't be back the next time I have to leave?"

"Maybe. I'm not sure."

"Why would you think that?"

"Because it has happened to me before. Hannah's father left me. The next man who took me in betrayed me, too. I've been with more than one man. I was never married, Joshua. Hannah is an illegitimate child."

"I know that."

Mary frowned. "You do? How could you know this?"

"Delbert mentioned it the first day I met him. I asked him if he knew your husband and he said he didn't think you'd ever been married but he didn't hold that against you. It is a grave matter, but it is in the past. We will never mention it again. I love you and I love Hannah."

"You've known since then?" A sob escaped her and suddenly she was crying as she hadn't cried in years. She had been so afraid and all this time he knew.

"Don't cry. It doesn't matter. I love Hannah. She is the daughter of my heart." Joshua drew Mary into his embrace and held her. He gave her his handkerchief and she cried until she didn't have any tears left.

When she grew calm, he knelt in front of her. She dried her eyes and blew her nose.

"Are you okay now?" he asked.

She had a headache and her eyes were burning as if they were full of sand, but she ignored those minor discomforts. "I'm better than I have been in a long time."

"If you are ready to go back, I'm sure they have a birthday cake for you."

"*Nee*, stay. I'm ready to tell you what happened."

"You don't have to do that."

"I do. I want you to understand what I was going through when I made some horrible decisions."

He took a seat on the tree trunk beside her. "Okay, I'm listening."

She gazed up into the beautiful sky and prayed for courage. "My father died when I was only six. I vaguely remember him. My mother remarried when I was ten. My stepfather was a good man, but he wasn't an affectionate man. He needed a wife to help him raise four sons and my mother fit the bill. I was an extra mouth to feed. My mother died in a buggy accident four years later. My stepfather didn't waste time remarrying. I never felt like I was part of the family after that."

"I'm sorry you were left alone."

"I found a job as a live-in maid with a family in Canton when I was fifteen. The husband was so nice to me. I just wanted to be loved. He saw how vulnerable I was and took advantage of that. He seduced me."

"Is he Hannah's father?"

She nodded. "When I suspected I was pregnant, I told him and I was promptly fired. He was terrified his wife would find out. I went back to my stepfather, but I wasn't welcome there. I was alone and out on the streets. I turned to my church for help, but the bishop called me terrible names. I was shunned. That's when I met someone who said he wanted to take care of my baby and me. I was so naive. You'd think I would have been smarter about men at that point, but I wasn't."

"We are taught to trust in the goodness of all men. Who was he?"

"A truly evil person. He took me in and took care of me. I thought I loved him. I began to suspect he was dealing drugs on the side, but I didn't want to believe it. I couldn't be that wrong about another person I wanted to love."

"What happened?"

"I overheard him making arrangements to sell my baby when it was born. He knew someone who would pay a lot of money for a white child. They would pay more for a son, but they would take a girl. I was sick with fear for my baby. I had nowhere to go. He made me believe I couldn't escape him."

"But you did."

"I couldn't let them have my baby. God was watching over her. I went into labor one night when he was gone and delivered Hannah by myself. I had nothing for her. I stole a quilt off the clothesline of a neighbor and wrapped her in that. I knew I had to hide her. I knew he would be back at any time. There was a convenience store not far from our place. I used to see Amish buggies parked there. There was one in the parking lot that night. I put Hannah in the basket on the backseat and I left a note begging the Amish family to take care of her. I told them to meet me in the same place in a week. I needed time to gather enough money so we could get far away from him. I believed he would find us and take her if I didn't."

"That was an incredibly brave and unselfish thing to do. Did the buggy belong to Ada?"

"*Nee*, it belonged to Levi Beachy. His brothers, Atlee and Moses, had taken it without his knowledge and met up with some girls to see a movie. They didn't know Hannah was in the backseat until they were almost home. She started crying and they panicked. They couldn't take her back. They couldn't take her home with them or their brother would know they had sneaked out without his knowledge. They were passing Ada's farm and it occurred to them that she didn't have grandchildren, so they left Hannah on her doorstep. They never saw my note. They never told anyone about her. She was found by Miriam. She saw an Amish buggy leaving and thought some unwed mother didn't want her baby. Miriam and Ada found the note and waited for me to show up at the farm. I didn't. I was in the parking lot of a convenience store praying the people I left Hannah with would bring her back. When they didn't return, I knew I'd lost her forever."

"What about the man who wanted to sell her?"

"I told him the baby was stillborn. He was furious, but he believed me. He still thought I was in love with him, but I knew I was nothing to him. I was nothing to anyone."

"That is never true. We are God's children. He is always with us, even in the dark times."

"I know that now, but I didn't believe it then. Nick and Miriam were investigating and trying to discover the identity of Hannah's family when I was taken to the hospital. I was…sick."

She wasn't ready to tell him that she had tried to end her life. She didn't have the courage. Not yet.

"Eventually, they figured out who I was and they gave Hannah back to me. I couldn't believe it. I had my baby in my arms and I had people who cared about us. Nick and Miriam were amazing. They gave me a home when they took me to live with Ada. They gave me protection and security by adopting me. God saved more than my life. He gave me a family. How can I expect anything more than that?"

"I think you are selling God short. I think He gets to decide how much joy and how much sorrow comes into our lives. His love is limitless."

Did she doubt God's mercy and goodness?

"Does Hannah's father know he has such a beautiful daughter?"

"He died in a small plane crash when she was eight months old."

"What happened to the man who wanted to sell her? I can't believe Nick would let him go unpunished. It is not the *Englisch* way to forgive."

"He was arrested for the drugs and then charged with

second degree kidnapping, too, because I was a minor. It was then he learned my baby was still alive. I testified against him in court. If I hadn't, he would have gone free. I know it is not our way, but I believe he would've found another girl in trouble and sold her baby. I could not be a party to that. He made many threats against me. After only four years, he's getting out on parole. Nick and Miriam are worried that he will try to find me. That's why I was so upset about seeing my face on television." Emotionally drained and exhausted, Mary closed her eyes.

"Do you believe he will?"

"I do. That's why I changed my name to Kaufman when Miriam adopted me. It was at Nick's urging. He knew it would make it harder for Kevin Dunbar to find me. There are a lot of Mary Kaufmans among the Amish."

"Did you say Kevin Dunbar?"

The strain in Joshua's voice caused Mary to open her eyes. "Do you know him?"

Joshua rose to his feet and walked a few feet away. He raked a hand through his hair. "No, but I've heard my brother mention someone by that name. It might not be the same man. There could be more than one Kevin Dunbar in the world."

"The Kevin Dunbar I know is in the Beaumont Correctional Facility."

Joshua stared at her in shock. This could not be happening. Mary could not be the woman he had been sent to look for. He paced back and forth in front of her.

"Joshua, what's wrong?"

How much information about her had he shared? He

racked his brain trying to recall all the times he had mentioned her in his letters and spoken of her when he was with Luke. Had Luke shared that information with Dunbar? Was it enough for Dunbar to figure out it was the same Mary? Maybe.

Luke was waiting for Joshua to contact him with more information. His brother needed to know Dunbar wasn't being honest with him. Joshua needed to find out exactly how much the man knew about Mary Kaufman, if anything. What if he had put her in danger?

"I know it's a lot for you to take in, Joshua. I understand that. I wouldn't blame you if you packed up and went home. I'm not exactly the kind of girl you want your parents to meet." She rose to her feet.

He stopped pacing and reached for her. "Mary, you're the only woman I'd like my parents to meet. I *am* going to pack up and go home, but I'll be back. I want you to believe that. I love you. I want us to be together, but I have to take care of something else first."

"Does it have to do with your parole?"

Joshua's jaw clenched. He had a meeting this evening with Officer Merlin at the inn. He would have to miss it. The man would be furious, but Mary was more important. Joshua had to make sure her identity was still safe.

"It's family business. It could take a couple of days. After your party, I'll catch a ride home with the man that's picking up Oscar." From there, he could get a ride with a local man to see Luke.

"But you will be back. I believe that. I love you."

He saw the soft glow in her eyes as she spoke. He pulled her into his arms and kissed her gently. "I love you, too. God willing, we will have many years to whisper those words to each other."

Joshua was shocked at the change in his brother when he visited him the following morning. Luke was hollow-eyed and shaking. "You look terrible."

"So do you. So what? What do you want?"

"I found the woman you asked me to look for. I found Mary Shetler, but you can't tell Dunbar anything about her."

Luke laughed but there wasn't any humor in it. "I didn't have to."

"What are you saying?"

"All I did was tell him my brother was courting the *Englisch* sheriff's adopted Amish daughter. I thought it was a *goot* joke considering you're on parole. Does she know that? It turns out Dunbar knows Sheriff Bradley rather well."

"Oh, Luke. You have no idea what you've done."

"I helped a friend find his daughter. Not that he turned out to be much of a friend."

"You're using again, aren't you?"

"I'm going cold turkey this time, thanks to my *goot* buddy."

"Dunbar was supplying you drugs in here? That's the kind of man you helped find an innocent woman and child?"

"Hey, keep your voice down. Do you want the guards to hear? I'm not a rat."

"Dunbar isn't Hannah's father. He tried to sell her on the black market when she was born. Mary was fifteen and homeless when he found her and took her in.

Not because he cared about her, but because she was pregnant. Apparently, some people will pay large sums of money for a white baby."

Luke lost his smug look. "I don't know what you're talking about. Kevin said he was her father."

"He lied to you. Hannah's father died in an accident months after she was born. Kevin is looking for Mary because she testified against him. She's the reason he's in here."

"I didn't know any of this."

"You know what kind of man he is. You know he is dealing drugs and you would do anything for them. Did he see my letters? Does he know where she lives?"

"I'm sorry, Joshua. You have to believe that I'm sorry. He saw your letters. He was paroled two days ago."

"What is Bella barking at?" Ada looked up from her needlework.

Mary laid down the book she was reading. "I'll go see. Did Hannah come in?"

"I don't think so."

Rising from her chair, Mary went to the window to look out. There was a black car parked on their lane. Was it a driver bringing Joshua back? "I see a car at the end of the drive."

"Are they coming to the house?" Ada rose to join Mary at the window.

"*Nee*, it's just sitting there."

"Perhaps someone is lost."

"Maybe Joshua has come back." She was so eager to see him. Eager to explore the future with him.

Ada remained at the window. "I thought he said it

would be several days. Now they are coming this way. You might be right."

"I'll go see." Mary hurried through the house to the kitchen door. She paused before opening the screen to still her racing heart. It might not be him. But it might be.

Bella's barking intensified, then she yelped once and was silent. Hannah screamed. Mary pushed open the screen door and rushed out. Her heart dropped to her feet when she saw Kevin standing beside the car. He had Hannah in his arms. She was struggling to get free and crying. There were two men with Kevin. Bella lay sprawled on the ground at the feet of one of them.

Mary ran toward Kevin. "Don't hurt her. I'm begging you, don't hurt my baby."

"You should have kept your mouth shut. None of this would've happened if you had just kept your mouth shut."

Mary reached Kevin's side but one of the men stopped her when he wrapped his arms around her. She tasted the salty tears that streamed down her face. Clutching her hands together, she pleaded with Kevin, "Please, if you ever had any feelings for me at all, don't do this."

"That's just it, Mary. I never did have feelings for you. The baby was all I wanted and now I've got her. She's still worth money, although not to the same people. Tell your boyfriend I appreciate him finding you for me." He looked at his men. "Let's go."

The man holding Mary threw her to the ground. Before she could get up, they were all in the car. She grabbed the door handle, trying to reach Hannah. Her baby was screaming. Her baby needed her, but she couldn't hold on as the car drove away.

She fell to a heap in the driveway screaming Hannah's name.

Chapter Fourteen

Joshua jumped out of the van before it pulled to a stop in Ada's yard. Bella lay on the porch with her head on her paws. There was blood on the left side of her face. As soon as he saw Mary walk out of the house, his heart leaped. She was safe. He ran toward her. "Mary, I have to talk to you."

She didn't speak. She didn't move. His steps slowed as he approached her. Her face was streaked with tears. It twisted with agony. "Why did you do it? Where is she, Joshua? I can forgive anything else. Just tell me where she is."

"What are you saying? Oh, please, God, don't let it be Hannah." He caught Mary by the arms. The raw pain in her eyes was unbearable.

"He took my baby. I couldn't do anything to stop him. Why did you tell Kevin where we were?"

"I didn't, Mary. You have to believe me. I never told him anything."

Nick Bradley came out of the house. "Mary, get inside."

She ducked her head and turned away. Joshua

reached for her, but Nick grabbed his arm, twisting it behind him and forcing Joshua up against the side of the house. "Joshua Bowman, you are under arrest for violating your parole and for conspiracy to commit kidnapping. You have the right to remain silent. If you give up that right, anything you say can and will be used against you in a court of law."

Joshua knew his rights. He ignored Nick as he continued to recite them and focused on Mary where she stood only a few feet away. "Mary, let me explain."

Nick jerked Joshua around. "You were in on this with Dunbar from the beginning. Where is she? Where did he take Hannah?"

"I'm not working with Kevin Dunbar. I don't expect you to believe me, but Mary, you have to believe me. I would never hurt you. I would never hurt Hannah."

"Then tell us where he took her," Nick bellowed, anger blazing in his eyes.

Joshua recoiled from the sheriff's rage. What would Nick do if he learned of Luke's part in this? Joshua didn't believe Luke had known Kevin would harm Hannah or Mary, but he had given away their location in exchange for drugs. That alone would add years to Luke's sentence. Joshua struggled with his need to protect his brother and to find Hannah.

"I don't know where he took her." He bowed his head. He didn't expect Nick to believe him.

"Wrong answer." Nick yanked Joshua toward his SUV.

"Wait." Mary touched Nick's arm.

He stopped. "I'm not Amish. I don't get to forgive and forget. I have to uphold the law."

"I need to hear what he has to say."

Nick shook his head, but took a few steps away.

Mary placed her hand on Joshua's chest. Her heart was being torn to pieces by her frantic grief, but she knew—she knew in her soul that he was telling the truth. He loved her and he loved Hannah. She had to trust that love. If she couldn't, then she truly was a broken human being. Joshua had kept things from her, but she had kept things from him, too.

"I believe you when you say you didn't have a part in this, Joshua. I trust you. I'm sorry I accused you."

When she looked at him, his eyes were filled with tears. She loved him so much. "God sent you to save us once before. Can't you help save her now?"

Nick came to Mary's side. A tense muscle twitched in his cheek, but he had his anger under control. "Tell us what you know. I don't want to make this harder for you. I just want our little girl back."

Joshua had no choice. Hannah and Mary needed him. He had to put aside his distrust and fear of the *Englisch* law and believe that God was in charge of his fate and of Luke's. He faced Nick knowing his words might condemn his brother to more years in prison.

"I wrote home about Mary and about Hannah and their lives here. I wanted my family to know what an amazing woman she is. My mother forwarded all my letters to my brother Luke the way the Amish do with their circle letters."

Nick crossed his arms. "How did he know you were seeing Mary Shetler?"

"He didn't. Kevin saw Mary in one of the news reports about the tornado. He knew she was in Hope Springs. Luke knew I was here, too. He wrote that he needed to see me. When I went there, he told me about his friend, a guy who had been in love with an Amish girl before he went to jail. He said she was pregnant and went back to her Amish family. He saw Mary on the news. He knew she was in Hope Springs. He wanted to make sure she and his child were okay. I said I would ask around. Something about Luke's behavior bothered me. I thought he might be using drugs again, but I had no idea how he could be getting them."

Mary wiped at the tears on her face. "You never asked me about Mary Shetler."

"The only person I asked was Wooly Joe. He said what I was already thinking—that it was better to let Mary Shetler's child grow up without knowing he or she had a drug dealer for a father."

Nick pushed his hat up with one finger. "Do you think Dunbar was supplying your brother with drugs in exchange for information?"

"I can't be sure, but I think he was. I told Luke that Mary had been adopted by you. Luke thought it was hilarious—I was fresh out on parole and dating the sheriff's daughter. He shared the story with Dunbar. The man figured out that Mary Kaufman and Mary Shetler were one and the same. When Mary told me about her relationship with Dunbar, I was sick with worry that my letters would lead him here. I went to see Luke. That's why I missed my meeting with Officer Merlin. As soon as Luke told me Dunbar had been released, I came to warn you."

"Why didn't you call me?' Nick demanded. "I could have stopped him."

"Because I didn't trust you. I was afraid if you knew about Luke's dealings with Dunbar, you'd make sure he stayed in prison."

"So now Dunbar has Hannah and we're still no closer to knowing where he took her."

"Luke once mentioned Dunbar was going to set him up in business when he got out. With some of his friends in Cleveland. They're brothers who run a salvage yard."

"There are a lot of brothers in Cleveland. You're gonna have to do better than that."

"That's all I know. Luke may know more."

"You had better hope he does. He's going to tell me everything."

Joshua understood Nick's anger. "He might not talk to you, but he'll talk to me."

Nick turned to Mary. "Get your things together. You and Ada are leaving this afternoon. Miriam has a safe place for you. I want you out of harm's way in case that maniac comes back." Nick pulled open the rear door and pushed Joshua in.

"I'm coming with you. I'll be as safe with you as I am with Miriam. If Joshua's brother knows where Hannah is, maybe I can convince him to tell us."

"All right, get in."

Joshua remained silent on the long ride to the correctional facility. Mary didn't speak to him. She didn't even look at him. He could hardly blame her. She had to be terrified. The handcuffs were cutting into his wrists by the time they arrived, but he didn't complain. It was nothing more than what he deserved. Nick was right. If Joshua had only trusted Nick enough to call him, Hannah might be safe.

Mary and Joshua were seated at a wooden table when they brought Luke into the interview room. Nick leaned against the cinder-block wall. Luke wore a defiant look. "So you couldn't keep your mouth shut, little brother," he said in Pennsylvania Dutch. "You had to involve me."

"Sit down and speak English." Nick pushed away from the wall and shoved Luke into a chair. Luke glared at him.

Mary clasped her hands together on the table. "Please help us. Kevin has taken my daughter. Her name is Hannah. She is only four years old. I know she must be so frightened. I only want to get her back. Anything that you can tell us may help us find her."

Joshua added his plea. "Please, brother. I know you would never hurt a child. I know you didn't mean for any of this to happen."

Some of Luke's bluster slipped away. "I thought he was the kid's father. A father has a right to see his child."

Nick struck the table with both hands, making everyone jump. "Do you know where he took her?"

"I don't."

Joshua said, "You told me Kevin had friends in Cleveland who would set you up with a job when you got out."

"He probably lied about that. He lied about everything else. He said he'd take care of me but the minute he got out, the supply dried up."

"Was he smuggling drugs to the inmates here?"

Luke hunched forward and rubbed his arms as if he were cold. "He still has friends inside. I can't tell you anything."

Nick pulled up a chair and sat beside Luke. "Hannah

is the sweetest child you have ever met. Her eyes are as blue as the sky. She doesn't deserve to be punished because Kevin Dunbar wants to make Mary suffer. She did the right thing when she testified against him."

"I forgave him for what he tried to do to me, but I could not let him do it to someone else," she said.

Nick patted Mary's hand and then looked at Luke. "I know it will take courage to tell us what you know. Do you have as much courage as this woman does?"

Luke sat back. "The name is Sanders. They own an auto salvage lot on the west side. They've been helping Dunbar smuggle drugs into here. I don't know how. That's all I know.

"Thank you." Nick jumped up from his seat and left the room.

"Danki," Mary said, and followed him.

Joshua gave his brother a tired smile. "You did a good thing."

"It doesn't make up for all the wrong things I have done."

"Maybe not. But it's a start."

"This means I'm going to be in here for a long time."

Joshua stared at the door. "Maybe they will give us a cell together."

Perched on the end of his cot in the county jail in Millersburg, Joshua prayed, not for his release, but for Mary's and Hannah's safety. The last thing he wanted was to hurt them, and yet he had led a vicious man to their door. He didn't know how he could live with himself if anything happened to Hannah. All things were according to God's plan, but it was hard to see that when his heart was breaking.

He heard the cell-block door open. He looked up as Sheriff Bradley paused in front of his cell. Joshua jumped to his feet. "Did you find her?"

The sheriff looked tired and worn. "My family is no concern of yours."

"I just want to know that she is safe. Please, can you tell me that much?"

Nick sighed heavily. "We found her. She's frightened but safe. We arrested two men, but Dunbar got away."

"Where is Mary now? Can I see her?"

"She and Hannah are safe with an Amish family in another community."

"Thank God." Joshua gripped the bars and laid his head against the cold steel. It didn't matter what happened to him now. He would go back to prison and finish out his sentence, but he could face that knowing they were safe.

Sheriff Bradley unlocked the cell door and held it open. "You're free to go home if you agree to follow the conditions of your original parole."

"I don't understand."

"You had a valid reason for missing your meeting with your parole officer, but it can't happen again. Do you understand?"

"Why are you doing this?"

"Because I think you love my daughter."

"I do. I love her more than life itself and I love Hannah like she was my own child."

"Then I'm sorry, but you are going to have to forget about them. They are no longer your concern. The only way to keep Mary and Hannah safe is to keep them hidden."

"If I could just say goodbye to them. That's all I'm asking. That's all I'll ever ask of you."

"No."

Hope died in Joshua's chest.

"There's a car waiting outside that will take you home."

"What about my brother? What will happen to him?"

"I'm not at liberty to talk about an ongoing case. Go home. There's nothing you can do for them."

"You have to eat something. You're going to dry up and blow away. Who will take care of Hannah then?" Ada pushed a plate piled high with meat loaf, green beans, mashed potatoes and gravy across the table to Mary.

Mary pushed it aside. "I'm not hungry, and I'm not about to dry up and blow away. I will always take care of Hannah. You should stop worrying about me."

"How can I stop worrying when there is such sadness in your eyes?"

"If you're worried that I'm going to do something stupid, don't be. I was very young and very foolish when I tried to commit suicide. I have learned that I can bear all things if I trust in the Lord. This too shall pass." They were hard words to say while her heart was breaking, but she spoke the truth.

Her daughter was safe. Bella was making a good recovery from the blow to her head. Ada hadn't suffered any ill effects from the fright and stress. It had been two weeks since Hannah's abduction and Mary had no idea if she would ever see Joshua again. She missed him dreadfully.

The outside door opened and Miriam came in. "They caught him."

Mary jumped to her feet. "They caught Kevin Dunbar?"

"He was trying to cross into Canada."

Ada patted her chest. "The goodness of the Lord be praised."

"Amen," Mary and Miriam said together, and smiled at each other.

"Does this mean we can go home?" Hannah was sitting at the table eating her green beans and dropping a few to Bella, who was on the floor at her feet.

Miriam grinned at her. "According to Papa Nick, you can."

Mary laced her fingers together and squeezed hard. "When can I see Joshua?"

"Nick is going there tomorrow. He wanted to know if you would like to go, too?"

Mary squealed in delight. "I do. I do want to go."

"Me, too," Hannah shouted.

"Me, three," Ada shouted, and they all laughed.

Miriam looked over the table. "We're to meet him there at ten o'clock. This looks good. Can I join you?"

"I will get you a plate." Ada hurried to the cupboard.

Mary sat back and gave silent thanks. The dark clouds covering her days had been blown away. If only Joshua could accept her family and her family accept him. It was a tall order, but nothing was impossible in the sight of God.

Joshua was cleaning Oscar's stall when he heard a car drive in. He put aside his pitchfork and headed to the door. It wasn't his day to meet with Officer Merlin. Who was here?

He recognized Nick Bradley's SUV and his heart

thudded painfully. Were Mary and Hannah okay? Had Dunbar found them again?

Nick got out and opened the back door on the passenger's side. Joshua couldn't believe his eyes when Luke got out. He glanced toward the house. His father and mother had heard the vehicle, too, and had come outside. The joy that spilled across their faces took his breath away.

He hurried forward and held out his hand. His brother was still pale, but his eyes were clear. "Luke, I can't believe it's you. What's going on?"

"I got an early parole."

"How?"

Nick closed the door and folded his arms over his chest. "Your brother is cooperating with our investigation into drug-smuggling activities at the Beaumont Correctional Facility. In the interest of his safety, the judge has granted him parole. You might also want to know that Kevin Dunbar was arrested this morning trying to cross into Canada. He's going away for a long, long time, without the possibility of parole."

Another car turned into the drive. It was a blue sedan. Joshua didn't recognize it. By this time, all of Joshua's brothers were standing behind his parents.

Luke rubbed his palms on his pant legs. "Reckon it's time to get a tongue lashing from dear old *daed*."

Joshua slapped him on the shoulder. "It won't be as bad as you think."

As his family went into the house with Luke, Joshua stayed behind. "Was this your doing, Nick?"

"A little. I thought your family deserved a break after what happened to you."

The car pulled up behind Nick's vehicle. Joshua went weak in the knees when Hannah burst out of the backseat and came running toward him. He crouched down and gathered her in his arms. "Hannah Banana, it is so good to see you."

She squeezed his neck in a huge hug, then leaned back and patted his face with both hands. "I'm not a banana."

"I guess you aren't. You're getting to be a very big girl." Joshua put her down. He saw Miriam get out of the driver's side and open the back door. Ada got out. Then the beautiful woman he was dying to hold in his arms stepped out, too.

"Mary." He breathed her name into the air.

She slowly approached him. He'd thought about her so often, agonized over what he might say to her. Wondered what she might say to him. Now that she was standing in front of him, words failed him. He wanted to drop to his knees and beg her forgiveness.

"Hello, Joshua." Her voice was tentative, hesitant.

"Hello, Mary." He wanted to tell her how beautiful she looked in the morning light. He wanted to tell her how much he had missed the sound of her voice, the curve of her lips when she smiled, the soft blush that stained her cheeks so easily.

Miriam took Nick by the elbow and Hannah by the hand. "Let's go inside and meet Joshua's family. I'm sure they have a lot of questions for us."

Joshua shoved his hands in his pockets. He had no idea where to go from here.

Mary couldn't believe how nervous she was. Once she had Hannah safely in her arms, the only thing she'd wanted was to tell Joshua how much she missed him. Now that he was standing in front of her, she couldn't think of a thing to say. She just wanted to be in his arms. Why was he just standing there? Couldn't he see how much she loved him?

He raised his face to heaven. "When you look at me like that, I can't think straight."

"How am I looking at you?" she asked softly, stepping closer.

"Like you need me to hold you."

"I do, Joshua. I need you to hold me all the days of my life." He groaned as he pulled her close and her joy filled her to the brim. He was strong and solid—this wasn't a dream. She wouldn't wake and find she was alone in her bed in a strange house. She was finally where she belonged. She was afraid to breathe, afraid he would pull away and she would never feel this complete again. She cupped his face with her hands and gazed into his eyes. "You are a wonderful man. I don't deserve you."

He gave her a wry smile. "I'm the one who doesn't deserve you. I understand if you would rather have Delbert Miller."

Mary's heart soared as she realized her life was about to take an amazingly wonderful turn with this amazing and wonderful man. She grinned happily. "He's a fine fellow, but I think Hannah likes you better."

"What will she think about having me as a father?" His voice was hesitant. Didn't he know Hannah already loved him, too?

"She will be delighted."

"Are you sure?"

"I'm very, very sure. There's no one in the world who will be a better father than you, Joshua. I believe that with all my heart."

He brushed his lips tenderly over hers. She raised

her arms to circle his neck as he crushed her close. She wanted to be held by him this way for a lifetime. When he drew away, she missed his warmth and the feel of his heart beating against hers.

Drawing a shaky breath, he said, "That still leaves one obstacle."

"I don't see any." She needed his lips on hers. She tried to pull him back, but he resisted.

"What about your father?"

"Nick? What about him?"

"Mary, my brother and I are felons. Your father is a sheriff. He's not going to like having ex-cons for in-laws. Neither will your mother."

"Oh, Joshua, you underestimate Nick and Miriam. They fell in love young, but theirs was not an easy path. Nick was English, Miriam was Amish, but there was much more. Nick was responsible for the death of Miriam's only brother."

Joshua's eyes widened with shock. "How?"

"Miriam's brother had stolen a car. He was desperate to reach the English girl he loved before she left town. Nick gave chase, not knowing who was driving the stolen vehicle. He ran the car off the road in an attempt to stop it and Miriam's brother was killed in the crash. It took a long time for Nick to forgive himself and much longer for Miriam to forgive him. A baby left on Miriam's doorstep years later brought them together."

"Hannah?"

Mary slipped her arms around Joshua's waist and laid her head on his chest. "*Ja.* It was Hannah. The baby I gave away."

When his arms closed around her, she knew he was the one God had chosen for her. "Isn't it amazing how the Lord uses us to reach others in ways we can't imagine? Nick and Miriam understand that people make mistakes, but those mistakes do not define who we are. What we do with each new day that God gives us defines who we are in His sight."

"In that case, Mary Kaufman, will you marry me? I love you. I don't want to face a life without you. Every morning and every night I want my love for you to define who I am in the sight of God."

Sweet bliss filled her heart and surged through her veins. She hated doing it, but he had to know one more thing before she gave him her answer. She stepped back and pulled up her sleeve. Her scars stood out puckered and white on her wrists. "You know what these are from?"

"I don't, but it must have hurt you very much."

"I don't remember it hurting. I did it to myself, Joshua. I tried to kill myself with a broken piece of bathroom mirror. I cut my wrists open and waited to die."

She expected the shock she saw in his face, but she hadn't expected how quickly his expression changed to compassion. "You must have been terribly alone."

It was so long ago, but she could feel the cold creeping over her even now the way it had as she lay dying. "You can't know what it's like to reach the point where you believe in your soul that you and everyone else will be better off if you're dead. After I lost Hannah, I had nothing to live for. I wasn't sick when Nick and Miriam found me in the hospital. I tried to commit suicide."

He caressed her cheek with his fingers. "I'm sorry you went through such a terrible ordeal, but I rejoice that your life was spared. Mary, it doesn't change the way I feel when I'm with you."

"Truly?"

"Truly."

She let out the breath she had been holding. "In that case, I would love to marry you."

He pulled her close and kissed her again, with infinite tenderness and passion. Mary saw just how wonderful their life together was going to be.

The door to the house opened and Hannah came out with a cookie in her hand. "Joshua, your mother is a *goot* cook."

"I'm glad you think so." He picked her up and sat her on the hood of Nick's SUV. "Hannah, I have a serious question for you."

"I haven't blamed Bella for anything she didn't do."

He glanced at Mary and chuckled. "I'm glad to hear that. I need your permission for something important. I would like to marry your mother. What do you think about that?"

Her mouth fell open. "I thought you were going to marry me?"

"I love you dearly, but your mother is already twenty. This might be her last chance to get a husband."

Hannah thought it over, and then nodded. "Okay. Can I get another cookie?"

Laughing, Joshua took one of her hands and Mary took the other. They swung her off the hood and walked into their future together.

* * * * *

A HUSBAND FOR MARI

Emma Miller

A friend loves at all times…
—*Proverbs* 17:17

Chapter One

Wisconsin

Mari rolled up her grandmother Maryann's red-rooster salt-and-pepper shakers in a stained dish towel and stuffed them into a canvas gym bag. "What time is your boyfriend picking you up?" she asked her soon-to-be-ex roommate.

Darlene pulled her head out of the dark refrigerator, a carton of milk in her hand. There wasn't anything left but condiments, two eggs and the quart of chocolate milk. With the electricity shut off for the past forty-eight hours, Mari wouldn't have touched the milk. Darlene took the cap off and sniffed it. "Twenty minutes." She wrinkled her nose and took a swig. "You want the eggs?"

Mari shook her head. "You take them. I can hardly carry them to Delaware, can I?"

Darlene, thin as a rake handle, features embellished by enough dollar-store makeup for all the participants in a toddlers' beauty pageant, tucked the egg carton into a cardboard box. "Suit yourself." She picked up a green rubber band that had once secured celery and gathered her dyed midnight-black tresses into a ponytail. "I'm gonna run next door and use the bathroom before Cassie goes to work."

Mari nodded; they'd been using their neighbor's bathroom since the electric was disconnected. Darlene went out the front door, inviting an arctic blast in, and Mari shivered.

She sure hoped it would be warmer in Delaware. Wisconsin winters were brutal. If it wasn't for the kerosene heater, they couldn't have stayed there the past two days. She rewrapped the wool scarf she wore and gazed around. There wasn't anything about the old single-wide trailer with its ratty carpet and water-stained walls that she was going to miss. She had very little to show for eighteen months in Friendly's Mobile Home Park: few belongings and no real friends. She and Darlene had become housemates only because they worked on the same assembly line at the local plant and were both single mothers. They weren't really friends, though. They were just too different.

Feeling the need to do something besides stand there and feel sorry for herself, Mari grabbed a broom and began to sweep the kitchen. She couldn't wash out the refrigerator or wipe down the cabinets, but she could sweep at least. That didn't take water or money, which was a good thing, because she didn't have either. She almost laughed out loud at the thought.

Money had been short since the plant closed and her unemployment ran out. Even shorter than it had been before. Jobs were scarce in the county. Mari had picked and sorted apples, cleaned houses and even tried to sell magazines over the phone. She read the want ads every day, but employment for a woman with an eighth-grade education and few skills was nearly impossible to find.

She pushed her hand deep into her pocket to reassure herself that Sara Yoder's letter was still there and that she hadn't just dreamed it. Sara, an old acquaintance from her former life, was her only option now. If it hadn't been for Sara's encouraging letters and her unsolicited invitation to come stay with her in Delaware, Mari didn't know where she and Zachary would be sleeping.

Mari swallowed hard. She shouldn't dwell on how bad things had gotten, but it was hard not to. First her car had died, and then she couldn't keep up with her cell phone bill. She'd found a few days of work passing out samples of food in a supermarket, but, living in a rural area, without transportation, it was impossible to keep even that pitiful job. Her meager savings went fast; then came the eviction notice.

Mari had tried her best these past few years, but it was time to admit that she was a failure. A bad mistake, poor judgment and a naive view of the world had gone against her. She had nothing but her son now, and she was worried about him. Worried enough to move a thousand miles away.

At nine years old, Zachary was becoming disillusioned with her promises and forced optimism. She was always saying things like "When I find a better job, we'll rent a place where you can have a dog." Or "I know it's a used bike, but maybe next year I'll be able to buy you the new bike that you really wanted for your birthday." Secondhand clothes, thirdhand toys and a trailer with a leaky roof were Zachary's reality. And her bright, eager child was fast becoming moody and temperamental. The boy who'd had so many friends in first and second grade now had to be dragged away from watching old DVD shows on the TV and coaxed to get out of the house to play. In the past month, he'd brought home two detention notices, and most mornings he pretended to have a stomachache or a headache in an attempt to avoid school. She was equally concerned about the envy Zachary had begun to exhibit toward other boys in his class, boys who had name-brand clothing, cell phones and TVs and PlayStations in their bedrooms.

She'd wanted to dismiss Zachary's unhappiness as just a stage that boys went through. A few bad apples in his classroom, a difficult teacher, an ongoing issue with a school bully, would make anyone depressed. But those were all excuses.

Mari knew she had to do something different. She couldn't keep relying on neighbors or roommates to keep an eye on Zachary while she worked odd shifts and weekends. She needed a support system, someone who cared enough about them to see that he got off to school if she had to leave early, someone to be there if he was sick or she had to work late.

Mari had thought she could raise him alone, but she was beginning to realize she couldn't do it. Love wasn't enough. It was her concern for her son that had given her the courage to agree to move to Delaware. She needed to provide for her child, and she needed to give him what he had never had: structure, community and a real home where he wouldn't be ashamed to bring his friends.

Seven Poplars, Delaware, the town that Sara Yoder

had moved to, had become a refuge in Mari's mind, the hope of a new beginning. In her dreams, it was a place where she and Zachary could make right what had gone wrong in their lives. Sara had offered her a room in her home and the promise of a job. There would be a tight-knit community to help with Zachary, to watch over him, to teach him right from wrong. And if it meant returning to the life she'd thought she'd left behind forever, that was the sacrifice she would make for her son's sake.

The groan of brakes one street over told Mari that Zachary's bus had entered the trailer park. She put away the broom and began to stack the few bags they had on the couch. Sara had hired a van and driver to take them to Delaware.

The door banged open and Zachary came up the steps and into the trailer, head down, his backpack sagging off one shoulder.

"I hope you had a good last day." She tried to sound as cheerful as she could as she closed the door behind him to keep out the bitter wind. "There's still a couple of things—" She halted midsentence, staring at him. He wasn't wearing a coat. "Zachary? Did you leave your good coat on the bus?" Her heart sank. It wasn't his *good* coat; it was his *only* coat. She'd found it at a resale shop, but it was thick and warm and well made. "Where's your coat?"

He shrugged and looked up at her with that expression that she'd come to know all too well over the past months. "I don't know."

Mari suppressed the urge to raise her voice. "Did you leave it on the bus or at school?" She closed her eyes for a moment. There was no time to go back to school to get his coat before the hired van came for them, and she had no way to get there even if there was.

Zachary dropped his old backpack to the floor. He was wearing a hooded sweatshirt, hood up, but he had to be cold. He had to be frozen.

"I'm sorry about the coat," he muttered, not making eye contact. "But it wasn't all that great. The zipper kept getting stuck." He hesitated and then went on, "It wasn't in my cubby this afternoon. I think one of the guys took it as a joke. I looked for it, but the second bell rang for the buses. I knew I'd be in trouble if I missed my ride home." He swallowed. "I'm sorry, Mom."

She took a breath before she spoke. "It's all right. We'll figure something out." She dropped her hands to her hips and glanced down the hall. "You should see if there's anything left in your room you want to take. Check under the bed. The van will be here for us soon."

Zachary grimaced. "Mom. I don't want to go. I told you that. I won't have any friends there."

And how many do you have here? she thought, but she didn't say it out loud. "You'll make new friends." She forced a smile. "Sara said the kids in the neighborhood are supernice."

He wrinkled his freckled nose, looking so much like his father, with his shaggy brown hair and blue eyes, that she had to push that thought away. Zachary was his own person. He wasn't anything like Ivan, and it was wrong of her to compare them.

"You're talking about Dunkard kids," he said.

"Not Dunkards. That's not a nice word. I'm talking about Amish kids. It's an Amish community. Sara is Amish, and she's—"

"A weirdo," Zachary flung back. "I told you I don't

want to go live with her. I don't even know her. I've seen those people in town. They wear dumb clothes and talk funny."

Mari pulled her son into her arms and held him. He didn't hug her back, but at least he didn't push her away. "It'll be all right," she murmured, pulling back his hood to smooth his hair. "Trust me. You're going to like it there."

"I'll hate it." He choked up as he pressed his face against her. "Please don't make me go. I don't want to live with those weirdos," he sobbed.

"Zachary, what you don't realize," Mari said, fighting her own tears, "is that *we* are those weirdos."

Seven Poplars, Delaware, three days later...

The rhythmic sounds of rain drumming against the windows filtered through Mari's consciousness as she slowly woke in the strange bed. She sighed and rolled onto her back, eyelids flickering, mind trying to identify where she was. Not the trailer. As hard as she'd worked to keep it clean, the mobile home had never smelled this fresh. Green-apple-scented sheets and a soft feather comforter rubbed against her skin. Mari yawned and then smiled.

She wasn't in Wisconsin anymore; she was in Delaware.

There was no snow, but there was rain. They were farther south, and the temperature was warmer here. They'd driven through a winter storm to get to Delaware. The van drivers, a retired Mennonite couple, had been forced to stop not for the one planned night, but two nights because of icy conditions and snow-clogged roads. Mari and Zachary had finally arrived, exhausted, sometime after eleven the previous night.

Mari rubbed her eyes and glanced around the bedroom; there were two tall walnut dressers side by side on one ivory-colored wall and simple wooden pegs on either side of the door for hanging clothing. Simple sheer white curtains hung at the windows. It was a peaceful room, as comfortable as the beds. *An Amish home*, she thought sleepily, as plain and welcoming as her grandmother's house had always been but her uncle's never had. And this one had central heat, she realized as she pushed back the covers and found her way to the chair where she'd laid out her clothes the night before.

She could hear Zachary's steady, rhythmic breathing. She considered waking him, but decided that he needed his sleep more than he needed to be on time for breakfast. Sara had told her that they ate early so that Ellie could be at the schoolhouse on time.

Ten minutes later, face washed and teeth brushed, Mari came down the wide staircase to find Sara in the living room. "Good morning," Mari said.

"I thought you'd sleep in." Sara, short and sturdy and middle-aged, smiled. She was tidy in her blue hand-sewn dress, black stockings and shoes, and white apron. Her crinkly dark hair was pinned up into a sensible bun and covered with a starched, white prayer *kapp*. "But I know the girls will be happy to have you join us for breakfast."

"Should I wake Zachary?" Mari rested her hand on the golden oak post at the foot of the steps.

"Let the child catch up on his sleep. I'll put a plate on the back of the stove for him. What he needs most is plenty of rest first, then pancakes and bacon."

The sound of a saw cutting wood on the other side of the wall startled Mari, and Sara gave a wave of dismissal. "As you can hear, we're in the midst of adding a new wing onto the house. I apologize for the noise this time of the morning, but the boys like to start early so they can get in a full day's work and still get to their chores at home after. Hope they won't wake Zachary."

"It's fine," Mari said. "Once he's asleep, he sleeps hard. Never hears a thing."

"Good. When I bought the house, I thought that it would be big enough," Sara explained, folding her arms across her ample bosom. "But I didn't realize how many young people would want to stay with their matchmaker. I've got a girl living here now, Jerushah, who leaves for her wedding in Virginia in a few days."

Sara was speaking English, for which Mari was grateful. *Deitsch* was the Alemannic dialect brought to America by the Amish and used in most households, but she hadn't spoken *Deitsch* in years, and Zachary didn't understand it at all. That was another adjustment he'd have to make if they remained in the community for any length of time, which she hoped wouldn't be necessary. In light of Zachary's reluctance to make the move to Delaware, the language difference was something she hadn't mentioned. Mari suddenly felt overwhelmed.

What had she been thinking when she'd agreed to come to Seven Poplars? A new school, new customs *and* a different language for her son? How could she expect a nine-year-old, raised in the English world, to adjust to living among the Amish? Even temporarily? Zachary had never lived without modern transportation, electricity, cell phones and television. And he'd never known the restrictions of an Old Order Amish community that largely kept itself separate from Englishers.

But what choice had she had? Apply for state assistance? Take her child into a homeless shelter? She could never blame those mothers who had made that choice, but if it came to that, it would snuff out the last spark of hope inside her. She would know that she was as stupid and worthless as her uncle had accused her of being, the same uncle who had offered to let her come home if she put her baby up for adoption.

Mari mentally shook off her fears. It never did any good to rethink a decision. She would embrace the future, instead of looking backward at her failures. She would make this work, and she would secure a better life for her and her son. "So the job at the butcher shop that you mentioned in your last letter…it's still available?"

"Sure is." Sara's lips tightened into a firm pucker while her eyes sparkled with intelligence and good humor. "Not to worry. I told you that if you came to Delaware, we'd soon straighten out your troubles."

In spite of her jolly appearance, Mari knew that Sara Yoder was a woman who suffered no nonsense. Fiftyish and several times widowed, shrewd Sara was a force to be reckoned with. Like all Amish, her faith was the cornerstone of her life, but she'd been one of the few who'd not condemned Mari when she'd gotten with child out of wedlock and run from her own Amish community.

"Thank you." Mari sighed with relief.

"Enough of that. You'll do me credit. I'm sure of it. Now, come along and have a good breakfast." Sara bustled toward the kitchen, motioning for Mari to follow. "And don't worry about the job. I told Gideon that he'd best not hire anyone to run the front of the store until he'd given you a fair shot at it." She glanced back over her shoulder, her expression clearly revealing how pleased she was herself. "I found the perfect wife for Gideon, and he owes me a favor."

Sara had written that Gideon was looking for someone to serve customers, take orders and deliveries, and act as an assistant manager of his new butcher shop, where he'd be featuring a variety of homemade sausages and scrapples. Sara had explained that he needed someone fluent in English and able to deal easily with telephones and computers, someone who could interact with both Amish and non-Amish. She hadn't mentioned what the wages or hours would be, but Sara had assured her that Gideon would be a fair employer. And, most important, someone would always be at Sara's house to watch over Zachary while she was at work.

The smell of dark-roasted coffee filled the air. Sara's home was a modern Cape Cod and laid out in the English rather than the Amish style, but in keeping with Plain custom, she had replaced the electric lights with propane and kerosene lamps. As Mari walked through the house, she felt herself being pulled back into her childhood, although the homes she'd grown up in were never as nice as this. Sara's house was warm and beautiful, with large windows, shining hardwood floors and comfortable furniture. Sara had apologized that Mari and Zachary had to share a room, but it was larger and nicer than anything either of them had ever slept in. Mari only hoped that someday she could find a way to repay the older woman's kindness.

"There you are!" Ellie declared as they entered the kitchen. "I was hoping to see you before I left for school." Ellie, the vivacious little person Mari had met the previous night, stepped down from a wooden step stool beside the woodstove and carried two thick mugs to the long table that dominated the room. She couldn't have been four feet tall. "How do you like your coffee, Mari?"

"With milk, please," Mari replied, returning Ellie's smile.

It was impossible to resist Ellie's enthusiasm. With her neat little figure, pretty face, sparkling bright blue eyes and golden hair, Ellie was so attractive that Mari suspected that had she been of average height she would have been married with a family rather than teaching school.

Already at the kitchen table was shy and spare Jerushah, the bride-to-be whom Sara had spoken of. "Sit down, sit down," Sara urged. "Ellie has to leave at eight." Sara gestured toward the silent, clean-shaven Amish man at the end of the table. "This is Hiram. He helps out around the place."

Hiram, tall, thin and plain as garden dirt, kept his eyes downcast and mumbled something into his plate, appearing to Mari to be painfully shy rather than standoffish.

Ellie pushed a platter of pancakes in her direction. "Don't mind Hiram. He's not much for talking."

"Shall we take a moment to give thanks?" Sara asked.

Mari bowed her head for the silent prayer that preceded all meals in Amish households. That would be another change for Zachary. Oddly, she felt a touch of regret that she hadn't kept up the custom in her own home.

"Amen," Sara said, signaling the end of the prayer. And although they were all strangers to her, except for her hostess, Ellie and Sara began and kept up such a good-natured banter that it was impossible for Mari to feel uncomfortable. Again, all the conversation continued in English. Jerushah's barely audible voice bore a Midwestern lilt with a heavy *Deitsch* accent, but Ellie and Sara spoke as if English was their first language. Hiram didn't say anything, but he smiled, nodded and ate steadily.

"You have the buggy hitched?" Sara asked Hiram. "Rain's let up, but it's too cold for Ellie to be walking."

"Ya," Hiram answered. No beard meant that he wasn't married, but Mari couldn't have guessed his age, somewhere between forty and fifty. Hiram's sandy hair was cut in a longish bowl-cut; his nose was prominent and his chin receding. His ears were large and, at the moment, as rooster-comb red as Sara's sugar bowl. "Waiting outside when she's ready," he said between bites of egg.

Hiram had slipped into *Deitsch*, and Mari was pleasantly surprised to realize that she'd understood what he'd just said. Maybe she hadn't forgotten her childhood language.

One bite of the blueberry pancakes and Mari found that she was starving. She polished off a pancake and a slice of bacon, and she was reaching for a hot biscuit when she became aware of the sound of an outer door opening and the rumble of male voices.

"My carpenter crew." Sara slid a second pancake onto Mari's plate. "Better put on a second pot of coffee, Ellie."

Mari suddenly felt self-conscious. She hadn't expected to meet so many people before eight in the morning her first day in Seven Poplars. Now she was glad that she'd chosen a modest navy blue denim jumper, a black turtleneck sweater and black tights from her suitcase. And instead of her normal ponytail, she'd pinned up her hair and tied a blue-and-white kerchief over it. She wasn't attempting to look Amish, but she wanted to make a good impression on Sara's friends and neighbors. Not that she'd ever been one for the immodest dress many English women her age went for; she'd always been a long skirt and T-shirt kind of girl.

Five red-cheeked workmen crowded into the utility room, stomping the mud off their feet; shedding wet coats, hats and gloves; and bringing a blast of the raw weather into the cozy kitchen.

"Hope that coffee's stronger this morning, Sara," one teased in *Deitsch*. "Yesterday's was a little on the weak side. It was hard to get much work out of Thomas." The speaker was another clean-shaven man in his late twenties or early thirties.

"That's James," Sara explained in English. "He's the one charging me an outrageous amount for my addition."

"You want craftsmanship, you have to pay for it," James answered confidently. He strode into the kitchen in his stocking feet, opened a cupboard door, removed a coffee mug and poured himself a cup from the pot on the stove. "We're the best, and you wouldn't be satisfied with anyone else."

"Nothing wrong with Sara's coffee," chimed in a second man, also beardless and speaking English. "James is just used to his sister's. And we all know that Mattie King's coffee will dissolve horseshoe nails."

He glanced at Mari with obvious interest as he entered the kitchen. "This must be your new houseguest. Mari, is it?"

"*Ya*, this is my friend Mari." Sara introduced her to the men as they made their way into the kitchen and began to pour themselves cups of coffee. "She and her son, Zachary, will be here with me for a while, so I expect you all to make her feel welcome."

"Pleased to meet you, Mari," James said. The foreman's voice was pleasant, his penetrating eyes strikingly memorable. Mari felt a strange ripple of exhilaration as James's strong face softened into a genuine smile, and he held her gaze for just a fraction of a second longer than was appropriate.

Warmth suffused her throat as Mari offered a stiff nod and a hasty "Good morning," before turning her attention to her unfinished breakfast. She took a piece of the biscuit and brought it to her mouth, then returned it untasted to her plate. She kept her eyes on her pancake, watching the dab of butter slowly melt as she felt the workmen staring at her, no doubt curious about her presence at Sara's. Mari didn't want anyone to get the idea that she'd come to Seven Poplars so Sara could find her a husband. That was the last thing on her mind.

"Thomas would rather drink coffee than pound nails any day," Ellie teased as he took a seat at the table.

"And who wouldn't, if they were honest?" Thomas chuckled. "Pay no attention to her, Mari. Any of these fellows can tell you what a hard worker I am."

"I hope you're not disappointed we've got rain instead of snow this week." James pulled out a chair across from Mari. He unfolded his lean frame into the seat with the grace of a dancer. He wasn't as tall as Thomas. His hair was a lighter shade, and his build was slim rather than broad, but he gave an impression of quiet strength as he moved. "I know you had plenty of snow in Wisconsin."

"I don't mind the rain," Mari heard herself say. "And I definitely appreciate the warmer temperature."

Her comment led to a conversation at the table about the weather, and Mari just sat there listening, wondering why she felt so conspicuous. Everyone was nice; there was no need for her to feel self-conscious.

"Well, I hate to leave good company," Ellie said, getting to her feet. "But if I'm not at school when Samuel's boys get there to start the fire, they won't be able to get in." She tapped the large iron key that hung on a cord around her neck. "They'll be wet enough to swim home." After putting her plate in the sink, she picked up a black lunch box and a thermos off the counter. "Are you ready, Hiram?"

Hiram wiped the last bit of egg from his plate with a portion of biscuit and stuck it into his mouth. "Ready."

Ellie smiled at Mari. "See you after school?"

"Of course. Unless…" Mari glanced back at Sara. "Unless I'm supposed to go to work today."

"Ne," Sara assured her. "Not today. Gideon and Addy have just thrown open their doors, so the pace is still slow. Gideon said tomorrow would be fine. Give you a chance to settle in."

"Going to be working for Gideon and Addy, are you?" James remarked as he added milk to his coffee from a small pitcher on the table.

Mari slowly lifted her gaze. James had nice hands, very clean, his fingers well formed. She raised her gaze higher to find that he was still watching her intently, but it wasn't a predatory gaze. James seemed genuinely friendly rather than coming on to her, as if he was interested in what she had to say. "I hope so." She suddenly felt shy, and she had no idea why. "I don't know a thing about butcher shops."

"You'll pick it up quick." James took a sip of his coffee. "And Gideon is a great guy. He'll make it fun. Don't you think so, Sara?"

Sara looked from James to Mari and then back at James. "I agree." She smiled and took a sip of her coffee. "I think Mari's a fine candidate for all sorts of things."

Chapter Two

The following morning dawned cold and clear. Mari had risen early to help with breakfast and make certain that Zachary was dressed and fed before she left him in the care of Sara for the day. "Wake up, sweetie," she said, shaking him. "Time to rise and shine."

"I want to sleep some more." Zachary tried to roll over, away from her.

"Nope." She put her arm around him. "No can do. I start work this morning."

Zachary rubbed his eyes. "I don't like it here. I want to go home."

Mari ruffled his hair. "We can't, and you know that. We can't go back to Wisconsin because there's no money and nothing to go back to."

"Can't I go with you to work?" He stared up at her with large, sleepy eyes. "I don't know these people."

"You'll be fine." Mari got up and laid out a pair of jeans and a faded flannel shirt for him. "Sara has been good to us, and she's doing everything she can to make this easier. I told you she'd be keeping an eye on you for a few days while I'm at work. As soon as I can, I'll get you enrolled in a new school. You'll make friends, and before you know it, I'll have enough money so that we can move into a place of our own."

Zachary's chin quivered, and he looked as if he was about to burst into tears. "My stomach hurts," he said, not sounding very convincing.

"Don't even try that trick." She'd heard his attempts at malingering before, only to see him devour two bowls of cereal once the school bus went by. "What you need is breakfast. Sara makes great pancakes."

He looked up at her. "I don't want pancakes. I want to go home."

She sighed. "I know this is hard—it's hard for me, too." *Though maybe not for the same reasons*, she thought to herself. She hadn't been prepared for how comfortable she would feel in Sara's house. She leaned down and kissed his forehead. "I need you to try, Zach. Can you do that for me?"

His eyes narrowed. "For how long do I have to try?"

She thought for a moment. She hadn't really given herself a timeline. Had she subconsciously done that on purpose? "Three months," she said off the top of her head. "Promise me that you'll do your best to help me make this work."

He considered. "Three months is a long time. How about one month?"

Mari shook her head. "Not long enough. We have to get our feet back on the ground. I have to earn and save money to get us started again. And even though Sara has been nice enough to let us stay here, I still have to pay for our food and such."

They were both quiet for a second, and then he said, "All right, Mom. Guess I can try."

"Is that a promise?"

"Three months," he said. "But if it doesn't work, if I still hate it, then what?"

Mari walked to a window and stared at the barnyard below. James and his crew had just arrived and they were unloading tools from a wagon. Her gaze fell on James's broad shoulders and lingered. She turned back to Zachary. "I don't know what we'll do then," she answered him honestly. "If we can't make it here in Seven Poplars, I don't know what we'll do." She turned back to him. "But I'll think of something. And that's a promise."

"Okay."

"Good." She smiled at him. "I knew I could count on you. Sara told me that there will be a van here at eight o'clock to pick me up, so we have to hurry. Up and into your clothes, favorite son." She gave him a tickle under his chin.

"I'm your only son!" Giggling, Zachary rolled out of his bed and scrambled for his clothes.

A short time later, Mari was downstairs pouring orange juice at the kitchen table for Zachary. "I'm so glad my new boss is providing transportation to work. I was wondering what I'd do until I could buy a car."

Sara passed the plate of pancakes to Hiram so he could have another helping. "It was Addy's idea that Gideon hire a driver to pick up all his workers and drop them off at the end of the day. Good way to make sure everyone's on time."

"Addy's Gideon's wife," Ellie explained.

Jerushah nodded. "Gideon's wife," she repeated.

Mari buttered a slice of rye toast. "I suppose I expected the Amish employees to walk or come to work by buggy."

"Most of us do use horse and buggy to get around," Sara said. "At least locally."

"Or a push scooter," Ellie put. "I usually ride mine to the school, unless the weather is bad."

"We'd rather keep the horses and buggies off the main roads," Sara explained. "Because of the traffic. But we like horse power, especially for visiting back and forth in our community and for worship services or grocery shopping. Farther than Dover and most people usually hire a driver. And it's reasonable if more than one family shares the price."

"And if the employees drove a horse to Gideon's shop, the animals would have to stand outside all day," Hiram added. "Not good." It was a long speech for him, Mari realized, and as if he'd used up his allotment of words, he reddened, put his head down and concentrated on his third stack of pancakes.

The loud sounds of hammering and sawing drifted from the direction of the addition. "I hear they're at it already," Mari said.

"Ya." Sara added sugar to her coffee. "James is a hard worker."

Zachary slid his plate back. Mari noticed that he'd eaten part of a pancake and pushed his scrambled eggs around, but he hadn't really eaten much. "Can I go watch the men working?" he asked.

"I think you'd better stay in the house out of their way. I'm sure they don't want boys around. Dangerous tools and stuff," Mari explained.

"Oh, let him," Sara suggested gently. "Like as not, they could use some help. There's always something another pair of hands can do, even if it's just fetch and carry. How else is a boy supposed to learn how to do something, if not by watching and learning?"

"Please, Mom?" Zachary begged. "I won't touch anything. Please? There's nothing to do in here. I can't watch a DVD or play a video game. What am I s'posed to do?"

Mari felt her cheeks grow warm. "I'm sorry, Sara," she apologized, meeting her hostess's gaze. "I explained to him about electricity, that you didn't watch television or listen to the radio, but—"

"But it's all new to him," Ellie finished for her.

"So spending time with James's crew might be the best place for him." Sara added a pat of butter to the top of her pancake. "Unless he wants to help me and Jerushah wash clothes." She raised her eyebrows at him.

The look on Zachary's face made it clear he wasn't interested in doing laundry. He turned to his mother. "Please, Mom?"

"If you're certain you won't be a nuisance," she said, relenting. She met her son's gaze. "Promise me that you'll stay back out of the men's way?"

"I will, Mom. Honest." He got to his feet, picked up his plate and carried it to the sink.

"Put what you didn't eat into that pail for the chickens." Sara pointed to a stainless-steel container with a lid sitting just inside the utility room. "Nothing goes to waste here."

"Chickens eat eggs?" Zachary asked. "Yuck. Cannibals."

"Chickens eat most anything," Hiram said. "Even boys if they sit still long enough."

Zachary glanced at him, curious and suspicious at the same time. "Would they?"

"*Ne*, Zachary," Sara assured him with a chuckle. "My chickens would not eat you. I think you are probably too tough to chew."

Zachary laughed, realizing that Hiram had been teasing him, and made a dash for the back door.

"Get your heavy hooded sweatshirt," Mari called after him, making a mental note that she needed to ask Sara where she could buy a decent used coat for him.

"I'm not cold."

"Your hoodie," Mari insisted, rising as she glanced at the clock on the wall. If she wanted to be outside waiting for the van when it came up the lane, she needed to get ready to go. "I don't want you catching cold. Tomorrow or the next day, we'll register you for school."

"Not this week," Zachary protested. "We just got here. I don't want to start a new school in the middle of the week." He stood in the doorway and scowled at her.

"It isn't your decision," Mari reminded him quietly. "I'm the mother." She closed her eyes for a second, suddenly remembering with a sinking feeling that she'd never made arrangements to have his records forwarded. She'd intended to call, but then in all the commotion of packing to leave, it had slipped her mind. She wondered if there would be a phone she could use in the butcher shop. Surely there would be. But what if her new boss didn't want employees using his phone? A lot of places she had worked didn't allow personal calls.

"We're not staying here that long," Zachary said. "So there's no sense in me starting school anywhere." He headed for the back door again. "I'm just going to stay here and build stuff with the men until we go back to Wisconsin." Seconds later, the back door slammed with a bang.

"I apologize for Zachary's behavior," Mari said to Sara and the others at the table. "He's never like this. Honestly." She exhaled, resting one hand on her hip. "At least not often. Excuse me." She turned to follow him.

"Grab a coat on your way, Mari," Sara ordered. "Plenty in the laundry room. If he's going to catch his death, there's no need for you to, as well."

A minute later Mari opened the back door and was hit with a blast of cold air. This might not be Wisconsin, but it was still January and bitter. She was glad she'd taken Sara's advice and taken a barn coat from the assorted outer garments hanging on the wall. She'd also gotten one for Zachary; it would be big on him, but at least it would be warm. There was no way she was going to let him outside in just jeans and a flannel shirt.

Mari crossed the porch and then went down the steps to the sidewalk that ran around the house. She followed it to the new construction, a two-story addition, and caught sight of her son at once. He was standing near a pile of new lumber watching as two men eased a new window into place on the ground floor. "Zachary!" she called.

He turned and hurried across the barnyard. Either he hadn't heard her in the wind or he was pretending he hadn't heard her. She exhaled, debating whether or not to go after him. She didn't have time for this this morning. How was it that children picked the worst times to misbehave?

She was still debating when James came walking toward her.

Suddenly she felt flustered, standing there in the yard with a boy's coat in her hand. "My son…" She lifted the coat and then lowered it. "He's staying here today while I work. Sara's going to keep an eye on him. She said it was okay if he came outside to see what your crew was doing."

"But he forgot his coat." James's kind eyes were now twinkling, as if he and Mari were sharing some sort of private joke between them.

She felt herself relax a little. "Actually, *his* coat is in Wisconsin." She exhaled. "Long story."

James glanced in the direction Zachary had just gone. "What's his name?" He slipped a hammer back into his leather tool belt and smiled at her reassuringly.

She hugged the barn coat against her chest. "Zachary."

James nodded. "Eight or nine?"

"Nine."

"Hard age. Changes are tough for boys. But he'll be fine. He just needs time and patience to adjust."

James's accurate perception of the situation surprised her. "He's a good kid, really," she said. "It's just…a lot for him. For both of us," she amended. "Moving and all."

"And you need him to show more maturity than he's doing right now."

"You must be a father." She looked at him and smiled, then felt awkward. James had no beard. If he had no beard, he was unmarried. If he didn't have a wife, he shouldn't have a child, and she'd just inferred that—

"Nephews," he explained, smoothly ignoring her mistake. "Four of them."

"Nephews," she echoed. "Then you know how boys can be."

He rested a broad hand on his tool belt. "Sometimes boys can try a mother." James stood there for a minute, then said, "Would it be okay if I talked to him? I could take the coat to him. He's got to be freezing." He held out his hand.

"I don't know. It's nice of you to offer, but—" She stopped and started again. "It's just that he doesn't know you."

"But I'm a man." He took the coat from her. "It may be he just needs to talk, one man to another."

The van driver would be here any minute to pick her up for work. She needed to run inside, brush her teeth and grab her lunch box. But she didn't know if she felt right, just leaving Zachary with this man she didn't know very well. Of course she wasn't really leaving him with James. Sara was there and it had been Sara's suggestion that Zachary hang out with the workmen; it had to be safe.

"He'll be fine," James said gently, seeming to know exactly what she was thinking. "Go to work and Zachary will be here waiting for you when you get home with a smile on his face. You'll see."

She met James's gaze, and the strangest thing happened. She believed him.

James watched Mari hurry off into the house before turning back to study the six-over-six wooden-framed window Titus and Menno had just set in place. It looked straight to his eye, but he'd been accused more than once of being a perfectionist. "Best be sure before you nail it in place," he said, picking up a level and tossing it to Menno. "You know Sara. She'd have us take it out again and reset it if it's a sixteenth of an inch off."

Menno grinned. "And she'll be out here with her own level as soon as we leave."

James chuckled and glanced in the direction of the barn where Mari's boy had gone. "Get the next window in once you're finished. I'll be a few minutes. I might have found a young man to sweep wood shavings and the like."

Leaving the men to continue their work, James crossed the yard to the barn and stepped inside. Out of the wind, with the heat of the animals to warm the space, it was almost comfortable. Light filtered in through a high window, but the stalls remained in shadow. At one end, a wooden partition divided the stalls from the hay and feed storage. His horse, Jericho, stood, ears erect and twitching, watching something of interest near the grain barrel.

James suspected that Zachary was hiding there, but he didn't let on. Instead, he tossed the barn coat Mari had given him on a hay bale and approached the horse. Jericho nuzzled him with his nose, rubbing against James's hand affectionately. "Good boy," he murmured as he stroked the animal's head. How a man could become attached to a motor vehicle, James couldn't imagine. No pickup ever nickered a greeting in the early dawn or ran to its owner looking for a treat.

Jericho nudged him, and James dug into his pocket and came up with a piece of raw carrot. Holding his hand flat, he watched as the gelding daintily nibbled it.

"I didn't know horses liked carrots," Zachary said from the shadows.

"Apples, carrots, even turnips. But Jericho likes sugar cubes most of all." James didn't look in the boy's direction.

Zachary climbed up the half wall of the stall and peered at the bay gelding. He was a little small for his age: brown hair, blue eyes. A nice-looking boy. But he didn't look like Mari, and James couldn't help wondering about his father.

"He's pretty big," Zachary said.

"Just under sixteen hands. He's a Thoroughbred, foaled for racing. But he wasn't fast enough, so he ended up at auction. That's where I bought him."

"They auction off horses?" Zachary stared at the horse.

"They do." James glanced at the boy. He seemed wary, prepared to run if Jericho made any sudden moves. "Have you been around a lot of horses?"

"Not a lot of horses in a trailer park."

"Probably best. Not a lot of pasture in a trailer park." He looked past Zachary to where bales of sweet timothy hay were stacked. "Toss Jericho a section of that hay, will you?"

Zachary didn't move from the stall's half wall. "That his name?"

"It is."

"Horses on TV have better names."

James leaned on the gate. "Such as?"

Zachary thought for a minute. "Lightning. Thunder."

"Thunder. Hmm. Don't know if I'd feel easy hitching a horse named Thunder to my buggy." James glanced Zachary's way. "Nippy out here. You can put that coat on if you want."

"Nah. I'm good." Zachary slid down, broke off a section of the hay bale and stuffed it through the railing. Closing his eyes, the horse chewed contentedly. "He's pretty neat. For a horse. But buggies are dumb. Why don't you buy a car?"

"I had a truck once, but I sold it when I bought Jericho."

Zachary's eyes got big. "You had a truck?"

"A blue Ford F-150 pickup," James answered.

Zachary watched Jericho eat, seeming to be fascinated. "Horses are too slow."

"Depends on how big a hurry you're in, I suppose. Sometimes, you notice things you'd miss if you were in a hurry."

"It must be boring. Being Amish. No video games or Saturday cartoons."

"No, we don't have those things. But we do lots of things for fun. Baseball, fishing, ice-skating, hayrides, family picnics and work frolics."

"What's a work frolic?"

James noticed that while Zachary's voice gave the impression of boredom, his blue eyes sparkled with curiosity. "Well, say someone needs a new barn. Either lightning has struck his old one and burned it down, or a family is starting out on a new farm. A work frolic would be when the whole community pitches in to help build that barn. There might be as many as fifty or more men all working at once."

Zachary frowned. "Sounds like a lot of hard work."

"If you're with friends, all laughing and joking, it is fun. There's nothing like watching a barn rise up from an empty pasture in one day." He smiled. "And then there's all kinds of great food. Fried chicken, shoofly pie, ice cream. And we have games after we eat— tug-of-war, softball, even sack races. Winter is a slow time, because of bad weather. But if you're here in May, you'll see lots of work frolics."

"Oh, we won't be here," Zachary assured him. "We're going back to Wisconsin. I've got friends there. In my old school."

The boy's voice sounded confident, but the expression in his eyes told another story, and James felt a tug of sympathy in his chest. "Must have been rough, leaving all those buddies behind." He leaned on the stall gate. "Coming to a new place where everything is strange. I can see how you wouldn't much care for it."

"I'm not saying this to be mean, but the whole Amish thing?" Zachary said. "It's kinda weird."

James nodded solemnly. "I can see how you'd feel that way. Everybody dressing differently, eating different food."

"The food's not bad."

"I guess your mom's a good cook."

"The best. Great. But Darlene wasn't," Zachary clarified. "She and her daughter lived with us at the trailer until we got evicted. Darlene couldn't even cook mac and cheese out of a box."

James grimaced as much from the idea of Mari and her son being evicted as the thought of macaroni and cheese out of a box. "I don't think I'd enjoy her cooking," he told Zachary.

"Who would?" Warming to his tale, Zachary elaborated. "One time, Mom got this coupon for a free turkey. If you buy enough stuff, the supermarket gives them to everybody. It's not charity or anything."

"No," James agreed. "It wouldn't be if anyone could get one."

"Right. But you had to buy so many groceries and save the receipts. Anyway, Mom got this turkey for Thanksgiving, but she had to work, so Darlene tried to cook it herself." Zachary made a face. "Can you believe she didn't take the guts out? She just stuffed the bird in the oven with the plastic bag of guts inside and ruined it."

James chuckled. "Sounds bad."

"It was." The boy kicked at the bottom rung of the stall rhythmically. "You said you sold your truck. How come they let you have a truck? Mom said Amish drive buggies."

"They do. If you want to be a part of the Amish community and the church, you have to agree to follow the rules. And the rules say no cars and no electricity."

"They think cars and TV are bad?"

James shook his head slowly. "Not necessarily bad, just worldly. Things like electricity link us to the outer world. They take us away too easily from the people and things that mean the most to us."

"So how'd you have a truck? I'd guess you got in big trouble."

"Some but not much." James took his time answering, taking care with the words he chose. "When you become a young man or a young woman in the Amish community, you get to decide how you want to live. Do you want to be Amish, or do you want to join the English world? No one can force you to be Amish, so many Amish young people go out into the world to see if they like it better than this one. That's what I did. I left Seven Poplars and got a job working construction."

"You just packed up and went?"

James nodded again. "I did. My sister begged me not to go. She's older than I am, more like a mom than a sister, because our mother died when I was little."

"No mom. Tough," Zachary said. "My father died, but I never knew him, so I didn't care much."

"Your mom didn't remarry?" James asked.

"Nope. And she doesn't go out with guys like Darlene did. Mom says I'm her guy." He gave a little smirk.

James smiled to himself. He was glad to know that Mari wasn't attached; maybe because he didn't like the idea of her being with someone who clearly hadn't been taking good care of her. He tapped the toe of his boot against the stall. "Listen, I have to get back to work, but I was wondering if you'd be interested in helping us out today. We need somebody to sweep, fetch nails and tools. Stuff like that."

Zachary's eyes narrowed. "Would I get paid?"

"If you do the work, sure. I know you'll be going back to school soon, but—"

"I'm not starting school here," Zachary interrupted. "I tried to tell Mom that."

"You and your mom butt heads a lot?"

"No, not so much. I mean, she's great and all. Really. But when she can find a job, she works a lot. Overtime. Sometimes two jobs at the same time. So a lot of times, I was with babysitters and after-school care. Mom thinks I'm a kid still. She's kind of bossy."

James had to press his lips together to keep from chuckling. "My sister can be like that."

Zachary grimaced. "Girls."

"Hard to understand them sometimes."

"Yeah. But I could probably help you out until Mom figures out we don't belong here."

"I don't know your mother well, but she seems like she cares a lot for you. Like she's trying to do the right thing."

"She's the best. But this was a bad idea, coming here. It's better back in Wisconsin. You're probably nice people and all, but we like cars and TV and electric. I hate it when the electric gets turned off in our trailer."

"Gets turned off?" James asked.

"You know." Zachary frowned. "When you can't pay the bill."

Now it was James's turn to frown. He could imagine how hard it must have been for Mari as a parent, trying to care for her son. "That happen a lot?"

"Mom does her best. Electricity and car insurance are expensive. We make out all right. It's just that Mom lost her job and then we got kicked out of our trailer for not paying. But something will come along. It always does." The boy reached out boldly and patted Jericho's broad back.

They were both quiet for a minute. Sara had told him a little about Mari the week before, that she and her son needed a fresh start, but she hadn't told him that Mari had lost her job and her home. His heart went out to her. He couldn't imagine what it was like for a woman to be alone with no family, no friends, trying to raise a boy properly.

James glanced at Zachary again. "Sounds like what I'm hearing you say is that you might like to earn a little money. And be a help to your mom." He didn't know that the bit of pocket change Zachary might earn would really help Mari's situation, but he did know that even a boy Zachary's age wanted to feel as if he was needed. "Take some of the strain off her?"

"Yeah. That would be good," Zachary agreed.

James crossed his arms over his chest. "And from me and my crew." Again, he was quiet before he went on, "Zachary, I think your mom was pretty upset when she left for work. This move, losing her home and all, has been pretty tough on her. I think maybe she could use a hug from you when she gets home."

"Probably." Zachary looked thoughtful.

"I don't know why you quarreled, but a man's got to show respect to his mother."

Zachary looked up at him. "I'm a boy, not a man."

"But you're old enough to have responsibilities. And it looks to me as though the most important one is to take care of her. Treat her right."

He twisted his mouth thoughtfully. "Guess I should say sorry when she comes home tonight."

"Sounds good to me. So let's shake on it, you doing some work for me." James extended his hand and Zachary took it. Zachary had a firm grip, and James liked that. "But if you're serious about working with my crew, you'd better go put that barn coat on. All of my men come dressed for work, no matter the weather."

"Okay," Zachary agreed. He grabbed the jacket and put it on. "What's your name?"

"James. James Hostetler."

"I'm Zachary. Zachary Troyer."

"Glad to have you on my crew, Zachary." He didn't allow his amusement to show in his expression. *Zachary Troyer*, he mused. *Not so different from us after all*. James had never met a Troyer who wasn't Amish or who didn't have Amish ancestry. Maybe Zachary wasn't as far away from home as he thought.

Chapter Three

When the van dropped Mari off at Sara's after work, she had them let her off at the end of the lane to give herself a couple of minutes to decompress. Her day had been hectic and overwhelming; but she was definitely going to like the job. Gideon and Addy Esch were good people to work for, just as James had said they would be. Gideon laughed and teased her so much, she wasn't always sure how to take him. And Addy had seemed pleased with her, though it was obvious she was going to be the one who would be a stickler for doing things the way she liked them. Still, it had been a fun first day at work, and Mari was looking forward to seeing everyone at the shop the next morning.

Inside Sara's house, Mari found the kitchen a beehive of activity. The delicious smells of baked ham, biscuits and gingerbread swirled through the kitchen. Pots steamed and dishes clattered as Sara, Jerushah and Ellie stirred and tasted. Mari was pleasantly surprised to find that Zachary was part of the activity, carefully placing silverware on either side of blue-and-white willow-pattern plates at the large table. And just as James had predicted, he seemed perfectly content.

"How was your day, Zachary?" Mari walked over to the table. She wanted to hug him or at least to ruffle his hair, but she didn't want to embarrass him in front of the others.

"It was good," he said enthusiastically. "I helped work on the addition! I learned how to use a level and how to swing a hammer." He talked faster and faster as he went, as if he had so much so tell her that he was afraid he'd leave something out. "James's hammer was kind of big, but he said he had one at home my size that he'd bring tomorrow. Not a toy hammer. A real one. One that fits better in my hand. A good weight for me, James said. He said I could call him James. That's okay, right? He says that's the way they do it here. Amish people. Kids call adults by their first names."

Mari couldn't resist a big grin. Zachary was so excited and happy that she barely recognized him as the sulky boy who had ridden in the van with her from Wisconsin a few days ago.

"And, oh!" Zachary put down the handful of silverware and dug in his pocket, coming up with a five-dollar bill and some ones. "See. I made money, too." He pushed it into her hand and beamed at her. "For you. You know. To buy us stuff we need."

Tears sprang to Mari's eyes. Zachary could be such a kindhearted boy. She didn't know why she worried so much about him; he really *was* a good kid. "Honey, you earned that money," she said gently, holding it out to him. "It's yours to buy what you want. You could save for a handheld video game or something like that."

He thought for minute and then shook his head. "I

think we better save it for a car, but I can hang on to it for us." He put the money back in his pocket and reached for the silverware, then dropped his hands to his sides.

Mari knew that look on his face. He'd done something wrong. Her heart fell. If Zachary couldn't behave himself when he was at Sara's, she didn't know what she was going to do. She exhaled. "You have something to tell me?" she asked quietly.

He nodded, staring at the floor. But then he looked up at her. "I just wanted to say I was sorry." He spoke so softly that Mari had to lean over to hear him. "I shouldn't have been mean to you this morning. I should have gone and gotten my hoodie when you told me to."

"Oh, Zachary." Mari couldn't help herself. She wrapped her arms around him and hugged him tightly. "I know this is hard, and I'm so proud of you." She kissed the top of his head before letting go of him.

"James says it's important that a man know how to say he's sorry." He picked up the silverware and went back to setting the table.

Mari just stood there for a minute, her heart just a little too full for words.

"What a good boy you are to want to give to your family," Sara pronounced enthusiastically. "I know your mother appreciates it." Then to Mari she said, "Glad to have you home—supper's almost ready. We're all eager to hear about your first day."

"Let me run upstairs and clean up," Mari said as she retreated from the kitchen. "I'll be right back down."

In the room Mari shared with Zachary, she hung up the two new plum-colored aprons bearing the butcher shop's logo. Then she slipped out of her work sneakers and into the only other pair she had.

As Mari tied her shoes, she thought about her day. It had been overwhelming but fun, too. She just hoped she'd be able to live up to Addy's expectations, which were pretty high. But she knew she could do it. She would do whatever she needed to do and learn whatever they wanted her to learn. The other employees were pleasant, including the butchers who worked in the plant, and she thought that dealing with a mix of Amish and English customers would be interesting. She did have experience taking orders because she'd worked at another job several years earlier where she sat at a computer all day selling items advertised on television. But she much preferred working face-to-face with people, and she liked meeting new challenges.

The job would be fine, she assured herself as she ducked into the bathroom to wash her hands and tidy up her hair. She and Zachary had been through a lot of bad stuff, but things were looking up since they moved to Delaware. It had definitely been the right decision; she knew that now. And maybe Zachary was beginning to see that, too. She was so relieved to come home to Sara's and find him smiling instead of sulking in their room. And the idea that he wanted her to have his money and then had apologized for his behavior that morning… It made her heart swell. And it also made her realize that she had some thanking to do, as well.

Once presentable, Mari hurried back downstairs and into the kitchen. "Sara, what can I do to help get supper ready?"

"Could you go outside and hunt down James—you remember which one is James?" Sara arched an eyebrow.

Sara hadn't changed a bit since Mari had known her in Wisconsin. People said that Sara had more energy than a March snowstorm. Some called her interfering and headstrong for a woman, but Mari had always admired her. Now she was once more a widow, but even as a wife, Sara had been direct and known for speaking her mind. Very much like Addy seemed to be, Mari thought. Maybe that was why Addy and her husband spoke so highly of Sara and respected her opinion.

"I know who James is." Mari suppressed a little smile. She had no idea what had gotten into her.

"Ask him if he would like to join us for supper. But not those Swartzentruber rascals. Just James. A new client will be arriving any moment. We're a household of women except Zachary, and I don't want him to feel awkward his first night here. A gaggle of women can be intimidating to a man."

"Of course we have Hiram," Ellie chimed in. The little woman was climbing on a three-foot stepladder to reach a serving plate in the cupboard.

"*Ya*, there's always Hiram," Jerushah said, "but he doesn't have much to add to the conversation."

"Exactly." Sara smiled. "James said his sister and the boys were going to her mother-in-law's tonight, so James will be on his own. Tell him that I'd consider it a favor if he could put his feet under my table and make Peter feel at ease. Peter's mother advises me that he's shy, so I doubt he'll talk much more than Hiram. We need to make him feel more at ease talking with women. James will help him relax."

"Whereas," Ellie declared from her perch on the ladder, "Titus and Menno would delight in telling Peter tall tales of the homely women Sara wants to match him with."

"Like they did with my prospective husband," Jerushah put in shyly. "They nearly frightened my John into backing out of the arrangement before he'd even met me."

"So no ham for Menno and Titus tonight." Sara gave a firm nod of her head. "They can go home, have cold liver and onions and pester their own mother."

"Like I do sometimes," Zachary chimed in.

The women laughed, and Mari glanced at her son. What had gotten into Zachary? He talked when they were alone together, but he was usually quiet around strangers. Apparently he'd finished setting the table; now he was holding a towel for Ellie. She'd just come down off the ladder to find hot mitts and slide a gigantic pan of gingerbread from the oven.

"So Zachary worked with the men today, I hear," Mari said. "I hope he wasn't any trouble. James said it would be fine, but I don't want to…" She searched for the right words as an image of James came to her and she felt her cheeks grow warm. What on earth was wrong with her, being so silly over some man she didn't even know? Just tired, she supposed. "I just wouldn't want to take advantage of anyone's kindness," she said.

"He was no trouble at all. What this house needs is some active children." Sara went back to the refrigerator and removed pickles and a crockery bowl containing chowchow. "Not only was he no trouble but he was helpful. First he worked outside with the men. Then he came in and made the gingerbread for dessert."

"Zachary made gingerbread?" Mari wanted to pinch

herself to make certain she wasn't dreaming. "I didn't know he was interested in cooking."

"Not cooking, Mom," Zachary corrected. "*Baking.* Sara said if I learn to make really good gingerbread, they'll sell it at the shop where you work and I could make money doing that, too."

Ellie carried a pan of gingerbread to a soapstone-topped counter and set it down to cool. "Addy was telling me she thought Sara's gingerbread would be a good seller. I know it's a butcher shop, but they want a couple shelves of baked goods, too."

"We didn't make it from a box," Zachary explained. "I mixed flour and eggs and ginger spice and stuff. It took a long time."

"I can't wait to taste it." Mari offered Ellie a smile of gratitude.

It usually took Zachary a long time to warm up to strangers, but he was acting as though he'd known Ellie for ages. Ellie obviously had a real knack for dealing with children.

Mari heard the sound of a car coming up the driveway, and Sara turned from the stove. "That must be Peter," she said, wiping her hands on her apron. "Ellie, watch that the potatoes don't burn. I'll just go out and welcome him. Mari, can you go fetch James?"

"Going."

"Plenty of coats hanging in the utility room," Sara instructed. "You might as well just save your own for good. On a farm, a sturdy denim is best, anyway."

Mari found a coat and slipped into it. Though the style was certainly utilitarian and obviously Amish, Sara's old coats were warmer than her own. Buttoning up, she dodged Hiram coming in with a bucket of milk and hurried across the back porch.

She walked around the house to find James using a power saw to trim a length of wood. Walking up make-shift steps into the still-open-to-the-elements addition, she called his name, but he couldn't hear her over the loud whine of the power tool. She waited for him to finish the cut and turn off the saw before speaking again. The gas-powered generator was still running, but it was far enough away that the noise wasn't too bad. "James?"

"Oh, hey." He turned toward her and smiled. "Sorry I didn't hear you, Mari. I was just finishing up here."

He said her name correctly—just like Mary. Some people wanted to call her *Maury* because of the way she spelled her name. It was short for Maryann, but she'd never liked that name, so when she started writing the shorter version, as a child, she decided to use an *i* instead of a *y*.

Mari's breath made small clouds of steam, and she pulled the coat tighter around her and suppressed a shiver. The walls and roof cut off some of the wind, but there was no heat. Her ears and nose felt cold, and she wondered how the carpenters could work outside in such bitter weather.

"What can I do for you?" James asked.

And then he smiled at her again, and she immediately became flustered. "Um, I— Sara—" Mari couldn't seem to speak, and she had no idea why. Obviously it had something to do with James, but she didn't understand her reaction. This was so unlike her.

Mari didn't dislike men, but she certainly wasn't in awe of them like other women her age she'd known.

She'd learned that a woman who wasn't looking for a boyfriend or a husband found life a lot easier. James was looking at her expectantly, but his expression was curious, not impatient. She glanced around at the half-finished space. There didn't seem to be any of the other workmen there, which made her mission easier since Sara had specified James and not any of the others.

"Sara sent me to ask you if you'd join us for supper," she said in a rush, then went on to explain why Sara was hoping that he'd join them.

James unplugged and wound the power cord for the saw. "I'd be glad to. I'd be having leftovers at home." He noticed her looking at the saw. "You're wondering about the electric saws and such."

She nodded. Sara had a lot more modern conveniences than the Amish community Mari had come from in Wisconsin. Her uncle hadn't even had a real bathroom; they still used an outhouse. Maybe this community was a lot more liberal, she thought.

"Gasoline-powered generators are okay," he explained. "Makes the job go faster. I can build the traditional way when I need to, but Sara wanted this addition done as soon as possible."

Mari took in the size of the structure. "She must be expecting a lot of company. Wanting more bedrooms."

"She's big business in Seven Poplars. Got a waiting list of folks wanting to come and stay and find a spouse." James placed the heavy saw on a stack of lumber and covered it with a tarp. "So how was your first day at the shop?"

"Um. Good." Her mind went blank. She studied him, wondering at his interest in her day. It had been a long time since anyone had asked her about her day.

James Hostetler appeared to be in his late twenties, maybe a little younger than she was. His height was average, maybe five-eleven, not as tall as the Swartzentruber brothers or Thomas. James was lanky, with slender, sinewy hands. His fair German complexion was suntanned, his eyes slightly oval and his hands and wrists calloused from a lifetime of manual labor.

James possessed a typical Amish face, more long than round; light brown feathery hair, very clean; a well-defined nose; and a wide, expressive mouth. He was handsome, though not overly so, with a friendly smile and the intelligent brown eyes she'd noticed on first meeting him. He moved easily, almost boyishly, with a bounce in his step. She didn't know James and she didn't give her trust easily, but she was inclined to like him. He seemed trustworthy, which wasn't a trait she saw often in her world.

Not that she was interested in him in any romantic sort of way. Her life was complicated enough without that. She'd proven with Ivan, Zachary's father, that she didn't have good judgment when it came to choosing a partner. And she had quite enough on her plate without more complications. A man was the last thing she needed.

She found her voice. "My day was good," she said. "Everyone was really nice. There's a lot to learn. I don't know anything about the business, but I want to know everything."

"I'd think Gideon would be an easy boss to work for. And Addy is fair. She speaks her mind and some might fault her for that, but there's not a mean bone in her body." He removed his heavy leather work gloves and shoved them into his coat pockets. "This can't be easy for you, losing your job, your home. Making the move with Zachary and starting over in a new town."

She looked up at him. How did he know about her being evicted from her trailer?

He smiled. "Sorry," he said, seeming to know what she as thinking. "Zachary told me all about it. I hope that's okay. He's a good kid, Mari," he added thoughtfully. "I don't think there's any need to worry about him."

She hesitated. "I wanted to thank you for letting Zachary help you today." She looked down at her sneakers and them up at him again. "And… I don't know what you said to him, but it must have been the right thing. I was afraid he'd be in a funk when I got home, but he's not. In fact, he's great. He seems so… happy. And he apologized to me for his behavior this morning."

The easy smile reached his eyes, lighting them from within and revealing hints of green and gray that she hadn't noticed before. If he'd been a woman, people would have said that they were her best feature. In a man, they were remarkable.

"*Ya.* We kept him pretty busy," James went on. "He carried a lot of coffee, fetched some nails and did some sweeping. We worked on how to drive a nail properly."

"He told me you were going to bring a hammer for him to use. He was really excited about it," she said.

"Good." James nodded his head slowly. "I like your Zachary. You must be very proud of him."

"I am." She smiled. "It wasn't necessary to pay him."

"But it was." He settled his gaze on her. "He earned it. I try to give fair wages for good work."

She pushed her cold hands into the pockets of the coat, trying to warm them. "It was still good of you to take the trouble to make things easier for him. Kids don't like change, and he's had more than enough of it."

"He was no bother. He really wasn't. In fact, it was fun having him with us today. I'm looking forward to spending time with him tomorrow."

James squatted in front of a wooden toolbox on the ground just outside the addition and began to unload his tool belt and fit everything inside. It was an orderly box, his tools clean and well cared for. Mari admired that. She liked order herself, when she could find it in her life.

"Zachary has a quick mind," James continued. "And he's not afraid to get his hands dirty. It's plain to see that you've done a good job with him."

"I try." She stood there for a minute watching him, then realized it was silly for her to just be standing there. She'd passed on Sara's message. There was no reason for her to linger. She put her hands together. "Well, I hope you like ham," she said. "I saw one in the oven. I think Sara and Ellie made enough food for half the county."

"Sometimes it seems like half the county's eating with them. Sara has an endless string of pretty young women and their beaus as dinner guests. She hasn't been in Seven Poplars that long, but she's made a lot of friends here, and there's no doubt she provides a much-needed service."

"Not for me," Mari blurted out, then felt her face flush. "I mean, I'm not here to find a husband. That's not why I came here. We're old friends. From Wisconsin. She's just giving me a hand until I can get settled here in Delaware. I came for the job."

He glanced up from his toolbox. "That's what Zachary told me."

"I'm not married. I'm not even Amish." She felt as if she was babbling. "Not anymore. I was, but—" She pushed her hands deeper into the coat pockets. "Not anymore," she repeated.

He nodded, holding her gaze. There was no judgment in his eyes.

"But you were born to Amish parents."

"Sara told you?"

James shook his head. "A name like Mari Troyer?" He smiled that easy smile of his again. "It's not hard to guess what your background is."

"I left that life a decade ago."

"It's hard, leaving. Hard coming back, too."

"Oh, I'm not… I didn't come to be Amish again. It's not who I am anymore," she added softly, wondering what it was about James that made her feel as if she could stand there in the bitter cold and discuss things she hadn't talked about in years.

"I think the people who raised us, our parents and grandparents and their kin, they're always a part of us, whether we want them to be or not."

"I don't know about that. I guess I'm part of the English world now."

He thought for a moment before speaking. "Has it been kind to you, that world?"

She glanced away. The way he was looking at her made her feel nervous about herself. About things she believed to be true. "Not particularly, but it suits me." She shrugged. "And I can't come back. It's too late."

She wrapped her arms around herself, feeling oddly wistful. "Zachary and I are just here for a little while. I've done fine out there. It was just that the plant where I worked closed down. Jobs were hard to come by."

James hefted the heavy toolbox. "I'll be pleased to join you for supper. Mattie, she's my sister, and the kids went to have supper with their *grossmama*. Mattie and her mother-in-law get on like peas in a pod. And Agnes can't get enough of the new twins." He took a few steps and then stopped, obviously waiting for her.

"Your sister has twins?" She caught up with him. "How old?"

"Six weeks last Sunday. William, he's the oldest, and Timothy. They're good babies. It's their big brothers who cause all the fuss in our house."

"How old are they?"

"Roman is three, and Emanuel is twenty-two months."

She couldn't help chuckling. "Bet they're a handful."

"Emanuel takes close watching. Turn your back on that one and he'll be up the chimney or have the cow in the kitchen." They reached the back porch and James carried his toolbox up the steps and set it against the wall of the house. "It will be fine here until morning. Saves Jericho, he's my horse, from hauling it home and back tomorrow." He opened the back door and held it for her.

Mari walked through the doorway into the utility room. Instantly, she was wrapped in the homey smells of food and the sounds of easy conversation and laughter. She slipped out of the coat, hung it on a peg. James did the same and began to wash his hands in a big utility sink.

Mari walked through the doorway, feeling as if she was drawn into the embrace of Sara's warm kitchen.

"Mari, James, this is Peter Heiser." She indicated a thin, beardless man in his early forties sitting at the table. "I know you'll help to make him feel at home here in our community."

"Peter," Mari said as she slid into an empty chair between Ellie and Zachary. "Nice to meet you."

Peter's mouth opened, then closed; then his lips moved, but no words came out. Sweat beaded on his acne-scarred forehead as he nodded in her direction. His pale brown eyes were wide and stunned in appearance, like a frightened deer caught in the headlights of a car. His lips parted again, and something like a croak emerged. Mari expected the poor man to leap up from the table and flee the kitchen at any second.

James came to his rescue, sliding into a chair. "Good to have you with us," he said to Peter. "Everyone. Shall we?" He closed his eyes and slightly inclined his head, a signal for silent grace.

Mari reached for her son's hand under the table. He gripped her fingers, his small hand warm, clinging to hers. She smiled at him reassuringly, and he nodded before closing his eyes and lowering his head in imitation of the men and women around him. Mari did the same.

Mari's head was still bowed when James opened his eyes. She looked so relaxed in prayer. *A brave woman and a good mother*, he thought. He didn't care what she'd said; life couldn't have been easy for her in the English world. It never was for those born into a different one. Not that the Amish lifestyle was a perfect one. Nothing on earth was, he supposed. But it was obvious to him that Mari's struggles must have been more difficult than his own, and he admired her for her pluck and fortitude.

Sara's cheerful urging for someone to pass the ham jolted James from his musing. He caught Peter's gaze and offered him a friendly smile. Poor Peter. No wonder he needed Sara's help to find a wife. The man was obviously terrified of women. Hands trembling, Peter almost dropped the plate of meat into Hiram's lap. Hiram caught it in time, moving faster than James had thought him capable. Peter went white and his ears reddened. He was so flabbergasted by his near mishap that he hadn't even taken a slice of ham for himself. Hiram, who never missed an opportunity to fill his stomach, helped himself to two pieces.

"*Ach*, I forgot the butter," Ellie said. She started to rise, but Mari was quicker.

"I'll get it." Mari moved gracefully to the refrigerator and came back with the butter, offering it to James.

James glanced at Peter and then back at Mari and wondered if Sara had any notion of matching the two of them. He doubted it. Sara was good at reading people; Mari's personality was too strong. Peter needed a gentle woman, maybe someone a little older than he was, someone who could overlook his social deficiencies. And Mari had made a point of saying she wasn't here to find a husband. James knew Sara well enough, though, to suspect that didn't mean anything to her if she set her mind to it. Sara could be a determined woman, especially when it came to the idea of there being someone for everyone. Of course Mari would have to join the church to marry an Amish man, but that wasn't a far-fetched idea, especially since she had grown up Amish.

Mari took her seat again, murmuring something to her son. James couldn't hear the boy's reply, but whatever it was, it made his mother smile. A warm expression lit her brown eyes. She was an attractive woman, probably around his own age. She was rounded rather than thin and not more than medium height for a woman, but she gave the appearance of someone much taller. Her hair was russet brown, her brows dark and arching over intelligent, almond-shaped eyes. Mari wasn't a flashy beauty like Lilly Hershberger, but James liked Mari's wholesomeness better.

"Pass the ham back to Peter," Ellie instructed.

Peter reached for the platter, his hands shaking.

James glanced at Ellie. Surely Sara wasn't trying to match Peter with Ellie. She was *definitely* too strong to make a wife for Peter. He was very fond of Ellie. He didn't care that she was a little person, but there was no spark between them. And he had no intentions of settling for a wife. Maybe he'd picked up too many English ideas about romance when he was out in their world, but he wanted more than a sensible partner who shared his Amish faith and had reached the age of marriage. He wanted someone to love, a woman who would love him. He wanted a smart, sensible woman who would light up his life. He'd been waiting for that lightning strike, but so far that special person had never crossed his path.

His gaze gravitated to Mari again. At least he didn't *think* he'd met *the one* yet.

It would be good to find the right woman, to move on from being alone to being the head of a family. He wanted a wife and children. He was ready to settle down, but he was a patient man. When the right girl came along, he'd court her properly, treat her tenderly and offer her his head and his heart for a lifetime.

Just as that thought went through his head, Mari met his gaze across the table and she smiled. He got the strangest feeling in the pit of his stomach. When he'd returned to Seven Poplars and been baptized, he'd made the decision to return to the Amish way of life, and that meant marrying an Amish woman. Mari had told him she had no intention of returning to her roots. She'd also said it was too late. But James knew firsthand it was never too late for God's work. Which made him wonder what God had in store for Mari Troyer... and him.

Chapter Four

The following day James pushed open the back door of his old farmhouse and was greeted by the acrid stench of something burning, the fretful cries of a newborn and the combined wailing of two small boys. "Mattie!" he shouted. In the kitchen, smoke was rising from the stovetop in clouds, and from the hall came the shrill blast of a smoke alarm.

James crossed to the gas range and turned off the flame. Using the corner of his coat to protect his hand from the hot metal, he slid the pot over onto a cool burner. "Mattie!" he called. "Everything all right?" The kids continued to cry, but he knew them well enough to know they weren't hurt. He opened a window to let out the smoke, dodged a yellow tabby cat that was fleeing for her life and scooped up twenty-two-month-old Emanuel, who was in hot pursuit of the cat.

The smoke alarm continued to squeal.

With his squirming nephew tucked football-style under one arm, James walked into the living room. Roman, age three, was sitting at the foot of the steps with his eyes shut and his hands over his ears, shrieking. "Roman," James said. "You're fine." Then he called up the stairs. "Mattie? You up there?"

"*Ya.* Just finished feeding the twins!" his sister called from upstairs. Both of the newborns were crying now. "Can you make that smoke alarm stop? I don't know why it went off! I almost had William to sleep!"

"That supper on the stove?" he called above the racket.

"What? Can't hear you!" Mattie shouted back.

James deposited Emanuel on the bottom step beside his sniffling brother and grabbed a broom from the corner of the hall to wave it under the smoke detector and clear the smoke. Some men might remove the battery, just to shut the contraption up, but not James. He'd heard too many tragic tales of smoke detectors without batteries; his family meant too much to him.

"What did you say? I couldn't hear you for that noise!" His sister, scarf askew and face red, appeared at the top of the landing. A fat little baby, six weeks old and as bald as an onion beneath his tight-fitting baby *kapp*, was screeching like a guinea hen.

Like his brothers, James thought. A healthy child with good lungs. The smoke detector finally went silent, and he lowered the broom. "I asked if that was our supper on the stove."

"Not the chicken stew? Did I burn it?" She looked down at the screaming baby in her arms, then at James. "Again? I ruined our supper *again*?"

"Not ruined." James waved her back. "You tend to the twins. I'll see what can be done about the meal."

Just then, Roman yelped, "*Mam!* Emanuel bit me!"

"Emanuel!" Mattie took a step down the staircase.

"I can handle this," James insisted.

She smiled gratefully. "You're a peach."

He picked up the nearest small boy. "Time-out for both of you." He pointed to a small wooden stool. "Three minutes for you, Roman, one for Emanuel." The oldest child started to cry, but James remained firm. "Three minutes." He put the second one on the sofa. "Stay there, Emanuel. If you get down before I say you can, no cookies after supper." Emanuel might have done the biting, but if he knew Roman, the older one, had done something to offend the younger. Easier not to try to figure out who was at fault each time.

James returned to the kitchen, found that most of the smoke had cleared out and closed the window. He removed his coat, hung his black wool hat on a hook by the door and rolled up his sleeves. "All right, Emanuel. You can get off the sofa," he called.

"Can I get up now?" Roman whined.

"Not yet. I'll tell you when." James washed his hands, went to the stove and tasted the stew. The burned taste wasn't awful, but it was there, and there was a thick layer sticking to the bottom of the pot. He carried the offending stew to the sink and poured it into the strainer. As he suspected, the stew in the bottom of the pot was unsalvageable, but large chunks of chicken, the carrots and the onion would be okay with a fresh gravy.

By the time Mattie came downstairs, the two boys were playing peacefully with a miniature horse and wagon, and James had whipped up a batch of corn bread to go with the stew.

Mattie was carrying one of the twins. "William won't go to sleep." She settled into the rocking chair in the corner of the kitchen and watched as he cut potatoes into small chunks, added them to the rescued stew, poured broth from a carton from the pantry into the pot and put the whole thing back onto the stove.

"I didn't get bread made today," Mattie said. "Not even biscuits." She sniffed, searched in her apron pocket, then sniffed again.

James removed a clean handkerchief from his own pocket and handed it to her. "No need crying over burned stew, Mattie. It will be fine. You'll see." He rummaged around on a shelf for some bay leaves, pepper and tarragon. He stirred the spices into the stew and adjusted the flame under it. "Shouldn't take too long to finish, And I've got corn bread in the oven."

"You shouldn't have to do this," Mattie managed, barely holding back tears. "It should be me. I'm not holding up my end."

James crouched down in front of her and patted her hand. "None of that, now. Who took care of me when I was growing up? It's only fair that I repay some of your kindness by helping out. You've got your hands full with four children so close together."

Their mother's death had made Mattie a mother to him when she was nothing but a girl and he was no older than Roman. They were closer than most brothers and sisters. She'd always been there for him, and he valued her wise council. With qualities like that, who cared if Mattie could cook or not?

"You should let me hire a girl to help for a few weeks," he told her.

"*Ne.*" Mattie sighed. "I can't let you spend money so recklessly. I'll be fine."

James shook his head as he rose to his feet. "I never

liked this idea, Rupert working away from home. You know he can come and work on my crew any day."

Mattie blew her nose again, threw the apron over her shoulder to cover herself and began to nurse little William again. "He wants to do this, James. Work is good. He's getting overtime every week. We should have enough money to start building our cabin in the spring." She smiled at the thought. "You should be happy. You'll get your house back."

"It's *our* house," he replied. It had never seemed fair to him that his father had willed the house and farm to him. James had given Mattie and Rupert twenty acres across the field to build on, though. Two years ago, when jobs had been scarce in Kent County, Rupert had taken a job in Pennsylvania with a small company that made log-cabin kits and shipped them all over the country. The money was good, better than James could have afforded to pay his brother-in-law, but it meant that Rupert could come home only once a month.

The baby began to make contented sounds, and the tension drained from Mattie's face. She looked up at James. "It's a chance for us. And it won't be long. Once Rupert starts work on our cabin, he won't work away from home any longer. We'll be grateful for a job with you then. And…" She threw him a meaningful glance. "You'll be able to start looking for a wife."

"I will, will I?" His finding a wife was one of Mattie's favorite subjects.

"Lots of nice girls available. You've been back home two years, and you've been accepted into the faith. It's time you thought about settling down ."

When James first returned to Seven Poplars, he'd felt self-conscious when reminded about the period he had spent among the English, but that had passed. Over time, he'd come to believe that his time in the English world had made him a better man. A better Amish man.

"Did you have anyone in particular in mind? For my wife?" he asked, amusement in his voice.

"You know I've always liked Lilly Hershberger. And then there's Jane. She likes you a lot."

"Jane Peachy?" He made a face. "Isn't she a little old for me? She's got to be eighty, at least."

She laughed. "You know perfectly well which Jane I mean. Jane *Stutzman*. She's a good cook. And I know she likes you. I've seen her watching you in church."

He gathered dishes and utensils to set the table for the evening meal. "I met a nice girl this week at Sara's," he said casually.

"*Ya?* Who? Sara's got so many coming and going these days, I lose track. Do we know the family?"

"Her name's Mari Troyer. She's from Wisconsin."

Mattie's eyes narrowed. "Troyer? You don't mean that girl who went English? Sara mentioned her Sunday last. She's going to find her a husband."

"You think?"

"Well, why else would she be staying with the matchmaker?" Mattie asked, sounding as if James was foolish not to have known that. "Of course, first she'll have to join the church. She was never baptized, according to Sara, so it's just a matter of taking the classes with the bishop and making the commitment."

He turned from the stove. "Mari's joining the church?" he asked, trying not to sound too interested; otherwise, his sister would get herself worked up. That wasn't what Mari had said to him. But there had been something in the tone of her voice that had made him think that she wasn't as sure as she wanted him to be-lieve.

Mattie narrowed her eyes suspiciously. "I don't think a girl like that is someone you should court, James. You haven't been back that long."

"Two years." He turned back to the stew.

"It's better if you marry a girl who hasn't been in-fluenced by Englishers. That way you won't be—"

"What?" he asked, staring into the pot and stirring it slowly. "Lured away by fancy cars and HBO?"

"I don't even know what HBO is, but you know what I mean." The baby started to fuss, and Mattie put him on her lap and began to pat his back. "This Mari has lived among the English. She might put ideas in your head to leave again."

James laughed and then frowned. "You think I can be influenced by every pretty English girl I meet?"

"She's pretty, is she?"

"*Ya.* And she has a way about her that's…endear-ing. One minute she seems confident and the next so unsure of herself," he said as much to himself as his sister. He looked over his shoulder at Mattie. "And she's a good mother."

"She has a *child*?"

"A boy. Nine years old. A man marries a woman with a boy nine years old and he's got an instant helper around the farm," he teased. "Makes sense to me. You know, rather than starting a family from scratch."

"James Hostetler," she admonished. "You're pull-ing my leg, aren't you?" She cuddled the baby against her. "Well, it's not funny. You've been baptized into the church. If you left again, you'd be lost to us…to me and the children." Mattie shook her head. "It's not a joke, brother."

He went to her and placed a hand on her shoulder. "I'm not going anywhere, Mattie. And I'm not running off with Mari Troyer." He kissed the top of his sister's head and wondered to himself what the chances were that Sara knew Mari Troyer better than Mari knew herself.

Friday was hectic at the butcher shop, but Mari already thought she was getting a handle on her responsibilities and a good working knowledge of how the scales and cash register worked. She'd even learned a bit about sausage and scrapple making from Gideon. There was a lot she had to learn, but whenever she hit a snag, Addy or Gideon was there to throw her a lifeline. Ending up in Seven Poplars was really quite a turn of events, when she thought about it. Of all the ways she'd tried to imagine finding self-sufficiency, she'd never thought it would be working in an Amish butcher shop and living with an Amish friend.

At five o'clock she hung up her apron and walked out the door feeling as though she'd earned her day's wages. Her only regret was that she had been unable to enroll Zachary in school. The local school secretary had been polite but firm. The school's policy was not to accept a new student without proper documentation, which meant waiting on the school records she'd requested Wednesday.

On the plus side, while at work, Mari had been confident that Sara, Jerushah or James was at the house and watching over her son. But it was unfair to expect them to take responsibility for Zachary when he should be in school. Zachary, however, was more than pleased that he couldn't start yet. And to hear him tell it, he was practically a member of James's crew and on his way to being a journeyman carpenter. As relieved as she was that Zachary was happy, she knew that she had to get him back into class before he fell further behind in his studies.

When the van dropped Mari off at Sara's, the house was quiet. Nothing bubbled on the stove, and the table was not set for the evening meal. Instead of the usual Friday evening supper, Sara was hosting a neighborhood evening meal in a barn that stood behind the stable where she kept her animals. Ellie had pointed it out earlier in the week and explained that Sara had purchased it in the summer for practically nothing because it was about to be torn down at its original location to make room for a development. With the help of friends and neighbors, James's construction crew had dismantled the barn and then rebuilt it on Sara's acreage.

Mari changed out of her work clothing, dressed warmly and followed the pathway through a grassy field to the barn, where light shone from every window. By daylight, it was a postcard-perfect gambrel-roofed building with a metal roof, red siding and jaunty rooster weather vane, but Mari couldn't imagine why Sara would plan a supper in a barn on a cold January evening. Once she pushed open the white wooden door, Mari was immediately reminded of why she should never doubt her friend. Sara's barn was amazing.

Mari gazed around at the interior, taking in the high ceiling, the massive wooden beams and the spotless whitewashed walls. Not only had the inside of the building been insulated, but the old wood floor had been sanded and refinished. Two enormous woodstoves stood in opposite corners, making the main room so warm that she was going to have to take off her coat. And it smelled so good, the scent of burning hickory mixing with one of Sara's cinnamon-and-clove potpourris bubbling on the back of one of the stoves.

The space was a beehive of activity. Men and boys were setting up long tables and arranging chairs while women in Amish *kapps* and starched white aprons carried in large stainless-steel containers and placed them on counters along one wall.

"Mari!" Sara waved to her from the food area. "What do you think of my hospitality barn?"

She laughed. "You can hardly call it a barn. It's beautiful."

This building was nothing like the barns Mari remembered from her childhood; some had smelled of hay and animal feed, but others were not so pleasant. She shivered involuntarily, remembering her uncle's dank and forbidding stable, all shadows, cobwebs and sagging doors and windows. She had spent many mornings and evenings there milking the cows in the semidarkness, and it wasn't a memory that she cared to linger over.

She walked over to where Sara was standing. "When you said you were having dinner in a barn, I wasn't thinking of anything like this. This is terrific." In her memories, her uncle's barn had always been damp and drafty, even in summer. This, in contrast, was a cheerful place, clean and welcoming.

"I'm pleased with how it came together," Sara said, planting her hands on her hips. "If you're looking for Zachary, I saw him just a few minutes ago. If I know Ellie, she's pressed him into service back in the kitchen. Tacos tonight, so there's a lot of prep work."

"There's a *kitchen* in your barn?" Mari asked.

"Right through that doorway." She pointed. "Every hospitality barn needs a kitchen, don't you think? You can go help if you like. I know Ellie needed someone to start the salsa."

"What exactly is a hospitality barn?" Mari hung her coat on a hook on the wall. More Amish were coming into the building now, and two teenage girls were spreading the tables with white tablecloths. "I've never heard of such a thing."

"Made it up myself. I wanted someplace larger than my home where I could get young people together," Sara explained. "For my matchmaking, so that men and women of courting age could meet. Also, our church community needed a safe place to hold youth meetings, singings and frolics. This barn was an answer to our prayers, and it practically fell into my lap. It's more than a hundred years old and is in wonderful shape."

"But the expense of moving the structure." Mari looked around, still in awe. "It couldn't have been cheap."

"A bargain at any price. A lot of Amish communities have problems with their kids being lured into bad habits by the free ways of the English. Even Amish kids need somewhere away from adults to let down their hair, so to speak."

Mari nodded in agreement.

"On Wednesday evenings our local youth group, the Gleaners, meet here. They do game nights, birthday parties and work frolics here, as well. It's good that Amish children learn the value of work and responsibility, but boys have a lot of energy. If we can channel that energy in a positive way, the entire community benefits."

"I didn't realize you were involved in so many projects," Mari said. "You haven't lived here in Seven Poplars that long."

"*Ne*, I haven't, but ours is a close-knit and caring community. I feel like I was called to come here."

"Sure seems nice." Mari smoothed her skirt. "Not anything like where I grew up. I don't think anything had changed in our town in a century."

"Tradition is good." Sara nodded thoughtfully. "It's served our faith well for hundreds of years, but as I see it, we don't live in a vacuum. We have to be open to change when it can be done without endangering our way of life."

Mari had known that Sara, who never had children of her own, had always been interested in kids, but she hadn't realized that her concern went so deep. "And you did all of this for other people's children?"

Sara chuckled. "Not alone. It's really for everyone. My socials are always open to the entire neighborhood. You rarely run into opposition from parents if you have a preacher or bishop present." She lowered her voice. "I'm an obedient member of my church, but some of my ideas do stretch the boundaries of tradition."

Mari nodded. She'd always admired Sara, and now she admired her even more. It was endearing to see that her kindness didn't extend to just old acquaintances who'd fallen on hard times.

Families were filing in, and Mari glanced around, hoping to catch sight of Zachary. So many people who all knew each other was daunting to her. She could imagine how it might be difficult to her son.

The main door swung open again, and James and another man entered, followed closely by Zachary. "Mom!" her son called. He said something to James, who smiled at him and waved him toward her and Sara. Zachary ran to join them. "Hey, Mom." He stopped short and shoved his hands into his pockets.

"I'll be in the kitchen," Sara said, giving Mari a pat on the shoulder. "Through that doorway."

"I'll be in in just a minute to help." Mari turned back to her son. His cheeks were bright red, and she noticed that the cuff of his hoodie was torn. She thought about telling him to run back to the house and grab one of the spare coats from Sara's house, but he looked so happy that she didn't want to seem critical. And to his credit, he was wearing a wool cap pulled down over his ears, like the other boys. She'd thought of Zachary often today, wondering how he was making out. It was a relief to see that he seemed in good spirits.

"I was helping James with the horses." Zachary bounced on the balls of his feet. "He's teaching me how to clean Jericho's hooves. Stones get stuck in there."

"He learns quick, your boy."

Mari looked up to see James walking over to join them. "I hope he isn't being a bother," she said.

James shook his head. "No. Not at all." The warmth of his expression told her that he wasn't simply being polite. "It's a good thing to find a young man who's interested in the care of animals." He raised one shoulder in an easy shrug. "With a horse, feet and legs are everything. They're surprisingly frail for such a large animal. You have to pay close attention to their health."

"Absolutely," she agreed. "My uncle had a horse that had to be put down because a sharp rock caused a hoof infection that spread up the animal's leg."

Zachary looked up at her with obvious admiration on his face. "You never told me that your uncle had a horse."

A lot I haven't told you, she thought. But she just smiled. There would be time when he was older to tell him the whole story of her life before he became her life. "I'm going into the kitchen to help Sara, Zachary. Want to come along?"

"Can't. James says the men have things to do." He glanced at James again. "I can't believe we're having tacos tonight. I didn't know you people..." Mari saw the hint of a flush creeping up his neck and face as he averted his gaze from James's. "Ate stuff like tacos," he finished, suddenly fascinated by the toe of one of his sneakers.

"I love tacos," James said. "And I like them spicy."

Zachary grinned, his eyes wide with admiration. "Me, too. And lots of sour cream."

James looked to Mari. "I could use Zach's help," he said. "If it's all right with you. I'd like him to meet some other neighborhood boys his age. We'll be right here in the barn."

"Please, Mom," her son begged. "I'll come and help you later. Promise."

James waved to a slender boy with an olive complexion. "'Kota, come here," he called.

'Kota ran to join them. Mari didn't think he was Amish because he had an English haircut, but his plain blue sweater and hand-sewn denim jacket were similar to what the other Amish boys were wearing.

"'Kota is one of Hannah's grandsons," James explained. "'Kota, this is Zachary. Do you think you could take him up to the hayloft? I'd like you two to roll down eight bales of straw. Sara says we're going to play a game later, and we'll need the straw."

'Kota nodded. "Sure. We can do that. Come on, Zach. It's neat up in the loft." The two boys dashed off together.

Mari watched Zachary follow 'Kota up a ladder and climb through a trapdoor overhead. It was all she could do not to call out to him to be careful. "Are you sure that it's safe?" Mari asked James. "Zachary hasn't had any experience in barns."

"Don't worry," James assured her. "Nine-year-old boys climb like squirrels. It comes as natural to them as breathing. 'Kota's a good kid. Zachary will be fine with him."

"Is he Amish?" Mari asked, her gaze still fixed on the now-vacant ladder.

"Mennonite. His mom, Grace, is married to John Hartman, the local veterinarian. You'll like Grace and John. They're good parents. And Zachary needs to make some friends in Seven Poplars."

"You're right," she said. "He does. And I appreciate your help." She smiled at him, thinking how nice it was that he was taking such an interest in Zachary.

She looked at him and he looked at her. He was dressed like all the other Amish men milling around inside Sara's barn, but there was something that made him stand out. "Well," she said, beginning to feel awkward. "Guess I'd better go give Sara a hand in the kitchen."

"*Ya.* Because there will be a lot of hungry people

here tonight." He returned her smile. "Me included." He paused and gave her a thoughtful look. "And no need to keep thanking me. I like Zachary, and I've spent enough time with him to already know he's going to be fine. You really don't need to worry about him. I think you just need to give him time and a little breathing room and he'll settle in just fine."

"Easier said than done." She chuckled. "The *don't worry* part."

"That's what my sister says. She tells me that it's part of the requirements for being a mother. But you need to give yourself some credit. You've done a good job with Zachary. He may kick up his heels at times, like any high-spirited colt, but he's got a level head on his shoulders. He's a son you can be proud of."

"Thank you," she said. "That means more than you can guess." She grimaced. "It's just been the two of us, and sometimes…" She hesitated, surprised that she was talking so easily about her private feelings with James. Again. But oddly, although she'd only known him a few days, James didn't feel like a stranger. He seemed like an old friend. "Sometimes I wonder if I'm being the kind of mother he needs."

"I'm sure you are," James said. "He thinks the world of you." He nodded. "Now I'd best get on with my assignments or Sara will want to know where her straw bales are."

He strode off in the direction of the loft ladder, and Mari found her way back to the well-equipped kitchen. A plump woman that Mari hadn't met was standing at a big gas stove, stirring sizzling ground beef in several cast-iron frying pans. "Reinforcements have arrived," Mari announced to Ellie. It was funny that she'd been tired when she walked to the barn but now she felt so full of energy. And happy to be included in the evening.

"Goot." Ellie was standing on a wooden stool to reach the counter. "Anna, this is Sara's Mari Troyer. Mari, Anna Mast, one of Hannah's daughters."

"Welcome to Seven Poplars." Anna smiled broadly. She was a big woman with bright red hair tucked under her *kapp* and a smile that warmed Mari to her toes. "Sara told us all about you. We're so glad to have you here. You want to take my place or start making up the salsa?"

"Whatever would help most." Mari liked Anna at once, with her warm expression and laughing eyes. "You're Grace's sister, right?"

"One of them," Anna replied. "Take my spatula and keep this meat from burning. I'll mix up the salsa. Watch me, and you'll know how to do it next time."

"Everyone will be starving," Ellie said.

Jerushah and another young woman who Anna introduced as her sister Rebecca came into the kitchen and began to chop onions and grate cheese. Soon the five of them were laughing and talking in *Deitsch*. Rebecca, a pretty girl a little younger than the rest of them, was as friendly as her sister Anna, and Mari liked her at once, too.

"Oh, don't forget," Rebecca said to Anna after a few minutes, "tomorrow is the coat exchange at *Mam*'s. She'll need help."

"I'll be there." Anna glanced at Mari. "You should come. Sara says you're a good organizer. We could use your help."

"Ya, come," Rebecca urged. "We have a good time, and our *mam* really does need extra hands."

"I'd love to." Mari added more fresh ground beef to a frying pan. "But I have to work until noon."

"Perfect," Rebecca said. "I'll pick you up a little after one. It doesn't start until two o'clock, but there's a lot to do there before the moms and grandmothers arrive. You have a son about... What is he? Eight years old?"

"Nine." Mari dumped the pan of cooked ground beef into a strainer.

"They grow like weeds at that age, don't they?" Anna asked. "Anyway, if you have any boots or coats, sweaters or hats that he's outgrown, bring them. We call it a coat exchange, but really it's a clothing exchange for our kids. The whole afternoon is a little crazy, but it's fun. You'll enjoy yourself."

Mari smiled but didn't say anything. She loved the idea of a coat exchange; she just wished she had a coat to contribute.

"And be sure to take something home with you," Rebecca insisted. "If you have a boy, you can always use another winter coat. We do this twice a year, mid-winter and summer before school starts."

Anna chuckled. "Mari may not want her Englisher boy wearing an Amish coat. They're warm, and they hold up good, though."

"You can meet our mother and most of the women in Seven Poplars," Rebecca offered. "And you and your son should stay for supper. My sisters will be there, and your son can meet our kids. It will be fun—I promise."

Mari wavered. "I'll be glad to help out, but I'm not sure that your mother will want me to stay for—"

"Our mam?" Anna laughed. "The more at our mother's table, the happier she is."

"She's coming," Rebecca told her sister. Then she glanced at Mari. "You'll have a good time, I promise you. And so will your son."

"All right." Mari gave in with a smile. Everyone was so nice that she wanted to pinch herself to prove she wasn't dreaming. "Thank you."

"Don't thank us yet," Anna teased. "Wait until you see how much work you've just agreed to."

Chapter Five

The coat swap was every bit as crazy as Anna had warned it would be. Dozens of children ran, climbed, crawled and tumbled through Hannah Yoder's kitchen. Babies cried, clapped their hands and squirmed in their mother's and older siblings' arms. School-age boys in lined denim coats and black wool hats were tugged into the parlor, which held piles of coats of all sizes.

The system was simple enough. People dropped off coats, found ones that fit their children and left. Between helping find sizes, Mari sorted through the trade-ins to see if they needed mending, washing or were too far gone to be used for another boy. Anything that couldn't be worn any longer, she'd been told, would be cut up to be used in rag rugs.

For two hours Mari worked. As fast as coats went out, coats came in, and soon her neat piles of particular sizes weren't so neat anymore. When there was a lull in activity and she found herself alone for a few minutes, she started trying to reestablish the piles according to size. Once she got the piles back in order, she wondered if she ought to go look for Zachary. She hadn't seen him since he'd spied 'Kota when he'd scrambled down out of Rebecca's husband's buggy and ran off after him.

"There you are, Mari!"

Mari looked up from where she knelt on the floor in the middle of piles of coats to see Rebecca Yoder standing in the doorway, a rosy-cheeked toddler in her arms.

"Have you been stuck in here all this time?"

"No, I grabbed a cup of tea earlier. And I don't mind," Mari assured her. "I like being able to help out."

"I really am glad you decided to join us today."

Mari held a little navy blue quilted jacket in her hands. "It was nice to be invited. I've met so many people that my head is spinning." She chuckled as she folded the garment.

Upon her arrival Mari had met Ruth, Miriam and the youngest of the sisters, Susanna, all redheads like Anna and Rebecca, and all with their mother Hannah's likable disposition. Leah, according to Anna, was serving as a missionary and teacher in Brazil. There was another sister, Johanna, who was expected later.

"So it looks like you're settling in nicely." Rebecca shifted the baby to her hip. "I heard from Addy that you're doing well at the shop."

Mari set the little coat in a growing stack and reached for another. "I really like it there. Everyone has been so pleasant. Not just at work." She glanced up at Rebecca, suddenly feeling very emotional. Sara had written to her about Seven Poplars, but never in her wildest dreams had Mari imagined it would be so nice. "Everywhere I go, people are so kind and welcoming."

"I'm so glad. You know, I saw you talking with James Hostetler last night before you joined us in the kitchen." Rebecca cut her eyes at Mari and smiled as if she knew some secret. "A very handsome, eligible man, that James Hostetler. He seemed very interested in your conversation. Interested in *you*."

Mari picked up another coat off the floor. "James is…very nice. I know him from Sara's. He's building her addition, so we see a lot of each other," she explained, wondering why she felt the need to explain.

"I see." Rebecca drew out the last word.

When Mari dared a glance up at Rebecca, she was still smiling.

Then she gave a wave of dismissal. "Oh, I'm just teasing you, Mari. I didn't mean to embarrass you."

"I… I'm not," Mari managed, still feeling the heat of a blush on her cheeks. "James has been very kind to me…to us. To my son and I. He… I think he'll be a good friend."

"A good friend, yes," Rebecca repeated, her tone still teasing. Her baby began to fuss, and she moved him to her shoulder. "You want me to take over here?"

"No," Mari said. "I'm fine. I'm determined to get these piles in order."

"Okay, well, give me a holler if you need help." She peered into the baby's face. "I think this one is hungry again."

After Rebecca left the room, Mari turned to pick through a pile of coats too worn to be handed out. She came upon a familiar gray hoodie in the pile of blue denim coats. Zachary's hoodie. *What in the world?* He must have slipped in and out again when she'd been in the kitchen having a quick cup of tea with the Yoders when she first arrived. She was holding it up, wonder-

ing what he was wearing, when she heard a familiar
male voice.

"Hey! I didn't expect to see you here."

She looked up to see James standing in the doorway
holding the hand of a small boy in a black hat and blue
denim jacket identical to his. Her first thought was one
of fear. He must have passed Rebecca in the hallway.
Had he overheard them talking about him? "James."

"My nephew Roman," he introduced him, pointing
down at the little boy.

If he'd heard any of her conversation with Rebecca,
he didn't give any indication, which made Mari sigh
with relief. Not that she'd said anything wrong or inap-
propriate, she just… *You just what?* She looked down
at the little boy.

The child eyed her suspiciously.

"Roman, here, is in need of a larger coat than the
one he has."

The boy ducked behind James's legs and buried his
face in his uncle's trousers.

"Hello, Roman." Mari rose from the floor. "Did you
come to find a new coat?"

James shook his head. "He doesn't understand English yet." He quickly translated for the child. Roman
peeked around James's legs at her and buried his face
again.

"Ne," Roman murmured.

"Ya," James corrected. Then he returned his attention to Mari. "My sister's twins were fussy today, so I
was elected to coat detail," he explained. "Do you think
you can help us? We're not trading in this one, because
there are three more boys younger than Roman, but
my sister sent a pile of mittens she knitted. They were

gone before I got through the kitchen." He reached behind him, scooped up the boy and tucked him under his arm. "Of course if we can't find something that will fit him," James said, switching back to *Deitsch*, "we'll just trade him for one of the bigger boys outside who comes with his own coat that fits." James didn't crack a smile and appeared perfectly serious.

Roman began to giggle, James broke into a grin, and Mari found herself chuckling with them.

"I'm sure we won't have to go that far," she said in *Deitsch* so Roman would understand her. She was amazed by how easily the language was coming back to her. "We can find something that will fit him. We probably have more of the smaller coats left than the ones for the older boys."

"So long as I go home with one boy and one coat," James said. "Otherwise, I'll have some explaining to do." He hesitated and then said, "Your *Deitsch* is good. I'd never have suspected you'd been away so long."

"Thank you." Mari turned away, suddenly feeling shy and having no idea why. "So…let's see what we can find."

Finding a coat for Roman at the coat exchange proved more difficult than James expected. Because all of the jackets had been handmade, nothing was marked with sizes. Some were too long, some too short. And every one of them looked just like the others to him until he got it on his nephew. And then once he found one that fit, the trouble was finding one that would be acceptable to his sister. One had been poorly patched, and others were badly worn or not sewn as neatly as Mattie would have liked. The denim coats were fas-

tened with snaps rather than buttons, and he'd been instructed not to bring a garment home that had missing
or broken snaps. Most of the jackets were lined, but
in different material and padding, and not all were as
warm as what James wanted for Roman.

"He's an outside boy and rough on his clothing,"
James explained to Mari in *Deitsch*. Roman beamed.
"He needs something that will protect him from the
cold and something that will hold up. Mattie wasn't
sure that she could trust me to pick out the right coat,
but I told her I could. So my reputation is pretty much
on the line here."

"Not to worry," Mari promised as she dug through
a pile of coats. "We'll find one here somewhere and
Roman will go home as warm as toast."

Roman wasn't happy about actually trying on the
coats, and he was soon squirming and whining in protest. James could understand the boy's reaction. Unlike his sisters, he'd never had the patience to stand
still while his *mam* measured him for new clothing or
had him try on new garments she'd made.

"There must be something suitable here," James
said to Mari, looking through another pile. "I promised
Mattie that I'd find him something that she wouldn't
be ashamed for him to wear to Sunday worship. She
was hoping to make him a new coat, but the twins keep
her pretty busy."

"Twin newborns?" Mari's smile lit her dark eyes.
"I'd think they would."

James decided she had a nice smile. "You should
hear William, the older of the twins. He has a set of
lungs on him."

"Bless her. I can't imagine how she does it. I was

at my wit's end with Zachary when he was a baby. I think raising a monkey would be easier than twins."

She was a woman with a sense of humor, and he liked that. He really hoped that she and Zachary would decide to stay in Seven Poplars because they would be a welcome addition to the community. And he couldn't help thinking how easily she seemed to fit in among them. He'd seen it at Sara's house and then at the dinner the previous night, too. Maybe she just needed a little encouragement and support from everyone.

"How about this one?" Mari held up another coat. "This would be fine to wear to worship."

"Let's hope it fits." He reached for it. "Are you coming tomorrow?"

"Coming where?" She looked up at him, another coat now in her hand.

He went down on one knee to wrestle Roman into the coat. "To worship. With Sara, Ellie and the others? Last Sunday was visiting Sunday, so we have worship tomorrow."

Mari's mouth tightened, and she visibly paled. "No," she said, shaking her head. "I'm not coming."

"That's too bad." He realized he had made her uncomfortable, and that hadn't been his intention. "We've got a good preacher. Caleb. He's a young man, but he knows the word of God."

She glanced at the coat in her hands, then up at him. "You might as well know right off, James, that I don't go to church anymore," she said quietly. "I haven't been to an Amish service since I left my uncle's farm when I was eighteen."

"Do you mind if I ask why not? Sara said you were raised in the faith," he said.

When he met Mari's gaze, he saw that her eyes suddenly glistened, and he wished he'd chosen his words more carefully. She looked as if she might cry. He released his hold on Roman, and the boy got down on his knees and crawled under a chair to pick up a wooden rabbit that some other child must have left behind in the parlor.

James sat down on a wooden stool and looked at Mari. He was already beginning to think of her as a friend. A very good friend. And he disliked the idea of upsetting her. "I'm sorry," he said. "I didn't mean to pry."

"No, it's all right." She swallowed, obviously trying to regain her composure.

He was quiet for a moment. Logic told him to change the conversation, but there was something about the look on her face that made him think that wasn't what he was supposed to do. It wasn't the Amish way to talk about God leading a person to do something or say something, but it *was* the Amish way to respond to such callings. "Do you miss it?" he asked softly in English, knowing she did. He could see it in her eyes.

"Sometimes," she admitted, meeting his gaze for a moment, then looking away. She hesitated and then went on in English, "It's hard to explain, James. Why I left the church. I don't think I've lost my faith in God, but... I think He turned away from me."

Someone or something had hurt her badly to make her say such a thing, and James instantly felt protective of her. His first instinct was to get up and go to her and put his arm around her. That wouldn't have been appropriate, of course. So he stayed where he was. "I don't think God ever turns away from us, Mari."

"It felt like it at the time." She hugged the little coat to her chest. "I wasn't welcome in my family's home anymore."

"Were you placed under the *bann*?" he asked.

Mari shook her head. "No. I left the morning of the day I was supposed to be baptized." Her lower lip quivered. Suddenly she seemed younger, more vulnerable. But she raised her chin and looked directly into his eyes. "I couldn't go through with it, and so I ran away."

"To the English world," he said, remembering so vividly the day he'd done the same thing. Only he'd been fortunate enough to not have to leave in the cover of darkness as many Amish did. His family had been there in the barnyard to say goodbye and to hug him and wish him well and encourage him to come home as often as he wished.

"Yes." A tear welled in the inner corner of her left eye, and she dashed it away.

"And you never went home again? Later, after the fuss of your leaving had died down?"

"I went to my uncle once, when I knew I was expecting." She didn't look at him when she said the words. "He said I would have to give up my baby in order to come home, so I didn't go back after that."

"Your brothers and sisters? Did they feel the same way?"

"My sisters were married and gone. I don't know where, but they were older, and we were never close. My brother...he died."

"I'm so sorry," he said, finding himself feeling the grief that clouded her beautiful eyes. "If you weren't baptized, there was no reason for them to treat you that way. Our faith gives each person the choice of baptism. Our church doesn't shun the ones who leave."

"Ours didn't, either. But my aunt and uncle were… not very understanding. He was a deacon, and he felt I had shamed him in front of the congregation."

They were both quiet for a long few moments and James knew he should let the conversation go, that he should take a coat and walk away, but he couldn't leave Mari like this. "Were you happy out there? Among the Englishers?"

"Yes," she answered too quickly. She set the coat in her arms aside and picked up another. "Well, sometimes…most of the time."

"But lonely," he said, seeing it in her face. "I know. I found that out for myself. I left Seven Poplars when I was twenty."

"You did?" She looked up at him with surprise. "That's hard to believe. You seem so…so Amish."

He had to laugh at that.

"You know what I mean." She smiled and dropped to sit on the edge of a chair, facing him. "You seem so content. So happy with your life."

"I am now." He held her gaze, smiling. "I can't believe Zachary didn't tell you I was English for a while."

"Zachary knows?" Again he could tell she was surprised. "He never said a word, that little rascal. How long were you gone?"

"About six years."

She was quiet for a moment and then she looked at him. "Can I ask you something?"

"Of course."

She met his gaze. "What made you come back?"

"Realizing this is where I belong. It's a good life

for some out there. But it wasn't for me. I learned a lot out there about people, about book stuff we don't teach in our schools, but I think that the most important thing I learned was that I belong here. Seven Poplars is my home."

"How long have you been back?" she asked. She held up a hand. "Sorry. I don't mean to pry."

"It's not prying. It's common knowledge in Seven Poplars. I've been back two years."

"And you've joined the church?"

He nodded. "*Ya*. First thing I did when I moved home. And it's brought me peace. Peace I never knew before."

"I'm glad for you," she answered, and he could tell she was being sincere. "But not everyone is meant for the life apart from the world like this."

"That's true," he agreed.

She met his gaze again, and he wanted to ask her how sure she was that she was one of those people, but the same feeling that he had a few minutes earlier telling him to press on told him to let it go. So he did. Instead, he reached for Roman, who was crawling past him with the toy rabbit. "There you are!" he cried, lifting the boy into his lap and tickling him.

"Try this one on him," Mari said, rising off the chair. She held up a small coat with neat stitching and a mended tear on the right cuff.

"I don't know about the mend," James said and then smiled. "Maybe Mattie was right. Maybe this job is too big for me."

"Absolutely not." Mari put the coat aside. "I think the ones in the baby room are too small for him, but…"

She picked up a garment that had fallen between the chairs. "Let's try this."

To James's relief, the coat she handed-him was only slightly big. "That should do it," he said, slipping it over his nephew's shoulders. The coat was sewn with stitches almost too small to see. The lining was quilted, and there were elastic cuffs inside the sleeves that would keep the winter wind from blowing up a boy's arms. Roman wiggled and shifted his feet, wanting to get back to his game with the rabbit, but Mari insisted on fastening all the snaps to make certain none were missing or broken.

"Nice fit" came a woman's voice from the doorway. "Be sure you grab one of those knit caps on the windowsill."

James looked over to see several small hats lying there. "Thank you, Hannah. I think we've found a coat that Mattie will like."

"And there's a little room for him to grow," Mari pointed out.

"He does that," James said. "I've tried putting him under the kitchen table and telling him not to, but every time I turn my back on Roman, he shoots up another inch or two."

The boy giggled.

"The fit looks perfect to me," Hannah said. "Find one to fit any better and a boy will outgrow it before he gets through the kitchen doorway." She shifted a fat-cheeked baby from one hip to the other. "I think Roman is our last customer." She glanced at the remaining coats. "At least we didn't come up short like last year. Ellie can take these spares to the school to see if anyone there can use one."

James helped Roman out of the coat, and as he did, he noticed the outline of a bee stitched into the inside at the back of the collar. "Look, Roman," he said to the boy. "Your new coat has a bee in it."

Roman laughed and scrambled to retrieve the toy rabbit.

"Johanna's work," Hannah explained. "She raises bees, and she sews a bee into her boys' coats. Our Johanna is an accomplished seamstress. Have you met her yet?" she asked Mari. Mari shook her head. "Well, you will because she and the children are coming for supper. Rebecca and Anna tell me that you're staying to eat with us, too. I'm so pleased to have you."

"That's not necessary," Mari replied. "You have a houseful already."

"*Ach*, the more at my table the happier my husband will be. He had no children of his own until he married me and inherited my lot. Now to see him, you'd think he fathered them all. And he spoils the grandchildren rotten."

"And you'd have to be foolish to turn down Hannah's invitation," James warned. "Everyone knows what a fine cook she is."

"Flattery will get you nowhere, James Hostetler," Hannah teased.

The baby popped a thumb into its mouth. James wasn't sure if it was a boy or a girl. "Not even an invitation to supper?" he said to Hannah.

She chuckled. "I was going to ask you anyway. Albert wants to ask your advice about a new shelter for the alpacas. My husband is mad for his alpacas," she explained to Mari. "We sell the fleece, and some girls in the neighborhood are learning to spin and weave the wool into yarn."

"I've heard that alpaca fleece brings a good price," Mari said. "Some of the expensive shops in Wisconsin sell alpaca hats and sweaters."

"Ya," Hannah agreed. "The fleece more than pays for the keep of the alpacas."

"Hannah will tell you that alpacas are Albert's hobby," James said, "but listen to her. She is fond of them, as well."

"I am," Hannah agreed. "Women who become skilled spinners and weavers can bring in extra money without leaving their homes. It helps our families and our community." She smiled at Mari. "Johanna teaches classes in her home one evening a week if you're interested in learning. Our Grace is picking up the skill quickly. I think you would like Grace. Her son, 'Kota, and your boy seem to have hit it off."

"Oh, my Zachary." Mari flushed. "I found his hoodie here in the pile of coats. I'm afraid he took one of the denim ones. We didn't bring a coat to contribute, so I can't—"

"Of course you can," Hannah scoffed, interrupting her. "What mother can't use another coat for her child? Look at what we have left. You're doing us a favor if you let Zachary keep it."

Mari appeared hesitant. "That's kind of you, but I wouldn't feel right about it."

"Why not?" Hannah asked. "You can always use it for him to play in. Zachary must have wanted to wear it or he wouldn't have traded it for his own."

"I suppose you're right," Mari agreed reluctantly.

"You can ask him at supper," Hannah said with a

smile. "I promise you he'll be on time for that. Because if there's one thing boys like more than playing, it's eating. 'Kota's staying to eat with us, as well as Johanna's J.J. and Jonah. They're close in age to your Zachary." She turned to go. "He'll fit in here like a pea in a pod."

Chapter Six

The family supper was at six and lasted until nearly eight o'clock. Mari enjoyed the meal, and—to her surprise—she had felt at ease with the Yoder family. She fit in as easily as, to borrow Hannah's expression, a pea in a pod. The huge kitchen had been warm and inviting; the food had been delicious. And she'd eaten far too much. What she didn't understand was how or why, exactly, she'd ended up agreeing to ride home to Sara's with James in his buggy.

"*Ach*, not to worry," Hannah had said, patting her on the forearm as they made their way to the utility room where everyone had left their coats and boots. "Everything is proper. No one will think anything of it. Your son is with you. And Johanna's J.J. and Jonah. James is dropping them off with their father. Anyway, James insisted he drive you. It's too cold out for you and Zachary to walk."

Anna pushed a wicker basket of leftovers into Mari's hand. "*Schnitz und knepp. Mam*'s dried-apple dumplings. Sara's favorite. And there's a tub of German potato salad and some roast duck with stuffing. For the

Sabbath." Anna's round face creased with good humor. "We don't cook on Sundays, and I know Sara always has company stopping in after church."

"Thank you so much," Mari said. She supposed it was a good thing she wasn't walking home. It was at least half a mile to Sara's, and both houses had long driveways.

"Sundays are a day of rest for the women, *ya*? It must have been a woman long ago who whispered that rule in her husband's ear. No work on the Sabbath." Anna chuckled as she scooped up an adorable little red-haired girl and wiped jam off her chin and planted a kiss on the child's rosy cheek. "My Rose," she said. Rose giggled and squirmed. "This one's ready for bedtime."

"How many children do you have?" Mari asked.

"There is Rose and Baby Naomi, little Mae and our Lori Ann. Then the boys Peter and Rudy. They're twins and rascals both. My dear Samuel brought me five of them from his first marriage, but I never remember which five they are." She leaned close and hugged Mari. "I'm so glad you stayed for supper, and so happy that you're staying with Cousin Sara. We all adore her, and we can see why she speaks of you so highly."

Somehow, amid the laughter and embraces Mari said her goodbyes, found her own coat and made her way to the kitchen door, where James and Zachary, now wearing identical blue denim coats, were standing amid a gaggle of boys.

Mari knew 'Kota and remembered that two of the boys belonged to Johanna, but she was at a loss as to who the others were. Zachary, however, seemed to know them all, and there was a great deal of teasing, pushing and shouted plans for some future enterprise as her son made his way out onto the back porch.

From the porch, Mari stepped outside into a brisk and bitter night. Since there were no artificial lights on the house or barn and there was no moon, the flashing battery lights on the buggy seemed startlingly bright. There was no heat inside the vehicle, but Mari knew the exterior would cut the wind. It had been a long time since she'd ridden in a buggy, and she wasn't sure whether it would bring back welcome or unwelcome memories from her childhood.

James walked around to the back and opened the door for the boys. 'Kota, J.J., Jonas and Zachary all piled in to sit on the facing backseats. James untied his horse from the hitching rail, wrapped the lines around a knob on the dash and followed Mari around to the far side of the buggy.

Mari quickened her step. The ground was frozen under her feet, and the cold seemed to leach up through the soles of her sneakers. She took hold of the buggy and started to climb up into the front seat, but she was in too much of a hurry. Her foot missed the metal bar that served as a step. She slipped and fell back, stumbling as she attempted to keep her balance.

James's strong hands closed around her waist and steadied her. "Sorry," he said. "I should have helped you up."

She looked over her shoulder at him, and he held her gaze for a split second. She remembered what Rebecca had said earlier in the day about him being interested in her. Surely Rebecca was mistaken.

"No, it was my fault," she said. His touch made her feel more off balance than her awkward attempt to climb into the buggy. Her hand tightened on the grab bar, and he boosted her up. She scrambled up into the seat. "Got it," she said. "Thanks."

He circled the front of the horse and buggy and climbed into the driver's seat. "Night!" he called to Albert and Hannah and the boys who were watching from the porch.

"This is cool," Zachary said from the darkness in the back of the buggy. One of the other kids said something in *Deitsch*, and they all giggled, including her son. Mari wondered if he'd understood what had been said or if he was just pretending he did.

A whip stood by James's left hand, but he never touched it. He made a low clicking sound, and the horse started off, first at a walk and then at a trot. The wheels made a familiar sound on the frozen ground, and the leather creaked. Mari closed her eyes and her mind returned to earlier times. Luckily, it was only good memories that came to her: memories of being cozy in the back of the family buggy with her cousins, memories of a feeling of belonging and safety.

They were halfway down the lane when James spoke. "Here. Put this over your lap. You boys warm enough back there?" he asked as he passed her a heavy woolen blanket. "Blankets under the seat."

"Wait!" Mari said, suddenly remembering how many boys had climbed into the back. "Did you forget Roman?"

James laughed. "*Ne*, Grace drove him home earlier. Mattie likes to have the boys in bed early. Grace had stopped to see if 'Kota was behaving himself. She was on the way to help her husband, John, with a late check on a horse. She's going to pick her boy up from Johanna's when they're finished."

Mari thought about how many times she'd struggled to find good child care for Zachary and the jobs and overtime she'd had to refuse because there was no one. "Must be nice to have so many willing babysitters," she said wistfully.

"Isn't that what family and friends are for?"

She glanced at James as they pulled out onto the road, surprised by how comfortable she felt with him. How at ease she'd felt all day, really. She was glad she'd come today.

"Glad you came today," James said.

She laughed out loud at the fact that the both of them had thought the same thing at the same time.

"What?" he asked, looking at her. "What's so funny?"

She shook her head and glanced away, feeling a blush creep across her cheeks. The longer she knew him, the more handsome he seemed to get. "It's nothing."

He smiled down at her. "I was just saying, I'm glad you came and I'm also glad you agreed to ride home with me, too. Otherwise, I imagine Hannah would have put some eligible unmarried girl in my buggy seat."

She lifted her brows. "Hannah's trying to fix you up? I thought Sara was the matchmaker in Seven Poplars."

"I think every woman over the age of sixteen sees herself as a bit of a matchmaker," he joked. "Half the women in my church are scheming to match me up with one of their sisters or daughters or cousins. Mattie won't stop bringing up the subject of my marriage to a nice girl. She's already picked out the bride."

Mari felt a sudden sense of disappointment and she didn't know why. "Someone in Seven Poplars?"

"*Ya.* And there's nothing wrong with the girl. I just don't know if she's the right one, and I refuse to let Mattie push me into courting someone." He shrugged. "I know it's not what's expected, but…" He sounded sheepish. "This probably sounds silly, but I'm looking for love, Mari. Real love."

Mari steadied herself as the buggy rolled over a pothole, trying to keep from brushing up against him. "Have I met this girl your sister likes for you?"

"She was at Sara's shindig last night. Lilly Hershberger. Curly blond hair. Dimples. Pretty girl. Smart. She'll make someone a good wife."

Noisy chatter came from the back of the buggy. The boys were obviously occupied with their own concerns, and Mari felt free to talk without fear of being overheard. "How does Lilly feel about you?"

James considered. "She's nice enough to me, but then Lilly's nice to everyone. My sister keeps mentioning Jane Stutzman to throw me off, but I know it's Lilly she wants me to walk out with."

He was talking to Mari as if she were a good friend. A confidant. Rebecca had obviously been mistaken when she said he'd been interested in her. James obviously saw her as a friend he could talk to. Why else would he bring up courting another girl? "So what are you going to do?"

"I don't know what to do. Do I give in to my sister? Maybe I should ask to take Lilly home from the next get-together. That's the way it usually starts here," he explained. "I ask one of her cousins or her friends if she'd be willing to ride home with me. They ask and then let me know. That way no one is embarrassed if she's not willing. If she is, I don't really have to say anything to her. It's just understood. We socialize with the rest of the group, and then when it's over, I ask her if she's ready to leave."

"So you don't take her to the frolic, like the English would. You just drive her home?"

"Exactly."

"And do you need a chaperone or do you have an open buggy? Most of the young men back in Wisconsin drove a courting buggy for their dates. In a closed buggy, like this, they'd have to have someone with them."

James shook his head as he turned the horse into a driveway on the left side of the road. "An open buggy or a chaperone isn't necessary, not if I'm just driving a girl home. If we were gone all day or went to Lancaster, maybe. But Bishop Atlee is reasonable."

"I guess our church was stricter," Mari said, liking the idea that she could bring up the life she used to have among the Amish and not feel uncomfortable. In the English world, she'd never talked about her life among the Amish.

She glanced out over the ears of James's horse; she could see the amber glow of lights, and as the horse trotted up the lane, the dim outline of Johanna's farmhouse became visible. There were no curtains at the windows, and the shades were still up. The house looked warm and inviting. James called over his shoulder, "Here we are, boys. And there's your *dat* at the door."

Home, thought Mari. As she watched the boys clamber out of the back of the buggy, she couldn't helping wishing the house was hers and Zachary's, and that she was coming home. The man in the doorway was a shadow, but he wasn't the attraction. And for an instant she was seized by the old desire to belong somewhere.

She glanced at James and felt a heaviness in her chest that she couldn't identify. A longing. She glanced back at the house.

Coming home. It was a dream that she cherished, a dream she didn't know would ever come true.

"Are you sure you won't come with us?" Ellie asked Mari the next morning. She and Sara were dressed for church, and Hiram had brought the buggy around to drive them all to Johanna and Roland's place. "You know that everyone would be happy to have you."

Mari nibbled on her lower lip in indecision. All night she'd wrestled with the dilemma of what to do about church. Sara and Ellie wanted her to go. And James had asked her to go, too. In their letters back and forth Sara had mentioned church, and relayed Bishop Atlee's invitation to attend, but Mari hadn't committed because she honestly hadn't known how she felt about it. Now that she was here, a part of her wanted to go, but part of her was afraid. What if she liked it? She'd told Zachary they would be in Seven Poplars until they got their feet back under them. They'd never really discussed staying. She hadn't even considered it... Had she?

She hesitated and then said to Sara, "I don't know. I'm not sure Zachary would want to—"

"I'll go!" Zachary declared excitedly. He was standing at the kitchen sink putting silverware in a pan of soapy water to be washed come Monday. When he turned so quickly to them, he sprayed little drops of water.

"You'll go to church?" Mari asked in surprise.

"J.J. asked me to come. He said we just have to be quiet for a little while. He said it's fun and his aunt

Anna is bringing pies." He glanced at Sara. "If Mom doesn't want to come, can I go with you, Sara?"

Sara met Mari's gaze. "I don't mean to put you on the spot. We all just think...you'd enjoy the experience."

Mari knew she shouldn't make the decision based on wanting to please her friends, or worse, to please James. Because at some point in the middle of the night, she realized she *did* want to please him. And that was dangerous. There couldn't be anything between her and James, and she needed to remember that. He was Amish and she wasn't, and even if that wasn't so, James didn't like her that way.

"Please, Mom? 'Kota won't be there. He goes to another church, but all the other guys will be there. J.J. says it's fun."

"Just to visit," Sara said softly. "To see how you feel about it."

"*Ya*, just come as a visitor," Ellie suggested as she tied her black bonnet over her *kapp*.

Mari watched Zachary dry his hands on a kitchen towel. "I can be ready in a minute, Mom. I promise I'll be good. Please?"

Mari smiled. How could she say no to her son when he was asking to go to church? And what harm would it do? It wasn't as if she had to decide on any lasting life changes today; like Sara said, she could go just to see how she felt about it.

So Mari went. And she sat on a bench with the other women, dressed in her long, navy blue skirt and scarf over her head, and she enjoyed the service far more than she anticipated.

When the final sermon and closing prayers of the

service were finished, the younger men moved the benches and set up the tables for the communal meal. The women were equally busy removing food from baskets and containers and serving. As no work was done on the Sabbath, most of the meal was cold, but thanks to Johanna's advance planning, there were kettles of thick broth and vegetable soup simmering on the stoves. As Johanna and Roland's house was not a large one, the meal was served buffet-style, with tables reserved for the oldest and youngest members of the flock, while others stood to eat or balanced plates on their laps where they sat on the remaining chairs and benches.

Other than a warm smile or brief "We're so happy to have you with us today" from friends and neighbors, no one made much of Mari's presence among them. The feeling she received was one of total acceptance, and that was far easier than being pointed out for special notice and attention. She joined the other women in the kitchen, glad for something to keep her hands busy, and grateful for the satisfying routine of breaking bread together.

Twice Zachary passed through the kitchen. Once he and one of Anna's older boys were carrying a table in from the bench wagon used to carry furniture from house to house for worship. The second time, he'd come with Johanna's Jonah to find a mop to wipe up milk that a child had spilled. Both times, he'd grinned at her but hadn't lingered to talk.

Mari helped in the kitchen until everything seemed to be done that needing doing, and then she found her coat, put it on and stepped out onto the porch. She just needed a minute to be alone and take in the day's experience. Closing the door on the laughter and talk inside, she inhaled deeply of the frosty winter air. A light dusting of snow had transformed the stables and sheds and farmyard to a Grandma Moses painting, complete with a black-and-white cow sticking her head out a barn window and a flock of sheep gathered in the shelter of a covered well. Mari sank down on the back step, hugged herself and closed her eyes.

How long she sat there thinking of the bishop's touching sermon and listening to the echoes of the hymns in her mind she couldn't say, but gradually she realized that she was no longer alone.

"It means a lot to me that you came."

Mari's eyes snapped open. "James?" Immediately she felt silly. Who else could it be? She would know that deep and tender voice anywhere. "I'm sorry—you startled me," she said quickly, trying to cover her blunder. "I was daydreaming."

"Thinking about Bishop Atlee's sermon, I hope," he teased, taking a seat beside her on the step.

She glanced at him shyly. "Actually, I was. He's not a shouter, is he? Our bishop at home—where I grew up, I mean—he shook the rafters when he preached. Your Bishop Atlee speaks softly, and everyone gets quiet and leans forward to hear him. I like that."

"He's a good man. He has a good heart and a way to remind us of God's word without raising his voice. Preacher Reuben, Addy's father, now, *he* can get loud. And his sermons are a bit long, but…" James smiled and shrugged.

"Well, I do like your Bishop Atlee. He seems a wise man."

"One you might want to speak with. If you have questions," he added hastily. "Or you want to talk."

"It's good to know," she replied. It was nice here, sitting with James, her mind at ease, not worrying about anything, just enjoying the moment. "You're a good friend."

"Am I?" He smiled again in that lazy way, and his eyes gleamed with warmth and compassion.

"You are," she said. "I've only been here a week, but it feels like it's been months. Years."

She rested a hand on the step between them. The wood was cold and slightly damp, but the overhanging roof sheltered the steps. She didn't want the moment to end. Tomorrow would bring work, decisions to be made and a need to plan, moving out of Sara's house. But for now, she didn't have to worry about any of that. She could just sit there with James and enjoy the peace of the snowy afternoon.

James smiled at her, and they sat there for a little while in silence. Then he put his hands together. "I don't know about you, but I'm hungry. I think I'm going to try some of Johanna's vegetable soup. Can I interest you in joining me?"

"Sounds good." She rose to her feet, returning his smile. And suddenly she was hungry, not only for food but for the company of the others inside. For an instant her gaze met James's, and then she nodded and followed him into the warm kitchen.

He's my friend, she thought, and her heartbeat quickened. *My friend.* The sound of it was sweet, but a part of her wished... She shook her head, pushing the unthinkable away. *It's enough*, she thought. *It would be greedy to wish for more.*

Chapter Seven

The next morning, when Mari passed the plywood partition that closed off the addition from the rest of the house, she noticed a crude window cut through the plywood. She couldn't resist peering through and when she did, she spotted James, crouched on the floor. "Good morning," she said, pleasantly surprised to see him.

He looked up from the measurements he was taking on a board and smiled at her. "Good morning."

She didn't hear the now-familiar sounds of the men working. "Here all alone today?"

"Just passing through. I sent the crew to do a quick repair on a roof for the day." He stood up. "I came by because I wanted to tell you we won't be working today. I'm going with Mattie up to Wilmington, so I can't keep an eye on Zach. Hearing tests for the twins at A. I. duPont Children's Hospital."

"Oh, my. That sounds serious."

"Probably not. Just a precaution. Their pediatrician thinks the boys are probably fine, but he suggested the testing just to be sure."

"Your sister must be worried."

"*Ya*, but Mattie worries a lot." James approached the makeshift window. "I tried to tell her that there are enough things to worry about that you are certain of. It doesn't seem right to worry about possibilities. With Roman, she was worried about his speech. That little chipmunk didn't say a word until he was two. No *mam*, no *daddi*, not even *ne*. Mattie didn't think he'd ever talk."

Mari drew closer to James.

"*Ne*, not a word," James continued. "And then one morning Mattie made oatmeal for breakfast and Roman said, '*Ne*, want pancakes. Booberry.' Mattie was so tickled that she sent me to Byler's store to buy blueberries."

Mari chuckled. "So he started talking, just like that?"

James nodded. "Started jabbering and hasn't stopped yet. Talk your ears off. Emanuel was the opposite. He talked really young. Shouts most of the time. I think the twins are used to hearing the older two make so much racket, they don't pay attention to the little beeps and bells in the hearing test."

"Let's hope that's what it is," Mari said. She knew Zachary would be disappointed to hear that there wouldn't be any working going on in the addition today. That meant he'd have to stay with Sara while she was at work.

James picked up a hammer. "Why don't you stand back and I'll open this up. Once the last plywood is on the exterior, we'll have to start using this entrance."

She moved back several steps.

In less time than she would have expected, James took

down two pieces of plywood, opening up an entrance-way that was the width of a double door. He stepped through with a flourish and a grin. "It won't be long now and Sara can start bringing in brides-to-be by the dozen."

"A dozen at a time? Goodness, that will be a full house!" Ellie came into the living room with three cups of coffee on a tray. As always, she was neat and pretty, blond hair peeking out from beneath her brilliant white *kapp* and blue eyes sparkling with energy. Ellie might have been a little person, but her personality was huge, and Mari liked her more every day.

"Big day," Ellie said, taking in the addition with a gesture. "It's actually starting to look like rooms." She offered Mari and James each a mug, indicating whose was whose. "Just the way you like it."

"Danki," James said. "Just what I need. I only got one cup this morning." He blew on the hot coffee and took a sip. "Where's Sara? She knew I planned on open-ing this doorway this morning. I thought she might want to see."

"She should be back soon. She had to make an early-morning phone call at the chair shop. Ruth's husband came to fetch her." She chuckled, looking at Mari. "A prospective client in Missouri with five unmarried daughters."

"Five?" James laughed. "Sara will find someone for every one of them. I don't know how she does it."

"Tell the truth, James," Ellie teased. "She's looking for someone special for you, too, isn't she? For all we know, Mattie could have hired Sara. I hear she's des-perate to see you married within the year." Her eyes twinkled as she glanced at Mari. "Sara never tells a cli-ent's business unless they want it told."

Mari smiled at the two of them. She liked how comfortable they were with each other. James was definitely a different kind of Amish man than the taciturn uncle and male cousins with whom she'd grown up. Even the boys she'd known in school and the neighborhood had been much more formal with girls and women they weren't related to. She found James's kind, easy manner refreshing.

James motioned to them both. "Come on in. Take a look. There's going to be a bedroom, a full bathroom and a big parlor downstairs, and three big bedrooms and another full bathroom upstairs. Plus some closets. Now that we have heat from the woodstove, the inside finishing will come together fast."

"I love all the windows," Mari said. "And the oak staircase will be lovely." Although the Sheetrock hadn't gone up yet, she could imagine what the space would look like once it was done. The wood-burning stove was a high-efficiency model made of soapstone from Sweden that was popular in Wisconsin and gave off a steady heat.

"I feel bad that I didn't let you know about not being able to keep an eye on Zach," James said to Mari. "There was a cancellation." He set down his coffee cup and picked up a broom. "The doctor's office left a message Friday on the chair shop's answering machine, but Mattie didn't get it until last night." He began to sweep. "Any progress on getting Zachary in school?"

She sighed. "The new school won't take him until they have his records, so that's what we're waiting on."

James swept the sawdust into a pile. "How long will that take?"

"I'm not sure. Honestly, it's my fault. It never occurred to me that they wouldn't take him without them," Mari said. She set down her coffee mug, picked up the dustpan and stooped to hold it for him.

"I'm sorry I can't spend time with Zach today."

"Oh, don't be silly. He'll be fine here with Sara." She glanced up at him. "Although I'm sure he'd rather spend the day working with you. Sara's liable to put him to work folding laundry or dusting furniture."

"Why don't I take him to school with me?" Ellie offered, sipping her coffee.

"I don't know," Mari said slowly.

"Can't I just go with James? I don't want to go to the Amish school."

Mari turned to see Zachary standing in the new door opening to the living room. He was wearing jeans and his pajama top. "Please don't be rude to Ellie," she said quietly. It hadn't been so much what he said as how he said it.

"Or to your mother," James said quietly.

Zachary's features lost their defiant expression, and he looked down at his feet. "Sorry," he mumbled. He looked up again. "But I don't want to go to school. I want to build stuff. Like James."

Mari emptied the dustpan into a bucket of trash. She rested the dustpan against the wall and went to her son. "Not going to school was never an option, Zachary. You know that."

He set his jaw. "It's not fair."

Ellie glanced at Mari, then at Zachary. "What I was wondering, Zach, was if you'd be willing to come give me a hand today at school? Not as a student. More of a helper."

Interest sparked in Zachary's eyes, but he averted his gaze. "Will I get paid?"

"Zachary!" Mari's eyes widened. "You don't ask people for money."

"I'll not give you a penny," Ellie said with a smile, not in the least bit fazed. "Just a big thank-you from me. James has been telling me what a help you are to his crew, and I thought I could borrow you for the day."

Zachary rubbed one stockinged foot against the other. "I don't know…"

Mari turned to James. Ellie's offer sounded like a great idea to her, but Zachary, realizing how she felt, might work against her. "What do you think, James? You think Zachary would be any help to Ellie at school?"

He nodded. "I do. He can be a big help, when he wants to be." He looked to Zachary. "I have to leave in a minute, but I could actually use your help right now moving a piece of plywood." He hooked his thumb in the direction of the far end of the addition. "You have time?"

Zachary looked to his mother, and she nodded. "Be right back," he said and ran after James.

Mari watched as Zachary followed James. Her son, she noticed, had thrust his hands into his pockets just as James had. "He has the magic touch, doesn't he?" she said to Ellie, watching them. "Zachary has taken to him. I'm constantly hearing 'James says this' or 'James does that.'"

"He's a good role model," Ellie agreed. "None better. He'll make a fine husband and a fine father."

Mari looked at her, suddenly wondering if she'd been so caught up in her own life that she'd missed something going on between Ellie and James. "Wait…" She pointed to James and then Ellie. "You and James, you're not—"

"Oh, no." Ellie laughed. "We're friends." Her smile was so wide that her dimples showed. "Good friends but just friends. We wouldn't be suited. I'm in no hurry to be wed, and I've made that clear to Sara. I'm a schoolteacher. It's a job I've wanted since I was six years old. If I marry, I have to give up the school, and I have no intention of doing that anytime soon."

Mari picked up her mug and took a sip of her coffee. "But all Amish women marry. At least most of them do. Don't you want a husband, a family?"

Ellie's features creased into a smile over the rim of her mug. "Sure I do. Someday but not yet. I'll teach a while first, get it out of my system. Then I'll let Sara find me a good man with broad shoulders and a gentle heart." She looked up at Mari. "How about you?"

"Me?"

"Would you like to be married?" Ellie asked.

Mari felt far more comfortable talking about Ellie's future than her own. "I… I don't know," she answered honestly. "I've been so busy trying to put a roof over our heads that I haven't thought much about it, I guess." She sighed. "I think I would like to be married again. To have a husband, but… I'm not sure I trust myself to choose a man I'd want to spend the rest of my life with." She pressed her lips together. "I made a pretty poor choice once."

Ellie caught Mari's hand and gave it a squeeze before letting it go. "That's why you let family or friends help you choose. Or a matchmaker." Her tone turned teasing. "Sara would make the perfect match for you—I know she would."

"You mean an Amish match?"

Ellie lifted one shoulder and let it fall. "If that's what you decide you want."

Mari found herself gazing off in the direction James had gone with Zachary, her hands wrapped around the still-warm coffee mug. "The thing is, I don't know what I want," she said softly.

"That's okay," Ellie assured her. "You don't have to know all the answers all the time. Sometimes we just need to sit back and see what God has planned for us. And *relax*."

Mari thought about the previous day, about church and how good it had felt to be there. And how she had felt a nearness to God that she hadn't felt in a very long time. So maybe Ellie was right. Maybe she did just need to relax and see what He had in store for her.

Ellie glanced down at the watch she wore attached to her apron. "*Ach.* Look at the time. I'd better get my lunch packed. And I think I'll pack one for Zachary, too. Just in case he decides to take me up on my offer."

"You don't have to do this," Mari said, on steadier ground talking about Zachary than herself.

"I want to. And he really would be a help. I know you probably don't always see it, but your Zachary is a very sweet boy."

"Who's sweet?" Zachary asked, coming toward them.

Ellie put a hand on her hip. She might have been barely as tall as Zachary, but she appeared imposing just the same. "Are you coming with me or not?"

"Yeah, I'll come," he agreed.

"*Goot*. Now, if you want anything besides egg-salad sandwiches, you'd best come give me a hand packing our lunches."

Zachary glanced at Mari and she nodded. "Go. Have a good day. And make sure you don't cause trouble. And thank you, Ellie," she called after her. "You're a lifesaver."

"Don't worry about the boy," James said quietly when Ellie and Zachary disappeared into the kitchen. "Ellie's tough. She won't let him get away with anything."

Mari sighed. "Sometimes, I don't think I'm tough enough. And other times I'm convinced that I expect too much of him." She offered James a grateful look. "I don't know what you said to convince him to go with Ellie, but thank you."

"No problem. He reminds me a lot of myself at that age."

She stood there for a minute in comfortable silence with James, then picked up his empty coffee mug to take it to the kitchen with her own. "Well, if you'll excuse me, I've got to eat something before I go to work. I hope everything goes well today. Safe travels."

"Mari?" he called after her as she turned away.

She turned back.

"I almost forgot," James said. "Mattie wanted you and Zach to come to supper tomorrow night."

"At your house?" She hesitated, wondering if she should. When she'd come to Seven Poplars, she thought it would be just a place to stop over on her way to a better life for her and Zachary. She hadn't expected to become so...*involved* in everyone's lives. She hadn't expected to make so many friends. And she couldn't help wondering if it was a mistake. If it would just make it harder when she left.

"Please come. I'll be happy to ride over and get you. It would be a big favor to me. Lilly's coming and bringing her cousin. Mattie is determined to throw Lilly and me together. And with her cousin, I'm afraid I'll be outnumbered, three to one. I need a friend to back me up."

Mari chuckled. "Well, when you put it that way." She gave a nod. "I'll be happy to have dinner with your family. I've been wanting to get to know your sister and the rest of your nephews." She liked the idea of him needing a favor from her. It was what friends did, wasn't it?

"Just be prepared for anything," he said with a grin. "And *never*, ever turn your back on Emanuel. The last time Bishop Atlee came to supper, he put a cricket in his soup."

As it turned out, Zachary didn't go with her to James's house for supper. Hannah Yoder was having some of her grandchildren over for an evening of homemade soup, corn muffins and apple pie. Zachary had explained after coming home his second day at the Amish school that they would make popcorn balls and hot cocoa the old-fashioned way at Hannah's and he didn't want to miss it. 'Kota, J.J. and Jonah would be there as well as a few boys from school. Anna's twins, who were older, were coming over to walk with him to Hannah's house and see him safely back to Sara's. Mari tried to explain to Zachary that he was expected to dinner at James's sister's house, but he couldn't be swayed. He really wanted to be with the other boys.

What could she do? She let him go.

"Don't worry about him," James said after she climbed into his buggy and explained why Zachary wasn't accepting Mattie's invitation. "Hannah will keep an eye on him. He won't get into any trouble on her watch. You want him to make friends, don't you?"

"I'm just amazed, I guess," she confessed. "In the community where I grew up, we never played with English kids. And we certainly didn't have English kids at school with us. Having worldly friends wasn't encouraged."

James snapped the leathers over his horse's back. "Walk on," he said to Jericho. And then to her, "But Zachary is a special case, isn't he? You were raised in the faith. According to our tradition, that makes your boy one of us, whether he likes it or not. In our eyes, he's no different than the other children in our community, because none of the children are baptized."

Neither of them said anything after that, and for a few minutes there was only the comforting rhythm of Jericho's ironclad hooves striking the blacktop. A few snowflakes were drifting down like confetti. The air was crisp and cold, and the quiet of the countryside surrounded them like a velvet cloak. It seemed nice to Mari to just be able to ride in silence with James. There was something comforting about their quiet companionship, something she didn't quite understand.

"So how did the twins' appointment go?" Mari asked.

"Great." He grinned. "The boys are fine. Hearing is fine. No need to see the specialist again."

"That must be a relief," she said. Then, after a few minutes, "I was thinking this morning. Do you know that no one here has asked me about Zachary's father?"

"They won't." He uttered a muffled grunt of amusement. "Well, Addy's mother, Martha, might, but no one would expect you to answer her." He cut his eyes at her. "Has anyone warned you about Martha?"

"Sort of. Gideon said if she came into the shop, let her have anything she wanted, free of charge. And not to do anything to ruffle her feathers."

"Smart man, Gideon. It's why he gets on so well with his in-laws. So long as Martha does nothing to upset Addy or cause trouble between him and his wife, Gideon lets Martha have her druthers."

"So Martha's something of a character, is she?"

She could see him grinning in the darkness. "You could say that. Gideon once told me that he suspects she eats unripe persimmons. Otherwise, she couldn't come up with all the sour things she has to say about her relatives and neighbors. But he says she has a good heart—she just doesn't realize that some of the things she says can be hurtful."

"It's hard for me to believe that there's not more than a little whispering going on about me. I'm a woman alone with a son. I know Amish. They're as human as anyone else, and, religious or not, they like to gossip."

"Some do," he admitted. "But we've all made mistakes. And Sara likes you. Gideon and Addy praise your work. And anyone who disagreed with them would have to face down Ellie. She's quite an ally."

"She is, isn't she?" Mari smiled at the thought. Ellie was probably one of the best friends she'd ever had. It seemed to have happened overnight. And so easily. She glanced at James. "What about you? Have you wondered about Zachary's father?"

James shrugged. "None of my business. I figured if

you want me to know, you'll tell me. I gather he's not really part of Zachary's life."

"No. He died." She let out a long breath, realizing that it felt good to confide in James. She waited for the old hurt to twist in the pit of her stomach, but all she felt was a twinge of sadness and regret for Ivan's passing. "He was Amish," she said. "We made a mistake and we ran away together, but he wasn't prepared for the outside world. He had a harder time adjusting than I did, maybe because he'd been baptized and he knew there was no going back."

"Mari, it's okay," James said quietly. "There's no need for you to share this with me."

She swallowed. "I don't mind. I... I'd like to tell you." He didn't say anything, just waited patiently, so she went on, "We were both young. I thought I was in love. Things just went too fast. We made some impulsive decisions. Then we had a new life to be responsible for. That was too much for Ivan. He turned wild. Fell in with the wrong crowd and did things I couldn't accept."

"He ran out on you."

She shook her head. "Not with other girls. He wasn't like that. He had a good heart in spite of his immaturity. But the things he was doing, the people he brought to our place? I didn't want them around our child."

"So you took on the full responsibility for yourself and your baby?"

"He left when I was seven months along. I tried to contact him when Zachary was born, but I think he was in jail. I never saw him again." She closed her eyes. "It was Sara who wrote to me and told me about the accident. Zachary was about four. Ivan and another ex-Amish boy were killed in a car accident. Ivan was driving."

James turned the horse off the road and onto his lane. "I'm so sorry, Mari. It must have been terrible for you."

"Terrible that I was so stupid, that I'd allowed such a thing to happen, that I'd left everything I knew and cared for behind. If Ivan and I had stayed, made confession and been forgiven, I'm afraid it would have been worse. I would have been married to a foolish boy who thought more about a good time than the fact that he was going to be a father."

"You told me that you went back to your uncle's that one time. Did you ever think about trying it again? Maybe going to some other member of the community?"

"I did." She sighed. "A couple of times...maybe a lot of times. But I was stubborn and proud. And I could never have stood in the church and said I had sinned and regretted what I'd done. My son isn't a mistake. He's good and pure and the most decent thing in my life."

"The faith can be hard to live by, but we really do believe in forgiveness. In God's mercy. In His love. I don't think anyone could expect you to deny your son's worth."

"My uncle did. He said the only way I could come back was to send him away, to let him be adopted by a married couple. Somewhere far away, where I'd never see him again. I couldn't do it. I *wouldn't* do it. So my aunt and uncle crossed my name out of the family Bible and said I was dead to them." Lights from the house grew larger as the horse approached it. She cleared her throat. "I'm sorry. I shouldn't have brought all of this up." She stared out at the gorgeous snowflakes, feeling a strange comfort in the sound of Jericho's hoofbeats. "I'm not much of a supper guest, am I?"

"We're friends, Mari, and this is what friends are for, right?" He reached over and patted her hand. "I'm honored that you'd share with me."

His hand felt good, the warmth, the security of it. But she also took note of the fact that he used the term *friends*. "I just hope we'll still be friends, now that you know what a wicked woman I am."

He laughed and took his hand from hers. "Hardly wicked. And don't worry. I don't discuss my friends' personal matters with other people, not even with my sister." He stopped the buggy at the front of the house. The door opened, and a man and woman stepped out. "There she is. Mattie," he said. "And her husband, Rupert. He surprised us by showing up this afternoon. You go in and get warm. I'm going to put Jericho in the barn."

Mari climbed down, and Mattie rushed out to meet her. "Come in—come in," she said cheerfully.

"Welcome," Rupert said.

"Everyone else is here," Mattie bubbled. "Lilly and her cousin can't wait to meet you. And the children are so excited that their *fadder* is home, they're worse than usual."

In minutes, Mari was inside and Rupert had taken her coat. Mattie, a smaller, rounder, ditzy version of James, had led her through the front room and into the kitchen and shown her to a chair at the round table. Scooping up a crying baby, she deposited him into Mari's arms and introduced Lilly Hershberger and her cousin Calvin, also a Hershberger. When James said Lilly was bringing her cousin, Mari had assumed he meant another girl. Calvin was a very tall, very slim man with yellow-blond hair.

Little William in Mari's arms was crying so loudly that she could barely hear what Lilly said to her. Trying to settle him, she rested him on her shoulder and bounced him. It felt surprisingly good to have a baby in her arms again.

"Wait," Mattie said laughing. "Let me trade you. You hold Timothy here. He never cries." She took a swaddled infant from Lilly and looked down into his face. "Or is this William?" A puzzled expression came over her face. "Lilly, did I tell you this one was Timothy?"

Lilly, who Mari had met at church Sunday, was a very pretty young woman with dimples on each cheek and curly blond hair much lighter than Ellie's. She laughed. "You said you thought he was Timothy, but you weren't sure."

Mattie met her husband's gaze.

"Don't look at me." Rupert grinned, holding up both hands. "You know I can't tell the twins apart except when you tie ribbons on their wrists."

James came in through the kitchen door just then.

"Sit there," Mattie instructed. "Next to Lilly." She handed him the baby she'd taken from Lilly. "We're not sure which one he is," she told James. "I'm going to start putting the food on the table."

"Can I help?" Lilly asked Mattie, while smiling at James.

"*Ne, ne,* you sit," Mattie said. The toddler Emanuel crawled out from under the table and seized a hold of his mother's skirts. "Emanuel. Up on your stool beside your *fadder*. Rupert, can you get him? Where did Roman get to? Roman? Come to the table." She rushed to the stove and began dishing up bowls of vegetables.

The baby that James was holding opened his eyes and began to whimper. James put him up on his shoulder and began patting the little boy on his back. The baby gave a loud burp.

Everyone laughed.

"I can see you're an old hand at that," Lilly said, clearly smitten with James. "You'll make some woman a *goot* husband."

Rupert took the now-sleeping baby from Mari's arms and laid him in a cradle near the stove and came back to retrieve the second twin from James and snuggle him in with his brother. Then Rupert put Roman on a stool beside James and went to help his wife bring the food to the table.

"Wait until you hear our news, James," Rupert said after he and Mattie had taken their seats and they had shared grace. "My mother has agreed to come live with us." He took two slices of ham and passed the platter to Calvin. "She'll be selling her house and helping us with the cost of putting up our cabin. Which means," he said, exchanging meaningful glances with his wife, "that you'll have your home to yourself much sooner than you expected."

Mari met James's gaze across the table. *See what I'm talking about*, he seemed to be saying. She had to look away to keep from laughing out loud.

Chapter Eight

For a second, James didn't respond to Rupert's obvious hint that once he and Mattie and the boys were gone, James would be free to bring home a wife. From across the table, he could see that Mari was trying not to laugh, her pretty eyes dancing. He almost started laughing himself, though he didn't know why. This wasn't a laughing matter. He really *was* going to have to sit Mattie down and have a talk with her. No underhanded or heavy-handed matchmaking his sister could do was going to sway him. He thought he'd made that clear to her. He wasn't going to marry Lilly Hershberger or any other girl just to make Mattie happy.

James grinned. "I'm in no hurry to be rid of you," he told Rupert as he threw out his hand to catch a glass of milk that Roman had just tipped over. James wasn't fast enough, but fortunately the three-year-old had already drunk most of the milk. James laid his napkin on the puddle as his sister leaped to her feet. "It's fine," he said. "I've got it."

"*Ne*, let me." Lilly offered James her napkin. "Cleaning up after children is women's work."

Calvin nodded. "Let her do it, James. It's always been that way in our family. Plenty of men's work outside, *ya*?"

"I'd say the wisest thing is that the job should go to whoever's closest," James replied. "And the one that will end up with milk in his lap if he doesn't jump fast." He chuckled, and the others joined in.

"I'm sorry," Roman murmured in *Deitsch*.

"No harm done," James assured his nephew as he eased back into his chair and reached for a bowl of green beans in front of him.

Calvin picked up a serving bowl and held it out to Mari. "Scalloped potatoes?"

"Thanks," Mari said.

Calvin took a generous helping for himself before passing the dish on to her.

As the evening meal progressed, it didn't escape James's notice that Lilly's cousin Calvin had been admiring Mari since they'd arrived. She had dressed modestly in a dark navy dress that he'd seen her wear before. She had pinned her hair up into a bun at the back of her neck, but she wore no head covering. Not that she should. It was only required for Amish, traditional Mennonites and other religious groups, not the English. But she was wearing nothing revealing, nothing that would not pass a deacon's scrutiny. She had dark stockings or tights on over her legs and sensible black sneakers. There was no reason for Calvin to keep staring at her, unless he found her attractive.

Not only had Calvin paid more attention to Mari than he should, he'd done a lot of talking to her about his plans to raise ducks commercially and for buying a farm in the area. He'd rambled on at length about the modern house he was looking for, emphasizing that he'd been single long enough and had reached an age to settle down and find a wife.

James glanced at Mari; he hoped she was having a good time. She seemed to like Mattie, and Mattie obviously liked her. If she didn't, James would have known. His sister was a force to be reckoned with and a woman who liked to have things her way, but in spite of all that he would truly miss her family when they moved into their own house. He loved Mattie and the children dearly, and he was very fond of his brother-in-law. But Mattie never let go of a notion once it had settled over her, and she always had *some* notion.

James took a bite of scalloped potatoes. Calvin was still talking about ducks. It was a shame that he and Lilly were related, because *they* would have suited each other. Calvin and Lilly both liked to talk about themselves best.

Calvin seemed nice enough, but it was obvious that he wasn't right for Mari. James seriously doubted that Calvin would understand the responsibility that came with taking a wife who had a nine-year-old son. The wrong husband and stepfather, and life would be unhappy for all three of them.

Rupert, probably tired of hearing about ducks, cleared his throat as Calvin took a breath and spoke quickly to get in before Calvin got wound up again. "How's the addition at Sara Yoder's going, James?"

"Well." He nodded, wishing he'd gotten up to get a clean napkin. He hoped he didn't have any potato in the corner of his mouth. He tried to wipe at it inconspicuously. "I opened the new rooms to the main house this morning."

"James is a wonderful carpenter." Lilly beamed at James. "He does beautiful work. Everyone says so."

"He's promised to build the cabinets for our new house," Rupert said. Emanuel chose that moment to slide from his stool to try to dive under the table. His father caught him by the back of the shirt collar and helped him firmly, but gently, back into his seat. "Sit still, son," he warned, "or no pie for you."

"Lilly brought two cherry pies for dessert," Mattie said. "Her cherry pie raised twenty-two dollars at the last school fund-raising."

Unfair, James thought. Mattie knew cherry was his favorite pie. He never could resist it, and he suspected that his sister had put Lilly up to baking it. He should have been pleased, but he felt like a shoat that was being funneled down a ramp into the slaughter room at the back of the butcher shop. Next Mattie would be talking about spring weddings.

"Muscovy or Runners. Both good layers," Calvin announced to the table and then moved on to the subject of different breeds of ducks and the possibility of finding a market for duck eggs.

James could see that Mari was trying to pay attention, but her eyes were beginning to glaze over. *So much for the duck farmer*, James thought. *He's duck soup.*

Eventually, Mattie took pity on them all and asked Mari about the different style of the women's prayer *kapps* in Wisconsin, and Mari gratefully gave her a detailed description of the head covering. Calvin, undeterred by his hostess's attempt to change the subject, asked Mari if she'd ever baked with duck eggs. When she admitted she hadn't but had seen her aunt use them in custards, Calvin seized the topic and explained why the larger duck egg was superior to a chicken's in bread pudding.

Somehow they made it through the supper, one twin's wailing, the cherry pies and a lopsided German chocolate cake that Mattie had baked, and Roman and Emanuel's protests at being sent to bed. The rest of the evening went fairly well, and James was just beginning to think about suggesting he hitch up Jericho to take Mari home. He'd had such a good time riding over with her that he'd been looking forward to the ride home all evening. Then Calvin beat him to it and offered to drive her home.

"We're going right past Sara's house," Calvin explained. "It would be foolish for James to go out when there's plenty of room in our buggy."

"It's not a problem," James said.

"Ne," Lilly chimed in. "James has to be hard at work at Sara's early tomorrow morning. We're glad to see her home. I insist."

A few minutes later, James followed Mari and the others out the door, amid a flurry of thank-yous and "You must come again soon," and helped her into the back of Lilly's father's family buggy.

"I hope you enjoyed yourself," James said to Mari as he found the lap robe under the seat and handed it to her. "I warned you that it would be chaotic."

"I had a great time." She smiled down at him. "The children are adorable."

"Even Emanuel?"

She chuckled. "Especially Emanuel."

James wanted to say something about the fact that he was sorry he wasn't going to get to drive her home, but he didn't know how to say it, so he just said good-bye. "I guess I'll see you tomorrow."

She smiled at him again, and James wished the evening wasn't over.

James returned to the kitchen to find Mattie settled down in her rocker near the stove, feeding the babies. He grabbed a clean dishcloth and started wiping off the table.

"So, James," Rupert said, a broom in hand. "Are you planning on asking Lilly to walk out with you?"

Mattie sighed. "Men." She rolled her eyes. "Not a clue. Didn't you see them together?" she asked her husband, though not unkindly. "I had high hopes, but James is as flighty as a yearling steer in fly season. He's not interested in courting Lilly."

Rupert paused to look at James. "I thought you were tired of the bachelor life."

"Lilly would make any man a fine wife." James leaned on the table to look back at his brother-in-law. "I like her, but that's not enough to make me choose her as my partner for life."

Mattie sniffed. "It's Mari Troyer who's caught his eye."

James glanced at her.

"Don't give me that innocent look of yours," she cautioned. "I saw the looks you two were giving each other across the table...*and* the dirty looks you were giving Calvin."

"I don't know what you're talking about." James wiped down the chair Roman had been sitting in, catching the crumbs with his hand. "But someone needs to tell that boy that there's only so much duck information a person can handle in one sitting."

"Don't try to skitter away from the subject," Mattie warned. "You like Sara's Mari."

"Of course I like her." James carried his handful of crumbs to the trashcan. "She's my friend."

"Just a friend?" Mattie asked. "The way you were watching her all evening? I'm afraid that it's more than just friendship there, brother."

"Oooh, getting warm in here." Rupert propped his broom against the wall. "Let me have those babies, Mattie, if they're asleep. I'll just carry them upstairs and tuck them into their cribs." Gathering up both babies, he gave James a glad-it's-not-me-in-hot-water look and made himself scarce.

"Don't you like her, Mattie?" James said quietly after his brother-in-law had left the room. "It seemed to me as if you two got on fine tonight."

Mattie rose and went to him, placing both hands on his shoulders. "Of course I like her. She's a good person. But you seem to be forgetting that Mari's not Amish. She walked away from the church."

"So did I, but I came back." He studied her face; she had their mother's eyes. "You saw Mari in church this week. Sara thinks she'll return to the faith. And so do I."

Mattie squeezed his arm. "You know how much I've always loved you and wanted what was best for you."

"I do." His voice came out thick and full of emotion. He loved Mattie, too, deeply, and he never wanted to hurt her. But sometimes they didn't see eye to eye, and he refused to give in to her just because he loved her. "And I gave you my word that I was back for good. I won't marry outside the church. You don't need to worry about that."

"How can I not worry?"

"I'm not the little brother who needs you to care for his skinned knees anymore. I'm a grown man, and I can take care of myself."

"It's not your knees I'm worried about. I'm afraid you're going to get your heart broken." She gazed up at him, her eyes teary in the lamplight. "Even if Mari does come back and accept baptism, how will you know that she won't leave again? Leave and take your children with her? Then you'd have to go, wouldn't you?"

"You have to trust me, Mattie. I know you mean well, but I'll pick my own wife when I'm good and ready."

"But not an Englisher. Promise me that," she begged. "And promise me that you'll think about what you're doing with Mari, the risk you're taking. You know, when I started to come of courting age, our *dat* warned me never to walk out with a man I wouldn't marry. I think it was wise advice."

"I'm not walking out with Mari. Mattie, you're the one who told me to invite her to supper. Tonight was just a supper with friends."

She gave him a look that made it clear she wasn't buying it. "Promise me," she repeated.

He exhaled. "I promise you I'll always take into consideration what you have to say. I value your advice, but in the end, the decision is mine. And you can rest your mind on one thing. I'd never consider an English girl."

"Have it your way," she said, releasing him and retracing her steps to the rocking chair. "Stay friends with Mari. And I'm not saying there's anything wrong with that. But find yourself a good Amish girl, someone who's never strayed from the fold, someone who will help you put down roots in this community. Marriage isn't just between a man and a woman. When you make your wedding vows, you marry a family, a community, and you make a commitment to your future children and grandchildren." Her gaze locked with his, and he felt the strength of her conviction. "Mari Troyer is a good woman and a good mother, but I don't want her as a sister-in-law. You think about that, James. And if you're wise, you won't let this *friendship* of yours go any deeper."

When business picked up late in the afternoon at the butcher shop, Mari left her desk in the office and went out to help wait on customers. She didn't mind the change of pace. She'd been working on orders and taking phone calls all day. Wrapping meat and ringing up sales was easy. She was just checking out a nice English woman with a toddler when she spotted James coming through the front door. Just catching sight of him made her smile. "Hi," she called to him. She handed the customer her receipt and her bag. "Thanks, come again," she told the customer.

James waited for the woman to walk away and then came to the counter. "I'd like four center-cut pork chops and two pounds of bacon, please," he said. "Mattie wants thick, lean chops."

"Sure." He was grinning, though why she didn't know. She couldn't help but grin back. "I'll be happy to get that for you. How was your day?" she asked as she pulled on clear plastic gloves and opened the meat display.

"Good. Good." He nodded. "Sara's addition is coming along. We'll be done before you know it. How about you?" He watched her place the chops on a piece of butcher paper on the scale. "Good day?"

"Great." And having him pop in like this made it better, but she didn't say that, of course.

He glanced at the big clock on the wall. "Don't you usually leave around this time?"

"About this time," she told him as she wrapped up his chops.

He nodded and slid his hands into his pockets. "Business good?"

"Picking up every day," she answered.

"Seems like you've settled in fast. Thomas mentioned to me that Gideon told him you were a great worker." He picked up a box of crackers from beside the register, looked at them and put them back. "I was wondering if you'd like a ride home to Sara's."

She looked up from the register at him in surprise. "That's nice of you to offer. I was going to take the van. They leave in half an hour." She gave him the total of his purchase.

James slid bills across the counter. "I know you can ride home with them, but I'm saying you should ride home with me. I have to stop at Byler's store, for Mattie. And Sara wants half-and-half for something, so I have to go by there on the way home anyway." He reached for the pork chops. "I figured you might like to go. You said you were getting your first paycheck."

"I don't know." She chewed on her lower lip. "Zachary might wonder where I am if I'm late," she said, although she really did want to go. To pick up a few things, of course. Not just so she could ride home with James.

"Funny you should say that because Sara said to

remind you that Zachary and Ellie would be late this afternoon. Something about an errand at Johanna and Roland's. So you don't need to worry about him."

"You told Sara you were picking me up?" she asked.

"I told her I was going to ask you."

Mari stood there, not sure what to do. She did want to buy deodorant and shampoo, and this would be the perfect opportunity. If she went with James now, she wouldn't have to try to catch a ride into town with someone in their neighborhood tomorrow.

Byler's was a Mennonite country store that had started out as a discount grocery and had grown to include kitchen goods, fruits and vegetables, frozen food and cold cuts. It was as large as many English chain groceries, and the prices were reasonable. Best of all, it was only two miles from the butcher shop.

James tucked the packet of chops under his arm. "Come on. You know you want to go. What's wrong with taking a ride from a friend?"

"Nothing, I suppose. Not a thing wrong with it," she said when she met his reassuring gaze. "But I have something I have to finish in the office. Can you wait ten minutes?"

He smiled. "And not five minutes longer."

She grimaced as she pulled off her apron and hurried toward the back to close out the last order of the day. "You've found my weakness," she called over her shoulder. "I tend to run late."

"Not for Byler's tonight, we don't. You run late and you'll miss your chance for me to buy you one of the best ice-cream cones in the county. They close at six o'clock in the winter, and it will be mobbed the last half hour."

They arrived at the store a little after five o'clock, and it was packed. The English shoppers, mostly senior citizens, outnumbered the Amish three to one, but she saw plenty of Mennonite and Amish families shopping. There was even a young Amish father shopping alone with an adorable little pigtailed girl in his cart and a four-year-old boy walking beside him. The girl wore a blue dress, black stockings and black boots, and a tight-fitting white baby *kapp*, while the boy was an exact copy of his father. Mari couldn't resist, and she waved and said hi in *Deitsch*. Shyly, the small boy hid his face in his father's pant leg, but his sister smiled and waved back.

James gave her a quick tour of the store; then they went their separate ways so he could pick up the spices and the raw sugar Mattie had requested. Mari grabbed what she needed and met him at the registers. By the time she got there, he had just paid for his items.

"I'll run these out and get our ice-cream cones— before they close," he told her.

"It's all right—we don't need ice cream. We'll spoil our supper," she teased, pushing her little cart forward in the checkout line.

"Never. It's like an appetizer," he insisted, tugging the brim of his black hat down. "And I already paid for them. Meet you right here in a couple of minutes." He backed away from her toward the door. "What flavor would you like?"

"Surprise me," she replied and shook her head, laughing as he hurried out the door.

A short time later James met her at the front of the store with two huge ice-cream cones. "That's more ice cream than we can possibly eat," she told him, unable to stop smiling.

"Bet it's not. Chocolate mint chip or butter pecan?" He held out the cones for her to choose.

It took her a second to decide because she loved both. "Chocolate mint chip," she declared.

He handed her the cone. "Want me to take your bag?"

"No, I'm fine." She found the ice cream to be every bit as creamy and delicious as he had described it on the way over.

"We can sit at one of those picnic tables," he told her, leading the way to a small eating area that was set up at the front of the store.

"That's fine." She followed him.

"And then we'll head home."

"Thank you," she said between bites when they were seated across from each other at one of the tables. "This is delicious." She was so glad that she'd come. Being with James was fun, and she found him so easy to talk to. She felt as if she could be herself with him. He made her comfortable with who she was, the good and the bad. "Be certain to tell Mattie how much I enjoyed her meal," she reminded him.

"I will. You know, she really likes you," he said. Then it seemed as if he wanted to say something more.

She took another lick of her cone and reached for the napkin holder in the center of the table. "But?"

He exhaled. "I probably shouldn't even say this but... I feel like we can tell each other anything. I mean, I know we haven't known each other long, but—"

"But I get you. And you get me," she dared, not knowing what made her so bold to say such a thing.

After all, they really *hadn't* known each other long. And what's more, their friendship wasn't typical. Amish men weren't usually friends with English women. They didn't shop or sit down to eat ice cream together. She passed him one of the napkins. "Tell me what Mattie said."

He exhaled. "She's worried that you could be a bad influence on me. Actually, I think she's worried that we'll be a bad influence on each other."

Mari frowned. "How?"

"I don't know. I'm not saying it makes sense. It's just what she said. She thinks that my being friends with you will make me want to return to the English world."

Mari thought for a moment before responding. It was upsetting to think that Mattie was concerned about her friendship with James, but she was glad he had told her. She could tell that it had been weighing on his mind. "Do I make you wish you were English again?"

He gave her a little smirk that made him look younger than he was. "Not hardly. I've had my fill of pickup trucks and wide-screen TVs. I belong in these clothes." He indicated his hat and denim coat. "Driving that buggy." He pointed to Jericho waiting patiently in the parking lot.

"James, I don't want to cause trouble between you and your sister," she said. "And it's certainly not my intention to convince anyone to leave Seven Poplars. I mean, I'm the one who came here from the big, bad world, and I have to admit, the change has been really nice. I like my life at Sara's and I like Seven Poplars." Certainly better than the life she'd had in Wisconsin.

"I told Mattie that."

She thought again for a minute. She was down to

the crunchy cone now. "You said she thought we were a bad influence on each other, but you're definitely not a bad influence on me." She hesitated. "You know, I think I went to church Sunday mostly because *you* wanted me to." She smiled. "But I'm so glad I did."

"I'm glad you came, too. Now, I don't want you to turn into a worrier. I told my sister that I choose my own friends and I meant it."

Mari picked up her napkins and wiped her mouth, trying to ignore the small twinge of disappointment. James had used that word again. *Friend.*

"James?" A tall, angular woman in a black dress and bonnet walked out of the checkout area. "I'm surprised to see you here at this time of the day. Cut out early, didn't you?" She was speaking to James but staring at Mari.

Mari recognized her as Gideon's mother-in-law, Martha.

"And Mari Troyer. I'm surprised to see you here." Her voice was as grating as fingernails across a blackboard. "Is Sara with you?"

Mari could tell by the woman's tone of voice that she knew very well that Sara wasn't with them. "She's not," Mari managed.

"Ellie?" Martha demanded.

James shook his head, finishing up his ice-cream cone and wiping his mouth with one of the napkins Mari had given him. "Afraid not."

Martha pursed her lips. "So you're here together? Unchaperoned?"

James chuckled. "Guilty, Martha."

Martha frowned, unfazed by James's charm. "You haven't been in Seven Poplars long, Mari," she said, turning to her again. "Not long at all. And I don't know what kind of rules you had in Wisconsin. But here, it's best if a young woman doesn't give others a reason to question her behavior." She glanced back at James. "Unless the two of you are courting and I haven't heard?"

She raised her eyebrows at James, and Mari was surprised when he didn't answer.

"Well," Martha huffed. Then she cleared her throat. "You know, Mari, some may think I'm a gossip, but I'm not. I'm just a woman who likes to speak her mind. So I'm coming right out and asking." She looked at James again. "Are you two walking out together?"

James got to his feet. "We're just buying groceries, Martha. I was coming to Byler's, and Mari needed a ride. The most scandalous thing we've done is eat ice cream before supper. But thank you for your concern." He balled up his napkin and tossed it in a trash can.

Martha drew herself up to her full height, and her eyes narrowed. "No need to get snippy with me, young man. I'm simply trying to point out to Mari that it's easy for a girl to be talked about. And Seven Poplars is not Hollywood."

Not sure what to say, Mari said nothing. She didn't want to get James in trouble. Martha held up her hand as if making a proclamation. "Enough said. Next time you'll know better. I'm surprised that Sara didn't have the sense to explain these things to you, Mari. But James certainly should have known better." She turned her censorious gaze on him. Then with a final sniff, Martha grabbed her shopping cart and walked out the doors to the parking lot.

Mari looked at James and saw that he was pressing

his lips tightly together to keep from laughing out loud. "Shh," she warned. Then she giggled. It really wasn't funny. Martha would tell everyone she knew, and probably people she didn't, that she had seen Mari and James having ice cream alone together. But seeing James laugh made it hard for Mari not to laugh.

Her groceries in one arm, he tugged on her coat sleeve and led her outside and around to where they'd left Jericho and the buggy parked.

"Stop laughing," she told him under his breath. "She'll tell Mattie, and then you'll be in trouble."

"I won't be in trouble." He took her hand to help her up into the buggy and leaned close to whisper in her ear. "But *you* certainly will be," he teased.

She sat down on the buggy seat, but he was still holding her hand. He leaned in so no one walking past them could overhear. "You're the one leading me astray, remember? First you sold me pork chops, unchaperoned, and now this."

Mari looked down at James and was so overwhelmed by the feel of his hand and his closeness that she suddenly felt dizzy. And happy. And guilty and scared and bold, all at the same time. "Get in the buggy," she whispered. "Before she comes back and insists on riding home with us."

He took one look at her and burst into laughter. She pushed him away playfully. "Get in the buggy."

He put her bag in the back and climbed up onto the seat beside her. As he picked up the reins, he leaned close to Mari and said, with a straight face, "Seven Poplars is *not* Hollywood."

And then they both burst out laughing.

"Seriously," James said as he guided his horse out

onto the roadway. "Don't let her upset you. Like I told you before, it may not seem like it, but Martha means well. And until you've been properly chastised by Martha, you haven't really become part of the community."

Mari wiped away the tears of laughter from the corners of her eyes, liking the idea that he now considered her part of his community. "Are we really supposed to be chaperoned to ride to the grocery store?"

"Only in Martha's mind. Neither of us is sixteen. And you're not even Amish. Of course if we *were* courting—" he looked at her "—I suppose we'd have to follow at least some of the rules."

Mari suddenly felt self-conscious and pretended to be absorbed in rewrapping her wool scarf. She couldn't tell if James was being serious or not. And, worse, she didn't know which she preferred.

Chapter Nine

When Mari climbed out of the van Friday afternoon, she was so excited that she didn't mind splashing through the half thawed, half frozen muddy yard to reach Sara's back door. She removed her coat and boots, left them in the utility room and hurried to find her son.

Ellie and Sara were in the kitchen making supper, and she gave them a hearty greeting. "Good news on the school situation," Mari announced. "I can't believe it. Zachary's records finally arrived. The school called me at work. I can take him in Monday morning and enroll him."

"I know you're relieved." Ellie's enthusiasm was lackluster. "But I'll miss him, and I know his friends at our school will miss having him there." She went back to peeling potatoes.

Sara laid down her rolling pin, brushed flour off her apron and offered a polite smile. "Good news, indeed."

"Where is Zachary?" Mari glanced around. The sound of hammering came from the other end of the house, and she knew the answer. "I suppose he's trailing James around again?"

"Lots done today," Sara observed. "The plumber hooked up the water in the bathrooms, and James's crew is going to start on the drywall on Monday. It won't be long before they'll be moving on to a new job. I'll be glad to have it done, but I have to admit, I'll miss the crew."

"I think we all will," Ellie said, eyeing Mari, a certain sparkle in her eyes. "Some more than others."

Mari looked at Sara and then back at Ellie. "You mean me?"

Now Ellie was grinning. "Guess who stopped by during lunch today to drop off a donation of spiral notebooks and pencils?"

Mari shook her head, but she could feel her cheeks getting warm. She had a feeling she knew what Ellie was going to say.

"Martha Coblenz."

"That was nice of Martha to donate to the school," Mari said.

"Sure was." Ellie turned to her, a potato in one hand, a peeler in the other. "She told me a crazy story about running into a couple at Byler's store. A couple who she felt should have had a chaperone. She took me to task for not being there."

"Why would Martha—" Mari clasped her hands together. "I'm sorry, Ellie. I didn't mean to get you into trouble. James and I, we just…" She stopped and started again. She knew her entire face must be bright red. She really didn't feel as if she and James had done anything wrong. It wasn't as if they had been holding hands. Then she remembered him helping her into his buggy and holding her hand as he'd whispered to her and her face got warmer. "He gave me a ride home and his sister needed sugar and—"

Ellie laughed. "It's all right, Mari. I'm just teasing you. Actually, I'm pleased you and James caught Martha's attention. She brought me so many new pencils that every student in the school got two."

"Poor Martha." Sara sighed. "Now that Addy's happily married and out of the house, she's looking for people to fuss with."

Mari looked to Sara. "We didn't do anything wrong, did we?"

Sara shook her head. "You're not teenagers. So long as you behave yourselves and don't do anything couples have been known to do, there's nothing wrong with riding with James in his buggy or getting me half-and-half at Byler's." She took a sharp knife and began to cut the dough on the table into long strips. "We do like to keep an eye on young folks courting, just because… Well, as my grandmother used to say, little lambs will play. But both of you are nearly thirty. I think you know what's acceptable and what's not."

Mari lowered her voice, afraid James or one of the other men might hear her. "But we're not a couple."

"Of course you're not, dear." Sara didn't look up. "You should probably tell Zachary the good news and let him know it will soon be time to wash up for supper."

"Tell Zach we're having one of his favorites, chicken and slippery dumplings," Ellie called after her.

Mari found her son halfway up the staircase of the new addition, holding a can of nails for James. "Hi there," she said. She leaned down and kissed the crown of his head.

Zachary made a face, but his protest was only half-hearted. "Aw, Mom. Not in front of the guys."

James turned his face away, but she caught the hint of a mischievous smile. "You look as though you had a good day," he said. His words came out slightly garbled because he was holding several finishing nails between his lips. He set one in place and drove it home with several well-placed blows of his hammer. Above the step where he was working, unfinished planks had provided a way up and down for the workmen, but now that the addition was almost done, he was replacing them with furniture-grade oak.

"I did have a good day." Mari looked up at him. "The stair treads are beautiful. Almost too pretty to walk on."

"I was fortunate that Sara had some oak left over from her hospitality barn project. Wide boards. They're hard to find anymore because most of the old growth timber was cut years ago. But the grain on this is beautiful." He ran his fingertips lovingly across the surface of the stair tread he was nailing in place. Without being asked, Zachary held out three more nails. James nailed them in place, one after another. Then he stood and rubbed the small of his back. "We had a good day, too, didn't we, Zachary? After he got home from school, he did some sweeping for me and now we've got this staircase project."

"See what James is doing, Mom? He's sinking the nails, and he'll fill the holes with wooden pegs. And when you stain and varnish it, they'll show up in a different shade and look cool."

"I see," she said. "I'm sure they will. And I have something cool to share with you, too. Your school records have arrived, so Monday morning you start at the new elementary school."

Zachary frowned. "Mom, we need to talk." He looked down. "I've thought about it and… I don't want to go to that school."

"Zachary, we talked about this. You have to go to school. You're too young to join James's work crew."

He glanced at James. "Yeah, James and me, we talked about that. I understand I have to go to school. I just don't want to go to that English school. I like Ellie's school. I don't want to leave my friends."

"Zachary." She exhaled in exasperation. He was wearing a blue hand-sewn Amish shirt and suspenders, much like the clothing that James and the other men were wearing. First he'd starting wearing Amish pants because they had better pockets. Then James had bought him a pair of work boots, just for on the job. Now Mari couldn't remember the last time she saw him in one of his own sweatshirts. She wasn't even sure where he'd gotten the pale green long-sleeved shirt he was wearing today. Sara, maybe. "I don't know what to say."

James began to hammer another nail down.

Zachary dropped down a step. "Mom, please? I really like Ellie's school."

She leaned on the rail. Never in a hundred years had she been expecting *this* conversation. A week ago, he hadn't wanted to go with Ellie for the day. Now he was talking about attending full-time? "Honey, you can't really go there. It's just for Amish children. Parents pay for their children to attend."

"But Ellie's the best teacher I've ever had." Zachary looked up at her with hopeful eyes. "I really like it there. Ellie explains stuff when I don't understand it. And the fourth grade is doing harder math than I was doing at my old school. It's fun. And I got a B on my test today."

"You took a test?"

Zachary nodded. "Yeah, and I got a B and I even helped Dora. She's in the fourth grade, but she's only doing third-grade multiplication. Ellie says it's okay if I help her with something if she needs it. Ellie says kids learn at different speeds."

"So you haven't just been helping Ellie?" she asked. "You're actually doing the lessons?"

"You're not mad, are you?" Zachary looked down at his dirty palms. "I didn't tell you because I thought you'd be mad. It's pretty neat, for school. At lunchtime we play games and do stuff together. And I get to carry in wood for the stove. They've got a woodstove right in the middle of the school. When you come in and your feet are cold, you prop them up on the railing and it's really toasty. And Ellie has cocoa on the stove. Anybody can have it. But only one cup a day because too much chocolate is bad for your teeth."

Mari sighed, glancing over her shoulder. "It sounds as if Ellie and I need to have a talk."

"Maybe you could ask her if I could stay?" Zachary begged. "It's so much fun there. The guys are neat, and nobody makes fun of anyone."

Mari pushed back a lock of hair that had fallen from her scarf. This was one of the hardest things about being a single parent—trying to do what was right with no one to talk to. She glanced up at James, who was now sitting on a step looking down at her. "What do *you* think?" she asked.

"It sounds to me as though you and Ellie do need to talk," James said. "And she would need to discuss it with the school board, but… Zach does seem to be doing well."

"You don't think I should send him to the school in Dover?"

"I think you should follow your instincts," James said softly, holding her gaze.

For a moment, Mari felt as if it were just the two of them alone. Just her and James. They weren't touching; he was four steps above her. But she felt as though he were resting his hand on her shoulder.

"My instincts," she repeated softly.

Zachary looked at her, then at James and then at her again. "So, it's okay? I can stay at Ellie's school?" he asked.

"I'll think about it. Maybe…" She lowered her gaze to her son again. "Maybe it might be the best thing, letting you finish out the year with Ellie. And then we can talk about starting at the public school in the fall. Especially if you can keep up with the fourth-grade work and be able to go on to the fifth in September. What do you think, James?" She looked up at him again.

"I think it might be a good solution," he replied, gathering his hammer and the can of nails. "I guess I'd best be getting on home. Mattie will have supper started, and I've got the cow to milk before we eat."

"Can I go tell Ellie?" Zachary asked her. "Not that I can definitely go to her school, but that you're going to think about it? I know she'd be happy to talk to you."

Mari sighed and smiled. He looked so happy. "Go talk to her, but the three of us are going to sit down together and have a talk, too."

She and James watched Zachary bound down the stairs and out of the addition into the main house.

Mari turned back to James, who was still standing on the staircase above her. "Thank you, James."

"No need to thank me," he assured her, coming down the steps. "It's always good when people who care about each other can talk things out."

She headed down ahead of him.

"Are you going to the birthday supper for Hannah's mother-in-law tomorrow?" James asked.

"Sure am. Anna stopped by the butcher shop and invited us all to come. I don't think Sara can make it, but Zachary and I can walk."

"Thomas said he's taking Ellie. Mattie and I and the kids are going. We'd be glad to have you and Zachary ride with us."

"Are you certain we'll all fit in your buggy?"

He grinned. "The more the merrier. Besides, if you come along, I won't have to drive with one of the twins in my lap. You can hold him."

She laughed with him. "I'd be glad to come with you," she said. And then she just stood there for a moment looking at him. *He's the best friend I've ever had*, she thought. *Better than any man I've ever known. I trust him to do what he says he'll do. And he's been so good to Zachary.*

"Good," James said.

She started to turn away, then looked back at him. "Oh, I almost forgot. Guess who paid Ellie a visit today to tell her about her trip to Byler's Wednesday?"

"Martha." James chuckled. "I knew it."

"James, she thinks we're dating. One of us is going to have to say something to her."

He hung his hammer on his belt. "Why's that?"

"Because she's going to tell people we're…you know. Courting. And—"

"And we're not," he said softly. Then he met her gaze and held it.

It was a strange moment, standing there in the addition, alone, her looking at him, him looking at her. As if there was something else to be said, but she couldn't think what it could be.

"See you tomorrow, James," she finally said, making herself walk away.

"See you tomorrow, Mari."

Sara sat at the desk in her office off the living room going over the letter of a young woman from an Amish community in Wisconsin. Sara prided herself on making marriages in difficult cases, but this one in particular was going to be a challenge. The contact had come from the girl herself, which was unusual since she lived with her parents. Usually a close member of the family initiated the arrangements. In this case, there was a serious medical problem, one that might be inherited by future children.

The obvious solution would be to arrange a union with an older widower who already had children. But the writer stated plainly that she wanted to have a child and would only consider a husband who accepted the possibility of a child with health issues and was willing to leave the outcome to the Lord. Sara wasn't sure how she felt about that. Was the young woman being selfish and irresponsible? It was an issue Sara felt she needed to pray on and maybe seek the advice of Bishop Atlee or possibly their preacher, Caleb Wittner.

A hesitant knock sounded at the door. Sara folded the letter, put it back into the envelope and slid it into her desk drawer. *"Ya?"*

The door opened slowly, and Sara saw Zachary standing there. "Ready, are you?" she asked.

The evening before, he'd asked her for an appointment. "It's important," the boy had whispered. "Don't tell anybody. It's *confidential*."

"Well, come in," she said, her curiosity piqued. "And close the door behind you."

Zachary's features were set in a serious expression, and for a moment she wondered if he'd gotten into some mischief and was trying to fess up. But as his attire registered, Sara realized that it was something else. Zachary had slicked back his unruly hair and put on the Sunday go-to-meeting white shirt and black coat she'd dug up for him. He was still wearing jeans, but she remembered that Mari had thrown Zachary's good pants into the wash that morning on her way out the door to do her Saturday-morning shift. The boy was carrying a quart canning jar with what appeared to be dollar bills stuffed inside.

Sara sat up straight, swallowed her amusement at his attempt to appear manly and regarded him with as much dignity as she could muster. "This must be important," she said. "Would you like to sit down?"

Zachary glanced around uneasily, then nodded and slid onto a straight-backed chair directly across from her desk. His lips were pinched tightly together; his eyes fixed on her.

After a moment of silence, she said, "So you have something you want to talk to me about?"

He nodded.

She waited.

"I want to hire you to…make a match," he said, all in a rush.

"I see." She nodded gravely. "Don't you think you're a little young yet to be thinking about finding a wife?" She liked Zachary and she didn't want to hurt his feelings, but it was all she could do to hide her amusement.

He shook his head. "Not for me. For my mom." He held out the canning jar. Cobwebs clung to the outside, and Sara guessed that he'd just retrieved his stash from the barn loft or the recesses of the cellar. "I can pay your fee. I've got money." He pressed his lips together. "It's mine. What I earned working for James. I wanted to help pay for a car, but…" He straightened his thin shoulders. "I don't think we need a car. We get along just fine here without one."

"So you're here to discuss a business arrangement?"

"Yeah, I mean…*ya*." Zachary nodded again. "I'm not sure how this is supposed to work." He placed his money jar on the floor by his left shoe. "This Amish stuff is pretty new to me."

"Well, when talking with a client, I usually start by having some refreshments. Would you like hot chocolate?"

"What are you drinking?" He glanced at her mug.

"Coffee."

"Then I'll have coffee, if it's okay."

"If you like." She held out her cup. "There's a pot on the stove in the kitchen. Refill mine and pour one for yourself. Lots of milk."

In no time, Zachary was back with two cups of coffee on a little wooden tray they kept hanging on the wall in the kitchen for just that purpose. "I put lots of milk and sugar in mine," he explained as he set the tray down on her desk and picked up his mug.

She motioned for him to sit. "Tell me about this match you'd like me to arrange."

"Everybody says that you're the best, and...and you're the only matchmaker I know." Zachary glanced down at the jar. "I don't know how much it costs, but I've got twenty-one dollars and eleven cents. If it's more than that, I can pay some every week."

"Let's set the finances aside for a moment." She removed her glasses and used the corner of her apron to clean them, a ploy she often used to give herself a moment to think of what to say. "Who would you like me to find a match for?"

"My mom," he blurted. "So we can stay here."

"I see." Sara reached for her coffee mug. "Have you thought this over carefully? You haven't been here at Seven Poplars all that long. And you're really just getting settled in our school. Are you certain you can be happy here?"

"Yeah. I think so. I mean..." He frowned. "I like Ellie and the school, and the kids are cool. Especially Jonah and 'Kota and J.J."

"You told your mother that you wanted to go back to Wisconsin. Have you changed your mind about that?"

"Yeah." He hesitated. "I like the stuff we do here. Working. And the horses. And we all play games at recess. Nobody pushes you around."

"Did people push you around at your old school?"

Zachary grimaced. "I'm not as big as some kids my age. At our old school, some guys thought they were all that. They took my coat, the one I told Mom disappeared. One of the older kids ran away with it."

"But you didn't tell a teacher?"

He shook his head. "Being a squealer could get you hurt. Everybody would gang up on you on the playground. I was scared of getting beat up."

"I'm sorry to hear that," Sara said. "But you should have told your mother."

"I guess."

"Does this happen at Ellie's school?"

He shook his head again. "No way. The bigger guys help you out. Peter showed me how to hold a baseball bat, and I got a hit. We were all playing ball after school yesterday." He wrinkled his nose. "It was a little slushy, but we didn't care."

She smiled. "I'm glad that this school is working out for you, Zachary. Amish don't believe in fighting. We don't believe in violence at all."

"That's what Mom said. She says Amish people are…gentle. It's why I want you to get a husband for her. So we can stay here."

Sara pursed her lips. She'd not expected this. But Zachary seemed serious, and she didn't want to hurt his feelings. "You understand that the matches I make are all for Old Order Amish couples," she said carefully. "Do you think your mother would want to marry an Amish man?"

"Maybe she would. I *think* she would. If we found her a good one. She likes it here."

Sara nodded thoughtfully. "And if I find her an Amish husband, she'd have to join the church herself. She'd be Amish. And so would you. How would you feel about that?"

"Me, too?"

Sara nodded again. "You wouldn't be expected to

join the church now. That's for adults. But you would have to go to church regularly. Can you do that?"

Zachary slid forward on his chair and balanced his mug on one knee. "It was okay. I think I could." He took a sip of the coffee and puckered his mouth.

"Maybe a little more milk," Sara suggested, pointing to a small pitcher on the corner of her desk. "And another sugar lump. It's a big cup."

"Thanks." Zachary carried his cup to the table and helped himself to both. He used the spoon to stir it and tasted the coffee.

"Better?" Sara asked. She'd never seen Zachary drink coffee before.

Zachary dropped in another cube of sugar. "This is good," he said. And then he added more milk.

"So you're okay with having an Amish father?" she asked.

"Yeah." He grimaced. "I hate moving to new schools. In second grade we moved twice. It's weird, you know. You don't know anybody. If Mom gets married to an Amish man, I can just stay at Ellie's school."

"I imagine moving has been hard on you."

He nodded. "Sometimes. But it's tough for my mom, too. Getting up the rent and money for electric." He offered a little smile. "No electricity bill if you're Amish."

Sara toyed with her glasses, rubbing a finger along the rim. "And how does your mom like the idea of an Amish husband? Do you think she'd agree if I found her a good match?"

"Oh, I've already picked out the guy for her. I just need you to convince her to marry him."

Sara raised her eyebrows. She had liked Zachary

the night he'd arrived, cranky and tired, but with every passing day, she liked him more. It was almost as if he was becoming the grandson she didn't have. "So this is all your idea?"

He nodded.

"And you haven't talked with your mother about a husband?"

He shook his head.

"I see." She didn't see at all. Lilly's cousin's mother had made an inquiry about Mari on behalf of her son Calvin, but the woman had quickly cooled when Sara had explained that Mari hadn't been baptized yet. She'd mentioned it to Mari, who'd chuckled and said that it was just as well because she wasn't certain she knew how to cook duck. It had seemed an odd reply, but Mari and Ellie had both laughed until tears rolled down their cheeks. So Mari definitely wasn't interested in the duck farmer. Who, then, did Zachary have in mind?

"You can't guess who I mean?" Zachary set his cup of coffee, barely touched, on a table beside his chair. "James, of course. He likes her. I know he does."

Sara lifted her brows, pleasantly surprised, not so much by the statement but by the boy's keen observation. *Out of the mouths of babes...* "James likes your mother?"

"Yeah." Zachary eyed an oatmeal cookie on a plate on her desk. "I just don't know if *she* knows. He looks at her all the time when she's not looking at him. And he smiles a lot when she's around."

"And you think they'd be a good match? Your mother and James?" She handed him the cookie, left over from her midmorning snack.

Zachary took a big bite. "They like to be together,

and she always asks him about stuff. James doesn't have a wife. And he needs one."

"He does?" Sara asked. "And why is that?"

"Because Mattie is moving into her own house and James will be all alone. He might be scared there by himself." He stuffed the rest of the cookie into his mouth. "And he wouldn't have anybody to eat with him and stuff." Zachary folded his arms over his chest. "I could help him, too. With his carpentry stuff and taking care of Jericho. James is teaching me how to drive. And if I was his son, he wouldn't have to pay me, and he'd have more money. So it would be better for both him and Mom." He looked down at the floor and slid one foot back and forth. "So what do you think? Will you do it?"

Sara smiled. "I think something can be arranged."

Chapter Ten

James came for Mari and Zachary on Saturday as he'd promised, and Mari felt a warm glow of excitement as his buggy stopped near Sara's back door. She and Zachary donned their coats and hurried out to discover that James was alone. "Your sister didn't come with you?"

"Emanuel and Roman both have upset stomachs," James explained as he came around the back to help Mari into the buggy. "Zach, you scoot up on the bench and sit between us," he said. "I promised to teach you the basics of driving, and this is as good a time as any to start."

"Yes!" Zachary fist-pumped.

"I'm sorry the kids are sick." Mari took James's warm hand and stepped up easily, settling herself on the cushioned seat. Amish buggies were all supposed to be alike, but they rarely were. Some, like their owners, were sparse, dusty and needed sprucing up, while others boasted black leather seats, an oiled dashboard and a spotless interior. There were no fancy red, white and blue blinking lights or extras visible inside James's vehicle, but the buggy had obviously been cleaned and recently painted inside.

"Mattie was disappointed to miss Lovina's birthday party," he said, "but Roman and Emanuel spent the afternoon sick to their stomachs. She could hardly inflict that on Anna and her guests."

"I hope the babies don't get sick, too."

"I doubt it's a virus," James confided. "I think the problem might be related to a jar of oatmeal cookies they got into while their mother was changing diapers."

Mari couldn't help laughing. "Those boys are a handful."

"That they are. The twins will have a high bar to get over if they want to match them for mischief. But Mattie has gone to so much trouble getting Roman and Emanuel to this age that I suppose she'll have to keep them."

Zachary, now sitting between them, glanced up at James, a worried look on his face.

"He's teasing," Mari assured her son. "Mattie loves all her children."

"She does," James agreed with a grin. "I think she even loves me, and when I was Roman's age, I was worse than he is, if you can believe what Mattie says. She was a good big sister, and she's a wonderful mother. She's smart and she's kindhearted. Women like that aren't easy to find."

"My mom's smart," Zach piped up, looking at James. "You could marry her, and then I could drive Jericho all the time."

Mari could feel the heat rising from her neck upward. Mortified, she didn't know what to say. As she opened her mouth to force something out, James laughed and tousled Zach's hair. "Now, that's an idea," he said, grinning as he pressed the reins into her son's hands. "This is how you hold the leathers. You have to be gentle but firm."

Mari looked away, touching her hand to her cheek. She had to be bright red with embarrassment. "So Lovina lives with Anna and her husband, doesn't she?" she asked. She knew very well that Lovina did, but she felt desperate to move the conversation to safer ground.

"She's been living with them for a while." James gently adjusted the reins in Zach's hands again. "That's right. Like that."

Mari had learned from Sara that Lovina Yoder, Hannah's first mother-in-law, had moved in with Hannah when she gave up her home in Ohio and moved to Seven Poplars. But the two never got on well. Anna was Lovina's favorite granddaughter and the only one with whom she never found fault. Apparently, Lovina was happier in Anna's home, and Anna and Samuel insisted that they loved having her with them.

"Lovina's strong-willed, as is Anna, so they're well suited to each other," James went on. "Everyone thinks it's a good solution." And then to Zachary, he said, "We call the reins *leathers*. You hold them firmly, but you don't jerk them or you'll hurt the horse's mouth. Jericho has a tender mouth, but he's a smart horse and eager to please. Not all animals are so easy to drive, but you need to treat them all with respect, even the difficult ones."

"James, you don't have to do this today," Mari said. "You could teach him another day, just around the farm." They'd be traveling on the paved road with motor traffic once they reached the end of the drive, and Zachary knew nothing of horses.

"Mom," her son protested. "I can do it. Peter and Rudy both drive on the road."

"Samuel's sons are older than you are," she answered. "I'm sure they weren't taking their parents' buggy on the road at age nine."

"This will be a short lesson today. Just until we get to the end of the lane." James nodded his approval. "That's it. Good grip. Now give him the order to 'walk on.'"

"Walk on," Zachary said, and he gave an excited sigh of delight when the horse obeyed.

Mari watched the serious way Zachary held the reins and felt a distinctly un-Amish pride in his first attempt at driving.

"That's right," James encouraged. He didn't touch the reins himself, but Mari saw that he was watching Zachary closely. "Good," James said. "You have a steady hand. Never let a horse know when you're frightened or unsure of yourself because they'll pick up on it and act accordingly."

"Addy said that Lovina is her grandmother, as well?" Mari asked, starting to relax. James didn't seem to be the least upset by Zach's remark.

"Yes, Lovina is Martha's mother. All right, Zach. I'll take over now." James took the reins, and Zachary dropped his hands into his lap.

"When can I drive again?" her son asked eagerly.

"Soon, I promise." James waited until a car passed and then eased the horse and buggy onto the blacktop.

With James driving, Mari felt herself relax. "Anna lives near the school, doesn't she?"

"Yeah, Mom," Zachary answered. "Right next door, just through the woods. Peter and Rudy just walk over. Most of the kids walk, and if I didn't ride with Ellie, I could walk, too."

Mari was still weighing the pros and cons of Zachary attending the Amish school, at least long-term as he was pushing for. She'd discussed it with Ellie at length and mulled it all over in her mind. But considering that Zachary wanted to go and was applying himself, she couldn't think of a good reason to forbid it.

Since the Mast home was near Sara's, less than two miles away, it didn't take long to reach it. Mari could smell food as she climbed down from the buggy. "You go on in," James told her. "Zachary and I will tie up Jericho."

Rebecca saw her as she walked toward the house, waved and hurried to welcome her. "I'm so glad you could come." Rebecca gave Mari a hug. "We're going to eat soon. Anna baked a huge pineapple cake, and *Grossmama* can't stop talking about it. She loves cake."

The warmth of the big farmhouse, even larger and finer than Hannah's, overflowing with relatives, friends and neighbors, enveloped Mari as Rebecca led her inside. Guests nodded, smiled and called out greetings to Mari and others who filed in behind her. The elderly Lovina was holding court in a high-backed, old-fashioned, cushioned chair near the woodstove that stood in one corner of the combination kitchen and dining room. Mari could see that the aging matron had once been tall and slim. Now she was rail-thin, her nose a sharp beak and her back bent, but her eyes as fierce as any hawk's.

When Mari went to say hello, Lovina peered at her

through her wire-rim glasses. "You have the look of your *grossmama*," she pronounced in a raspy voice when Mari greeted her.

Sara had warned Mari that Lovina's memory often failed her and that she suffered from early-stage dementia, but this white-*kapped* woman with the iron-gray hair who was sizing her up seemed alert and shrewd.

"*Grossmama*, this is Mari Troyer, Sara's friend," Rebecca introduced. "She's from Wisconsin."

"I know who she is." Lovina spoke in *Deitsch*. She stared hard at Mari. "You're Maryann Troyer's granddaughter."

Mari's mouth gaped in surprise. "You knew my grandmother Maryann?"

"Pfff, and why wouldn't I know her? We were second cousins. Grew up next door to each other. I've known Maryann since we were both in leading strings. She was Maryann Stutz then. She married some boy from Wisconsin and went off to live with his family."

Rebecca took a step closer. Someone passed her a plate of food. She placed it on the small table beside Lovina's chair and arranged a knife, fork and spoon where the elderly woman could reach it. "You and Mari's grandmother are cousins?"

Lovina scowled at her. "Didn't I just say we were? Second cousins, if you want to slice the ham close to the bone, but blood kin, all the same. So this skinny little thing from Wisconsin is family. Not only on my side, but on the Yoder side, as well. Double kin to you and your sisters. Maryann's people settled in the valley two hundred years ago." The beady eyes turned on Mari. "Glad you've had the sense to finally come to Delaware. Did you bring your grandmother?"

Mari shook her head. "She passed on."

"I'm sorry to hear it, even if she has gone on to her reward. You have the look of Maryann, child. Welcome to my home." Lovina turned abruptly to inspect her plate of food. "Stingy with the gravy, weren't you, Rebecca?"

Mari could see the corners of Rebecca's mouth twitching with amusement. "Anna made your plate, *Grossmama*. Just the way you like it. And you said not to give you too much gravy because you needed to leave room for cake."

With the older folks' and the children's plates made, everyone else got into line to help themselves at the buffet table. "Was my grandmother really a cousin to Lovina?" Mari whispered in Rebecca's ear when they were far enough away that there was no chance of Lovina overhearing.

Rebecca shrugged. "She must have been. *Grossmama* gets confused about a lot of things, but never about family ties. Wait until our *mam* and Sara hear. They'll be delighted." Rebecca hugged her again. "And that makes us cousins, too. Welcome to the family."

"Thank you," Mari managed. She was almost too astonished to speak. *Family.* She had *family* here in Seven Poplars. It didn't matter that the connections were old ones. Among the Amish any relative was important. If Lovina was right, she was a cousin to Hannah's daughters and to Sara, as well. It didn't seem possible. She'd thought that she and Zachary were alone in the world, but here were more relatives than she could count.

"I think *Grossmama* likes you," Rebecca said as they joined the food line.

"You think so?" Mari asked. "How can you tell?"

Rebecca laughed. "Oh, if she didn't, she'd have let you know. She and Aunt Martha both have a way of laying all their wash on the table." She shook her head. "The good thing about being related to *Grossmama* is that Addy's your cousin." She rolled her eyes. "And the bad thing is that Aunt Martha is bound to try and find fault with you."

"Oh, she's already done that." Mari hesitated, not sure if she should tell Rebecca about her and James at Byler's, but she had a feeling that even if Martha hadn't shared with everyone in Seven Poplars yet, it was only a matter of time before the word spread. She kept her voice low. "James gave me a ride home from work the other day and we stopped at Byler's for a few things."

Rebecca grabbed Mari's forearm, amusement on her face. "And she caught you two alone together?"

"Eating ice cream," Mari confessed.

Rebecca giggled.

"But we were just sitting at the picnic tables. We weren't doing anything wrong."

Rebecca gave a wave of dismissal. "Pay her no mind. She has this idea that she needs to monitor all the couples in the county. Some of the young folks are calling her 'the courting police.'"

The line had moved forward, and it was almost their turn to fill their plates. "James and I aren't a couple," she whispered. "I don't understand why everyone keeps saying that. I'm not even Amish."

Rebecca waggled her finger. "According to Lovina, you are."

Mari sighed. "You know what I mean. I haven't lived this life in a very long time. I haven't been baptized."

Rebecca took Mari's hand and looked into her eyes. "Do you want to be baptized?" she asked softly.

"I don't know," Mari whispered. "I think maybe yes, but…" She closed her eyes for a moment. "Rebecca, I'm so confused. If I'm honest with myself, I think James and I—" She exhaled. *James and I what?* "I don't want to take this step for the wrong reasons. I need someone to tell me what to do."

Rebecca squeezed her hand and let it go. "No one can tell you what's right for you. You need to pray about it. And you need to talk to the bishop. Maybe he can help you figure out where God is leading you."

"You think so?" Mari asked, wanting desperately to believe her. "He'd be willing to talk to me?"

"Absolutely. Now turn around—" she pointed over Mari's shoulder "—and grab a piece of fried chicken for me before it's all gone."

The thought that the Yoders were family warmed Mari throughout the evening, and she was still smiling when James brought the buggy to Anna's back door. "We don't need to wait for Zach. He's spending the night here with Johanna's boys." She made a face. "*Ach,* I hadn't thought this through. I hope this won't cause talk, you taking me home."

"No worry," he said, walking around to adjust a buckle on Jericho's harness. "Everyone in Seven Poplars has already heard we've been to Byler's for ice cream alone. Martha told Anna Yoder that we were secretly walking out together." He winked at her. "We'll be doing Martha a service, giving her something else to talk about."

She smiled hesitantly back at him, trying to read his face. She knew, of course, that he was joking, but was there something more in his voice? Did he wish it were true? Or was that just her own wishful thinking?

Mari made no move to climb into the buggy; instead, she watched by the light of the gas lamppost as James unbuckled Jericho's harness to make an adjustment. She hadn't been kidding when she'd told Rebecca that she was confused. She was *so* confused. About everything. About how she felt about God and the church she'd grown up in. About how she felt about James. About her whole life and where she wanted to go from here. She'd come to Seven Poplars thinking she'd stay a few months, then get a nice trailer for Zachary and her. But now she didn't want that. She wanted more. She wanted to belong to a community. She even thought that she wanted a family of her own: a husband, more children.

"Did you have a good time this evening?" James asked, still working on the harness. "I didn't get a chance to talk to you."

"I did." She tightened the wool scarf she wore around her neck. "Lovina says that she and my grandmother were second cousins. I never knew that much about my mother's family because I was young when she died. But I do remember my grandmother Maryann telling me that she grew up on a farm in central Pennsylvania and that they'd been very poor."

"And how do you feel about that?" he asked. "Being related to the Yoders?"

"I think it's great. Wonderful. You probably don't realize what it's like because you have family all around you, but I really like the idea of belonging somewhere. Belonging *to* someone."

"I know exactly what you're saying. I was away for a long time, and there's nothing like that feeling of coming home...of being among your own."

"You do understand," she said. She was so excited that she was at a loss for words. "I've always thought that Zachary and I were all alone in the world, and now... It's a good feeling."

He nodded.

She hesitated and then went on, "I talked a little bit with Rebecca tonight about church and...she suggested I talk with Bishop Atlee. And I was wondering..." She gazed out into the snowy barnyard. "I was wondering if you thought that would be a good idea."

He turned around to face her. "Can I ask why you'd like to talk to him?"

She clasped her hands, looking into his dark eyes. "I... I feel like God is calling me back, but I... I don't know, James." She suddenly felt herself tearing up. "But I want to be sure I'm truly being called. I don't want to become a part of the church just so I can be a part of all this." She waved in the direction of the Mast house, where light danced from the windows and the sound of laughter drifted through an open door.

They were both quiet for a second. She couldn't read his face.

Finally James spoke. "I think that talking to Bishop Atlee might be a very good idea. He can help you work your way through things. Pray with you. When I first came back, he was a lot of help. He has a good perspective. We did a lot of praying together."

Mari felt as though she couldn't breathe. She and James weren't touching, but the way he was looking at her made her feel as if he had wrapped his arms around her. His name rested on her lips, but she didn't say it.

"We should go," he said.

She nodded, turning to face the buggy, her emotions all a jumble. The decision had been made. She was going to talk to the bishop. But the decision to do it felt good. It felt right.

"I'd be happy to make the arrangements with the bishop for you," James offered. "He could come to Sara's, and you could talk in private in her office."

Mari reached up to grab the handhold on the buggy to step up, and he surprised her by coming up behind her, putting his hands around her waist and lifting her up. As she dropped onto her seat, her hand caught his. It was completely by accident, but then he squeezed it before letting go.

The intimacy of the gesture made her light-headed. She found herself surprised again by her own reaction. It had been a long time since she'd felt this way when a man touched her, almost too long to remember.

Flustered, she sat there in the moonlight, looking down at his kind, gentle face.

At that moment she felt as if he was going to say something, but then he turned and walked around the buggy to get in on his side.

It was still very cold as Jericho trotted down the driveway, but Mari didn't feel the chill because the memory of James's touch warmed her and filled her with a bubbly happiness.

Chapter Eleven

"Mari, could you give me a hand?" Sara asked. They had finished the last of the supper dishes and Ellie and Zachary were bent over a math problem at the kitchen table. "I want to take these extra jars of pickled green tomatoes down to the cellar and bring up applesauce and green beans for tomorrow."

"Sure. I'd be glad to help." Mari hung the dish towel over the handle of the woodstove and went to the counter to pick up a box of canned goods. "I know you didn't can tomatoes yesterday."

Sara shook her head. "No. Gideon brought them by. Careful with the steps. They're steep." She opened the door that led down to the cellar from the utility area off the kitchen.

The cellar was cool and dry with rows of metal shelving along two walls. Canned vegetables and fruits were neatly arranged in allotted sections, and there were wooden bins for potatoes, sweet potatoes, cabbages and turnips. "You could feed an army with all this food," Mari remarked.

"I hope not an army. But I could host more than a

few community doings." When they placed the jars
in their proper places and found the green beans and
applesauce for the next day, Sara motioned to the long
table in the center of the room. Benches ran on either
side. "I was looking for an opportunity to talk with you
alone," she explained. "I could ask you to my office,
but that might have Ellie or Zachary wondering what
business we're up to."

Curious, Mari took a seat.

Sara patted her hand reassuringly. "What I wanted
to discuss with you isn't a complaint, so don't look so
worried. It's an opportunity. But I'd like to ask something personal of you first."

Mari looked at her expectantly. "Of course." She
smiled. "We're family, remember?"

Sara smiled back. "Your meetings with the bishop?
Have they gone well?"

Mari folded her hands and placed them on the table.
She was so glad that Rebecca had suggested she talk to
Bishop Atlee and that James had been willing to make
the arrangements for her. She didn't know if she would
have been brave enough to do it on her own. As promised, Bishop Atlee had been wonderful at helping her
work through not only her past feelings about church
but her expectations for the future. She met Sara's gaze
across the table. "They've gone very well."

"I suspected so. You've seemed so happy lately."
Sara's dark eyes caught the light from the overhead
fixture and shone with compassion. "I don't mean to
pry. But whether or not you decide to return to the faith
has great bearing on the proposition I have to present
to you."

Mari stared at Sara across the table. "I don't understand."

"Someone, I'm not at liberty to say who, has come to me to request that I arrange a match for you with a man here in Seven Poplars."

"A match for me?" She knew her eyes must have grown as wide as saucers. "With an Amish man?"

"Of course. It's the only sort of marriage proposals I arrange."

"But...how could you... How could I..." She let out a breath that she hadn't realized she'd been holding. "I'm not Amish."

"Exactly. As I said, my proposal is contingent on your deciding to attend classes with the bishop with the intention of baptism into the Amish faith." Sara placed both elbows on the table and linked the fingers of both hands. "If you haven't considered returning to the church, then what I'm proposing is impossible. And my intention isn't to influence you. Marriage shouldn't be a reason for accepting our faith. It must be a call from God, and it must be deep and sincere."

A shiver went through Mari, and she wrapped her arms around herself. "I can't tell you if I'm going to join the church because I don't know what I'm going to do."

"But you have considered it?"

"Yes." She nodded. "Yes, of course, I've thought of it. I've thought of it almost every day of my life since I left my uncle's home. More so since I've become a part of this community. But I'm not sure. I could never... would never ask for baptism under false pretenses. If I do become Amish again, it will be with all my heart. It won't be to get a husband."

"Good." Sara smiled, and her shoulders relaxed their stiffness. "That's what I wanted to hear you say."

Mari narrowed her gaze. "Who came to you about finding me a husband?"

"As I said, I can't tell you that."

Mari thought for a second, fighting a sense of panic. Her heart was pounding in her chest. She couldn't imagine who would think she needed an Amish husband. "Who does this secret someone think I should marry?"

"Why, James, of course."

"James wants to marry me?" she asked when she recovered her power of speech. "*He's* the one who proposed this match?"

"That's not what I said. The person who came to me feels that the two of you would make a good couple, that you would be right for each other and would make each other happy." Sara's gaze sharpened. "Am I not wrong in thinking that you aren't opposed to such a union?"

First Mari was dizzy, and then she felt slightly nauseated. What a ridiculous thing for her to say. Now she'd embarrassed herself in front of Sara. Of course James hadn't come asking for her hand in marriage. "James doesn't think of me that way," Mari managed. "He…he considers me a friend." She dared a peek at Sara's face. "James doesn't know about this, does he?"

"I haven't approached James. That's not the way it works. I always go to the woman first. But I wouldn't have come to you at all if I didn't think this was a possibility." Sara's tone grew tender. "Remember, dear, I've been doing this a long time."

"But marriage with James?" Mari felt dizzy with the thought of it. "I… I don't know what to say. We're friends, yes, but I…" She stared at the tabletop, her eyes wide. "I never thought that it was more than that with him."

"That's for James to say. Many a solid marriage has started with friendship. And respect. You do respect him, don't you?"

Mari lifted her gaze to meet Sara's. "Immensely. He's a wonderful person. He'd make a wonderful stepfather to Zachary, but…" She shook her head. "This is too much to take in. I haven't known him that long. And I don't know if I can…if I will join the church. It's a decision that doesn't affect just me—it's my son's life, too. It's such a big step, to leave the world and become Amish."

"Not so great a gap to bridge if it's God's plan for you. Ours isn't a life of sacrifice, so much as one of joy. I believe you can find happiness in the church… in our community. And I think it would give Zachary the sense of belonging that he's lacked."

Mari's thoughts were flying in a hundred directions at once. Marriage to James. It seemed too good to be true. This wasn't a decision that could be rushed. She'd learned that with Zachary's father. "I can't agree to marry a man so quickly…not even a man like James."

"Are you refusing to consider the match?" Sara asked, seemingly choosing her words precisely.

Mari shook her head. "I'm saying that I need more time." She hesitated. "How does this work? If I *was* interested, does that mean I'm committing to marry him?"

"Not at all. If you are open to a match with the designated person, then I go to him. If both agree, then you start walking out together. Just as you would if a matchmaker weren't involved. Neither of you would make any commitment until you were certain."

Suddenly, Mari's life seemed full of possibilities. But could she trust her feelings? "How…how much time is to be allotted for this courtship?"

"There's no time limit. I had one couple that took two years to decide."

"And did they marry?" Mari asked.

"No, they decided against it. Each later married other people, and both the man and woman are content." She smiled. "I made the new matches. I doubted that the first would work out from the beginning, but the girl's parents insisted that he was the one. Time and common sense proved them wrong. And we were all happy with the outcome. Marriage is a sacred bond. You must be sure."

"It's why I want to wait." Mari rose slowly, barely aware of the words she was speaking. Someone actually thought she and James would be well suited to marry. She couldn't help but be thrilled by the idea. Even if it wasn't possible, it did her heart good to know that she hadn't imagined how well she and James got along. "To have time to know my own mind."

"Then that's what I'll tell the person who approached me about matching you and James. We'll table this whole thing at the moment."

"And you won't say anything to James?" Mari asked.

"Of course not." Sara smiled. "But you will consider the offer, won't you?"

"I will," Mari promised.

Mari stepped off the blacktop into the grass as a pickup truck whooshed past. The driver honked the horn, but it didn't faze her. She was in too good a mood to let anyone annoy her. In her denim coat and wool scarf, she was warm, and after the week of working at the butcher shop, walking to and from Bishop Atlee's house was a pleasant change of pace. It felt good to be outside in the brisk air, getting exercise and having some time alone to think.

She'd had a good afternoon with Bishop Atlee. His gentle wisdom and absolute faith in the goodness and mercy of God did much to ease her mind. Every Saturday afternoon and Tuesday night, he'd reserved an hour for her, and with each visit, she'd become more certain that this might be the right path for her and Zachary.

Mari's church attendance and visits with the bishop gave her an inner calm and a joy in everyday life that she hadn't had in a long time. It should have been enough for anyone, but strangely it wasn't. Because while every aspect of Mari's life seemed to be falling into place, there was one piece of the puzzle she just couldn't figure out. And that was James. Sara had been true to her word and not mentioned the proposal again, but that didn't mean Mari didn't think about it. She knew she had done the right thing in telling Sara she wasn't ready to think about marriage, to anyone, but a part of her wished she was. A part of her wanted to marry James and have his babies.

Wanting James as a husband went against years of conviction that she didn't need a man. She had Zachary, and she was able to work and provide for herself and her son. She'd given her heart to Zachary's father, and he had broken it. The pain had been devastating. Why would she want to risk everything again? She'd had her chance and failed miserably because she'd been a terrible judge of character. Ivan had been weak. He'd thought more of himself than the child they'd brought into the world. Ivan had been unwilling to make the sacrifices necessary to make a marriage that would protect and nurture Zachary.

It was a good argument against mooning over James like some love-struck teenager, but it fell flat. James was a strong and good man. He'd proved his worth many times over. And she loved him. She was *in love* with him.

But what if James didn't feel the same way about her?

Mari sighed and loosened her scarf. She was spending too much time dwelling on James. She had other things to think about, like where she and Zachary were going to live. Even if she did join the church, she couldn't board permanently with Sara, could she?

She wanted to remain within walking distance of her friends and her newfound family and the bishop's house. If she officially began lessons with him to prepare to be baptized, they would run a full year before she could be considered for church membership. And it had to be a place that was affordable on her salary. Apparently, someone in the next church district over had an empty *dawdi* house on their property they might be willing to rent. It wouldn't be too long a walk, but—

Her thoughts strayed to James again. In her mind's eye, she pictured his sweet smile and heard the sound of his voice when he laughed or said her name. When she closed her eyes, she could almost smell the scents of fresh-cut lumber and oiled leather that lingered in the air around him. She could see the way his lean hands looked when he clasped Jericho's reins or held a hammer.

Unconsciously, Mari picked up her pace. Sara's addition was done, and James's crew had started to work on a new job. But James still made a practice of stopping by sometimes to have coffee with Sara and the family before work or coming by to finish up a few odds and ends at Sara's. The previous Saturday, after her meeting at Bishop Atlee's, she'd seen James's buggy in Sara's yard, and she couldn't help hoping he might have come again today.

As much as she loved being with Zachary and with Sara and Ellie, Mari always had things she wanted to tell James. She'd share her experiences at the butcher shop with him, and he would tell her community news or funny things that had occurred with his nephews. It was James she could talk to about how to deal with a difficult customer, and it was James who gave her good advice on dealing with Zachary when he got into mischief.

She turned into the driveway and walked a little faster. James wouldn't be there, she knew he wouldn't, but she couldn't help hoping—

"Mari!"

She gave a small gasp of delight as she heard James's voice as she came into full view of the house. "James!" she called back, spotting him on the porch.

He walked toward her.

"I was hoping you'd be here," she called.

"You're later today than last week." He stopped and smiled at her as she approached. "How did it go?"

"Hey, Mom!"

Mari glanced toward the barn and saw Zachary. He and J.J. were standing in the open door of the hayloft.

Zachary waved. "I'm showing J.J. the new kittens. Lois said I could. She's in the house." He pointed. "Sara said Lois could keep an eye on me and J.J. while she was gone. She said I didn't have to go with her."

Lois was a new girl staying with Sara now; Mari liked her very much and trusted her completely. Mari waved to J.J. Then she said to both boys, "Just don't frighten the mama cat or she'll move them again."

"We won't!" Zachary shouted.

Mari met James's amused gaze. "See, I'm trying," she said quietly so the boys didn't hear her. "I didn't warn him to be careful even though I wanted to. I just keep seeing him tumbling out of the loft and me rushing him to the emergency room."

James chuckled. "Didn't you ever play in a hayloft when you were a kid?"

"I did," she admitted. "It was a favorite spot for me and my girl cousins to play house."

"And you never fell out of the loft window?"

She shook her head. "No, I didn't, but it's different when it's my child. And boys do fall, and sometimes they get hurt."

His eyes filled with understanding. "They do, but it's part of growing up. You can't protect him from everything. You have to learn to trust Zach's judgment. He's got a pretty good head on his shoulders."

"I know he does," she agreed. She headed for the porch. "You have time to sit a minute, or are you on your way out?"

James settled onto the porch swing as she took the rocker across from him. "I always have time for you."

Chapter Twelve

Mari stood at the kitchen window, her coffee mug in her hand. Hiram had already gone to hitch the buggy to go to church services at Roman and Fanny Byler's, and she was just waiting for Sara and Ellie. Zachary had spent the night at Johanna and Roland's and would meet her at church.

Mari watched as a bit of straw blew across the yard. The last of the snow had melted and the first green shoots of spring were popping up everywhere. The day before she'd spotted crocuses at the mailbox. She thought about how cold it had been when she'd left Wisconsin; it had felt as though she would never see the sun again. But here it was, with the first warm rays of the coming spring.

Her life seemed to be transforming with the weather. A short time ago she'd been in Wisconsin with no job, no home and no real hope. Then she'd come to Seven Poplars and everything had changed. Sara and the whole community had made her and Zachary feel so welcome. Her job was great, and Zachary had settled in at the little Amish school, doing better than he'd

ever done in a public school. And now she was taking classes with the bishop and making plans to join
the church.

She was happier than she had ever dreamed she
could be. And yet there was still something missing.
In the past week Mari had twice almost spoken to Sara
about the courtship with James proposed by the mys-
terious benefactor. Now that she had decided to join
the church, it only made sense to let Sara try to make
the match.

But there was a part of Mari that still held back.
She had no doubts about her feelings for James. She
knew she loved him; with each passing day that became more evident. And even though they were both
content to call each other "friend," she knew that he
had feelings for her, as well. But what if it was all her
imagination? What if Sara went to him and proposed
the courtship and he said no?

The truth was, she was madly in love with James.

Which made her question her decision to join the
church. What if somehow, subconsciously, she was
thinking she felt God's love, when it was James's love
she sought?

From somewhere in the house, Ellie's and Sara's
voices drifted down. Mari was dressed for church in
a beautiful blue dress Sara had made for her in the
Amish style. She wasn't wearing a prayer *kapp* yet,
but Sara had made her a scarf in matching blue fabric. With dark stockings and black leather shoes and
her hair up under the scarf, no Englisher would have
known she wasn't Amish.

Suddenly she felt overwhelmed. What if she was
just playing dress-up? What if God wasn't really call-

ing her? What if she was going to church and meeting with the bishop just because of James? What if she was wrong about her newfound faith?

Footsteps sounded in the living room: Sara's followed by Ellie's.

"Ready," Sara called.

When Sara walked into the kitchen, Mari backed up to the sink. Suddenly she didn't fell so well.

"We should go. Hiram's waiting," Sara said as she crossed the kitchen.

"Oh, good." Ellie tied on her black bonnet over her prayer *kapp* as she hurried behind Sara. "He's already loaded the vegetable soup and brownies. The soup will go well on a chilly spring day like this." She caught Mari's eye and halted. "Are you feeling all right?"

Mari pressed her hand to her forehead. "Actually… I don't think I am."

"Oh, dear." Sara sighed, throwing her black cloak over her shoulders. "That's the downside to working in a store. So many people. So many germs."

Ellie frowned, looking at Mari. "Do you think you have a fever? You look flushed."

"I…" Mari lowered her hand. "I don't think so, but I think I better stay home. Just in case," she added, feeling a little guilty. While she did feel light-headed and flushed, she knew it wasn't from a bug she'd caught at the store. "Will you just bring Zachary home with you this afternoon?"

Sara stood in the doorway, watching her closely. "Of course. But one of us can stay here with you, if you like."

"Oh no. I'll be fine." She waved them off. "I wouldn't

want you to miss service on my account. Go, and tell everyone I said hello."

Sara met Mari's gaze and Mari had to fight the urge to squirm. She really didn't feel as if she could go to church this morning. Her thoughts were too jumbled for worship.

"See you this afternoon, then," Sara called as she went out the door.

"Have some hot tea," Ellie advised.

Mari watched them go and then tied an apron over her pretty new dress. She'd clear the breakfast dishes, set the table for the evening meal and then maybe she'd go lie down for a while. Give herself some time to think. She'd have most of the day to herself. It was rare to have time where nothing was required of her, and she could just relax.

But as the minutes passed, she began to feel more and more uneasy that she'd made the wrong decision. Why had she stayed home from church? Out of fear? Was she afraid that God wasn't calling her? Or was she afraid He was?

After a few minutes, the feeling that she belonged at church service with her newfound friends and family grew stronger.

She glanced at the clock, not sure what to do. She knew what she *wanted* to do. It would take more courage to go than to stay home. So she rallied her courage. Removing the work apron, she found her blue denim coat and helped herself to one of Sara's woolen scarves. Because services were at Roman Byler's chair shop, it was close enough to walk.

"I'm going!" she declared to the empty house. Chin firm, shoulders back, she marched out of the house.

The walk down the lane, across the road and down the road wasn't far. It was cold and windy, but Mari didn't mind because the sun was shining, and when she tipped her head just so, she could feel its warmth. And better yet, its promise of warmer days to come. Every step made her more determined. Church was where she belonged. It was where she wanted to be.

As she started up Roman and Fanny's short drive, the line of black buggies between the house and shop made her slightly queasy again. What if she was making a mistake? What if God wasn't really calling her? A terrible thought crossed her mind. What if she wasn't worthy? Could God really accept her after she'd doubted Him for so long?

She reached the barnyard and stood there, uncertain. No one was in sight. Everyone had gone into the big shop where Roman made his chairs. She could run back to Sara's and no one would be the wiser. She glanced around. The barnyard was still and quiet except for the sound of a loose piece of tin on the side of a small shed. Suddenly losing her nerve, she ducked into the open shed.

Bales of hay were stacked against the far wall, and something gray slinked out of the shadows. Mari saw that what she'd feared might be a rat was a fluffy tomcat.

The friendly creature trotted over and rubbed against Mari's ankle. She stooped to pet it, and then a wave of memories swept over her as the air was filled with sound.

From inside the house came the achingly poignant resonance of joined voices singing an Old German hymn. The song was more chanting than modern words put to music. At the beginning of each verse a single wavering voice began alone and then a chorus of interwoven voices joined in praise, rich and sweet and so beautiful that she found herself in tears. Not of sorrow or fear, but tears of pure joy.

Step by step, Mari was drawn from the shed into the yard. Trembling, weeping, she made her way to the door of the chair shop. She let herself into the warm reception area of the shop. Two young mothers were there, one nursing an infant, another changing a toddler on a wide window seat. Both women stopped to smile at her, but neither spoke, unwilling to risk disturbing the singers in the main room of the building.

Mari removed her coat and added it to a pile on a chair, then quietly entered the much larger room. Workbenches and power saws had been moved so that rows of benches could be arranged in the open area. According to tradition, men and older boys sat on one side, women, girls and small children on the other. All three rooms opened into one another and were filled with worshippers. Everyone, other than a few elders, was standing, still singing the first hymn. There were many stanzas, and some hymns lasted more than half an hour. They'd not yet begun *The Loblied*, which was always the second hymn of every service.

Susanna King, Hannah's daughter, was in the last row, closest to the back of the room, and when she saw Mari, her round little face broke into a wide smile. Susanna moved over to make room for Mari and then took up the hymn again, her croaking voice never quite meshing with the others but filled with joyous enthusiasm. Mari drew in a deep breath and joined in. Susanna offered to share her hymnal, but Mari shook her head. She knew every note and every word by heart.

As everyone finished the last verse and began to settle onto the wooden benches, Mari glanced over to the men's side of the room. At the same instant, James, sitting in the fourth row, looked in her direction. Their gazes met and held. James smiled at her and nodded. Mari smiled back, felt a rush of heat in her cheeks and sank back onto her seat. A shiver of excitement ran through her, and her eyes misted with tears once more.

It felt right that she should be there. It felt safe and good, and she felt enveloped by the unity of the people around her. Suddenly she found herself wondering why she had struggled with the decision to come. She didn't feel like a fish out of water; she felt as though she had come home after being on a long journey.

The *vorsinger*, an older man with a long white beard and a cheerful round face, stood and began the second hymn. Behind Mari, a group of boys filed in, whispering among themselves. They found seats at the back of the men's section on the adjoining porch, and as everyone rose to join in the hymn, Mari saw her Zachary was among them.

Susanna reached over and touched her arm and smiled at her again. "Sing," she urged.

And Mari did just that, giving herself over to the familiar worship service, and setting aside her worries and her fears to let the peace of God's grace flow over her.

When the last hymn had been sung and the congregation broke for the midday meal, Mari remained where she was, her hands clasped. Eyes closed, she prayed silently, barely hearing the sounds of benches being moved, children running and laughing and women calling out directions to get the tables set for the meal. At last, when she had poured her heart out to God, she sighed with relief and opened her eyes, feeling a bit as if she'd been wrung through her grandmother's old-fashioned wringer washing machine.

Slowly Mari rose, taking in the activity around her. Although tables were already set up and young girls were laying out the place settings, there was plenty left to do. In the past few weeks she'd attended communal meals often enough to know what needed to be done, and she found it easy to join in. She was just leaning over to pick up the bench she'd been sitting on when James's sister, Mattie, caught her eye.

Mari smiled. She was used to seeing Mattie with at least one baby on her hip, but neither Timothy nor William was anywhere to be seen. Their father might have them, but it was more likely that one of the other women had swept the twins away, giving Mattie a much-needed break.

"Good Sabbath," Mattie greeted her.

Mari smiled. "Good Sabbath," she repeated, setting the bench down when she realized that Mattie was headed her way to speak to her. "Where are the babies?"

"I have no idea. Someone has them, I suppose." She chuckled, and Mari chuckled with her.

"I didn't see you when service started this morning," Mattie said, the bench between them. She was wearing a plain black Sunday dress.

Mari smoothed the scarf that covered most of her hair. Mattie was always pleasant to her, but Mari could always feel an underlying current of tension between them. James had warned Mari that Mattie was concerned about their friendship, but Mari kept hoping that with time, his sister would realize that she had no intention of kidnapping him and carrying him out into the big bad world. Didn't Mattie realize that world was what Mari had been running from when she came to Seven Poplars?

"I… I wasn't feeling well this morning," Mari explained. "But then… I felt better." She watched Susanna King carry a big bowl of macaroni salad toward the buffet table.

"Well, it's good to have you here with us." Mattie smoothed the bodice of her dress. "I understand you're seeing the bishop regularly and beginning classes to prepare for baptism."

"I am." Mari nodded, still feeling a little emotional from the service. "I hope to be baptized next year."

"And become a full member of the community?" Mattie asked.

Only then did Mari pick up on a certain tone to Mattie's voice. Mattie didn't seem pleased. "That's my intention," she said, taking a quick glance around, hoping James was nearby. Usually, Mari didn't talk with Mattie without James.

"Well, I'm very happy for you and for your son. I hope that you find peace here." Mattie hesitated. "But it's also my hope…" She exhaled and then started again. "Mari, I'm just going to come out and say this."

Now Mari was really beginning to feel uncomfortable. She was in a big room with at least thirty people, and yet suddenly she felt alone. "Yes?"

"You know how much my little brother means to me. You know how close we are."

Mari nodded, thinking to herself that Mattie was speaking of him almost as if he were still the little boy she had raised after their mother passed away. But it didn't seem right to say that. She just stayed quiet and listened.

"I just… I think you need to be absolutely certain that your desire to be a part of our community isn't—" She glanced away as if trying to get control of her emotions. "Mari, what I'm trying to say is that I'm worried that you're joining church in the hopes that James will marry you."

Mari felt a sudden rush of tears. She was tempted to just walk away. She was hurt that Mattie would suggest such a thing, but then hadn't she wondered the same thing just a few hours earlier?

Mari took a breath and slowly turned her gaze to meet Mattie's. The suggestion stung, but she had to admire Mattie for being willing to come directly to her. "I can't… I can't say that I don't care for your brother because I do, but I want you to know, Mattie, that I'm joining the church because this is where I belong." Her voice caught in her throat. "God is calling me to come back to the Plain life I knew as a child, and I've realized since coming to Seven Poplars that this is where I was supposed to end up. It's our home now, my son's and mine." She took a breath, feeling steadier. "And as far as wanting to be baptized just so I can marry James, that wouldn't make sense because I was already approached with the opportunity to enter a possible match with James and I said no."

"James asked you to marry him?" Mattie asked, clearly shocked.

"No." Mari shook her head. "Someone approached Sara to make a possible match between James and me." She gave a little laugh that was without much humor. "The person who hired Sara wanted to remain unnamed. I actually wondered if it was you."

"But James didn't initiate it?"

She shook her head.

Mattie crossed her arms over her chest. "I see."

Mari leaned down and picked up the bench. "I should get this to a table. It looks like it's time for the first seating."

Mattie sighed. "Mari, it wasn't my intention to hurt you. I only—"

"It's all right, Mattie." Mari didn't look at her. "I understand. You're only looking out for James and I'm glad." Emotion filled her voice. "I'm glad you are, because he deserves that. Now if you'll excuse me." Then she walked away.

Chapter Thirteen

After the morning services, James joined some other men outside and stood in the open carriage shed talking to Charley Byler. The sky looked as if it was going to rain. Church elders, married men and visitors were already seated in the chair shop, being served by the women. James usually waited until the second seating so that he could eat with his younger friends. Charley was telling him and the others about a new driving mare that he'd bought but James was only half listening.

Mari hadn't come to church with Sara and Ellie. Sara had explained that Mari hadn't been feeling well. James had been concerned and tempted to go check on her, but then had thought better of it. He could only imagine what Mattie would have to say. And Sara had assured him it was nothing for him to worry about. But then Mari had appeared, just as service began. Had she really just been feeling poorly, then felt better and decided to come after all, or was she experiencing spiritual doubts? When James first returned, even though he knew it was right for him, it still wasn't easy.

"James?"

He looked to see Mattie standing apart from the group of men. "Could I speak to you?"

She had one of the twins in her arms. Presumably, one of the other women had the other infant and the two older boys. That was the thing about community. A mother of young children could always count on help at any gathering. Relatives, friends and neighbors were always prepared to care for hungry, tired or rambunctious kids.

"Mattie looks like someone plucked the feathers off her favorite setting hen," Charley said, elbowing James playfully in the side.

James chuckled as he walked to meet her. But Charley was right. He could see by her strained face that she was upset. He wondered if one of the boys had misbehaved. "Something wrong?" he asked.

She motioned toward their buggy on the far side of the yard. Drops of rain sprinkled across his face. "I need to talk to you. Privately."

He glanced around. There were men in the barn, teenagers near the back of the house, women walking between the house and the building that housed the chair shop and factory. "Too cold out here in the yard for the baby," James said, taking the infant from her. The child was bundled in blankets, but the wind had turned raw. "Wait," he said. "Over there." He led the way to a toolshed. Inside, it was sheltered against the weather. He closed the door behind them. "Now, what's so important that—"

"I've been talking to Mari Troyer," she interrupted. He could barely see her face in the shadowy shed, but her posture was stiff, and he could almost feel the heat of her anger. "She said that someone approached Sara about a match for her. With you. When were you going to tell me? After the banns were read?"

He looked at her in disbelief and shook his head. "I have no idea what you're talking about."

"You know how I feel about this. I like Mari, but she's not right for you. Marriage is all about families. And if you marry her, you could tear our family apart." She gazed up at him, her eyes teary. "Are you willing to risk that?"

James was caught between feeling bad that Mattie was so upset and a strange excitement. Someone thought he and Mari should court? Who? Who would go to the matchmaker without telling him? It didn't make sense. Mari wasn't even a member of the church yet. Anyone who knew him well enough to know he secretly carried feelings for Mari would know he would never marry outside the church. He gazed down at his sister. "You're telling me that *Mari* told you that? You must have misunderstood."

"*Ne*, she told me not ten minutes ago. There's no misunderstanding. Didn't I warn you about this? I knew you were becoming too involved with her and her son. Was it you, James? Did you ask Sara to arrange a marriage?"

Still stunned, he stared back at her. "It's news to me," he said. "Who would be making a match for me?"

"I suppose she could have been telling an untruth, but she seemed sincere. She said that she'd refused the match. I don't know what to think. Why would she say such a thing, if it isn't true?"

Mari refused? His heart sank. "I can't say it any plainer, Mattie. I haven't proposed marriage to anyone. And I certainly didn't go to Sara."

The baby started to whimper, and he passed him back to Mattie.

"So, you didn't ask Sara to arrange a match between you and Mari?"

"No, I didn't."

She hesitated. "I saw you watching her during service."

He didn't reply. He just stood there.

"I thought… I'm sorry, brother. I was hurt by the thought that you might ask—"

"I just told you. I didn't."

Mattie sighed. "I'm sorry." She reached out with one hand and squeezed his arm. "I know you think I'm an interfering busybody. But you mean so much to me, to my children. I couldn't bear to see you make such a mistake."

He gazed out into the barnyard. He didn't know why he was upset. Mari had told him they were just friends. Anything he had read into their relationship was just his own wishful thinking. "I need to straighten this out," he told his sister.

"*Ya*, go to Sara. If Mari wasn't honest with me, you should know it."

"No, Sara's not who I need to talk to."

James found Mari in the reception area of the chair shop. She and Rebecca were carrying large pitchers of apple cider to the main showroom where the midday meal was being served. He stepped in front of her. "I have to talk to you."

"In a few minutes?" Mari asked, her mind seeming elsewhere. "Right now I have to—"

"Now," James insisted. He took the pitcher from her

and set it down on a table that held wood-stain color charts. "Please."

"I'll come back for it," Rebecca told Mari. She took one look at James and hurried off.

James took Mari's hand. "Come with me." Before she could protest, he led her through an office door and closed it behind them.

The room held a desk, a filing cabinet and several chairs. The outside wall was now taken up with a large window that opened on the yard. Although he didn't turn on a light, they could clearly see people walking past the window. The thought passed his mind that they could also see him and Mari. He didn't care.

"What is it?" Mari asked. "Has—"

Again, he cut her off. "Mattie said that you told her that someone asked Sara to arrange a match between you and me. Is that true?"

Mari stared up at him, wishing the floor would open up and swallow her. She wanted to look away, but she didn't.

"Is it true?" he repeated.

She couldn't tell if he was angry or hurt, but he was clearly upset. "Yes. Sara came to me and said so. She wouldn't say who had asked her."

"But you refused?"

Her mouth went dry. She could only nod.

"Why, Mari?" When she didn't answer, he continued, "Is it because you're not staying here? Because you want to take Zachary and go back to the English?"

"No." She shook her head again. "That's not what I want," she whispered. "I wasn't sure before, but I'm sure now. I belong here."

He took hold of her shoulders. His touch was gentle but firm. She sensed that if she pulled away, he wouldn't stop her, but she couldn't take a step. She could feel that there was something real between them, almost as solid as if she could see and taste it.

"I need you to be honest with me. Did you say no because you think of me as only a friend?" he demanded, his eyes searching her. "That you…" He stopped and started again. "That you don't see me any other way? That you could never see me as anything more than a friend?"

Mari didn't know what to say. If she told him she saw him as only a friend, it would be over. She wouldn't have to hear him tell her she'd been right in her decision. But there was something about the way he was looking at her that made her think something more was going on between them. The barest hint of possibility made her brave. "No," she whispered. "That isn't why I said no. But *you* said we were just friends. You said it over and over again."

"Because *you* said we were just friends. I knew within days, hours, maybe minutes of meeting you that my feelings for you were more."

Mari held her breath. They were practically in a fishbowl; anyone outside could see them standing so close, gazing into each other's eyes, but she couldn't move away from him. "I don't know what I want," she managed.

"I know what I want. I want you to stay in Seven Poplars," he said quietly. "I want you to be baptized into our faith, and I want us to walk out together. And if this is what I think it is, what I feel in my heart, I want you to be my wife."

She began to tremble. Tears clouded her eyes. "You

want to marry me?" she murmured huskily. "You want to be Zachary's father?"

"With all my heart," he assured her. "I want to be your husband and Zachary's father. But do you feel the same? You have to be absolutely honest here. Don't worry about hurting my feelings." He took a deep breath. "Are you willing to give us a chance to find out if we're meant to be together…as a family?"

"Yes," she answered. "Yes, I think I…" She looked down and then back up at him again. "If I could do anything, it would be marry you, love you."

He took both of her hands in his.

"But… I need time," Mari went on. "And *that's* what I told Sara. It wasn't that I didn't…" The words stuck in her throat. "It isn't you I'm not sure of. It's me. I have to know that I'm coming back to the church because it's what God wants me to do, not just because…because I think I love you." Suddenly, she became aware of a face close to the outside of the window. "James, someone's—"

"It's Martha." He looked from the window back to Mari again. "And I think we should give her something to see." James pulled Mari against him, tipped her chin with gentle fingers and kissed her full on the mouth.

Chapter Fourteen

"Why are you smiling?" James asked, tilting his menu so he could see her over the top.

Mari lowered her menu. "Why are *you* smiling?" she teased, leaning over so he could hear her above the hubbub of a birthday party going on on the far side of the restaurant.

They were sitting across from each other at a table for two in a pizza place near Byler's store. They'd made plans days earlier for him to pick her up from work and stop for supper. While they spent most of their time together in the presence of others at church, or on visiting Sunday or at a friend's or family member's house, they had both agreed that they would spend time together alone once a week. Now that they were officially courting, it was important to them that they spend time really getting to know each other. Secretly, they called it *date night*. It was an Englisher term the Amish never used, and Martha certainly would have disapproved, but it was a little joke Mari and James shared.

"*I'm* smiling because I've looked forward to this all

week and now finally here you are." He slid his hand
across the table toward hers.

It was all Mari could do to make herself pull her
hand away before they touched. She and James had
discussed their idea of spending time alone together
with both Sara and Preacher Caleb, and everyone had
agreed that because of their age, it would be okay to
occasionally go somewhere alone. But they had also
agreed that the rules of propriety had to be followed.
Among the Amish, there was no kissing until marriage,
and there wasn't supposed to be hand-holding, at least
not until a wedding date was set, but since they had
already broken the kissing rule in front of their entire
church, they'd both agreed to take care in their physical expression of their feelings for each other.

But now that they were courting, she wanted to hold
hands with him. And she wanted to hurry up and marry
him just so he could kiss her again.

James sighed, frowned and glanced at his menu.
"I'm so glad you like pizza. It's one thing I haven't
been able to give up since I came back."

"I don't think being Amish means we can't eat
pizza." She picked up her menu. She didn't know why
she was looking. They'd end up getting the same thing
they always got: a large veggie pizza with red peppers,
artichokes, mushrooms and eggplant.

"It doesn't, but there are some people who think
being in a place like this—" he lowered his voice
"—where alcohol is served, is wrong."

She nodded, setting aside her menu. She was so
happy to see James; they didn't get a chance to see each
other every day. On days when she didn't see him, it
seemed as if she constantly wanted to tell him some-

thing. There were definitely times when she wished they had phones to call each other, but as Sara had pointed out to her, in some ways it made being together better. Maybe there was something to be said about absence making the heart grow fonder.

A waiter came by and took their order; sure enough, they agreed on their usual. Once he was gone, Mari leaned back in her chair. She'd dressed with extra care, wearing another new dress Sara had made her; this one was rose colored. And with it, she wore a matching scarf over her hair. "Did you ever drink alcohol when you were living among the English?" she asked him.

"I tried it." He shrugged. "I had a beer a couple of times. I even tried a shot of whiskey once." He shuddered. "If that's what makes a man a man, I guess I'm not." He slid his hand across the table again and just touched her fingertips. "You?"

"I tried one of Ivan's beers once." She made a face. "That was the worst stuff I've ever tasted in my life. I spit it out in the sink."

He laughed with her.

"I've never understood why Ivan and his friends liked to drink alcohol," she went on. "I don't understand why they liked the way it made them act." She looked down at their hands on the table, almost touching, yet not quite. "Ivan wasn't a very nice person when he drank beer."

When James didn't say anything, she looked up at him. "I'm sorry. Does it bother you when I talk about Ivan?"

"Not the fact that you were married to him," he explained. "Just that he didn't treat you the way you deserved to be treated. That's what I find upsetting."

Mari could feel her heart swelling. James was so sweet. So kind and good to her. She could barely believe that all of this was happening. She was going to join the church and be baptized. And in a year or two, she and James were going to be married. She knew that the idea of courting was to get to know each other, but they'd agreed within days of their kiss in the chair-shop office, it was just a formality. They were getting married. There was no doubt in either of their minds.

"I try not to think about Ivan as being a big mistake, because I never felt that Zachary was a mistake. I mean… I wish we'd been married first. Before…" She met his gaze. One of the best things about James was that he was so nonjudgmental, particularly about her past. He told her all the time that what she was doing *today*, what she planned to do *tomorrow* with her life, was what mattered. She felt a faint blush. "You know what I mean. I regret Ivan, but I don't regret Zachary."

"Two root beers," the young waiter announced, setting mugs on the table between them. He pulled straws out of his apron and placed them on the table. "And your pizza's in the oven. Be right out."

"Thanks," James and Mari said in unison. They both laughed as they opened their straws, dropped them into their glasses and took a sip. They were always talking over each other, saying the same thing.

"Okay, so I have to admit, I'm still curious as to who went to Sara to arrange our match," James said.

"Me, too," Mari agreed. "But Sara won't say a word. She said it was an agreement between her and the other party, and it was their wish that we not know."

He played with the paper from his straw. "I just can't imagine who it could have been."

"Well, we know it wasn't your sister," she said with a grimace.

He laughed. "No, it wasn't Mattie, but she's coming around. I think she's beginning to see that we really are meant to be together."

"She's been very nice to me. Never a harsh or critical word. I think she genuinely believes that she was looking out for your best interests when she said she didn't think we should court."

"She still feels guilty about that. I think that job she got me was her way of trying to make up for it."

"Oh, the new job! I'm sorry. You met with clients yesterday. I completely forgot." His sister had an English woman who bought eggs from them regularly and when the customer had said she was looking for a contractor to build her new house, Mattie had introduced her to James. "How did it go?"

"Great. I'm hired. We go to contract next week. I'm building a three-bedroom house with a garage. She may want a barn, as well."

Mari clapped. "That's wonderful news. I'm so happy for you."

"I'm happy for *us*." He beamed. "I'll be able to save plenty of money. I was thinking that after we marry we'd take a trip. A honeymoon."

She stared at him. "Do Amish do that?"

"Sure. Sometimes. Well, mostly we go visit out-of-state relatives, but I was thinking maybe we could go to the beach. You said you've always wanted to swim in the ocean."

She looked down at her Amish-style dress. "I'm pretty sure the bishop wouldn't go for me in a bathing suit."

"So we'll just wade in. Together."

"Sounds wonderful," she said, unable to take her eyes from his.

He took her hand in his before she could pull away and squeezed it before letting go. "I think every day we spend together is going to be wonderful, Mari Troyer."

"Catch!" James, who'd been washing dishes, tossed a bowl to Mari.

"Don't!" she warned, but the brown pottery bowl was already in the air. She made a grab for it and managed to snatch it out of the air. "Don't do that," she protested. "What if I'd missed?"

He laughed. "But you didn't, did you? You have a good eye and good instincts. You need to trust yourself more."

"Who says I don't?"

His beautiful eyes gleamed. "We have to risk to get the most out of life."

"I'd say I'm risking a lot walking out with you," she teased.

He grinned at her, and her heart skipped a beat. Funny, sweet and tender, James was everything she'd ever wanted in a man. She couldn't believe that they were officially courting. He'd made both her and her son so happy that it was like a dream come true.

James rinsed a serrated bread knife under the faucet, shook off the dripping water and raised one brow in a mischievous expression.

"Don't you dare."

He shrugged, offered a sad face and meekly passed the knife to her, handle first.

She suppressed a giggle, dried the knife and returned it to the wooden rack. "Sara won't let you in her hospitality kitchen if you keep taking chances with her good dishes," she admonished. It was a Monday evening and the two of them had volunteered to help Charley and Miriam chaperone an impromptu meeting of the Gleaners in Sara's barn. The youth group had met to make plans to help out elderly or infirm members of the Amish community on Saturdays. It was after 9:00 p.m. The boys and girls had already departed, and the four adults were just finishing the cleanup.

"Seriously, Mari," James said. "You would make a good catcher. I think you should try out for the women's softball team this spring."

"Here in Seven Poplars? An Amish team?" He nodded, and she asked, "Are they all unmarried girls who play?"

"No. Lots of young mothers. Miriam coaches. Rebecca, Grace, even Addy plays. And Miriam—"

"What about Miriam?" She came into the kitchen with a tray of glasses. Like all Hannah's daughters, Mari thought she was a beautiful young woman who appeared younger than her years. Miriam wore a neat plum-colored dress with a white apron and a crisp white prayer *kapp*. And, being Miriam, there was a bounce in her step. It was difficult to remember that she was old enough to be the mother of two children and not a Gleaner herself. "This is the last of it," Miriam pronounced. "Charley's sweeping up."

James took the tray. "I was just telling her about your softball team."

Miriam chuckled. "We're always looking for players. No tryouts. If you want to play, show up in sneakers. But I warn you, James throws a mean pitch. When we challenge the men's team, we make them hit opposite-handed." She beamed with good humor. "We'd love to have you join us, Mari."

"Mari!" Charley pushed open the door from the main room. "Bishop Atlee is here to see you. You, too, James."

"The bishop?" James looked at Mari. "Do you have any idea what this is about?"

She shook her head. She undid her apron, hung it on a hook and hurried to meet Bishop Atlee. He was the one who'd been giving her instructions on joining the church, and she was scheduled to meet him again the following night. She couldn't imagine why he'd come to speak to her tonight.

As she approached the gray-haired man, Mari saw that his mood was somber. Behind her, Charley and Miriam called out a hasty good-night.

James glanced from the bishop to Mari. "Should I—" He hooked his thumb over his shoulder, indicating he could excuse himself.

"Ne." Bishop Atlee motioned to a table. "This concerns you both. I stopped at your house and Mattie told me that I'd find you here." He took a seat at the head of the table, and she and James sat to one side, facing him.

"This is awkward," the bishop said. "It's not a situation I've encountered before, and I've served in Seven Poplars for years." He was quiet for a moment, seeming to gather his thoughts. But the silence went on long enough for Mari to begin to feel uncomfortable.

"Mari," the bishop said, "it's my custom to always contact the previous church elders to inquire about the history of someone who wishes to become a member of our district. Soon after you began consulting with me,

I wrote to your old community. I wasn't prying. I simply had to confirm that you left your own church and entered the English world before accepting baptism."

"Yes." Mari nodded. "I can see how that would be something you'd need to know." Though her running away had caused much scandal at the time, she'd been unbaptized. The difference was a difficult one for outsiders to understand. Accepting baptism into the Amish church and then leaving was a terrible sin. It meant that the person had broken their faith, not only with the community but with God. That person would be formally shunned. Members could not eat with them. They could not ride in a car or a buggy driven by the shunned person and, in most cases, would not even speak to them.

Her aunt and uncle had refused to allow her to enter their home, but everyone in the county didn't accept their strict interpretation. Many, especially Sara, felt that Mari's family had been unnecessarily cruel, and their beliefs and actions had not prevented her from being welcomed into the Seven Poplars Amish neighborhood.

"This afternoon, I received this letter." He handed it to Mari. "You may read it." And to James, he said, "I'm afraid that plans for Mari's baptism and your marriage must be called off. She can't marry you because the current bishop states that she was already baptized into the Amish faith. Apparently, Mari made her promise to God and later went back on her word. Then she further compounded her error by coming to Seven Poplars and Sara's home under false pretenses." He folded his hands and placed them on the surface of the table. "I can't offer you membership into our church community at this time. I'm not saying it's not possible, ever. We can sit down and talk once we've both had time to think, but I know you understand that this changes everything."

Mari looked at Bishop Atlee and then back at the letter. Her hands shook so hard that she could barely make out the words. But the name at the bottom of the page was plain. The signature in tiny cramped letters was her uncle's. "My uncle wrote this?" she managed.

"Ya." Bishop Atlee folded his hands. "He recently became the bishop of his church. As your senior relative and your religious leader, he felt that he had to share this information with us."

She shook her head. "No. He couldn't have. That's not possible." She looked down at the letter again, hoping that she'd read it wrong.

"Mari, James… I'm so sorry," Bishop Atlee said, getting to his feet. "If you wish to discuss my decision further, I'll be at home on Saturday afternoon."

"There has to be some mistake," James protested.

"There has been," the bishop agreed. "And I'm afraid it was Mari who made it. But God is merciful. No one is beyond redemption. And if she truly repents of her rash actions, she can, in time, be forgiven." He nodded to them both and then walked out of the barn.

James stared at Mari. She could see the heartbreak on his face. "Is it true?" he asked. "Were you baptized?"

She tried to answer, but the words wouldn't come. How could he believe such a thing of her?

"I'm asking you, Mari. Say something."

"You actually think I'd lie to Sara…to you…to everyone about whether or not I was baptized?" She pushed her hands against the table and rose to her feet. "If you think that, you don't know me well enough to court me. And if you think that—" she choked on her tears "—you'll never know me well enough to marry me."

"Mari—"

Ignoring him, she ran to the door. He started after her, but she whirled on him, her face streaked with tears. "I'd believe you," she cried. "No matter what you told me, I'd believe you."

"Mari, please—"

"No, James. It's over between us."

"We have to talk about this."

"There's nothing more to say. I did make mistakes when I was nineteen, and I made another one when I thought we could have a future together. Goodbye, James." She ran through the darkness toward Sara's house.

Chapter Fifteen

James ran after Mari to the house, catching up to her at the porch. He asked her again if they could talk, but she refused. She went inside, closing the door behind her.

For a moment he just stood there, stunned. He didn't know what to do. If he and Mari couldn't discuss the problem, how could they work it out? He wanted to believe her, but the facts seemed to state otherwise. He wanted to put his arms around her and tell her that he would make everything right—that they would be married as they planned. But he couldn't let himself be blinded by love. If there was a chance that she had deceived him, it would be difficult to get past it. But to his shame, he had to admit that it wasn't breaking the *ordnung* that mattered to him as much as whether or not she'd told him an untruth.

James's sister's warnings rose in his mind as he walked to the barn. Could Mattie be right about Mari breaking his heart? In his gut, he knew that Mari wasn't capable of such a ruse. There *had* to be an explanation. But what was it? One of them had to be wrong. Was it Mari, or was it the bishop?

The questions preyed on James's mind all the way home. He wasn't ready to give up on Mari and Zachary, but her refusal to talk to him was disturbing. When he put his horse in the barn and went into the house, it was dark. Everyone was asleep. He lit a single propane lamp, took a Bible from a shelf in the living room and sat down at the kitchen table to read.

The familiar words that usually brought him so much peace didn't answer his questions. He closed the Bible, bowed his head and prayed.

Mattie found him there sometime after midnight. "Brother, you're up late," she said as she padded into the kitchen in her fuzzy slippers. Her hair was down around her shoulders, and she was wearing a robe over her long nightdress. "Is something wrong?"

He sighed.

She took a seat across from him. "Whatever it is, you can tell me." She waited, then asked, "Is it to do with Mari?"

He nodded. And when she said nothing, he found himself telling her the whole tale. She didn't say a word until he finished.

"And Mari insists that she told the truth?" Mattie asked quietly. He nodded. "And you believe her?" He nodded again. She took his hand and squeezed it.

"Mattie, I know you're against this marriage but…" He could feel his eyes tearing up, and he was embarrassed. "I love her."

"James, you're mistaken. I'm *not* against Mari. I'm against anything that would take you away from me, from our family and from our church." There was no accusation in her voice. This was his Mattie, the person he'd confided in and depended on since he was a child.

"I told you that I would never leave the faith again. If Mari and I marry, we'll make our home here, our faith will be hers."

"And she makes you happy?"

"She does."

"I've watched Mari, and despite my concerns, I do believe she loves you. All I want, all I've ever wanted, is your happiness. And if it's Mari who makes you happy, then I'll accept and love her, too."

"But this…" He shook his head. "I don't know what to make of it. Why would her own uncle tell an untruth?"

"Sara believes her to be unbaptized, doesn't she?"

He nodded. "Yes, but they never went to the same church and this… It would have been a long time ago." Then he let the question that had troubled him most fall between them. "And if Mari is telling the truth, why did she shut me out? Why was she so angry?" He rested his forehead on one hand. "It makes no sense to me. All I said was 'Is it true?' What kind of man wouldn't ask that question?"

"Maybe asking it caused her to doubt you," Mattie suggested. Her oval face was soft in the lamplight. "And maybe she was so hurt that she just lashed out like our sweet colt did last summer when he caught his leg in that wire. He was in so much pain that he couldn't think straight."

He raised his gaze to hers. "What should I do, Mattie? What would you do?"

"It's different. I'm a woman. I know what I'd do, but what's important is what *you* want to do."

"I don't know." He shrugged. "My first impulse is

to hire a driver. Go straight to Wisconsin. Find out the truth for myself. Clear Mari's name."

She laid her palm on the kitchen table. "Then that's what you should do. Go first thing in the morning."

"You don't think I'm a fool for doing that?"

She chuckled. "I think you're a fool if you don't."

Mari took another towel from the laundry basket and pinned it on the clothesline. Sheets flapped in the wind as the late-morning sun warmed the air. She loved the smell of freshly washed clothes that had been line-dried, and normally she didn't mind doing the wash. Today, her heart wasn't in the familiar chore.

Although it was Saturday morning, a refrigeration problem the previous night had forced the butcher shop to close. She would rather have been at work. Gideon had assured everyone that they would receive their regular pay for the missed hours, but she regretted the forced holiday. When she was working, it was easier to forget that her uncle's letter had ruined everything between her and James, and that she had only compounded the problem by refusing to discuss the problem with him.

Her first thought had been that James's failure to believe her meant that he didn't love her enough, that he didn't trust her. Her own pride and insecurity had caused an ugly exchange of words—words she hadn't meant and would give anything to take back.

Thinking about it rationally, James hadn't accused her of lying to him, he'd simply asked if her uncle's accusation was true. She couldn't blame him for that. All she would have had to do was deny it. Her behavior was both immature and hurtful to the man she loved.

And now she would pay the price. And she couldn't blame Bishop Atlee. He was acting as the shepherd of his church. He'd not accused her or rejected her. He'd simply told her that her baptism and wedding would be postponed.

Sara, as always, remained her rock. When she'd spilled out her story to Sara, her friend had sympathized with her and had offered her usual dose of sage advice. "Baptisms aren't performed in secret," she exclaimed. "Not even in the wilds of Wisconsin. I'd have heard if you'd been baptized."

Of course, Sara was right. When a young man or woman pledged his or her life to the faith, the entire community stood witness. Her uncle's false tale couldn't hold water, because other members of the church would verify her story. She didn't know why he had done it. She wouldn't want to think that he held such animosity against her that he would want to ruin her opportunity to return to the Amish faith and to make a good marriage.

Sara had only shrugged. She would write her own letters, she insisted. She had many contacts in Wisconsin, and she would ask them to confirm Mari's innocence. "It might take time," Sara said, "but we'll straighten this mess out and get you and James back together."

Mari wasn't so sure. Five days had now passed without a word from James. She hadn't seen him and he hadn't sent word by way of anyone else. It was obvious the life she had dreamed of these past few weeks was over before it ever began. Of course she realized that staying in Seven Poplars didn't depend on her marrying James or anyone else. Her precious son was happy here, and she was, too. But she'd wanted more. She'd dreamed of being James's wife, of having children together. Because of her own foolish words, that dream had dissolved. Now he might never allow her to mend the breech between them. And that loss would linger with her the rest of her days.

She reached for another towel, but her basket wasn't where she thought she'd left it. Puzzled, she looked around, then ducked under the line of wash.

And there stood James, wooden clothespins in his mouth and a damp sheet in his hands. He appeared to be looking for the corner of the sheet, but he'd succeeded only in making a muddle of it.

She laughed. She'd never been so happy to see anyone in her life.

He laughed, and the pins dropped out of his mouth onto the grass. Then he gave her a smile that melted her heart.

"Oh, James." She tried to find words, but they wouldn't come. What did come were tears.

He dropped the sheet and took hold of her shoulders. He pulled her close and looked down into her eyes. "It's all right," he said. "Stop crying. I can't stand it when you cry."

She cried harder, and he cradled her head against his chest. "I thought you were never going to speak to me again," she managed between gasps and sobs. "I was so wrong to run away from you like that, to say such things. I didn't mean it, James. I didn't. I love you so much…and now—"

"Now it's all right, Mari. Everything's all right. I went to Wisconsin and brought back proof that you were telling the truth."

"You went to Wisconsin?" She sniffed. "How?"

"Stop crying and I'll tell you." He pulled a handkerchief from his pocket and wiped away her tears.

"Why did my uncle tell such lies about me?"

"He's ill. My guess is that he's probably suffering from Alzheimer's. Your aunt says he's not himself. She says it comes and goes. Some days he gets lost on his own farm and one of his grandchildren has to find him and bring him back."

"But he said he was the bishop."

"And he is. No one in the church will take that office from him, but his preachers are understanding. They help him perform his duties. But a neighbor said the mental loss has done nothing good for his temperament. He did you a great wrong, but he needs our prayers more than condemnation." James took both her hands in his. "Can you do that? Can you have the grace to forgive him? Not just for this, but for all the ways he failed you? He should never have turned his back on you the way he did. To turn you away when you came to him in need. It's not what we're taught."

She pressed her lips together. "I'm sorry you had to hear those things."

"I'm not. But what's in the past is in the past. Whatever he's done, it's not for us to judge him. He will have to face a higher judgment." James took hold of her chin and raised it tenderly. "Can you pray for him?"

She nodded. Whatever bitterness she'd felt had evaporated with the sight of James's face. He was right. Who was she to judge anyone? "Can you forgive me?" she asked him.

"There's nothing to forgive. You were hurting and you reacted." He took her hand. "I want you to come to Bishop Atlee with me. We'll tell him the good news."

Doubt pierced her joy. "Will he believe you? Did you bring letters from anyone else?"

"No letters but something better." He grinned again. "Caleb. When Mattie told Rebecca that I was going to Wisconsin, she insisted that her husband accompany me. Caleb is one of our preachers. Everyone knows his word is good, and he witnessed the same statements that I did. He spoke with your uncle. We both did. And we could see that he wasn't behaving rationally."

"And Caleb will speak for me?"

"He will. He was going home to see Rebecca and the children, and then he's going straight to the bishop."

"We have to tell Sara," Mari said. "She believed me, but we have to share this wonderful news with her."

He looked down at the sheet on the ground. "Maybe we'd best finish this chore first. I don't want to be the one who tells Sara that I kept you from hanging out her laundry."

Mari looked at the wet sheet and then at him. "And what do we do about this?"

"Hang it up and hope for the best," he ventured.

"You seem to be all thumbs when it comes to hanging wash," she teased.

He chuckled. "That's what Mattie says."

She found a corner of the sheet and passed it to him. "So your sister knows you went to Wisconsin?"

"She knows," he replied as he retrieved the fallen clothespins. "She's the one who urged me to go."

"Then she won't stand in the way of our courting?"

"No, darling, Mattie won't stand in our way. It eases my heart that the two women I love best aren't at odds, but what Mattie wanted would never have made a difference. As much as I care for her, it was never her decision." He leaned over the clothesline until they were nose to nose and he gazed into her eyes. "You're the one I intend to marry, if you'll have me."

"I will," she promised. "I will, forever and ever."

Epilogue

Mari paused by her kitchen sink to gaze out the open window. It was a beautiful spring day, warm and full of the sweet scents of herbs and the fresh-turned earth of her kitchen garden. Just outside, a Carolina wren whistled a merry tune as it scratched at the base of the bird feeder James and Zachary had built for her the previous fall.

In the meadow, Mari could see Zachary and James heading toward the house, leading a brown-and-white pony hitched to a child's cart. She needed to get supper on the table; she was running behind because she'd been cooking for the following day's worship service. But now that Mari had everything ready for the Sabbath, she could take the time to feed her own family properly.

Tomorrow would be their second wedding anniversary, but because it was also a church Sunday, she thought it would be fine with James if they celebrated a day early. It didn't seem possible that so much time had passed since they'd stood in front of the elders and pledged their lives to each other. It seemed like only yesterday. *I'm happy*, she thought, *happier than I ever would have thought possible*. Life with James fulfilled all her dreams, for her and for Zachary.

The change in her son since they'd come to Seven Poplars was more than she'd hoped for. All he'd needed was a place to belong. And a father to guide him. Now, at eleven, going on twelve, he had not only grown in height and breadth, but in maturity and wisdom. He went willingly to school and kept up a B average, but his first love was being in the woodshop with James. Zachary said that he wanted to be a carpenter, and Mari thought that was a fine ambition. After all, hadn't Lord Jesus been a carpenter?

The odor of browning biscuits drew her away from the window and her musing, and she grabbed a hot mitt and opened the oven door.

"Something smells good," James said.

Mari smiled as a warm joy filled her. Would the day ever come that she could see him and not feel a burst of happiness? She hoped not.

"Zach will be in in a minute—he's putting his pony up." James came up behind her, slipped an arm around her waist and gently kissed the nape of her neck.

"Behave yourself," she protested, laughing. "What if Zachary comes in and sees you?"

James chuckled. "And what if he does?"

Laughing, she pushed him away and went to the refrigerator for butter.

"I brought you something," he said.

Pleased, she turned to see him holding a brimming handful of wildflowers. "Oh."

"Happy anniversary," he said.

She blinked back tears and smiled at him. "Beautiful," she managed. Multicolored blooms cascaded out of the bouquet, prettier than anything a florist could have arranged. "Thank you."

"Thank you," he murmured, pulling her against him and kissing her mouth tenderly. "These last two years have been the best of my—" An indignant wail broke through his words, and he released her to turn toward the cradle. "And what's wrong with you?" he crooned. "Is *Dat*'s little man hungry?"

"I'll get him," Mari said.

"Let me." James crossed to the cradle and scooped up their six-week-old Samuel. "I haven't gotten to hold him all day. Isn't that so?" he murmured to the baby. He settled into the rocking chair, shifted Samuel onto his shoulder and began patting the infant's back.

Samuel let out a loud burp, and both Mari and James laughed. "So that's all he needed," Mari said.

"No, all he needed was some *Daddi* time," James teased.

"Supper ready?" Zachary asked as he came in the door. "I'm really hungry."

"Wash up and pour iced tea for you and your father," Mari said.

A few minutes later, Mari lowered her head and closed her eyes for grace. *Thank You for Your many blessings, for this food, for the roof over our heads and for our two healthy sons. Thank You for my good and loving husband*, she prayed silently. *And thank You Lord for making a place for me at Your table.*

Mari had no illusions that her future would be free from worries and loss, but with love and faith she also knew in her heart that as a family, they would find a way to make it through. They would strive to serve their community and their faith. And they would be happy forever and ever. Together. Because she was finally home...

* * * * *

*Be sure to turn the page to get a glimpse of
author Patricia Davids' Amish romance
THEIR PRETEND AMISH COURTSHIP.*

Which New York Times *bestselling author
RaeAnne Thayne called
"Tender and gentle, with two delightful characters
who truly belong together. A lovely read."*

Chapter One

"You are going and I don't want to hear another word about it, Fannie. Nor from you, Betsy. Do you hear me?"

When Fannie's mother shook a wooden spoon at one or both of her daughters, the conversation was over.

"*Ja, Mamm*." Betsy beat a quick retreat out of the kitchen.

Fannie glared after her. The little coward. Without her sister's help, Fannie had no chance of changing her mother's mind. Seated at the table in her family's kitchen, Fannie crossed her arms on the red-checkered tablecloth and laid her head on her forearms. "*Ja, Mamm*, I hear you."

There had to be a way. There just had to be.

"Now you are being sensible." Belinda Erb turned back to the stove and continued stirring the strawberry jam she was getting ready to can. "I will write to my *mamm* and *daed* tomorrow. They insist on sending the money for your bus ticket. I expect you'll be able to leave the middle of next week. It will be a relief to know one of us is helping *Daed* look after *Mamm* while she recovers from her broken ankle."

"A week! That isn't much time to get ready to go to Florida." How was she going to come up with a plan to keep from going in a week?

"Nonsense. It's plenty of time. You have two work dresses and a good Sunday dress. What else do you need?"

Fannie sat up and touched her head covering. "I need another *kapp* or two."

Her mother turned around with a scowl on her face. "What happened to the last one I made you?"

"I lost it."

"When you were out riding like some wild child, no doubt. It's time you gave up your childish ways. Anna Bowman and I were just talking about this yesterday. We have been too lenient with our youngest *kinder*, and we are living to rue the day. She is putting her foot down with Noah, and I am doing the same with you. When you come back from Pinecraft at Thanksgiving, you will end your *rumspringa* and make your decision to be Amish or not."

Fannie had heard about Anna's plans to see Noah settled and she felt sorry for him, but she had her own problems.

Her mother turned back to the stove. "I have given up on seeing you wed, though it breaks my heart to say so."

Here came the lecture about becoming an old maid. She wasn't twenty-two yet, but she had been hearing this message since she turned nineteen. That was how old her mother had been when she married. Why did everyone believe the only thing a woman wanted was a husband? "Betsy isn't married and she is two years older than I am."

"Betsy is betrothed to Hiram. They will marry next fall."

Fannie sat up straight. "When did this happen?"

Why hadn't her sister mentioned it? Betsy and Hiram had been walking out together for ages. Fannie thought Hiram would never get up the courage to propose.

"Hiram came to tell your father and me last night."

"Then why does Betsy want to go to Florida?"

Fannie's mother took her time before answering. "She loves her grandparents and wishes to spend time with them while she can. As you should."

After pulling the jam off the stove, Fannie's mother came and sat beside her at the table. "Why are you so dead set against going?"

Fannie knew her mother wouldn't approve of the promise she'd made. "I have made plans with my riding club for this summer."

"Your horses and your club won't take care of you when you are old. *Mamm* writes that there are plenty of young people in Pinecraft during the fall and winter. You may want to stay longer."

"Young people but no horses."

"Enough about horses!" Fannie's mother rose to her feet. "You have chores to finish and I must get these jars of jam done. It's a wedding gift for Timothy Bowman and his bride. Timothy's mother told me they plan to leave on their wedding trip after the school frolic."

Fannie clamped her lips together. Her mother wanted to change the subject. It wouldn't do any good to argue; Fannie knew she'd only be wasting her breath. She left the room and found her sister gathering clothes off the line in the backyard. Fannie joined her, pulling down stiff wind-dried pants and dresses. "*Mamm* said you went and got engaged to Hiram."

"It was time. I'm not getting any younger."

"That's a poor reason to marry."

"It's reason enough for us. We are content with each other. You are blessed to have this opportunity." Betsy clutched a pillowcase to her chest. "I have always dreamed of seeing the ocean. I can't imagine how big it must be. Hiram has no desire to see the sea."

"Doesn't he have a desire to please you?" That, in a nutshell, was what was wrong with getting married.

"It would be an expense we couldn't afford. Perhaps someday."

"I would gladly send you in my place, but I don't imagine Hiram would be happy about…that…" Fannie's words trailed away as an idea took shape in her mind. "That's it. I need a Hiram."

"What are you babbling about now?"

It was so simple. "Betsy, would you go to Florida if I couldn't? What if *Mamm* decided you should go instead of me? Would Hiram understand?"

"He knows we must honor our elders. I would gladly take your place, but *Mamm* has her mind made up."

"If she knew I was being courted, she would bend over backward to keep me here. She is desperate to see me wed."

"She's desperate to see you interested in any young man instead of your horses. Who is courting you? Why didn't you tell me about him?"

"I have to go." Fannie shoved the clothes in her arms at her sister. There was only one fellow who might help her.

* * *

"Noah, where are you? I need to speak to you."

Working near the back of his father's barn, Noah Bowman dropped the hoof of his buggy horse, Willy, took the last nail out of his mouth and stood upright to stare over his horse's back. Fannie Erb, his neighbor's youngest daughter, came hurrying down the wide center aisle, checking each stall as she passed. Her white *kapp* hung off the back of her head, dangling by a single bobby pin. Her curly red hair was still in a bun, but it was windblown and lopsided. No doubt it would be completely undone before she got home. Fannie was always in a rush.

"What's up, *karotte oben*?" He picked up his horse's hoof again, positioned it between his knees and drove in the last nail of the new shoe.

Fannie stopped outside the stall gate and fisted her hands on her hips. "You know I hate being called a carrottop."

"Sorry." Noah grinned as he caught the glare she leveled at him.

He wasn't sorry a bit. He liked the way her unusual violet eyes darkened and flashed when she was annoyed. Annoying Fannie had been one of his favorite pastimes when they were schoolchildren.

She lived on the farm across the road where her family raised and trained Standardbred buggy horses. Noah had known her from the cradle, as their parents were good friends and often visited back and forth. Fannie had grown from the gangly girl he liked to tease at school into a comely woman, but her temper hadn't cooled.

Framed in a rectangle of light cast by the early-morning sun shining through the open top of a Dutch door, dust motes danced around Fannie's head like fireflies drawn to the fire in her hair. The summer sun had expanded the freckles on her upturned nose and given her skin a healthy glow, but Fannie didn't tan the way most women did. Her skin always looked cool and creamy. As usual, she was wearing blue jeans and riding boots under her plain green dress and black apron.

He preferred wearing *Englisch* jeans himself. He liked having hip pockets to keep his cell phone in, something his homemade Amish pants didn't have. His parents tolerated his use of a phone because he was still in his *rumspringa*. He knew Fannie used a cell phone, too. She had a solar-powered charger and allowed other Amish youth to use it if they didn't have access to electricity.

"What do you need, Fannie? Did your hot temper spark a fire and you want me to put it out?" He chuckled at his own wit. He and his four brothers were volunteer members of the local fire department. Patting Willy's sleek black neck, Noah reached to untie the horse's halter.

"This isn't a joke, Noah. I need to get engaged, and quickly. Will you help me?"

He spun around to stare at her in shocked disbelief. A marriage proposal was the last thing he'd expected from Fannie. "You had better explain that remark."

"*Mamm* and *Daed* are sending me to live with my grandparents in Pinecraft, Florida, until Thanksgiving. I can't go. I've told my folks that, but they insist. Having a steady beau is the only way to get them to send Betsy instead."

At least Fannie wasn't suffering from some unrequited love for him. He should have been relieved, but he was mildly annoyed instead.

He opened the bottom half of the Dutch door leading to the corral and let his horse out. Willy quickly trotted to where Fannie's Haflinger mare stood on the other side of the fence. The black gelding put his head over the top rail to sniff noses with the golden-chestnut beauty.

Noah began picking up his tools. "I hear Florida is nice."

Fannie grabbed the top of the gate. "Are you serious? My grandparents get around on three-wheeled bicycles down there. They don't have horses. Can you imagine staying in a place with no horses?"

He couldn't, but he didn't think much of her crazy idea, either. "I'm not going to get hitched to you because you don't want to go to Florida."

Indignation sparked in her eyes. "What's wrong with getting hitched to me? I'd make you a *goot* wife."

She stepped back as he opened the stall gate. "Fannie, you would knock me on the head with a skillet the first chance you got. You have a bad temper."

"Oh!" She stomped her foot, and then sighed heavily. "I do have a temper, but I wouldn't do you physical harm."

"Small consolation considering how sharp your tongue is. Ouch! Ow!" He jumped away from several imaginary jabs.

Her eyes narrowed. "Stop teasing. I don't want to actually marry you, *dummkopf*. I said *engaged*, not *married*, but I guess it doesn't have to be that serious. Walking out with me might do. If not, we can get engaged later. Anyway, we will call it off long before the *banns* are announced and go our merry ways."

He didn't like being called a dumbhead, but he overlooked her comment to point out the biggest flaw in her plan. "You and I have never acted like a loving couple. Your parents would smell a rat."

"Maybe, but maybe not. *Mamm* has been telling me for ages that it's time I started looking around for a husband."

He closed the stall gate and latched it. "Better go farther afield for that search. The boys around here all know you too well."

She wasn't the kind of woman he'd marry. He might enjoy teasing that quick temper, but he wouldn't want to live with it.

Her defiant expression crumpled. She hurried to keep up with him as he went outside. "Don't be mean, Noah. I need help. I can't go to Florida. My *daed* has two mares due to foal this month."

"They will foal without you, and your father can certainly handle it."

She walked to her mare standing patiently beside the corral. "Trinket will miss me. I can't go months without seeing her."

Fannie loved horses, he knew that, but he sensed she wasn't telling him the whole story behind this scheme. "Trinket will survive without you. What's the real reason you don't want to go?"

She sighed heavily and folded her arms tightly across her chest. "You may have heard I took a job working for Connie Stroud on her horse farm."

"*Mamm* mentioned it." His mother kept up on all the local news. How she was able to learn so much about the community without the use of a forbidden telephone was a mystery to him.

"Connie raises and trains Haflingers. Trinket was one of her foals. Connie's father passed away two years ago and she is having a hard time making a go of the place. She gives riding lessons and boards horses, but she needs to sell more of her Haflingers for a better price than she can get around here if she is going to make ends meet."

"If she can't sell a horse without you in the state, she's a poor businesswoman."

He walked over to two more horses tied to the fence. One was his niece Hannah's black pony, Hank. The other was Ginger, a bay mare that belonged to his mother. Speaking softly to Hank, Noah ran his hand down the pony's neck and lifted his front foot. He found the shoe was loose and too worn to save. He checked the pony's back foot, expecting to find it in the same condition.

Fannie walked over to Hank and began to rub him behind his ears. The pony closed his eyes in bliss and leaned into her fingers. "I'm deeply beholden to Connie. I need to help her save her stable."

Noah glanced at Fannie's face and was surprised by the determination in her eyes. Fannie might be hot-headed and stubbornly independent, but she was clearly loyal to this friend. "How does pretending to be engaged help her?"

"It keeps me here. Not a lot of people know what amazing horses Haflingers are. I came up with the great idea of an equine drill team using Connie's Haflingers plus my Trinket. We are going to give exhibitions at some of the county fairs and then at the Ohio State Equine Expo. I have seven Amish girls from my riding club who have already joined us."

"Your parents are permitting this?" It was an unusual undertaking for an Amish woman.

She looked away from him. "We haven't been told we can't do it. You know how crazy the *Englisch* are for anything Amish. If we can generate some interest, show what Connie's horses can do, I know it will help her sell more of them. Besides, everyone in the group is depending on me to teach them—and the horses—the routines. Our first show is in a week."

Fannie had a way with horses that was unique. He'd always admired that about her. "I'm sure your parents will come around if you make them see how much you want to stay."

"*Mamm* won't. She has her mind made up. She says Betsy is more help to her than I am because I'm always out in the barn. Betsy likes to cook, sew, mend and clean, while I don't. I'll die down there if I have to give up my horse." Fannie sniffled and wiped her eyes with the back of her hand.

Noah put Hank's hoof down to stare at Fannie. He considered putting his arm around her shoulders to comfort her, but thought better of it. "Would it help if I talked to your folks?"

"*Nee*, it won't do any good. *Mamm* will know I put you up to it."

"I'm sorry, Fannie, but don't you think your idea is a bit dishonest?"

She shook her head. "If you ask to court me today, *actually ask me*, then it won't be a lie. I can tell *Mamm* we are walking out with a straight face and a clear conscience."

"I don't see how, when you concocted the whole thing."

"You have to help me, Noah. I don't know what else to do. Betsy would *love* to spend a few months with our grandparents and see the ocean. You don't have to tell anyone you are dating me. All you have to do is take me home after the singing on Sunday and I'll do the rest. Please?"

Why did she have to sound so desperate?

Fannie wasn't making enough headway in swaying Noah. She took a deep breath and pulled out her last tool of persuasion. "What are your plans for this summer?"

He looked suspicious at her abrupt change of topic. "We are putting up hay this week. We'll start cultivating the corn after that if the rain holds off."

"I didn't mean farmwork. Are you playing ball again this summer?" She flicked the brim of the blue ball cap he wore instead of the traditional Amish straw hat. Once he chose baptism, he would have to give up his worldly dress.

He ducked away from her hand. "I'm in the league again with the fellas from the fire department. I'm their pitcher. If we keep winning like we have been, we have a shot at getting into the state invitational tournament."

She twined her fingers in Hank's mane. "You must practice a lot."

"Twice a week with games every Saturday. In fact, we have a makeup game tonight with the Berlin team, as we were rained out last weekend."

"You wouldn't mind missing a few of your practices or even a game for a family picnic or party, would you?"

"What are you getting at, Fannie?"

"I'm not the only one you'll be helping if you go out

with me. Your mother has been shopping around for a wife for you. Did you know that?"

His expression hardened. "You're *narrisch*. Up until this minute I was starting to feel sorry for you."

She almost wavered, but she couldn't let Connie down. "I'm not crazy. With all your brothers married, you are the last chick in the nest."

"So?"

"So she's worried that you are still running around instead of settling down. She has asked a number of her friends to invite their nieces and granddaughters to visit this summer with the express notion of finding *you* a wife among them. They'll be here for picnics and dinners and singings all summer long, so you can size them up."

"*Mamm* wouldn't do that." Amish parents rarely meddled in their children's courtships.

"Well, she has."

"My mother isn't the meddling sort. At least, not very often."

Fannie shrugged. "Mothers are funny that way. They don't believe we can be happy unless we are married, when you and I both know we are perfectly happy being single. Are you ready to spend the summer dodging a string of desperate-to-be-wed maidens?"

"*Nee*, and that includes you and your far-fetched scheme. No one will believe I'm dating you of my own free will."

She felt the heat rush to her face. "You kissed me once."

He arched one eyebrow. "As I remember, you weren't happy about it."

"I was embarrassed that your brother Luke saw us.

I regretted my behavior afterward, and I have told you I was sorry."

"Not half as sorry as I was," he snapped back. "That glass of punch you poured on me was cold."

She *was* sorry that evening ended so badly. It had been a nice kiss. Her first.

She and Noah had slipped outside for a breath of fresh air near the end of a Christmas cookie exchange at his parent's house the winter before last. She had been curious to find out what it would be like to be kissed by him. Things had been going well in his mother's garden until Luke came by. When Noah tried for a second kiss after his brother walked away, she had been so flustered that she upended a glass of cold strawberry punch in his lap.

"That was ages ago. Are you going to berate me again or are you going to help me?" Fannie demanded.

He leaned over the pony's back, his expression dead serious. "Find some other gullible fellow."

Her temper flared and she didn't try to quell it. "Oh! You're just plain mean. See if I ever help you out of a jam. You were my last hope, Noah Bowman. If I wasn't Amish I might actually hate you for this, but I have to say I forgive you. Have fun meeting all your prospective brides this summer." She spun on her heel and mounted her horse.

"If I'm your last hope, Fannie Erb, that says more about you than it does about me," he called out as she turned Trinket around.

She nudged her mare into a gallop and blinked back tears. She didn't want him to see how deeply disappointed she was.

Now what was she going to do?

Chapter Two

Noah regretted his parting comment as he watched Fannie ride away. She didn't have many friends. She was more at ease around horses than people. Her reputation as a hothead was to blame but he knew there wasn't any real harm in her. Her last bobby pin came loose as she rode off. Her *kapp* fluttered to the ground in the driveway.

Willy raised his head and neighed loudly. He clearly wanted the pretty, golden-chestnut mare with the blond mane to come back.

"Don't be taken in by good looks, Willy. A sweet disposition lasts far longer than a pretty face. I don't care what Fannie says—*Mamm* isn't in a hurry to see me wed."

He walked out and picked up Fannie's *kapp*. At the sound of a wagon approaching, he stuffed it into his back pocket. His cousins Paul and Mark Bowman drove in from the hayfield with a load of bales stacked shoulder high on a trailer pulled by Noah's father's gray Percheron draft horses. The *chug-chug* sound of the gas-powered bailer could be heard in the distance where Noah's father was pulling it with a four-horse hitch. Noah's brothers Samuel and Timothy were hooking the bales from the back of the machine and stacking them on a second trailer.

"Who was that?" Mark asked.

"Fannie Erb." Noah watched her set her horse at the stone wall bordering her family's lane. Trinket sailed over it easily.

"She rides well," Paul said with a touch of admiration in his voice.

"She does," Noah admitted.

"What did she want?" Mark asked.

Noah shook his head at the absurdness of her idea. "She's looking for a beau. Are you interested?"

Mark shook his head. "*Nee*, I'm not. I have a girlfriend back home."

His brother Paul nudged him with an elbow. "A man can go to an auction without buying a horse. It doesn't hurt to look and see what's out there."

Mark and Paul had come from Bird-In-Hand, Pennsylvania, to stay with Noah's family and apprentice with Noah's father in the family's woodworking business. The shop was closed for a few days until the Bowmans had their hay in, and Noah was glad for the extra help.

Mark scowled at his brother. "A man who doesn't need a horse but goes to the auction anyway is wasting a day *Gott* has given him. You know what they say about idle hands."

"I won't suffer from idle hands today—today—today. I'll have the blisters—blisters—blisters to prove it," Paul called out in a singsong voice. The fast-talking young man was learning to become an auctioneer.

Mark maneuvered the hay wagon next to the front of the barn. The wide hayloft door was open above them, with a bale elevator positioned in the center of it. Noah pulled the cord on the elevator's gas-powered engine. It sprang to life, and the conveyer belt began to move upward. Noah glanced toward the house and saw his brother Joshua jogging toward them. Noah sat on the belt and rode up to the hayloft. Joshua came up the same way and the two men waited for the bales their cousins unloaded.

After stacking the first thirty-five bales deep in the recesses of the hayloft, Noah and Joshua moved to the open loft door to wait for the next trailer load to come in from the field.

Joshua fanned his face with his straw hat and then mopped his sweaty brow with his handkerchief. "It's going to be another hot one."

The interior of the barn loft would be roasting by late afternoon, even with the doors open. Noah pulled off his ball cap and reached into his back pocket for his handkerchief, but pulled out Fannie's *kapp* instead.

The silly goose. Did she really think he would agree to court her at a moment's notice? Only she could come up with such a far-fetched scheme. He tucked her *kapp* back in his pocket and wiped his face with his sleeve, determined to stop thinking about her.

He leaned out of the loft to see how close the second wagon was to being full. "Looks like I'll have time to finish putting a new horseshoe on Hank before they get here. We have some pony-size shoes, don't we?"

Joshua nodded. "On the wall in the tack room. I had John Miller make a full set for Hank right after I brought him home."

"Goot."

"I can take care of him later," Joshua offered.

"Checking the horses' feet is my job. I only have Hank and Ginger left."

"What does Ginger need?"

"I noticed she was limping out in the pasture. I haven't had a chance to see why."

"I can take care of her. I know you want to have your work done before you head to your ball game."

"Danki, bruder."

"You can return the favor some other time. I'm looking forward to your game next weekend. It should be a *goot* one. Walter Osborn can knock the hide off a baseball when he connects."

Walter was an English neighbor and volunteer fire fighter. Part of his job was to gather the Amish volunteers in the area and deliver them to the fire station when the call went out. He was also a good friend of Noah's.

"Walter is the best catcher in the league and our power hitter. If we can get into the state tournament, he'll have a chance at being scouted by the pros. Those men don't come to these backwater places. Walter deserves a chance to show what he's got."

Joshua settled his hat on his head. "Are you hoping to be scouted by a pro team?"

"Where'd you get that idea?" Noah avoided looking at his brother. He'd never told anyone about his dream.

"Mamm and *Daed* were talking about it the other

day. Your coach has been telling everyone you have a gift. It's easy to see how much you love the game, but you'll have to stop playing soon. You will be twenty-two this fall. Your *rumspringa* can't go on forever."

Noah gave the answer he always gave. "I intend to enjoy a few more years of my running-around time before I take my vows. I'm in no rush."

Giving up his English clothes, his cell phone and the other worldly things he could enjoy now would be easy. But could he give up the game? That would be tough. He loved playing ball. Out on the pitcher's mound, with the pressure mounting, he felt alive.

He suspected that Fannie felt much the same way about her horses. She would hate giving up her riding but she would have to one day. Riding a horse astride was considered worldly and only tolerated before baptism. A rush of sympathy for her surprised him.

He pushed thoughts of Fannie and her problems to the back of his mind as he climbed down the ladder in the barn's interior and headed to the tack room. He needed to concentrate on winning the game tonight. It would bring him one step closer to his goal.

To find out if he was good enough to play professional ball.

If he was good enough, he believed it would be a sign from God to go out into the world and use his gift. If he didn't have the level of talent that his coach thought he did, that would be a sign, too. A sign that God wanted him to remain in his Amish community. Either choice would be hard but he had faith that God would show him the right path.

He was finishing Hank's shoeing when he heard the sound of a buggy coming up the lane. His mother and his sister-in-law Rebecca pulled to a stop beside him in Rebecca's buggy.

His mother graced him with a happy smile from the driver's seat. "We have just heard the nicest news."

"What would that be?" He opened the corral gate and turned Hank in with the other horses. The second hay wagon was on its way.

"The bishop's wife told me two of her nieces have arrived to spend a month visiting them. I have invited them to supper this evening," his mother said quickly.

"And I received a letter telling me my cousins from Indiana are coming to visit." Rebecca smiled at the baby in her arms. "I'll certainly be glad to have a pair of mother's helpers with me for a few months. This little fellow and his brother wear me out."

"So, both your cousins are girls?" he asked trying not to appear uneasy. Had Fannie been right?

His mother exchanged a coy glance with Rebecca. "They are, and all the young women are near your age. I'm sure you'll enjoy getting to know them. Maybe one will catch your eye. I might even talk your father into hosting a few picnics and singings this summer. Won't that be *wunderbar*?"

"Sounds like fun, but you know I'll be gone a lot this summer, and I have a ball game this evening."

His mother frowned. "It won't hurt you to miss one of your silly games. I insist you join us for supper and meet the bishop's nieces."

"The team is depending on me. I can't cancel now. It's important to them."

A stern expression settled over his mother's face. "And this is more important. Noah Bowman, we need to have a talk."

His heart sank when his mother stepped out of the buggy. She rarely took the lead in family matters. Normally his father took him aside for a talk after some indiscretion. Rebecca drove the buggy on to the house, leaving them alone.

His mother folded her arms over her chest. "Your father and I have spoken about this and prayed about it, and we have come to a decision. My *sohn*, you are our youngest. Your father and I have been lenient with you, letting you dress fancy and not plain, letting you travel with your team and keep your cell phone, but you are old enough to put away these childish things as all your brothers have done. It's time you gave serious thought to finding a wife."

He leaned close trying to cajole her with his smile. He didn't want her to worry about a decision he couldn't make yet, so he told her what he thought she wanted to hear. "You don't have to worry about me, *Mamm*. I plan to join the church in due time. If that is *Gott*'s will."

"You give lip service to this most solemn matter, but nothing in your actions gives me cause to believe your words."

He took a step back. She was dead serious. If his parents forbade his ball playing, he would have to do as they asked or leave home. He wasn't ready to make that choice.

The odds of getting picked up by a major-league team were a thousand to one against him, but he needed to know if he was good enough. Why had God given him this talent, if not to use it?

What could he say that would change his mother's mind?

He shoved his hands into his hip pockets and rocked

back on his heels. His fingers touched Fannie's *kapp*. Would she still agree to a courtship or had he burned that bridge with his taunting?

Swallowing hard, he pulled the *kapp* from his pocket and wound the ribbons around his fingers. "I didn't want to say anything, but I have plans to see someone before my game tonight."

His mother glanced from his face to the head covering in his hand. "Who?"

"Fannie. Fannie Erb."

His mother's eyes brightened as she smiled widely. She took his face between her hands and kissed his cheek. "Oh, you sweet boy. You don't know how happy I am to hear this. The daughter of my dearest friend. Why didn't you tell me?"

"I thought I had a plan to stay, but it fell through." Fannie and Connie had finished exercising two of Connie's horses and were brushing them down before returning them to their stalls.

"What plan was that?"

"I asked Noah Bowman to pretend to court me and he turned me down." Fannie patted Goldenrod's sleek neck and ran her fingers through the mare's cream-colored mane. She hated to admit her failure to her friend.

Connie swept a lock of shoulder-length blond hair away from her face and gave Fannie a sympathetic smile. "Thanks for trying. Don't worry so. The team will carry on without you."

"Will they?"

The girls were all younger than Fannie was. They didn't believe in the project the way she did. They weren't beholden to Connie the way she was. If Connie had to sell her property, Fannie would lose more than a friend. She'd lose the job she loved. Riding and training horses was more than a childish pastime. It was what Fannie wanted to do for the rest of her life.

Fannie's Amish upbringing put her squarely at odds with her dream. Although some unmarried Amish women ran their own businesses, it wasn't common. Some worked for English employers but only until they chose to be baptized. Most worked in their family's businesses. Her parents and the bishop wouldn't approve of her riding once she was baptized, she was sure of that. Unless she chose to give up her Amish faith, it was unlikely she could follow her dream.

Could she leave behind all she had been raised to believe in? She wasn't ready to make that decision. Not yet.

"I think the team will do fine," Connie said, but she didn't sound sure.

Fannie pushed her uncertainty aside to concentrate on her friend. "I wanted to do this for you. I owe you so much."

Connie continued to brush her horse. "You have to get over thinking I did something special, Fannie. I didn't."

"You kept me from making the biggest mistake of my life. That was something special."

"It was your love of horses that led you to make the right decision. I only wish those other young people had made the same choice."

"So do I." Fannie cringed inwardly as she thought about the night that had ended so tragically less than two months after her seventeenth birthday.

"Have you settled on the number of patterns the

girls will perform?" Connie clearly wanted to change the subject, and Fannie let her.

"Not yet, but I will before I leave. Have you had any inquiries from the ad you ran on the Horse and Tack website?"

"Lowball bids, nothing serious. Maybe I'm just a poor marketer. These horses should sell themselves. If I had the money, I'd have a professional video made. That might do the trick."

"My father says the *Englisch* want an angle, a story. A good horse for sale isn't enough. It has to be an Amish-raised and Amish-trained horse. That's okay for him, but it doesn't help you."

"I can always say raised near the Amish and trained as the Amish would, but that lacks punch even if it is accurate."

Fannie shook her head and realized her *kapp* was missing. *Mamm* would be upset with her for losing another one. She pulled a white handkerchief from her pocket. She always carried two for just this reason. She folded it into a triangle and tied it at the nape of her neck.

A woman should cover her head when she prayed, and Fannie was in serious need of prayers. She couldn't believe it was part of God's plan for her to abandon her friend and to leave her beloved horses behind. "It amazes me how the *Englisch* think anything Amish must be better. We are the same as everyone else."

"You're right. There are good, hardworking people everywhere. If only hard work were enough to keep this place going. I'm glad my father isn't here to see how I've run it into the ground."

"You took care of your father as well as any daughter could. It wasn't possible to grow the business while he was so ill. You had a mountain of your father's medical bills to pay and you have done that. You will get this place back to the way it was and even better."

Fannie followed Connie's gaze as she glanced around the farm. Only four of the twelve stalls in the long, narrow barn were being used by boarders. The barn was beginning to show signs of wear and tear. The red paint was faded and peeling in places. Cobwebs hung from the rafters. A soggy spot at the end of the alley showed where the roof leaked, but all the Haflinger horses in the paddock and pasture were well cared for, with shining coats that gleamed golden brown in the sunshine. Connie took excellent care of her animals.

Attached to the barn was an indoor riding area where Connie's nine-year-old daughter, Zoe, was practicing her trick-riding moves on her Haflinger mare. Connie had once crisscrossed the United States performing at rodeos and equestrian events as a trick rider herself. She paused in her work to watch her daughter.

"I have got to make a go here, Fannie. I have to leave my daughter something besides tarnished belt buckles, fading ribbons and debts. I don't want to sell any of this land. My father made me promise that I wouldn't and I want to honor his wishes. After I'm gone, Zoe will be free to sell or stay. That will be my gift to her. A woman should be able to choose her own path in life."

"I couldn't agree with you more."

Connie shot her a puzzled glance. "Strange words coming from an Amish lass. I thought an Amish woman's goal in life was to be a wife and a mother."

"It is for most of the women, but I can't imagine being so tied down. I certainly don't want to marry and give some oaf the right to boss me around." To give up riding horses was like asking her to give up part of her soul.

"Does that mean you are thinking about leaving the Amish? I know some young people do, but won't you be shunned if you decide to leave?"

"My church believes each person must make that choice. If I leave before I am baptized into the faith, I won't be punished, but I know my parents won't allow me to continue staying at home. If I do decide not to be baptized, I was hoping I could work for you full-time and get my own place someday."

"If your plan with the drill team works out, I sure would consider taking you on full-time. I've never seen anyone as good with horses as you are. But don't give up on the idea of marriage. I can't see you settling for an oaf. It will take a special fellow to get harnessed to you, but I think he exists and I can't wait to meet him."

"I don't think he exists and I'm sure not going to waste my time looking for him."

"If I'd had that attitude before I met Zack, I wouldn't have Zoe now. It was a fair trade. Look at that girl go. She is fearless." Maternal pride glowed on her face as she watched her daughter circling the arena on her horse.

"She's really getting good," Fannie said. Trick riding was something she had always wanted to try.

"Better than I was at her age. I shouldn't encourage her, but I can't help it. The girl is like a sponge. She soaks in everything I tell her. I guess I'm one of those mothers who relive their glory days through their kids."

"Do you miss it?"

Connie paused in her work. "Sometimes I do, but that life is behind me along with my failed marriage to Zoe's father. Dad's illness was the excuse I used to come home, but that wasn't the whole truth. I missed staying in one place. Zack was the one with a restless spirit. Besides, I didn't want Zoe to grow up in a camper, always headed down the road to the next rodeo. I wanted her to have a home—a real home—and Dad gave us that."

She cupped her hands around her mouth. "Point your toes down, Zoe. Keep those legs straight and arch your back more."

"Like this?" Zoe shouted.

"That's better. That's a pretty good hippodrome stand."

Zoe grinned and waved one hand in acknowledgment as she stood atop the back of a gently loping golden horse with a wide white blaze down its face.

"Zoe is going to miss you," Connie said, turning back to Fannie.

"Don't give up on me yet. I may still find a way to stay." Fannie had no idea what that would be, but she wouldn't stop trying.

Connie put down her brush and motioned toward a pitchfork leaning against the wall. "Good. Until then, you still have work to do. I don't pay you much, but I expect you to earn it."

Fannie laughed as she picked up the fork. "I would exercise your horses for free, but cleaning stalls will still cost you."

Connie untied the lead ropes of both horses. "I'll put

these two away. You start on stall five and work your way down. George should be here soon. That man is always late. I wish I hadn't hired him."

George was another part-time stable hand at the farm. Connie insisted she couldn't afford full-time help, but in Fannie's eyes, George wasn't worth even part-time wages. He spent most of his time flirting with the girls in Fannie's riding group—or any woman who came to the farm.

Connie motioned toward her daughter. "I'll be back after I help Zoe with her technique. She's getting flat-footed again and that's dangerous, even on Misty."

Fannie set to work in the stall Connie had indicated, but her mind wasn't on the tasks before her. She still had to find a way to convince her parents that Betsy was the one they needed to send to Florida. No amount of pleading by her and her sister had changed their mother's mind so far. Their father might be persuaded, but their mother was adamant.

If only Noah had agreed to her plan. She wanted to be angry with him, but she couldn't. He was right. Her idea bordered on being dishonest, even if it was for a good cause. She didn't want to be courted by anyone, but having Noah reject her outright was humiliating. She wasn't that ugly, was she? There had been a time when she liked him—a lot. She tossed a forkful of straw into the wheelbarrow at her side.

She had liked being kissed by him, too. A lot. Jabbing the fork into the pile of dirty straw, she tried to forget about that night. She was the *dummkopf* for dumping her drink on him. He sure wouldn't try that again.

"Fannie, can I talk to you?"

She shrieked and spun around at the sound of Noah's voice, sending her forkful of dirty straw flying in his direction.

Don't miss
THEIR PRETEND AMISH COURTSHIP
by USA TODAY *bestselling author*
Patricia Davids,
available June 2017 wherever
Love Inspired Books and ebooks are sold.
www.LoveInspired.com

Love Inspired®

Save $1.00

on the purchase of any
Love Inspired®,
Love Inspired® Suspense or
Love Inspired® Historical book.

Redeemable at Participating Walmart Outlets.

Save $1.00

on the purchase of any Love Inspired®, Love Inspired® Suspense
or Love Inspired® Historical book.

Coupon valid until September 30, 2017.
Redeemable at Participating Walmart Outlets. Limit one coupon per customer.

52614822

5 65373 00076 2 (8100)0 12279

® and ™ are trademarks owned and used by the trademark owner and/or its licensee.

© 2017 Harlequin Enterprises Limited

LIINCICOUP0617

SPECIAL EXCERPT FROM

Love Inspired®

*Will a pretend courtship fend off matchmaking mothers,
or will it lead to true love?*

Read on for a sneak preview of
THEIR PRETEND AMISH COURTSHIP,
the next book in **Patricia Davids**'s
heartwarming series, **AMISH BACHELORS**.

"Noah, where are you? I need to speak to you."

Working near the back of his father's barn, Noah
Bowman dropped the hoof of his buggy horse Willy, took
the last nail out of his mouth and stood upright to stare
over his horse's back. Fannie Erb, his neighbor's youngest
daughter, came hurrying down the wide center aisle,
checking each stall as she passed. Her white *kapp* hung
off the back of her head dangling by a single bobby pin.
Her curly red hair was still in a bun, but it was windblown
and lopsided. No doubt, it would be completely undone
before she got home. Fannie was always in a rush.

"What's up, *karotte oben*?" He picked up his horse's
hoof again, positioned it between his knees and drove in
the last nail of the new shoe.

Fannie stopped outside the stall gate and fisted her
hands on her hips. "You know I hate being called a carrot
top."

"Sorry." Noah grinned.

LIEXP0517

He wasn't sorry a bit. He liked the way her unusual violet eyes darkened and flashed when she was annoyed. Annoying Fannie had been one of his favorite pastimes when they were schoolchildren.

Framed as she was in a rectangle of light cast by the early-morning sun shining through the open top of a Dutch door, dust motes danced around Fannie's head like fireflies drawn to the fire in her hair. The summer sun had expanded the freckles on her upturned nose and given her skin a healthy glow, but Fannie didn't tan the way most women did. Her skin always looked cool and creamy. As usual, she was wearing blue jeans and riding boots under her plain green dress and black apron.

"What you need, Fannie? Did your hot temper spark a fire and you want me to put it out?" He chuckled at his own wit. He along with his four brothers were volunteer members of the local fire department.

"This isn't a joke, Noah. I need to get engaged, and quickly. Will you help me?"

Don't miss
THEIR PRETEND AMISH COURTSHIP
by Patricia Davids, available June 2017 wherever
Love Inspired® books and ebooks are sold.

www.LoveInspired.com